PRAISE FOR BIOME

"An indelible red-planet backdrop enhances an already rugged, tenacious story. The ending, meanwhile, satisfies on every level."

—Kirkus Reviews

"Superb. The Martian meets The 100. Fast-paced young adult sci-fi that combines all the action of a psychological thriller with the angst of coming to age. A fascinating premise deftly executed."

—Tosca Lee
New York Times bestselling author of *Forbidden*

"The twisting plot and fleshed out characters lead to a satisfying ending."

—The BookLife Prize in Fiction

"[E]xtremely engaging. I can't wait to read a sequel."

—Hannah Alexander
author of The Hallowed Halls series

"Within the first few chapters I gave up trying to predict where the story would go and simply let it carry me on a wild, extraterrestrial ride."

—Anne Elisabeth Stengl
award-winning author of *Heartless*

"A real page-turner, reminiscent of both *The 100* and *Doctor Who*, *Biome* is a refreshing take on Young Adult Science Fiction."

—India Edghill
author of *Wisdom's Daughter*

BIOME

To Aunt Elaine and Uncle Scott.

Thank you for supporting the dream. I wish you the best!

All the love.

R. Galloway

A novel by

RYAN GALLOWAY

STRANGER

All rights reserved. Published and distributed in the United States and Canada by Stranger Fiction LLC in Portland, Oregon.

First edition, December 2016

Summary:
When seventeen-year-old cadet Lizzy Engram of Mars Colony One wakes with a head full of stolen memories, she has six days to uncover what the doctors are hiding before they realize what she knows—and erase her from existence.

ISBN: 978-0-9978558-2-1 (paperback)
ISBN: 978-0-9978558-0-7 (ePub)
ISBN: 978-0-9978558-1-4 (Kindle)

For a glimpse into how *Biome* was self-published, visit strangerfiction.co/biome.

To Carissa—

For showing me the world through your beautiful eyes.

Chapter One

Something is missing at the back of my head. It eats at me slowly, dripping like a faucet, tapping just under the surface. I can never place what it is, exactly. Maybe a forgotten name. Or a warning.

Whatever it is, I have a feeling that it's important. That if I don't remember, something terrible will happen. And soon.

But I don't remember.

So it keeps on tapping.

This is how I feel all the time. As if I've had a leak in my brain since we landed on Mars. As if everything on this planet, from the soil that stains my weighted boots to the dust-red world outside my porthole, reminds me of something.

Maybe tomorrow, when we're finally allowed to leave the domes and see the planet for ourselves, I'll know what I've been missing.

Yet for reasons I can't explain, that idea only fills me with dread.

"How is the harvest coming?"

A rustle of ferns precedes Doctor Conrad's approach through the recessed herb garden. I straighten, shaking off my troubled thoughts.

"Getting there," I say.

"Looks to me like you've finished early. As usual." Conrad's gaze sweeps the herb bed, his brows raised approvingly. I can tell he likes me. But not because of my personality or anything. It's only because I'm more efficient than the other greenskeepers.

"Am I getting predictable?"

"Reliable is the word I'd use." He looks at my face for the first time, concern making the cross-hatched wrinkles around his eyes tighten. They always remind me of dried-out clay. "Are you feeling all right, Elizabeth?"

"I'm fine," I reply automatically. To be honest, I feel exhausted. But I feel that way most of the time. Not so long ago, we were in cryosleep for the interplanetary trip. You don't just bounce back from an eight-month nap.

How long has it been since we landed—three months? Four? It feels like a decade. Which is kind of funny, if you think about it. Martian days, called "sols," are thirty-nine minutes longer than a day back home. That means time is moving faster on Earth, depending on how you look at it.

Conrad consults a tablet pulled from the pocket of his white lab coat.

"You're one of Shiffrin's patients?" he observes, fingers scurrying over the glass.

"I wouldn't exactly call myself patient."

He either doesn't get the joke or doesn't think it's funny. I watch him nod and jot out a note with a swollen finger, skin cracked at the knuckle.

Here in the Forest and Woodland Biome, it can be easy to get dehydrated, at least during the artificial dry season. Warm air strokes the brushwood at our knees, moving out over the olive trees at the bottom of the slope, their limbs twisted behind a line of jagged, toothy rocks. All of this is housed inside the geodesic dome we currently stand in: saplings, bushes, herbs, and undergrowth. All pioneers on an alien world, like me.

For now, the edible varieties augment our food supply. Once the terraforming is complete and the atmosphere can support organic life, their seeds will be the first inhabitants of the newly transformed planet.

Sometimes when I'm working with my hands in the dirt, I forget I'm inside a giant, billion-dollar golf ball.

Conrad finishes with his notes and stoops for a look at the rosemary growing in one of the divided herb blocks. Beside it are genetically enhanced strains of lavender, garlic, dill, and chives. Fast-growing versions of their earthly cousins.

"Incredible," he murmurs. "It looks like this one is already beginning to flower again. We'll want to trim it back to ensure it doesn't harden." He dusts off his hands and rises, looking at me a bit sternly. "You seem fatigued, Elizabeth."

"I'm fine," I say again. "Just homesick, I guess."

The words are out before I can stop them.

"For Earth?" He seems surprised. "Well, you'll speak to Doctor Shiffrin about it tonight, I trust. You've got First Expedition tomorrow."

"Right."

"Got to keep in good health," Conrad says briskly. "Mentally, emotionally, and physically." It's practically a motto for him. He turns on his heel. "If you're finished, go ahead and take your produce to the kitchen for dinner."

Watching him go, I secretly resent him. Not because he doesn't care. It's because he views me the same way he views the plants.

This week alone I've been reminded about the importance of my general health probably a hundred times. The constant questions and reminders, the note-taking—it makes me feel like another root in an herb block. And what's it matter? Who ends up reading the notes anyway?

As for First Expedition... I don't want to think about that right now.

Clutching my bucket of herbs, I trace a path along a walkway bordered by Aleppo pine. The warm, slightly bitter scent of tree resin tickles my nose. It reminds me of our family trip to Italy when I was ten. I try to picture my mother and father ambling the cobbled streets of Florence. Their faces are blurry, I realize.

Do other cadets forget what their families look like so quickly? I feel a stab of guilt. It's strange, but the truth is I'm *not* homesick. I don't really miss the people from home, from my old life, at all. I just feel lonely.

But for who? And for what? Even if I could go back, it's been almost a year since I entered cryosleep. Things are different now.

The path crawls up a gentle incline, past quartered patches of Meyer lemon and sweet Seville orange. I catch a glimpse of the swamp at the north curve of the dome just as I reach the portal, which regulates humidity and temperature. Each biome has its own atmosphere to ensure that the plants are growing in optimal conditions.

Here on Mars we have no bugs, blights, or parasites. And everything grows like a weed.

The door whooshes open and I feel a rush of cool air, a ghostly caress against my skin. As I step into the hall, there's a melodic *ding-dong* on the overhead speakers. A pleasant female voice informs me that it's now seventeen hundred hours—or five o'clock, Earth time.

I'm almost an hour early with my harvesting. Most cadets are still scattered throughout the various biomes, performing tasks such as watering, pruning, trimming, mulching, fertilizing, irrigating, and so on. Glamorous, astronaut-y duties.

When we all auditioned to be the first cadets on Mars, I'm not sure anyone realized just how much yardwork would be involved.

The kitchen area is a wide hall of cabinets and drawers, with a hexagonal ceiling like a Chinese checkerboard. Every surface gleams.

Chloe, a fellow cadet, is unloading a crate of bell peppers onto a counter. Willowy and fair, she has long chestnut hair and giant green eyes that look even bigger behind her glasses. She's bright, kind-hearted, and an excellent listener. Admired by almost every cadet on the colony.

I'm nothing like her.

"Hello, Lizzy," she says. Though she spent only her summers with her grandmother in France, Chloe still has a slight accent. It shows up most in her habit of dropping the "h" out of words, making *hello* sound more like *ello*. "Good harvesting today?"

As I open my mouth to answer, it happens. The sense that something is missing, that something is forgotten, suddenly grows louder, taking shape, washing over me in a thousand tingling needle-pricks of familiarity. It's as if I've seen this before—this, exactly this moment, exactly this way: Chloe, the bell peppers, the light catching the rim of her glasses. Even my hesitation in the doorway.

But I haven't seen it, and I know it. Which again leaves me dizzy with the feeling that there's still something I'm missing.

"Hey," I manage.

"What's wrong?" Chloe asks.

"Nothing," I say as I place my bucket on the counter. She raises a quizzical eyebrow. Chloe has an uncanny way of reading me.

Also, I'm a terrible liar.

"It's just..." I begin. "Do you ever feel like you want to say something, and it's on the tip of your tongue, but you can't find the words?"

She considers this a moment, a frown tugging her lips.

"What would you be trying to say?" she finally asks.

"I don't know. Just... never mind."

"Have you been having déjà vu again?" she guesses.

"Well, 'again' would imply that I ever stopped," I say irritably. "And since I've had it almost every day this week, I think that—"

"*J'y crois pas!*" Chloe bursts out. "Every day? Lizzy, this is serious. Have you spoken to Doctor Shiffrin?"

Immediately I regret telling her. I know that look, that tone, when someone starts trying to fix me. That's why I don't talk about my déjà vu. Or my family and how I don't miss them. Letting people in only makes you vulnerable. And I'm not about to be anyone's project.

"I'm sure it's nothing," I say. "Hallucinations are pretty normal, you know."

Her mouth drops open in a hybrid of worry and disbelief.

"Lizzy, hallucinations are *not* normal," Chloe tells me. "They are a very serious symptom of several potential neurological disorders. You need to speak to a doctor."

Chloe isn't great with sarcasm. I begin removing cilantro stems from my bucket and their sweet, zesty aroma fills the air.

"I promise to speak with a doctor about my very serious hallucinations," I reply. "Okay?"

"That *does* sound serious," says a sugary voice.

Another cadet glides into the kitchen, smooth and graceful. She pulls open a drawer and scans the contents, then bumps it shut with her hip. "And you know, if you have even a minor illness, you can't go on First Expedition."

Terra usually tends the Arctic and Alpine Tundra Biome. This week, a few of my fellow greenskeepers got sick, so Terra was commissioned to help out with our agrarian and culinary duties. She has an annoying habit of eavesdropping on my conversations.

I'm counting the days until she goes back to her side of the colony.

"It was a joke," I say flatly.

"You shouldn't joke about that," replies Terra, tugging her bright hair back into a ponytail, revealing a thumbprint-sized birthmark on her neck. "Especially on Mars. Getting sick means getting quarantined. But of course, you know procedure."

"What are you looking for, Terra?" Chloe asks.

"Cutting board."

"That one on the left."

"Oh, thanks." Terra pulls open the cabinet. "Anyway, Doctor Harris said I'll be leading a gathering crew on First Expedition. I'll get to handpick who to take with me." She smiles at me, her dimples like pinpoints. "Probably Chloe, for starters."

"Good for you," I say, biting back a harsher response. All week she's been at me for no apparent reason, trying to lure me into a fight. Or make me jealous. Or something. I don't know what her problem is.

"Well, I hope you feel better," she says sweetly, then trots away to the other end of the kitchen. Chloe is silent.

"What's going on with you two?" she finally asks.

"I don't know. But I'm going to Terra-form her face if she doesn't leave me alone."

Chloe giggles as she retrieves her own cutting board and a vegetable knife. Wordplay, she can understand.

"What do you think we'll find out there?"

"During First Expedition? I'm betting on troubled Martian youths," I say, allowing myself a small smile.

"Oh, yes." Chloe sighs as she chops up a green pepper, tossing the seeds and core into a compost bin. "The terraforming is probably speeding up their hormones."

"Soon they'll be starting a band. The Martian Boys."

"They'll be too popular for us."

Other cadets stream in, lugging their own buckets of produce from the biome or unloading transport carts of fruits and greens from a neighboring climate. Their chatter echoes loudly off the flat surfaces of the kitchen as Doctor Bauer breezes in.

"Elizabeth," she calls out, her dark curls bouncing around an even darker face with smooth, high cheekbones. "Did you see that the rosemary is already flowering again?"

"Yes." Honestly, I don't know what she's so excited about. Like Conrad said, flowering means trimming. Just more yardwork for us cadets.

"Isn't it wonderful? Healthy, flowering rosemary on Mars." She clicks on a convection oven and puts her hands on her hips. "You're not excited enough, Elizabeth."

"I guess not," I say, though I can't help but laugh. Doctor Bauer is one of my favorite people in the whole colony.

"Fine. Then we're having Mexican tonight. If you can't be happy about fajitas, you have no business being on the planet. Chop up that cilantro."

When I turn, Chloe has already slid me a cutting board.

"Thanks."

She nods slowly.

"Are you sure you're okay?" she presses, just loud enough for me to hear. "You look... tired."

"Well, so do you," I snap, annoyed to be having this conversation again. "We all do. It's hardly been a year since we left Earth, Chloe. It takes time to adapt."

For some reason, the duration sounds different out loud. By the time my family makes the trip, another eight months will have passed. But that would be if they left right now—and they won't. Because of how the planets orbit, the next mission won't leave for two years. In total, that means almost three years will pass before I see my parents again. By then I'll be twenty.

Whatever they remember of me, I'll be an entirely different person. And they'll have changed too.

"You don't have to be so defensive," says Chloe quietly, withdrawing.

"I'm not," I say, but my voice sounds harsh even in my own ears. "I promise, I'm fine. Let's just talk after dinner, all right?"

"Okay."

Her smile doesn't reach her eyes. As she walks away, I concentrate on cutting the cilantro, trying to push down what I really feel. No more thoughts about home, I tell myself. Focus on something else. Like cooking.

You wouldn't think so, but the food on Mars isn't bad. For breakfast we have scrambled eggs, which are pumped out of a 3D printer using protein filament. Once you cook in the fresh rosemary and add sautéed onions, biscuits, gravy, and soy bacon—or "fake-on," as we all call it—it ends up tasting like a better-than-average hotel meal.

For lunch, some days we have burgers made of lentils and beans with printed whole-wheat buns. Fresh yams and potatoes from the biomes, which we hand-cut into fries. Dinner is usually extra special: fajitas, or sushi, or zucchini pasta topped with lemon avocado sauce, plus a chopped side salad of nuts and seeds, and maybe soft, grilled apricots for dessert. We even make ice cream from cashew milk.

I guess that makes us all vegetarian out here, but it isn't that bad. We ration what we can't grow and get creative with what we can.

After dinner, cadets are allotted two hours of free time. Most of us read, watch movies, play video games, or have tournaments in ping-pong or cards. Some make a habit of sending messages to friends and family back home, but a disruptive solar wind has recently made it tough to get signal from Earth. Something about a geomagnetic storm.

I don't feel like talking anyway, not even to Chloe like I promised. Instead, I decide to take some time for me—to distract myself from First Expedition, from Terra, from the déjà vu and whatever it is that I can't remember. I decide to go for a run.

In my sleeping pod, I wiggle out of my jumpsuit, pull an eco-latex tank over my head, cinch up my shorts, and step into weighted running shoes. The soles are relatively new but already beginning to show wear. I'm glad the 3D printers can manage fresh tread. It'll be a dark day indeed if we ever run out of rubber filament.

Run out, I think to myself as I triple-knot my laces. *Ha.*

Responsive lights bloom when I step into the Fitness Center, the eco-bulb system taking a moment to warm up. Around me, various exercise machines rest like dormant robotic insects. Most of these function on resistance rather than weight because of the gravity variance from Earth. With only a third of the pull we're used to, cadets would need to lift several hundred pounds just to get a workout.

It's the same reason we all wear heavy shoes. Without them, the energy we use to take a normal step would send us leaping down the halls.

Anyway, I'm not here for weight training. There's only one type of machine I ever use.

It's called a holotrek.

I step onto the platform and clip the safety tab to my shorts. The holographic display appears around me. As I thumb down the list, I pick one of my favorite paths: Wildwood, a trail from back on Earth.

Gel treads shuffle under my feet and begin to move, molding and tumbling to give the sensation of running on packed dirt and stone. At the same time, trees bearded in moss sprout up on either side, the mountain path unfolding as if I've stepped off the colony and into a North American park. Iridescent birds flit through the branches, their twittering vibrant and free. Running in their illusory presence, I feel free too.

One kilometer becomes two, then three, then five. I try not to think about my parents and how they must have changed during my absence. How everything must have changed.

Is it strange that I chose to leave? I don't even remember the moment I made the decision. NASA was looking for the best and the brightest, and I was one of them. It just didn't seem like something to miss.

With each kilometer, I outpace my feelings until my breath is coming in short gasps. But I grit my teeth, unwilling to give in, unable to quit until I've pushed myself as far as I can go.

Finally, I allow myself to press the stop button. The tread returns to a smooth sheet beneath my feet, and I step down, legs wobbly.

It was stupid to go that far after already running this morning. I'll regret it tomorrow.

"Good run?"

I almost cry out as the voice breaks my feeling of solitude. A cadet sits on a weight machine two rows over. His name is Noah. One of the medical cadets.

Tall and lanky, Noah is the only red-haired boy on the planet.

Possibly because his hair and height are so conspicuous, he hardly ever speaks. I think his quietness makes the other cadets think he's mature. It also makes it easy to forget he's even around until he finally *does* say something—and then everyone is kind of surprised, as if a piece of furniture joined the conversation.

In general, he makes me uncomfortable.

"Why are you in here so late?" I ask. It comes out like a demand.

"I missed fitness hour earlier," he explains, his face flushing. He acts as if he's embarrassed to be talking to me or something.

"Oh. Were you sick?"

"No."

Silence.

"Okay. Well, I've got to go talk to Doctor Shiffrin."

"I'm seeing Doctor Brink," he says quickly. He leans forward on the arms of the weight machine conspiratorially. "Are you... nervous?"

"About First Expedition?"

He nods.

"No," I lie. "Are you?"

"A little," he admits. "I've just been thinking all week... what if we get out there and it's not what we think?"

"What are you talking about?"

"I don't know," he shrugs. "What if it isn't like Earth at all?"

I can't help but wonder what he expects. From what I've seen, it's nothing but rocks and dust and the sad yellow sprouts that've been growing as a result of Aster, the terraformer. That, and the storms.

Every few days we get a fresh downpour of hail rattling along the dome roofs, complete with flashes of eerily silent lightning. The doctors keep saying we're on the edge of a breakthrough. As if once we get one tree going, the rest of the plants will fall in line.

I think they're being optimistic.

"It won't be," I say. "Look out the portholes, Noah. It hasn't changed much. And even after it terraforms, it still won't be Earth.

That's kind of the point, isn't it?"

He doesn't have an answer. I suddenly realize how cold I'm being. What is wrong with me? Why am I so harsh with him?

But I know the answer to that question. Because I have the same fear he does: that we left our home behind and nothing will be like it again. Ever. We'll learn that the terraforming is impossible. And so is a return trip.

As irrational as it may be, I'm not scared of what I will find, but of what I won't.

"I've got to talk to Shiffrin."

Before he can reply, I step through the sliding door.

My shower is brief, as always. Even with advanced water rec-lamation, there isn't a lot to go around. But I savor every second, letting the hot liquid run into my mouth, down my back, and over my ears, closing my eyes as I block out anything but the cleansing flow.

After showering as long as I dare, I towel off and zip into my jumpsuit, then pad down to the Wellness Suites, untangling my wet hair with my fingers as I go. It's kind of odd that, on a space colony, we brought along more psychologists than chemists. I guess they were really worried about us going stir-crazy out here all alone.

When I arrive for my time slot, Doctor Shiffrin is waiting.

"Elizabeth," she says warmly, standing. She's only middle-aged, but her hair is mostly grey as it hangs to her rounded shoulders, framing soft features and an aquiline nose. Reading glasses are tangled in her dull, wavy locks. In certain, ways she reminds me of my grandmother. "How are you feeling?"

There's that question again.

"Fine," I say.

"Tea?"

"No, thanks."

"Have a seat."

The Wellness Suites are among the best-furnished rooms on Mars. Music drifts in from the ceiling, a soothing cello playing some-thing classic. A diffuser puffs citrus-scented oil into the air. And here and there are holographic accents, such as a fireplace burning with crackling logs and a window looking out onto a beach. I can even hear the tranquil roll of the ocean.

Dropping into one of the overstuffed armchairs, I feel like I've stumbled upon a tiny piece of Earth.

Also, it's nice to sit after a five-mile run. That's putting it mildly.

"So," Shiffrin says. "Tell me about your week."

"Not much to tell," I reply. "Normal cadet stuff."

"Was any of this stuff... troublesome?"

"The plants have been growing since I trimmed them. They keep doing that. Sometimes I feel like I'm just reliving the same day over and over, chopping the same dumb bushes."

"Life can be that way," she replies.

"Boring?"

"Driven by habit."

I pick at the frayed armrest. Therapy is not something I enjoy. It almost never helps me. I guess. Mostly, I just don't like talking about myself. In a normal situation, I'd simply say as little as possible and then slip away once it was socially acceptable. Here, I have to sit and squirm while I'm examined like a baffling strain of bacteria.

Anyway, I never seem to remember what we talk about. The time evaporates, and we haven't solved anything. I still can't remember what I'm missing.

"So, what are we talking about today?" I finally ask.

"You."

"But there's nothing to talk about. I feel fine."

"Do you?" asks the doctor. "I'd say you seem tired."

"I did run twenty kilometers today. Ten this morning, ten tonight."

"Sounds like overtraining. A coping mechanism, maybe?"

"Why don't we just talk about First Expedition?" I suggest impatiently. "You're supposed to make sure I'm fit for duty tomorrow, right?"

"In time," the doctor replies. "First, I'd like to explore what's going on inside that brain of yours, if you don't *mind*."

She's trying to loosen me up. In spite of my annoyance, I smile.

"You're getting *a-head* of yourself, doctor," I reply.

Shiffrin laughs.

"I had a visitor today," she says casually. "She informed me that you've been having hallucinations."

"Terra."

"Yes."

"I thought if someone confided in you, you had to keep it secret," I say in surprise. I'm a little impressed. "Aren't you, like, breaking the law?"

"We're not on Earth, Elizabeth," she chides. "And anyway, that law only applies to *my* children. I don't owe anything to a stranger. And you're changing the subject. Would you like to talk about what happened?"

"No."

We just stare at each other for a few moments. Out of the corner of my eye, I notice a security camera watching us. Black and unfeeling, the size of a softball. Like a giant doll's eye. Time stretches until I'm convinced that Shiffrin won't speak again until I do.

"Okay," I finally give in. "I had déjà vu today. In the kitchen with Chloe. I've had it four other times this week. Gathering tomatoes, brushing my teeth, sitting in one of Meng's talks, and entering the code to my sleeping pod. It happens again and again, and I don't know why. I don't remember dreaming about this stuff. But somehow it feels connected. Like, somehow it's all reminding me of a single, bigger thing. I just... I can't put my finger on what it is."

"And how does that make you feel?"

"Like it's crazy. Like *I'm* crazy."

"I see." Shiffrin reaches for a plastic cup on the table beside her. As she blows on it, the tab of her tea packet flutters like a moth. "And you believe these... *experiences* are a kind of hallucination?"

"I never said that," I say defensively. "Terra said that."

"Ah. So what do you believe?"

"I don't know," I pause, growing frustrated. "Nothing."

"We all believe something, Lizzy," the doctor replies.

A part of me wants to tell her exactly what I'm thinking. That it's no one's business what goes on inside my head—not hers, not anyone's. And by the way, how is this meant to help me? Comments like that only make me angry.

"Can we talk about something else, please?"

"Of course," says Shiffrin soothingly, as if sensing that she's hit a wall. "Are you anxious about First Expedition?"

"No."

"Not even a little?"

"No."

"And nothing else is wrong? Nightmares, depression, lack of appetite?" I shake my head through the list. "Fights with other crew members? Dizziness? Trouble sleeping?"

"Just impatience with therapy, I guess."

The doctor smiles again.

"Fair enough."

She stands and steps toward a series of cabinets. From within one, she takes a small white case with a latch. Pulling a chair close to my seat, Shiffrin cradles the box in her hands like a collection of mementos.

"Taking my vitals?" I ask.

"Not quite. I need to inoculate you for the mission, to boost your oxygen capacity and regulate capillary pressure. Wouldn't want you passing out on the edge of a crater, would we?" She clicks the latch.

"Is it a shot?"

"Just a cap."

Shiffrin opens the box and produces a thumb-sized plastic tube. It looks like an inhaler, with wings on one end. Holding my forearm, she pushes the inoculator into my skin. I hardly even feel the dozens of tiny nano-needles. The tube is released as the dose readout transitions from green to red. Then a tingling sensation flows backward up my arm, like warm honey.

"Nothing else happened this week?" Shiffrin clicks a penlight, shining it into my eyes and blinding me. "Nothing that made you uncomfortable?"

Though I'm still sitting, I suddenly feel off-balance, as if the whole planet has suddenly pitched to the left. Instinctually, I grab the armrests.

"This is making me pretty uncomfortable."

She clicks off the light.

"And you didn't have any memory lapses? Difficulty remembering names or where you put a personal item?"

"Not that I r-remember," I stammer. My tongue feels too big for my mouth, my head now heavy and swollen. "You sure... that was a... booster?"

Shiffrin doesn't answer. She swims before my eyes as she stands and glides toward the cabinets, punching a code. I'm woozy, as if I've suddenly entered a dream world. My head sags against the headrest, and then Shiffrin is beside me again, holding a sort of latticed, glimmering device. I can't seem to focus on it.

"Just relax, Elizabeth," says Shiffrin's voice.

My eyes flutter. I feel a dull pinch as something tight slides around my head. The lights in the ceiling warble and start to spin; shadowy fingers blot out my vision. I mean to say something, but I don't.

The next thing I know, it's morning.

Chapter Two

My head is going to explode.

That's my first thought when my sleeping pod blooms to life, LED fixtures stabbing my eyes like needles. I pull the sheets over my head and groan.

"Lizzy, are you in here?" a voice whispers.

"Go away."

The door snicks shut and I hear padded, hesitant footfalls.

"You should've been up an hour ago," Chloe's voice says. "You're really late."

"Late for—?"

My stomach lurches. First Expedition is today. We'll be suiting up right after breakfast. I'm abruptly nervous—and grateful I don't feel well.

"I can't go on First Expedition. I think... I'm sick."

"What are you talking about?" Chloe asks, now closer. "First Expedition is next week. What doesn't feel good?"

"Huh?" I clutch my blanket more firmly and roll over. "No, it's not. It's today."

A hesitation, and then—

"Should I get a doctor?" Chloe asks.

I try to breathe slowly. All I have to do is convince her I'm unwell, and she'll leave me alone. But that's the easy thing to do—the cowardly thing to do. I ball the blanket into my fists, disgusted with myself. No matter what waits on the other side of the airlock, I'm not going to hide from it. Especially not just because of a stupid headache. That's not the kind of person I am.

And anyway, like Terra said, the alternative is getting quarantined.

Forcing myself to sit up, I shake off the covers, squinting into the flood of light. When did I even get in bed? I can vaguely recall being inoculated and getting drowsy... was I drugged?

"Turn off the overheads, will you?"

"Uh, okay."

Chloe flips the switch. Instantly the room goes dark, save for the small green emergency diodes in the baseboards. I gingerly swing my aching legs out of bed and stand. In the shadows, Chloe's face is a mask of concern.

"Do you want me to get Doctor Zonogal?" she asks again.

"No." Faltering, I clutch her shoulder for support. "I'm fine."

"But you said—"

"It's just a headache," I say. "Trust me, I'm okay. I just need some aspirin or something."

I dress in darkness and then step into the blinding hall, awash in light from the glowing ceiling tiles. Chloe stays close, as if scared I'm going to collapse. I try to rub the sleep out of my eyes but just end up making myself dizzy.

"How ironic is it that I'm seeing stars in space?"

Pressing her lips into a thin line, Chloe hands me a granola packet from the kitchen.

"Eat this," she instructs. "The Sick Bay is right up here."

The Sick Bay is like a pharmacy from the hospitals back on Earth, a few stubby aisles stocked with anything you'd need to patch a cut or treat a burn. In the back, behind frosted glass, is an operating room. As far as I can remember it's never been used. But then as we step up to the counter, I smell antiseptic and it happens again—déjà vu, the feeling that I've done all this before.

But it doesn't end there. The dripping in my brain becomes a flood rushing in, and my subconscious is overwhelmed by a full-on memory.

It was my first week on Mars.

I was harvesting the already-thick stalks of rhubarb, which were rapidly growing behind the lupines. The shears slipped, cutting through my glove, right into the artery in my wrist. For a second it didn't hurt. I just saw the blood pulsing out of my body, shooting in a ruby arc that stained a half-meter line in the soil.

Then the pain lit my wrist like fire, white hot, and I knew I was in trouble. Stumbling down the dirt path, I nearly vomited.

When I reached the Sick Bay, I was pouring sweat and barely on my feet. Doctor Zonogal saw me first. Face pallid, she barked orders at the medics. One of them was Noah. He led me over to a chair, telling me I'd be okay. An oxygen mask was slipped over my ears. I looked up into his eyes, honey brown and filled with concern, and I wondered if I was going to—

"Lizzy?"

Behind the counter, Noah stares at me with an expression hauntingly similar to the one I was just remembering.

"Huh?" I return his gaze, confused, rubbing my wrist. But when I look down, there's no cut. Not even a scar.

What was I thinking about?

"She isn't feeling well," Chloe explains. "Bad headache."

"Four hundred milligrams?" asks Kellen, one of the other medical cadets. He smiles at me sympathetically, his white teeth almost glowing against the charcoal black of his skin.

"I'll get it," says Noah. He ducks down one of the med aisles and returns with two cups, one of water, the other with two pink pills at the bottom. I put the capsules on my tongue, swish twice, and swallow. The water makes me feel a little better. But only a little.

"Don't forget to sign," Kellen tells me. He slumps into a chair, locking fingers behind his shaved head. "How about you, Chloe? Nervous about First Expedition?"

A holographic sheet appears on the counter as I tap it.

"Oh, I guess," Chloe says timidly. Then her gaze flits to Noah.

"Are you?"

"A little."

"He's afraid it might not be like Earth," I say.

As soon as the words are out of my mouth, I wish I could take them back. Not so much for Noah's sake, but for mine. Chloe and Kellen are staring at me, waiting for an explanation. But the last thing I want is to discuss First Expedition again, or why Noah was sharing his fears with me in the Fitness Center.

I look at him, expecting to find hurt or anger in his gaze for so freely sharing his confided thoughts. But he only seems confused.

"We talked about it yesterday," I tell him. "Remember?"

"No, we didn't," he says as his face begins to redden. Why is he trying to deny it? Is he afraid Kellen will make fun of him?

"Maybe it was a dream you had," Chloe suggests.

"Sure," I say flatly. Whatever game he's playing, I don't have the mental energy to go along with it. I scribble my finger over the projection and it disappears. "Come on, Chloe." As I turn, the tapping in my head grows into a full-on pounding.

Chloe almost has to trot to keep up with my brisk pace.

"What was that about?"

"Just Noah Hartmann being weird as usual," I grumble.

For a second she's quiet. Then she asks hopefully, "You seem like you're feeling better?"

"So much," I reply. I've only been up for twenty minutes and I'm having hallucinations, for real this time. Chloe doesn't pick up on my sarcasm. "Wait, we're going the wrong way."

"No, we're not."

"The airlock is that way."

"It's Monday, Liz," Chloe says patiently. "We're going to Group, like normal."

I try to connect the name to something that matters, and it comes to me: Doctor Meng's lectures on history and art. Two things that mean absolutely nothing to cadets who live on Mars. My stride slows considerably.

"Either I really *am* dreaming, or you need to find a calendar. We've got First Expedition today. It's the only thing I've been hearing about all week."

"It's next week," Chloe assures me. "I wonder if you have a fever?" She puts a hand to my forehead. "Or maybe you're just nervous—"

"I'm not."

"Okay, well then a fever."

"Maybe," I concede, pushing her hand away. "I do feel nauseous."

"Do you think you might throw up?"

"I will if I have to listen to one of Meng's talks."

Chloe smiles and grabs my arm, pulling me down the hall.

Only medical cadets like Noah and Kellen are on duty during mandatory functions such as Group. As a result, the corridors are empty. We take the Wheel, the circular hall at the center of the colony. It links the various domes without passing through the giant biomes, which makes it the quickest way to get around. Our footsteps echo off sterile, polished surfaces that gleam like fresh-blown glass.

In total, there are five biomes on our colony. And truthfully, Chloe and I are fortunate to be assigned to one of the more temperate climates. Other cadets, like those who tend the Arid and Coastal Desert Biome, spend their days roasting in a chalky bubble.

Back when we arrived on Mars, the psychologists decided it would be a good idea for us to name our dome subset, to help us "feel more at home." My fellow cadets named us Scrubs, in honor of the small, scrubby bushes that we never stop trimming.

A few of us wanted to be called Pyros, because back on Earth, controlled fires were often used to renew ecosystems like ours. And really, after a few months of fighting the relentless plants, turning a few of them into kindling starts to sound like a pretty nice idea.

But you've got to be careful with stuff like this. Take the cadets from the Grassland and Flora Biome, for example. They call themselves Clovers because they were so "lucky" to get picked for the most pleasant habitat on the colony.

Everyone just calls them grassholes.

As we exit the Wheel, Chloe leads me through another airtight portal and into a smaller dome. This is our theater. Arranged in a tiered semicircle, the seats face a table at the front of the room, upon which is a giant lens. It looks like a deconstructed telescope, gazing upward.

For some reason, it's always freezing in here.

Meng has already begun his lecture. A holographic image floats above the iris: a satellite with a white dish and feeble metal arms. Every seat is filled except for two. One on either side of Terra Donahue.

I'd officially like to nominate this as my worst day on Mars.

"Good morning, cadets," says Doctor Meng with a hint of annoyance. "So glad you could join us."

Not another word is said as I slip into the seat nearest the aisle, allowing Chloe to pass ahead of me. I would usually be self-conscious about everyone's staring, but at the moment I'm too irritated—and miserable—to care.

"Where was I?" Meng asks. "Ah yes, the probe." He walks around the desk in a clipped circle, as if he's marching. He taps a button and the image rotates slowly. "Voyager 1 is another example of what I'm talking about. Like all its brother probes, it carries a gold-plated disc. These discs contain audio and visual samples of our race, like the collective memories of humanity. Poetic, isn't it? Some of you must have questions. Come, don't be shy. Daniel?"

Near the front, a cadet stirs.

"What kinds of memories?" he ventures, almost managing to sound interested.

"Sounds, such as songs or a baby's cry. Various languages. If a probe were to encounter an intelligent life form, or if humanity ceased to exist, these discs would carry on the essence of our race." He turns his attention back to the translucent model of the antiquated probe. "In that way, our biomes perform a similar function.

They preserve the plant life of Earth for generations to come, here on Mars."

Terra nudges me sharply with her elbow.

"You slept late," she whispers, a hiss.

I clench my teeth but succeed in holding my tongue—mostly because my head is still too muddled to produce an adequate comeback. When I don't rise to her bait, Terra shifts her attention onto Chloe.

"Did you hear about Doctor Atkinson?"

It's almost hard to watch Chloe try to decide what to do. Talking during the lecture would mean breaking the rules. But ignoring Terra would mean hurting her feelings. After squirming for a few seconds, she hesitantly shakes her head.

"He attacked Doctor Conrad," Terra informs her.

"What?" Chloe is astonished. "Why?"

"No one knows. But this morning Conrad had a black eye, and no one's seen Atkinson. They probably had to lock him in the Helix, if he's dangerous."

"But... I don't understand. Why—?"

"Excuse me," Meng interrupts. His eyebrows scrunch over his glasses like great black caterpillars. "Are you listening, Miss Donahue?"

"Yes," Terra replies quickly. Everyone turns to stare again, but this time not at me. I feel slightly gratified.

"Well, since I've got your attention, why don't you tell us all why we bother studying the past in the first place?"

"Because... we can learn from it."

Meng's face pinches in what could be an attempt at a smile.

"Partly true. What I was saying is, we study the past because we tell ourselves stories. What does that mean? It means everyone has their own version of things, yes? We see things *our* way, from our *own* perspective. History is no exception. However, when we can agree on the facts and set them in a permanent record, like on Voyager 1, we can all see things the same. That's a beautiful idea, because it unites us as a single life force. Without that unity, humanity could never have created even half of its wonders—the pyramids, the Internet, or a colony on Mars. The human spirit is indomitable when it sets itself toward a common goal."

The cadets are all nodding along, but my headache is growing worse and the motion makes me queasy. Meng begins changing dials on the holographic imager, pulling up probes and satellites. I can't seem to focus on his words. More than anything, I just want to lie down and close my eyes.

I'm drawn out of my daze by a beeping coming from the overhead. It sounds like an alarm. Meng seems confused, and has just opened his mouth when the lens switches, projecting the image of a man.

The way the light shapes the figure, it turns his cropped white hair into a kind of halo, reflecting in his round spectacles, glistening along the oxygen tubes that run around his ears and into his nose.

He looks familiar. But not in a déjà vu way. I seem to remember speaking to him before. In a cold room across a metal table, my wrists tied down, his gentle voice asking question after question, telling me I couldn't leave until we'd finished, keeping me from water, from food, from rest, until he had the answers he wanted.

It occurs to me that maybe I really *am* hallucinating.

"Doctor Dosset," Meng says. "Um, good morning."

"Hello, Charles," the man called Dosset replies.

The image smiles. His posture is stately, paternal, even harmless. A little like Shiffrin. But it's his eyes that give him away—they're as sharp and exacting as chips of ice. Just the sight of them sends tiny spiders of dread skittering down my spine.

"I apologize for interrupting," he says to Meng. "But I have an announcement to make. It should only take a minute."

"Of course."

Anyone who dared whisper or fidget while Meng was talking has now grown very still. I try to keep calm, but my pulse is racing so fast, I actually wonder if Terra can hear it beside me. Dosset seems to enjoy the quiet. Why am I so afraid of him?

"News travels quickly," he says. "Especially on such a small colony. No doubt, many of you have noticed Doctor Conrad's injury."

When no one speaks, he goes on.

"It seems that Doctor Atkinson contracted a fever last night and became delirious. When a number of his fellow doctors attempted to help him, Doctor Conrad was inadvertently harmed. I assure you, there is nothing to worry about. Doctor Atkinson is resting in his sleeping pod and his fever is now under control."

He's lying.

That's my first reaction. I don't know why, but it is. Suddenly my headache spikes, acid screeching on my brain. I have an overwhelming urge to dig my fingernails into my thighs, or to scream, or to run out of the room.

What's happening to me? Where are these thoughts coming from?

"For now, the illness is quarantined," Dosset is saying. "But in close quarters, sickness is among our greatest threats. If anyone presents with symptoms of delirium or confusion, please report them to a doctor at once. They will need immediate medical assistance."

I stare at the chair-back in front of me, smooth plastic with a rubber seam, trying to keep my bearings. At the edge of my vision, I can see Chloe watching me. I know what she must be thinking, that I've been delirious and confused all morning.

But it isn't a fever. And even if it is, I'd rather go for a walk in a Martian hailstorm than let Dosset anywhere near me.

"Thank you for your attention," the hologram says.

Smiling at us all, he reminds me of a wolf. I fight off a shiver as the image vanishes, reverting to a model of a spacecraft.

I don't even hear what Meng says after that. I just focus on breathing, on keeping the headache under control, wondering if it will split my skull open.

As soon as the other cadets begin moving, I'm out of my seat and through the door, stumbling half-blind toward my pod. When I get there, it takes four tries to get the access code right. The whole world seems skewed somehow, as if light is coming from all the wrong angles.

At last I stumble in, and the darkness envelops me like a cold compress. In my head I can see him, Dosset, sitting in a chair in just the same way he did on the hologram, asking me questions. He holds a webbed sort of crown, white pearly electrodes spread across a thin mesh. He calls it a Stitch. Says it won't hurt.

I ask him what it's for as Shiffrin enters the room. As he slides the Stitch over my head, she looks as nervous as I feel. One of those tablets is in Dosset's hands. He taps away. What is he doing? Is he scanning my brain?

There's a pinch in my scalp, but it's deeper than that—it's inside my head, and I gasp in surprise and stumble, my knee crashing into the plastic end table as I'm drawn out of the memory, back into my sleeping pod. I fall, taking the lamp down with me. It thuds on the floor. I remember more snaps across my temple, bees stinging the surface of my brain, buzzing angrily. It's so vivid, it feels as if I'm reliving it.

As if I'm losing my mind.

Tap, tap.

I sit up, panting, and push my hair off my forehead, damp with sweat. Is someone at the door? Or am I hearing the echo of Dosset's fingers drumming along the tablet? Maybe he sensed my terror even through the hologram, the way a shark smells blood. He could be right outside my pod, holding the Stitch, his instrument of torture.

Deep breaths. I take deep, slow breaths. Thinking back, I try to carefully recall what happened. Dosset asking me questions, taking notes, sending electric darts across my scalp. I become incoherent. Shiffrin suggests they give me a painkiller, but Dosset wants me conscious. When they're finally done, she presses an inoculator into my arm, a drug she calls Verced. Says it will calm me. That it will help me forget.

The room grows fuzzy, collapsing in a whirlpool as the drug takes effect. I wake up the next morning feeling groggy and disoriented.

But that's it.

"I didn't remember," I whisper aloud.

How is that possible? How could I forget something so traumatic? I cast back for more memories. It didn't happen just once. I can remember another instance—was it only a week later?—of Shiffrin asking me questions. Putting the Stitch on my head, giving me a dose of Verced. In the morning I wake without remembering what happened. Without remembering a lot of things. And the next week, she does it again.

So I begin to understand. They weren't scanning my brain. They were changing it. Erasing memories. The realization makes me cold and weak. And then, slowly, the questions emerge from the tumultuous waves of my mind.

Why would they do something like this? What could they possibly gain?

As I sink back to the floor, the numbness spreads over me. I can't bring myself to accept it. There's no reason good enough, no plausible explanation. Maybe I *am* sick. Yet the memories are there, adrift in the painful throbbing.

Another *tap, tap, tap*. This time, clearly a knock on my door.

I try to get a grip. Most likely it's just Chloe. But what if it's Shiffrin or one of the other doctors? I straighten my jumpsuit and tuck my hair behind my ears. Whatever happens next, I have to pretend that I don't know a thing. That everything is fine.

Tap, tap.

"Just a second." My voice is hoarse. I force myself to take a few more deep breaths. Then I open the door.

Chapter Three

"Are you okay? I heard a crash and I thought—"

Before she can finish, I pull Chloe inside and shut the door. I swiftly press my ear to the reinforced plastic. It hums like a tuning fork with the vibration of the oxygenators, the air purifiers, the myriad machines that run the colony. After a moment, feet shuffle by. Then it's quiet. Little by little, I begin to relax. They must not realize what I know.

Yet.

But what do I know? That's the burning question still bouncing around inside my head. That, and about twenty million others. Such as where these memories came from, and whether or not they're real. My brain feels raw, like fresh rug burn.

"Lizzy," Chloe speaks deliberately, adjusting her glasses in the dark. "What's going on? You're starting to scare me."

"I'm starting to scare me too," I say.

She gives me a funny look.

"What Doctor Dosset said, about that virus..." She gently touches my arm. "I think you might have it. And if you do, we need to tell Doctor Meng or—"

"No!" I blurt out more loudly than I'd intended. I cast a glance back at the door, feeling as if it might burst open at any second. I lower my voice. "No. I can't talk to him."

"Why not?"

"Because he... can't help me."

Chloe gives me a sympathetic smile, her teeth neon green in the gloomy lights. Like she thinks I'm completely insane. Sweaty, unshowered, hiding in a dark room. Yeah, I probably look like a raving lunatic.

I kind of feel like one too.

"You were just saying how awful you felt two hours ago," Chloe says delicately. "Doctor Dosset said that Doctor Atkinson had a fever—"

"Which I don't."

"—that he was delusional—"

"Which I'm not."

"—and that he was confused. Don't take this the wrong way, Liz, but you've been acting kind of, um, out of control all day."

"Well, it's been kind of an out-of-control day."

There are so many things I want to tell her, but it's as if they're all stuck. I can't begin to explain these memories or where they came from. It suddenly occurs to me that, if the doctors can erase what we recall, they might be able to give it back as well. But why would Shiffrin just up and give my memories back after erasing them over and over? I press the side of my head with a fist to stop the spinning.

Chloe turns on the light and I flinch. My eyes immediately begin to water.

"Come on." She rolls up her sleeves and folds her arms to show she's not kidding. It's the closest she'll ever get to intimidating. "If you're contagious, you're risking a lot more than your own health by hiding in here, and you know it."

I mean to answer, but something shiny catches my eye. It's a thin white line that runs along the inside of Chloe's wrist. A scar. I've never noticed it before. It reminds me of the cut I got from the shears, the one that I remembered in the Sick Bay.

Only I don't think that memory was mine.

"Chloe," I say faintly. "Where did you get that scar?"

Her frown is impatient, as if I'm trying to distract her.

"From... back on Earth, I suppose."

"Are you sure?"

"Yes," she says brusquely.

"You didn't get it from the shears while you were harvesting rhubarb?"

She opens her mouth, but then she closes it again. Finally, she says, "What... what are you talking about?" I try to cast back, thinking about the accident. As I do, I realize I can recall other things about her. The old code to her sleeping pod. How she'd journal every night before the colony stopped allowing personal tablets. The way she'd secretly go out of her way to talk to Noah Hartmann as much as possible.

Concentrating like this makes the headache so much worse. The memories threaten to overwhelm me, emotion boiling over as it did in the Sick Bay. But I manage to push through, to shove down the pain and, since I don't know what else to do, close my eyes as I narrate the memories to her. She listens in stunned silence. When I get to Noah, she abruptly grabs me by the shoulders.

"Stop it!" She shakes me hard, eyes wide with terror and confusion. "How do you know that? Who told you that?"

"No one, I just... I remember."

And so I tell her what I know about the doctors, even though it sounds crazy. From what I can piece together, they've been changing our memories since a few months after we landed. Even as I'm saying it all, I wonder how it feels to know that someone has a window into your personal memories and there's nothing you can do about it.

Chloe's expression is blank, the blood drained from her cheeks. Slowly her arms fall to her sides as if overcome by gravity.

"I don't understand," she says. "That can't be true. You're just... you're delirious. Why would they do that?"

My only reply is, "I don't know. But the memories—"

"It doesn't make sense." Her eyes are welling with tears. "There must be a mistake."

And again I remember how it felt when they took away her tablet. As if by taking away her journal, they'd taken away a part of her. With the memory comes a wave of sadness and loss swelling inside my ribcage. They erased the experience. She hasn't had to feel robbed, exposed, cheated. She didn't even know what was taken. Now, only I do.

To my surprise, tears fill my eyes as well. It's the first time I've cried in a long time.

"You believe me, right?" I ask, suddenly desperate to be sure I'm not alone in this. "You believe me, don't you?"

Chloe looks startled. She squeezes my arm.

"Whatever's happening, we'll figure it out together," she assures me. "We'll talk to Doctor Zonogal and she'll—"

Annoyed, I swipe at the tears.

"You don't get it, Chloe. The doctors are behind this. We can't trust them."

"None of them?"

"I don't think so."

She hesitates, and her gaze falls to the floor. It's just like it was in Group, when she had to choose between being polite to Terra and breaking the rules. If Chloe believes I'm right, then she'll have to believe that the doctors are wrong. It means picking a side. That's not exactly one of Chloe's strong suits. And to be honest, I don't blame her for doubting me. I'm not even sure I believe myself.

At length, she sits down on my bed and waits until I do the same, legs crossed beneath us like we've done a hundred times. She takes my hands.

"Okay, how about this," she says slowly. "Let's watch the doctors and see what they do. If they really are, um, brainwashing the cadets, there'll have to be proof of it somewhere, yes? And if they're not, and these are just hallucinations or something, I'm sure waiting a day won't infect the entire colony."

Though I've never had a hallucination before, I feel pretty certain they don't work like this—thousands of them all at once. But

I'm not ready to do this alone, and I can tell there's some sense in what she's asking me. If the doctors are as sinister as my memories suggest, there should be some kind of evidence.

"All right," I say, but she's not finished.

"In the meantime let's go to the Sick Bay again and see if you've got a fever."

"No way. I'm not risking it."

"Lizzy—"

"Do you trust me?"

There's that hesitation again. Finally, Chloe nods. "Yes, I trust you. But—"

"Then no doctors. Don't tell anyone what I told you. Until we know more, we can't trust anyone else. Got it?"

"Fine."

"No one."

"I said fine!" she says in exasperation.

I take a deep breath and let it out slowly, finally calming a little. It's such a relief to shift some of the weight off my shoulders by sharing the burden with her. But I can almost see her sag under the pressure.

Sweet, caring Chloe. How much would it take to crush her gentle spirit? I make a mental note to be careful how much I put on her.

"So where do we start?" I wonder aloud.

"The last time-statement I heard was at eleven hundred hours," Chloe says. "So we're late for our morning duties."

"Oh, yeah. Duties."

She's right, of course. If we hope to keep our secret and investigate the doctors, we'll need to pretend that everything is normal. That means fulfilling my duties, being on time, and talking to my friends as usual.

Well, if I had any friends besides Chloe. For now, I'll just have to be patient. Something I'm not particularly good at.

Usually, our day begins at eight hundred hours, with basic hygiene and exercise in the Fitness Center. From there we head to the showers, then breakfast prep, the meal itself, and cleanup. Next comes Group with our dome subset. After that are morning duties, which vary daily. Some cadets, such as Noah, have special duties—caring for minor wounds as they arise or running healthcare diagnostics.

Most cadets are greenskeepers. We're assigned an area of plant life and a duty to go with it.

But today we've missed our briefing, so Chloe decides we're better off going straight to lunch hour. Doctor Bauer won't ask too many questions.

Which is good, considering that Chloe is also a horrendous liar.

"I'm really a terrible influence on you," I say as she leads me down the corridor. The bright ceiling tiles are putting my headache into hyperdrive again. I wonder if this is what a migraine feels like.

"What do you mean?"

"I made you late to Group, and now you've missed your duties..."

"Everyone misses duties once in a while," says Chloe in a superior tone. "Besides, I skipped for a noble reason. A friend in need."

"Very charitable of you," I say. It's meant to be a joke, but I wonder how true it is. Chloe is my only friend, but *she* has friends all over the colony. Cadets who aren't always snapping at her or being evasive like I am. So why does she bother?

The lights are really doing a number on my head. Even though I squint, my eyes water uncontrollably. By the time we reach the kitchen, tears are running freely down my cheeks. Which is lucky, because when we enter the glistening hallway, Doctor Bauer isn't alone.

"Lizzy, are you hurt?"

At the sound of Shiffrin's voice, I freeze. Chloe tugs me forward as the doctors surround me, talking over each other. It's just like my reaction when I saw Dosset during Group. Now that I know the role Shiffrin played in erasing my memory, I'm hyperaware of how close she is. As if she's a predator. My only thought is whether I can reach the exit before she pounces.

"What happened?" asks Doctor Bauer.

"Nothing," I say. My voice is thick and my face feels puffy. I must look like a total wreck.

"It doesn't look like nothing," says Shiffrin gently.

And that's when Chloe says something brilliant. Something I would never think to say in a thousand years.

"Just... boy problems."

Both Shiffrin and Bauer take a breath, then sigh with almost theatric sympathy. Stunned at the profound effect these three words have had on the doctors, I wipe my nose on my sleeve and do my best to look like this isn't a surprise.

"Whoever he is, I bet he's a moron," says Bauer softly. "Why don't you two have a seat? We'll manage the kitchen without you today."

I can only nod. Shiffrin leans close, patting my arm.

"We'll talk about it later, hm?"

I try not to bristle under her touch. Even if I don't want to tell her, she'll just read my mind in a few days anyway, won't she?

It occurs to me that if all the doctors are in on this conspiracy, then Bauer must be as well. The idea makes me sad. I'd always felt that, deep down, she at least was on my side.

I'm ushered into the cafeteria. Above our heads, a hanging trellis is suspended from hooks and wires in the dome ceiling. Tendrils of ivy have wound up, around, and down through its silver holes, hanging playfully over the ranks of tables. Like everything else on Mars, it serves a purpose beyond appearances: the plant naturally cleans allergens and mold spores from the air. Still, on rare pasta nights, when the doctors turn down the lights and play opera music, I swear it feels just a little like Italy.

After pointing me toward a chair, Bauer squeezes my shoulder and vanishes into the kitchen. Not a minute later, Chloe appears with raspberry popsicles.

"They said this might make you feel better," she says, alighting on the edge of the chair beside me. Sometimes the way she moves reminds me of a bird.

"Boy problems, huh?" I say with a smile. "Let me guess—Martian youths?"

She blinks at me.

"What?"

"Oh." My heart sinks as I realize she no longer has that memory. "Uh, never mind."

Dry, chilly flavors thaw across my tongue. For a minute neither of us speaks, and I can't help but feel that these memories have somehow created a wall between us. I distract myself by focusing on the simple pleasure of an unexpected treat, biting off chunks as I dare, careful not to give myself a brain freeze. With everything swirling around in there, I don't want to make it more painful than it already is.

By the time we're finished, more Scrubs have begun to enter the room, groups of twos and threes. Those not on cooking duty begin to fill out the tables around us, and with the cadets comes the noise—laughing, shouting, teasing. I bite my lip, trying to ignore the effect it all has on my headache.

A few of the cadets stop to say hello, but it's obvious their words are intended more for Chloe than for me. It doesn't feel as if they're being exclusive, though. More like they've taken some sort of hint. What the hint is, I have no idea. I'm not an unkind person. I just don't like sharing my personal thoughts. Why is it that someone like Chloe can be so warm by instinct, while I have the social inclinations of a cactus?

The truth is, I wish I made friends so easily. But it seems like every time someone asks me something personal, I feel a tension in my shoulders—an aversion running icy fingers down my spine. In some way, it's as if I'm afraid of them. Not that they'll hurt me but that they *could* hurt me if I allowed them in. And from the very moment we're introduced, I know that's something I'll never do.

Picking at my jumpsuit, I let my gaze wander the room. Two tables over, I notice a boy. High forehead, big smile. He's laughing with his friends. He doesn't notice me, but something about him holds my attention. I realize that it's how natural he seems, talking with them. And I can't help but wonder—does he have problems like mine? Does he fear trusting the people around him?

It doesn't seem like it. Actually, it seems like he's happy. Like everyone else is happy. Each with a place to fit in, to be understood.

And then, as I stare at him, a name flits across my mind: Derek Allen Jones. But that's not all. I also remember a birthdate—his birthdate—and a hometown, and a house on the end of a street lined with maple trees, and a bedroom painted sunset orange, a color he liked when he was five, and how many stairs led up to that room, and which ones creaked when he snuck down in the middle of the—

Pain shoots through my head like lightning. I wince and turn away, biting my lip again. Too hard, this time. Blood begins to blossom in my mouth.

"You okay?" Chloe whispers.

"Give me a minute."

Deep breaths. Those seem to help. Inhale until my lungs are full, then exhale slowly, counting to ten. I don't remember learning to do that, but it feels right. So I keep going, sucking my lip until the room isn't spinning and the pounding has quieted. There's talk going on around me still, but I try to block it out. Then one voice breaks through. One I recognize.

Noah Edward Hartmann, born July 17—

"Shut up," I whisper, digging my knuckles into my forehead as the room begins to wobble again. What's he doing in here? He should be on the other side of the colony with his own dome subset.

Above me, his voice takes on a concerned quality.

"Just wanted to see how she was feeling," he says.

"Um, yes, she's fine..."

Their voices grow vague and distant, replaced by another memory. Just as happened before in the Sick Bay, the recollection takes over. As if I'm reliving the moments right now. As if I've stepped inside a holographic imager, projections illuminating my mind.

I'm in the tundra habitat, shivering as I wait for something. Or someone. Gauzy light drapes everything in a gray sheet. I hear the chatter of voices drifting through a stand of evergreens, moving across rows of plants: bearberry, liverwort, reindeer moss.

Directly ahead of me is the craggy hill at the center of the dome, its slopes patterned with frost. To my left, across a truncated field, the ice cave looks like the frozen knuckles of a giant's fist. It was built from Martian boulders. Back when we landed on Mars, the doctors used Mechs to haul in the dirt and rocks we would need for growing plants inside the biomes.

In that way, the soil was a trial run of the landscape. A kind of litmus test for the larger project of terraforming the planet.

Looking at the boulders now, you'd never guess they belong to an alien world.

As I'm waiting, I notice how nervous I am, thinking that this is a horrible plan. But what *is* the plan? She doesn't want to talk to me. She probably doesn't even know I exist.

It's so strange, having these thoughts bounce around my head and this feeling of shivery terror that squeezes my lungs and makes my knees shake. I can tell these sensations aren't coming from me, from Lizzy. They belong to someone else.

So whose memory is it? The cadets who tend this habitat call themselves Polars, which is about as uncreative as it gets. No surprise, Terra is one of them.

I look down at my hands for a clue and find them pale as bone in the cold. They look so much bigger than my own. The nails have been bitten down to almost nothing. And there are freckles. Lots of freckles.

I hear the voices, closer. Then I see her.

Elizabeth.

"Hello, Noah," Chloe calls out.

Belatedly I realize that she's talking to me. That I'm reliving one of Noah's memories. But the impact of this revelation is robbed by how *strange* it feels, watching Chloe and myself move along the path from his perspective. He straightens, stomach tightening with anxiety.

"Uh, hey," he manages in return. Through his eyes, I look at myself—the other Lizzy—and I'm momentarily stunned.

Noah sees me... differently. I'm captivating. Not at all the cold, awkward person I feel like in my own skin. My unwillingness to meet his gaze is just timidness, not avoidance. My eyebrows scrunched low on my forehead make me look less angry than troubled.

His eyes follow the angle of my cheek, brushed pink by the cold air. The way my wavy blond hair bounces as I walk toward him, like the sweeping curtains of a willow. He begins to blush as he studies me this way. Or I do. My head is growing cloudy, blurring the lines between which feelings are his and which are mine.

"Are you waiting for us?" Chloe teases, coming to stand before him. "You must be cold."

His lips answer her as the memory continues, but it's all getting fuzzy, like a camera with the focus thrown off. As if the world has begun to tilt back and forth. I feel nauseous.

Stop it.

I shake my head as if to clear it, and a terrible pain shoots through me. It's like a flare turning my vision white. But I'm still there in the Polar Biome, tongue frozen in my mouth, not from the cold but from fear, for other-Lizzy is looking at me with those bright blue eyes made electric by the surrounding frost, an ionized aurora, mesmerizing and—

"Stop it!" I shout, trying to regain control, to push the memory away. Again the pain hits me. Knocks me to my knees. My vision clears enough for me to catch another glimpse of white. Only this time it's carbon tile. When I'm able to gather the strength to sit up, I find an entire cafeteria of cadets staring at me.

A deathly quiet hangs in the air.

"Lizzy?" Chloe asks, her voice tight with worry. She's trying to pull me to my feet. I look over my shoulder and see Bauer and Shiffrin watching me as well. And in Shiffrin's eyes, I find a glimmer of surprise and understanding.

She knows.

Chapter Four

Yes, she knows. Or at least she suspects. Which is essentially the same thing.

I don't know where I'll go, but I have to get out of here.

"Just a headache," I mutter thickly, and I force my legs to bend, to pick me up, to carry me toward the door. It's like trying to move in zero gravity, my efforts hardly yielding any effect. I've barely reached the other end of the dome before I hear clipped footsteps close behind.

There's no way I can run. I'm still just trying to focus on walking. That, and not vomiting up my popsicle. If only I could've made it to my afternoon duties and lost myself in the wooded undergrowth of the Scrub Biome. But it's far too late for that now.

"Elizabeth."

Shiffrin adopts a warm, friendly tone as she catches up to me, matching my halting pace. I try to smile at her, but it probably comes out more like a grimace.

"Um... hey."

"How are you feeling?"

"Fine."

"That's good." Shiffrin takes my arm and forces me to stop. I consider resisting, but I doubt I could. Bile is at the back of my throat. I never knew a headache could make me sick like this. But then, this is no natural headache.

I stare at a scuff on my left shoe, concentrating on something simple, fighting to remain calm. Presently I realize I'm wearing my running shoes. I must've accidentally put them on this morning in the confused darkness of my sleeping pod.

More feet approach behind us.

"Ah... hello, doctors," says Shiffrin, and I'm surprised by the edge in her voice. When I turn I see the approaching forms of Sarlow and McCallum. Stocky and broad-shouldered, the pair serves as the joint maintenance directors of the colony.

"Good afternoon," says Sarlow. It sounds like a question, as if she's checking.

"Do you have time for a little walk, Lizzy?" asks Shiffrin. "I was hoping we might chat."

"Well, I—"

"This way." And I'm marched off like some kind of criminal, Shiffrin at my right, McCallum at my left, and Sarlow right behind. Silence fills the air, broken only by the squeak of our rubber shoes. For a second I wonder where we're headed, but then we take a turn and I know at once.

We're going into the Helix.

The colony is divided into a series of domes. Largest are the biomes, five immense bubbles that house the assorted climates. Attached to these domes are smaller versions, where the kitchens, sleeping pods, wash areas, and various other facilities are kept. It all makes a sort of clustered ring. At the center of that ring is the Wheel—and at the center of *that* is a sort of tower, called the Helix.

Swirling to a point like a screw, dotted with dishes and antennas, the Helix relays messages to and from Earth. Once it was the spacecraft that brought us to Mars. Now it serves as living quarters to the doctors—probably along with other, more sinister purposes.

As I stumble along, panic mounting, I suddenly wonder just how many memories are inside my head. I've got Chloe's and mine. And I guess Derek's and Noah's. It hits me that I might have more—possibly all of the memories of every cadet on the planet. And if that's true... if that's true, I should know anything they know. Or rather, what they knew. Shouldn't I? Such as, what's inside the Helix, a structure I've never entered.

Gritting my teeth against the tempest inside my brain, I hopelessly try to recall anything I can about the central building. But nothing comes to mind.

"We missed you at breakfast," Shiffrin says in her usual placid tone.

"I wasn't feeling well," I mumble without thinking. Then hastily add, "I feel fine now."

No answer.

As we round a bend in the Wheel, I see the entrance to the Helix—a silver door at the end of an empty hallway. This door looks different from the others on the colony. Shiny chrome instead of carbon, and no handle to be seen. Dread settles in my chest.

Why has no one been inside? Or maybe I just don't know how to reach those memories. Unless cadets *have* gone inside but never left. Maybe the doctors don't need to brainwash you in there. Maybe they lock you inside a cryobed, leaving you adrift in a world of endless dreams.

Maybe that's where Doctor Atkinson really is right now, sealed in a frozen coffin.

We've reached the door. Cameras leer at me from every angle as my heart begins a staccato beat, adrenaline kicking in. I can't go in there. If I do, I might never come back out.

"Have you ever been inside the Helix, Lizzy?" Shiffrin smiles over her shoulder as she puts her thumb up to a reader. Is she really asking? Because she must know I haven't. If I had, we might not be having this discussion.

"No," I barely whisper.

The reader glows a malevolent green.

"Well, this should be educational, then."

I look down at my shoes. Still plenty of tread. But am I in any shape to run? Before I can decide, the door slides open.

"If we just—"

Clenching my jaw, I leap to the left, pumping my arms to gain an extra burst of speed. The move is sluggish, but I manage to duck out of McCallum's reach, feeling a *whoosh* by my ear as his arm swings wide. Shiffrin is shouting, but I don't hear a word. I concentrate on staying upright and putting as much distance between me and them as possible. Down one hall, then another. The world ripples in waves.

I tear into the Tropical Rainforest Biome, and the heat hits me like a wall. The plants here grow so fast that they're already tall, five meters, maybe six, sheltering the path in a tattered canvas of shadow and light.

Down a slope, past tiny, pungent fields of cocoa, spices, and nuts. Beneath my jumpsuit, sweat is already dribbling down my spine. I run beneath the canopy walkway as Bolos—the cadets who tend the biome—peer over the edge. Their faces pull names to mind. Edgar. Anika. Savannah. Paolo. Pushing the thoughts aside, I slam the door panel and take off down another series of hallways.

The Polar Biome is a welcome change after the rainforest climate, like sinking into an icy bath on a blistering summer day. But each biome is a full three kilometers across. By the time I make it to the other side, I'm fatigued and shivering. My sweat has turned to ice.

When I reach the airlock I finally stop, gasping for breath. It's funny, I didn't intend to end up here. But it makes sense, doesn't it? I have to get away, and they can't chase me out there. At least, not easily. I reach for the access panel and a code pops to mind from a latent memory.

Incredibly, it works.

The great locking mechanism begins to spin, like on some colossal vault. My lungs are shuddering. But it's not just the sprint that's got me short of breath. I realize that I'm about to actually go out onto the Martian landscape. I try to recall if any other cadets have been outside the domes. But just as with the Helix, it's a blank. Like trying to remember the face of a person I've never met.

The door opens and I step into a square chamber about the size of a two-car garage. Spacesuits are lined along the walls like suits of armor, sentries at attention. As I move toward one, I hesitate.

What am I thinking? If I leave, I'll only get about six hours before I start running out of oxygen. And then they'll catch me. That or I'll die out there, alone with the rocks and dust.

I know one thing: I'm not ready to die. I'm not even sure I'm ready to fight. In the corner of the room, I notice another security camera watching me. Rage swells. Isn't it enough that they pry into our minds, taking whatever they like? What gives them the right to watch us so closely, making judgments about who we get to be?

Without thinking, I rip a glove off one of the suits and throw it across the room. My aim is better than I expected; the metal fist obliterates the delicate plastic iris, leaving it hanging at an angle like a broken wrist. Then the glove falls with a clatter into an empty gathering crate.

No one can see me now.

How long until they catch up? I'm quick, but once they realize where I've gone, I'm sure Sarlow and McCallum won't be far behind. A minute, tops. This moment is all I've got.

Think, Lizzy, I tell myself furiously. They brought us to Mars for our brains, didn't they?

I stare at the gathering crate, and suddenly an idea pops into my head. Because I'm out of time, I don't stop to question it. I start moving, disassembling the rest of the suit whose glove I threw. Then I dump the whole thing into the same crate. It fits, but barely. I shut the lid.

Next I dash from suit to suit, sliding down the reflective golden sun visor on each helmet. Then I drop the bottom half of the last suit, duck, slide my arms up into the top half, and pick up the heavy white pants, buckling the two halves together.

The whole process takes less than a minute, but I can already hear footsteps racing along the hall. I punch the airlock button, opening the door to the outside.

Immediately, red lights begin to spiral and an alarm goes off. The door leading back into the colony seals up as I pull on my gloves. I hear a number of loud clicks and metallic thumps.

Thirty seconds. That's how long it takes for the airlock to seal and begin depressurizing. Anything inside the airlock that isn't maintaining an atmosphere of its own will be choked and frozen before it can even shiver. Or at least, that's how it was when we first landed. Now that Aster has been terraforming for a few months, it could take longer. If shrubs can take root out there, it can't be entirely hazardous, can it?

As soon as the depressurization is complete, I begin to grow lightheaded. It takes me a few seconds to realize that my oxygen isn't flowing. I fumble with the controls on the front of my suit as the other end starts to open. Then I look up.

It's so desolate.

A gentle slope shoulders upward, dust and rocky terrain scattered with tufts of yellow plants and cactus-like growths. Even through my visor the sunlight is stark, only hampered by a gale of dust that's just begun to kick up, reducing visibility.

What's out there? I can't help but wonder. And for a fraction of a second, I'm tempted to find out. Are fragile, single-celled organisms wiggling to life in a desert puddle even now? Have entire ecosystems formed in some half-centimeter fissure just beneath the rusty surface?

For a prolonged moment, I just stare. It's funny, but until now I've never really considered how amazing it is that life is able to exist here. Or anywhere. The dust and dirt that blow into the airlock, once dead, can now support life again—even if it isn't much.

They say Mars was like Earth, billions of years ago. With time and care, is it possible we could bring it back? Looking out at it now, I can almost forget what waits behind me and dream.

Almost.

The alarm is going off again, and the door begins to close. This is my moment. I click off my air, let my arms hang as naturally as I can, and stand absolutely still. As soon as the airlock is sealed, the other door opens.

"I can't *believe* this."

Shiffrin is the first one into the room. Her usual cool demeanor has evaporated, leaving behind a woman on the edge of a breakdown.

"We should have been able to head her off before she ever reached an airlock. How did she get the access code? I mean, she... she could die out there!"

Sarlow and McCallum are next, wheezing. Then Conrad, and another doctor who I think is the agriculturalist from Polar. They've only just arrived when a beeping fills the room. Shiffrin begins fiddling with her watch. A holographic image blooms, a full-size, ghostly blue human projected into their midst.

Dosset.

An oxygen cart is at his side, tubes snaking up to his crinkled face. The rest of the doctors grow quiet, the silence interrupted only by the hiss and click of the respirator. It's as if they're afraid of him. Or maybe just respectful.

I attempt to slow my own breathing, to save what little air I have.

"Doctor?" asks Conrad hesitantly.

At first, Dosset doesn't answer. He's looking at the place where the now-hidden suit had stood, rubbing his stubbly jaw. Then the projection turns, as if drawn like a magnet toward the gathering crate. My heart stops.

But he doesn't seem concerned with the container. Instead, he tilts his head up, carefully examining the broken security camera.

"Well," he says, his voice muffled. "I'm genuinely surprised for once." It's hard to hear the hologram through my helmet, especially over the thundering of blood in my ears. Then, abruptly, Dosset laughs. The others exchange looks.

"Something amuses you?" Shiffrin asks.

"Our dear Doctor Atkinson," he replies once he's caught his breath. The hologram turns. From this angle, he's looking almost directly at me. Even though I know he can't see beyond my golden visor, it makes me want to start running again. "I believe we've just learned what he stole the Memory Bank for. Or rather, *who* he stole it for."

The full weight of his words hits me like a sledgehammer.

Atkinson.

Suddenly it falls into place. If Shiffrin didn't give back my memories, someone else must have. And Atkinson went missing the same morning I woke up with my headache. They must've known that he stole this... this *Memory Bank*, but they didn't know what he planned to do with it. That would explain why Dosset started the rumor about a virus, so that if a cadet woke with a head full of random memories, they'd just think they were sick and turn themselves in.

Like Chloe almost did with me.

Conrad is aghast.

"You think he uploaded the entire Memory Bank to a single girl?"

"It's not so unbelievable," Dosset replies. "Only two cadets ever learned the access code to the airlock, and Elizabeth Engram was not one of them. To my knowledge, neither cadet ever shared the code. If she doesn't have their memories, how else was Elizabeth able to leave?"

"But that many memories at one time," Conrad sputters. "He... it could've killed her!"

I can feel the air growing thin inside the suit. Just a little longer. If I can just hold on a little longer, surely they'll leave.

Shiffrin is nodding, looking lost.

"That's why the others—"

"Yes," says Dosset.

"And how he—"

"I believe so."

She wraps her arms around herself as if to ward off a chill.

"I never would've thought Atkinson capable of this."

"Which is exactly why we must continue to do as we always have," says Dosset. "His very actions prove the necessity."

"Did we at least learn why?" Conrad asks.

"Why?" Dosset repeats.

"Why he did this. What he must have told Elizabeth to do next. Surely he had a plan, in order to take such a risk?"

At first, there's no answer. Just the hiss, click. Hiss, click. Then—

"For now, focus your attention on Elizabeth. Whatever his motivation, you make a good point: Marcus still seems to underestimate the trauma involved with heavy memory alteration." He turns to the maintenance directors. "Jackie and Patrick, you go after Elizabeth. She'll be too disoriented to get far, but knowing her, my guess is that she'll keep running until someone stops her." Again he pivots, this time shifting his oxygen tank. "The rest of you, talk with her fellow cadets. See if she's told anyone what she knows. Anyone she considers a friend. I don't want loose threads."

"Understood," says Sarlow.

"Oh, and doctors?" They all look up. "Let's handle this delicately. We still have several days until the next Revision. The last thing we want is some kind of widespread panic."

"Of course."

Dosset pauses, and then he adds, "And let's have no more talk about Marcus Atkinson."

The holographic image vanishes. Shiffrin and the others hang about for only a moment, then hurry off without a word.

I don't even have time to worry about Sarlow and McCallum discovering me before they've chosen other suits, expertly stepping into the armor-like plates. Then the airlock opens again, revealing that the gale has intensified into a howling storm, obscuring the slope and the plants completely. The two hulking astronauts click on headlamps and start out into the swirling dust. Moments later they're gone.

Seconds crawl, my lungs trickling fire. The airlock door begins to close, and then it seals. Pressure returns and the lights click off, leaving only red emergency bulbs like giant, mounted fireflies along the wall. I claw to release my helmet.

The seal pops and I'm gasping, taking greedy gulps of air. I don't think about anything else until the burning in my chest has eased. When I feel normal again I shakily unbuckle the pants of my suit and slip out, hoping the doctors are far enough away to not hear the noise.

My sweaty jumpsuit clings to my body. I think about Chloe and feel a mixture of guilt and fear. I should never have involved her. They're likely on their way to find her right now. I wonder if she'll be able to lie when she tells them I've got the virus.

At this point, I wonder if she'll even think she's lying.

Slowly I sink to the floor as the wind picks up, sending tremors through the airlock. What am I supposed to do now? When Dosset's thugs don't find me out there in the dust, they'll eventually be forced to assume that I'm dead. Will they just erase me? Like a memory too dangerous to hang around, the déjà vu of a girl who had only a single friend.

I feel like I want to cry. But I can't. I'm either too tired or too numb. What I really want is for all of this to just go away. I'd love nothing more than to walk up to Dosset, tap him on the shoulder, and say, "Please take these memories. I don't want them." Then he'd pull out a Stitch and make it all disappear. Because that's what the doctors do.

But inside my head, I feel the voices swirling. The volume is low enough that I can think, but barely. Echoes of grief and embarrassment, stabs of guilt and pain. Many of the memories are negative, it seems. But as I vaguely recall getting caught in a lie, I realize it was what made me careful to be honest. And when I pushed that girl and called her those names, I didn't mean it. I was jealous. But

I never had a chance to be forgiven by her, and I never forgave myself.

Surging and crushing, the tornado of thoughts encircles me as I pull my knees up to my chest, cowering in the darkness. I feel the weight of distrust, unhappiness, and repeated mistakes, of passion and longing and hope. It's a black hole, and I want to escape, but I don't know how I can. I'm the only one who knows these memories were stolen. They're mine now. I can see myself as the victim, the aggressor, the fool. It feels as if each memory is a piece of my past. An act I personally committed.

"That's not me," I whisper to myself. Twisting, I grab my space helmet and gaze into the golden reflection just visible in the brooding light. Tears spring to my eyes after all. "I'm Lizzy. Those memories aren't me. I'm Elizabeth Engram."

I'm Elizabeth Engram.

And I remember everything.

Chapter Five

How long I sit in the airlock trying to sort out my thoughts, I can't say. My mind feels dull, almost paralyzed by the weight it now carries. But I force myself out of the memories and back into the present, wiping my nose as I set the helmet aside.

I can't stay here forever. And anyway, I'm being pathetic. It won't be long until Sarlow and McCallum return. I imagine how stupid it will look—Elizabeth Engram, threat to Dosset's brainwashing empire, found sniveling in the airlock. I should be forming some kind of plan, not wallowing in self-pity.

I decide to start with what I know.

From what I've gathered, the doctors have been altering our memories for weeks. To be sure we don't catch on to what's really happening, they keep a close eye on our movements—and they accomplish this in a series of ways.

First is the obvious. There are probably a few hundred cameras throughout the domes. With facial recognition software, they'll only need one good shot of my face to peg my location and send someone after me.

Second, there are dozens of cadets who will know me on sight. That's not even counting the forty or so doctors who've probably been alerted to my absence.

Third, they've got all my past memories. Dosset seemed to have a pretty good idea of what I'd do next—though already he's made a mistake. If I hope to elude capture, I'm guessing I'll need to be unpredictable. Which means returning to my pod is not an option.

What options does that leave me? I can't run away from the colony. And I can't just stay on the move. I'm already exhausted from the headaches, the sprinting, the barely consuming any food or water. Not to mention crying. My eyes feel as if they've been rubbed in rock salt. Really, my only option is to lay low with someone they wouldn't expect. Which begs the question: Who would I decidedly *not* go to for help?

Terra Donahue. My teeth clench involuntarily at the thought. Even if I were willing to seek her out, there's no chance she'd help me. But besides her, there's only one other person I go out of my way to avoid.

Noah Hartmann.

Just his name brings up memories of the awkward conversations we've had. But there are other memories, such as the one from the Polar Biome, flitting around in my head as well. For the briefest of moments, I allow one forward. I think it's of the first time we met.

We're in the Scrub recreation room, sprawled out on inflated chairs around the ping-pong table. And again, I look... like a different girl. Like the kind of person who could change your life with a smile. At least that's how Noah sees me. But he's too nervous to speak. Instead, he just watches, taking note of how I bite my lip when I'm—

I shake the memory off, my face growing hot despite the cold temperature of the airlock. Forget it. I'd rather not know. He doesn't remember, so it doesn't matter. The bottom line is that he makes me uncomfortable, and, in my own way, I make him uncomfortable too.

As far as places to hide, I'd say his sleeping pod is the safest place on the planet.

So that just leaves the problem of getting there.

Though I'm often aware of the cameras, I don't have their locations memorized. Not even close. And yet, as I think about them, I seem to recall one right outside the airlock, above the door. It should have a blind spot along the wall. If I slide past, I might be able to avoid its viewing range. And if I move down the corridor, there'd be another one on the far wall. If I edged beneath it, I could use the access door to cut through a utility dome, past the water reclaimers, and then take the next hallway...

As my plan unfolds, I gradually realize that I can visualize each and every dome along the path. And not just those domes, but others too—maybe all of them, as if I have a matrix of memories behind my eyes, forming an atlas of the colony.

I shove the images away, unnerved. I don't know whether I should feel exhilarated or terrified. Right now, I guess I don't have time for either. I've already lingered in the airlock too long.

Collecting my nerve, I press the button to cycle the airlock. I can only hope there aren't any passing doctors.

A few painfully loud thunks, and the door opens.

There's no one in sight.

"So far, so good," I mutter to myself.

Instantly I know that I was hiding for longer than I thought. The ceiling tiles have been switched off, leaving the halls lit only by soft green runner lights.

Every night after the cadets have gone to bed, all non-critical electronics get shut down: holograms, clocks, lights, everything. And it makes sense. With no power coming from the solar panels until dawn, we've got to regulate the biomes, the oxygenators, and other demanding systems on a limited energy reserve.

I'm actually surprised that the airlock is still on. This late, Sarlow and McCallum must've already returned from their search. I'll bet the storm drove them off course and they entered through another airlock.

It's all good news for me. Until sunrise, the halls will be dark and empty. And that means I might have a real shot at getting where I'm going, unnoticed.

Since I've already visualized my path, it's actually pretty easy to put it into action. Security is tight, but there are gaps. I tiptoe past the sterile gaze of the cameras waiting around every bend.

My evasive dance probably looks ridiculous, but there's no one here to see. I'm alone in these halls, each as familiar as if I've walked it a thousand times.

Cadet sleeping pods are divided by gender and situated on the top levels of their lavatory domes, just down the hall from their sub-set's biome. Though Noah is a medical cadet, he's also technically a Xeri: one of the cadets assigned to the Arid and Coastal Desert Biome. I guess they're named after xeriscaping, the scientific term for cultivating drought-resistant plants.

All Xeri vegetation—buffalo grass, agave, succulents—is dug out into switchbacks that form a deep, irrigated basin. It may seem pointless to bring a bunch of cacti to Mars, but these species will be first to survive out in the bitter, freezing wind.

In fact, many of the plants I tend will be last to adapt.

Up the stairs, I arrive in a spotless hallway with doors on either side. Even without the nameplates, I know which pod belongs to Noah. Near the end on the left. As I draw closer, I can't believe I'm actually about to go through with this.

Let's just hope he doesn't sleep naked.

"Four, four, one, eight," I whisper, punching the code. Recalling the numbers makes my head throb. It seems as if every time I pull up a memory, it fuels a new round of headaches. I'll have to make a note of that.

The inside of his room is, like all cadet pods, mostly bare. A plastic cube table. A lamp of three stacked orbs. A single chair with tripod legs, cradling an inflated seat. On the floor lies a crumpled jumpsuit, and the bed is a lumpy mass of sheets. I close the door with a careful click.

And then it hits me. Up until this moment, I haven't really con-sidered what I'm going to tell him. Because, of course, I have to tell him something. I can't just sleep here and run off in the morning.

What if he wakes first? Anyway, I'm in dire need of a friend now that the doctors have Chloe. But that leads me back to what I'm going to say.

Hey, I know you daydream about me, and it actually makes me super uncomfortable, but I was hoping I could sleep here tonight so the evil doctors can't brainwash me. Cool?

Yeah, Lizzy. Real convincing. You don't sound like a psychopath at all.

A *clack* on the ceiling makes me flinch. It's shortly followed by another. Then all at once the downpour begins, hail drumming along the thermoplastic that forms the outside wall. I creep over to the porthole, staring out as tiny chunks of ice bounce off the transparent film. The sound becomes an acoustic drone, a sharper version of the rain back on Earth. It's oddly soothing.

By now I'm so tired I can barely stand, so I allow myself to sink into the chair. "Incredible" doesn't quite cover how good it feels to rest on something other than the airlock floor. Just for a second I close my eyes, listening to the rattling cadence.

When I wake up it's still dark.

At first I'm not sure where I am, and I struggle out of the chair onto tingly legs. My panic subsides as I see Noah still sleeping, his face turned toward me, serene in the soft glow of the moon. It's not our moon. It's one of the moons of Mars—Phobos or Deimos. Probably Phobos, the larger and closer of the two. Deimos is so small, you could almost mistake her for a star.

I return to the porthole and see that the storm has ended. Since our colony is bordered by mountains, it's shielded from the worst of the weather—but it also means our portholes look out on nothing but clumpy red dirt. And since I've never been outside the colony, I've never actually seen the Martian stars.

It's weird to think that, since leaving Earth, I haven't seen the sky even once.

I remember one night when my cousins and I went camping. My parents let us have our own tent, pitched not so far from theirs.

After the adults fell asleep, we left the cocoons of our sleeping bags to stare up at the night sky.

That was the first time I saw Mars. Even to the naked eye, it was red—a dancing ruby in a swirl of diamond white. Gazing upward, I lost my balance. It felt as if I were adrift in those constellations. As if I'd already left Earth behind for a home on another world.

Then we heard a twig snap and a low growl. After hearing so many stories about coyotes, bears, and wolves around the campfire that evening, it took us exactly three seconds to get back into our tent, screaming as we went.

The next morning we found out that my dad and uncle had followed us, just to scare us silly. Mother had not approved of their antics, or of my sneaking out.

At the time I'd thought her fights with my dad were just part of being married.

"Noah."

He doesn't hear me the first time. I crouch and gently shake him by the shoulders. "Hey. Wake up." Fluttering eyelids, then he sees me. He recoils and knocks his head against the wall, crying out at the sudden pain.

"Shut up, dummy," I say desperately. "It's me, Lizzy."

"Lizzy?" he repeats, as if I've just claimed to be an alien invader.

"Yes. Keep your voice down before you wake everyone up."

"What... what time is it?"

I reach over to engage the backlight on his clock, but of course, it's dead. It could be two hundred hours, or five. At least there's no sign of dawn outside the porthole.

"It's late," I say quietly.

He's staring at me again.

"Okay. Uh... what are you doing in my pod?"

"Well, at the moment I don't really have anywhere else to go," I say. Here goes nothing. I pull the chair over to his bedside and lean forward, fists under my chin, elbows on my knees. "I have some pretty heavy stuff to tell you, Noah."

"Now?"

"Yep. Now."

He just watches me with those big brown eyes of his, one cheek still creased with sleep. Rubbing his face, he sits up a bit.

"Okay. I'm listening."

"All right," I say. "For starters, you should know there are things the doctors have been keeping from us. Intentionally."

"Like what?"

"A lot of things." How do I possibly say this? It sounds so outrageous. "They have this... device. It's called a Stitch. They use it to scan your brain. And if they find memories they don't like, they erase them. Well, technically I guess they steal them, because they keep a kind of copy in a Memory Bank. Are you with me so far?"

"Uh huh."

Sure, he is.

"Well, something happened to me last night after the Verced wore off. That's the drug they use to knock us out. When I woke up this morning, I had all those stolen memories in my head." Before he can laugh or shout for help or tell me I'm totally insane, I hurry on. "Yours, Chloe's, everyone's. At least the cadets. I don't think I have any from the doctors. I haven't remembered any yet. Which sort of makes sense. I mean, why would they be stealing their own memories?"

I almost laugh at myself. None of it makes sense. Why would they steal *our* memories? The whole thing is entirely unbelievable.

Noah has an incredible capacity for silence. He doesn't even move. He just watches me, like one of those paintings where only the eyes are alive.

"Look, I know it sounds crazy," I say, taking his stillness as an invitation to continue. "But I can prove it to you. Um, hold on a minute."

Scrunching my brow in concentration I dig deep, trying to pull up anything I can find. It's not easy to summon memories on command like this. It's as if I'm whipping through a flip book, trying to stop on a specific page. When nothing useful presents itself, I decide to just work with what I've already remembered. "Okay, well for starters, you... think I'm pretty, right?"

He blinks.

"H-huh?"

"I've got all these memories," I begin, averting my gaze. "Of you and me. Well, mostly of you watching me. Like the time we bumped into each other in the Polar Biome, you got really nervous..."

I risk a glance and see that, even in the darkness, his face is bright red. My cheeks are starting to burn as well. And my headache is returning. This is a disaster. Isn't there anything about Noah Hartmann that isn't so painfully awkward?

I need something else, something less embarrassing.

Again I try, and this time a new memory surfaces. At first, I'm relieved as the sensations take over. I find myself with a group of cadets in the Xeri cafeteria. I'm telling a story. Everyone is watching, having fun. And then it happens.

Slowly I become aware of their eyes. They're heavy, the way they hang on me. Then I become aware of my words. And suddenly I'm not thinking about what comes next in the story but fearing what will happen if I freeze up with everyone watching. It's a self-fulfilling prophecy: First I go numb. Then my chest tightens, my words tumbling to a halt. And the terror continues to grow, multiplying like a deadly virus.

Everyone is still staring, expecting me to go on, to finish the story. But the pressure is compounding, and the fear has become my reality. Smiles fade as they begin to look at each other, wondering what's wrong.

I want to run, or hide under the table—but I can't move. I sit there with icy palms. Tunnel vision. Mindless panic. Feeling as if I'm in front of an oncoming train racing along the tracks. As if the whole planet has somehow twisted itself into a knife, and it's pointed at my heart.

It's the most terrifying thing I've ever experienced. And I'm petrified.

With a shudder I push the memory back, sweat breaking across my forehead. It takes a second to catch my breath. I've never felt anxiety like that before. It was as if... I felt as if my life were ending. As if everyone wanted to hurt me.

And for the first time, I think I understand why Noah is so quiet in front of others.

"Panic attacks," I blurt. "You have... panic attacks. You had one during Group, when Doctor Hitch asked you a question. And the night before we were supposed to go out on First Expedition. And one when you got turned around in the Clover domes and were late to Briefing. And... well, you've had a lot."

Further silence. Then he sits up a little more.

"Yeah. I just had one this morning, actually." He looks at the floor, embarrassed again. "I don't remember when they started. To be honest, I don't remember the ones you just mentioned. But they sound right." He hesitates. "You said those memories were taken?"

"That's right," I say, nurturing a frail hope that he might yet believe me.

"So... how did you get them?" he asks.

"Doctor Atkinson, I think. I overheard some of the doctors saying he stole the Memory Bank. They think he had some kind of plan to put an end to the Revisions. That's what Dosset called the brainwashing technique. Anyway, they captured Atkinson before he could pull it off. He must've been trying to use me in some way. But I never got a chance to find out how."

And then a bizarre thought hits me. Up until now, I hadn't really considered why it was *me* that Atkinson chose. I've only been concerned with the fact that I have the memories and, as a result, I'm in danger.

"Now the doctors are all looking for me, to stop me from telling anyone what I know," I continue. "Dosset must be able to review the Memory Bank quickly, because he already knew who all my friends were. I think they got Chloe."

"Chloe Tindal?"

I nod.

For a minute the quiet is broken only by the steady, calming hum of the oxygenator vent. More of Noah's memories are trying to surface in my mind, stirred up like the bottom of a lake bed, turning my thoughts cloudy. But I manage to keep them down.

"So then, what's next?" he asks.

"Huh?"

"If the doctors know everything about us, we'll have to do something they don't expect." He pushes himself all the way into a sitting position. The sheets fall back, revealing a skinny white torso and arms. I look away as he grabs a t-shirt and pulls it over his head. "I mean, all those things you know about me, they know too, right?"

"I think so," I say slowly.

"Okay, so what's something they won't expect?" When I don't answer, he says, "Break Atkinson out of wherever they're keeping him, for starters."

I can't help but smile.

"And I thought I sounded crazy."

"No, you don't. We just need a good plan. And we'll have to be unpredictable." He smiles in return, a little boyish. "They brought us to Mars for our brains, didn't they?"

A balloon of hope dares to expand inside my chest. The voices of my memories grow a little quieter as if for the first time believing they might be heard.

Could we really outwit Dosset? Is there a chance we could get Atkinson back and finish whatever he started?

I can't believe how easily Noah trusts me. I'd half expected him to call for a doctor the moment I woke him up. But then as I sit back, I catch the way he's looking at me, just like he did in his memories. And it hits me why.

He loves me.

All the relief I just felt evaporates like a breath of freezing air.

That's it. He thinks he loves me. Which means from the moment he woke to find me in his pod, Noah has *wanted* to believe me. To be the hero and save the girl of his dreams.

I suddenly feel guilty, and acutely alone. This is why I don't tell people what I'm thinking. This is why I can't trust anyone. Because once you let someone in, you're vulnerable. They can use those feelings against you. Like I just did with Noah. Without even meaning to, I've manipulated him. What happens if he gets hurt, or locked up inside the Helix?

It'll be all my fault.

Now I wish I'd never come to his pod at all. But I know I need his help. I can't meet his gaze as I say, "Chloe will help us, assuming she hasn't been brainwashed. We'll have to be smart about how we contact her, but between the three of us, maybe we can make it work."

"We'll just be careful and take it slow," he says.

"Not too slow," I reply. "We've only got a week."

"A week?"

I nod, pushing the last of my misgivings away. It's not as if I had a choice. Noah is the only person I could turn to. "Revisions happen every Sunday night during therapy. If we can't find Atkinson before then, you and Chloe will have your minds read. Then they'll know everything, whether we tell them or not."

"That gives us... six days," he says.

I glance out the porthole and see that a vague glow has begun, casting the dusty rocks in a pallid gray. Even the mild light is enough to sting my eyes. "We should get some sleep."

Noah looks surprised.

"You're going to sleep here?"

"Where else?"

"Oh, uh... I didn't think about it. Here, you can sleep in my bed." He starts to rise.

"No," I tell him, pushing him back down. "Just give me a blanket and a pillow."

He quickly obeys and I wrap myself up like I'm camping, as far from his bed as I can manage. Even in the shadows, I can see his eyes watching me. Now knowing what the look means, my guilt returns in a fresh wave, followed by an erosive sense of help-lessness.

"And can you quit with the staring?" I say sharply. "It's kind of creeping me out."

"Oh. Sorry."

He rolls over and I try to get comfortable, burying my feelings for good. Just a couple hours until a new day begins. After that, I'll figure out what I'm supposed to do next.

"Hey, Lizzy?"

"Yeah?"

"Have there been any other cadets that were on the colony? Like, cadets they erased from our memories?"

Without even thinking, I know there are. One of them slept in the pod two doors down from Noah—a lanky girl with a dark pony-tail and bony arms. And a boy with freckles along his nose and a quirky laugh. He was a Bolo.

The headache spikes as I recall their faces, making me cringe. Other than hazy memories that haunt the edges of my subcon-scious, there's no trace of them. They've simply disappeared.

"No."

It's my first lie to him, but surely not the last. From here on out, the less I have to tell Noah Hartmann, the better.

Chapter Six

When I was little I'd have a recurring dream in which something was about to crush me. I'd be in its shadow, something so large I couldn't even see what it was. And that's what made it so terrifying—it consumed everything else, bearing down on me with the weight of the entire world. No matter how fast I ran, I could never escape it.

I'd always wake up screaming.

A hand closes over my mouth, and I bite down hard, drawing blood. The metallic taste fills my mouth, sickeningly warm. Someone groans and the hand vanishes. I spew the liquid, trying to get my bearings as an urgent voice speaks in my ear.

"Lizzy, be quiet or they'll know you're in here."

I recognize the voice.

Noah.

The nightmare ebbs as I blink away the tears, Noah's pod coming into focus. He cradles his hand, and I see that I've bitten him badly, almost tearing off a chunk of skin. Grabbing a shirt, he tightly wraps the wound as blood trickles down his forearm, dripping to the floor.

"Noah, I'm sorry, I didn't mean to—"

"It's okay, just be quiet," he insists.

I realize I'm still almost shouting, and lower my voice. "I'm so sorry."

"It's okay," he repeats. When he pulls away the t-shirt, blood immediately springs forth, ruby red. Like Mars from a distance. "I'll get some supplies from the Sick Bay. No one'll know." I'm shaking, but I nod. "What were you dreaming about?" he asks.

The question is so unexpected, it actually makes me flinch.

"I... don't remember," I lie, glancing at the door. He's either bad at reading people or he just trusts me that much, because he doesn't question my answer.

"Must've been pretty bad." He picks up a gym bag with his good hand. "I've got to get to fitness hour. After the Sick Bay, I mean. Can I bring you anything? Besides food?"

"Don't worry about it. I'm not staying."

"You're not?"

He's surprised. And a little disappointed.

"I need to talk to Chloe about our plan, assuming she still remembers me. And there are a few supplies we'll need if we actually hope to rescue Atkinson," I say.

"I could get them for you, so you don't have to—"

"No," I say firmly. "I can handle myself."

For a second I wonder if he'll push back. But he just watches me with those honey-brown eyes of his. In the daylight, emerald flecks ring his pupils. "Well, if I see any doctors running, I'll be sure to take a few of them out," he jokes.

Again I feel a twinge of powerless frustration. But I don't bother arguing because he's already walking out the door.

Once he's gone, I take time to consider my next move. As much as I'd like to leave Noah and Chloe out of this, I know I can't do it alone. But what am I trying to do—rescue Atkinson? It sounds crazy now that I've had a few hours to sleep on it. Still, I'm not sure what else to do. I have no idea what I'm up against. All I've got is a head full of memories that I can hardly keep straight. It would be nice to have someone to look to. Someone who actually knows what they're doing and has reason to believe I'm right for the task.

Again I decide to start simple. We need supplies. The kind of stuff to dismantle a lock, tie someone up, or break a camera.

A maintenance closet will have the basics: rope, wire, scissors, tape, pliers, wrenches, screwdrivers. But I don't want to take it all from one place, or someone might notice. Better to stop by maintenance closets in each dome, leaving smaller gaps in the resources.

It crosses my mind that if I'm apprehended I might need some kind of weapon. But the idea of intentionally hurting someone makes me fidgety. And yet, having already been chased by Sarlow and McCallum once, I can't take chances. I add a pruning sickle to the list.

At least I know that if anyone gets hurt, the Sick Bay will be able to patch them up like they did for Chloe.

Thinking of Chloe, I realize I'd better get going. She's always the first one done with her duties, usually reaching the kitchen around sixteen hundred hours. That gives me only the morning and early afternoon to work the domes and gather what I need; and since this time around the halls will be lit, it won't be as simple as last night. I'll need a disguise.

I take a look around Noah's pod and manage to scrounge up a surgical mask, a hat, and a jumpsuit from the back of a cabinet. After tucking my hair up under the cap, I slip the mask over my ears and thrust my hands deep into the pockets of the jumpsuit, zipped over my own. It's a couple sizes too big for me. But if I need to change quickly, I can just ditch the outer layer. Plus, with a Xeri badge, no one will suspect my identity.

At least that's the hope.

It's slow going, moving around the domes. My first instinct is to use the Wheel, but compared to the rest of the colony, it's practically bristling with cameras. Instead, I fall back on the biomes. The habitats take longer to traverse, but there are no cameras inside, likely because they don't attach well to the cladding panels of the high, gauzy ceiling.

My hat proves to be another problem. I keep it pulled low so no one can see my face. But that also makes it hard to see where I'm going. It's already easy to get lost if you aren't paying attention. The halls are all a uniform, immaculate white. Really, the only color on the colony is the vegetation in the biomes and the door markers.

Each dome subset is given a wayfinding color code so that we know where we are. Red for Scrubs, yellow for Bolos, blue for Polars, green for Clovers, and orange for Xeris. The markers show in descending order on the doorjambs, with your current location at the top of the archways—currently, orange.

But this means that in order to see where I'm going, I need to potentially reveal myself to a camera. A risk I can't really afford to take. So I keep my head down and rely on my hearing.

It's an odd experience, only glimpsing a few steps ahead of me. Never seeing who might be moving my direction or what they might be doing. As I trudge down a trail of packed dirt, even just the voices of my fellow cadets stir up memories. Yet I do better here than in the cafeteria. The secret, I realize, is to keep myself focused on something tangible, something real, such as the tightly woven texture of my jumpsuit or the gray pebbles that dot the soil on either side of the path.

No meltdowns. No freak outs. I simply can't afford them. For as long as possible I need to keep Dosset thinking I'm stranded on a Martian dune, gasping for my final breath.

Wire cutters from the Bolos, rope from the Polars, scissors and tape from the Clovers, and a few odds and ends from the Xeris later, I'm headed back toward Noah's pod. Then, as I pass a portable defibrillator on the wall, the sight causes a memory to surface. Some latent thought from a cadet I've never met: Romesh Dean, a Clover.

Stopping to consider his idea, I look over my shoulder and find an empty hall. Indecision settles in my gut. Usually, I'd just stick to the plan. That's what I'm good at—knowing my goal and reaching it. I've already got what I came for.

And yet, with these new memories come new perspectives. My lip begins to sting as I chew on the cut from yesterday, wavering. What could it hurt? Someone might notice it missing. But the possibility it represents...

I make up my mind. After disengaging the alarm, I shove the defibrillator into my pocket and hurry off toward Noah's pod, heart hammering along the way. I don't breathe easy again until I've locked the door and laid everything out on the floor.

Before I acknowledge the defibrillator, I examine each item twice. Then I sit back and swallow nervously. My eyes wander to the device.

Tentatively I cradle it in my hands. No bigger than a fist. Made of smooth, innocuous plastic. I'm being stupid. Cowardly. I scowl at the synthetic cover.

"Okay, Lizzy," I finally mutter. "Either Romesh Dean is a genius, or you're about to give yourself a heart attack—literally."

Closing my eyes, I recall the memory in the clearest detail I can manage.

It's a simple idea, really. A defibrillator is meant to shock a stilled heart to beating again. But if that person's heart is already going, the jolt would do the opposite: make it stop. If I can dial down the output so that it's not fatal, the defibrillator could be turned into a kind of stun gun.

Easy enough. Just so long as I don't shock myself in the process.

Pushing through the discomfort in my head, I focus on Romesh's thoughts. To begin, I pull apart the plastic casing, carefully laying out each half. Next is a metal sheath that surrounds the electrical components, protecting against energy spikes. That takes a little work, getting the safety valves to release. Then I strip the wire and alter one of the resistors to change the output. Finally, I attempt the tricky part—removing the failsafe, which prevents the device from shocking anyone who still has a pulse.

I'm amazed at how detailed Romesh's memories are. As expected, concentrating like this is giving me a titanic headache. The whole process takes longer than I anticipated. By the time I finally sit back and wipe the sweat from my forehead, I feel as if I'm going to throw up again. But it's done. Somehow I managed to pull it off.

"Thank you, Romesh," I murmur, picking up my new weapon.

It won't be very easy to use, since I still have to attach the patches to some part of my victim's skin. But it's better than nothing. It strikes me as kind of incredible that the idea of a total stranger has been so helpful to me. Though I guess we're not really strangers anymore, now that I have his memories. I might even know him better than some of his friends do.

With that realization comes something else—the understanding that these memories are more than just a reason I'm in danger.

They're also a tool.

On the overhead, fourteen hundred hours is announced. Not a moment too soon. The gnawing tooth of hunger has begun to wear into my stomach, and I've got a long walk ahead of me. It's time to find some food and talk to Chloe.

The trek to the Scrub kitchen takes me back through the stifling desert heat of the Xeri Biome, snaking down the mesa-like switchbacks to the valley floor. Here, the air hangs hottest. I've only been in a real desert once, when we drove through Death Valley on our way to the Midwest. Then and now it struck me as incredible how alien the topography can feel, even though deserts make up nearly a fifth of the earth's landmass.

At length, I reach the breezy calm of the Clover Biome. There are two halves to this habitat. On one side trellises of herb shelves extend two to three stories high, with pulley systems that lift green-skeepers up to reach them. In contrast to these latticed towers, the other half of the dome is packed with fields of plants and flowers, a patchwork of leafy vegetation. Seeing cadets up to their knees amid the crops, I'm reminded of the farmland near our house in northern Michigan.

But now the sight also calls up other memories: A view from the crest of a hill in Kentucky, or a hamlet in Poland woven into strips of packed wheat.

I still haven't quite gotten used to being "reminded" of things that I've never actually experienced.

The walk is over six kilometers in total, and by the time I'm out of the biomes and nearing the Scrub kitchen, my body has developed a whole new kind of ache. My feet throb. My lips are cracked. My joints move like rusted iron. It occurs to me that I haven't had anything to eat or drink since the popsicle yesterday. Water is now my top priority.

That's when I hear Doctor Hitch's voice, sharp and commanding.

"You—stop!"

I force my dogged steps to halt, and my legs begin to tremble. He's out of sight, just around the curve of the hallway. How did he see me? Was it the cameras?

"What?" asks a gruff voice. "I wasn't doing anything."

"That's not what it looked like," Hitch says, the edge in his voice like a piece of broken glass. With a flood of relief, I realize he isn't talking to me but to another cadet. "I shouldn't need to remind you that there is *absolutely* no physical violence on this colony. Got that? We don't tolerate it. Not under any circumstances."

"But I didn't do anything!" the voice protests in frustration.

I run twitchy fingers along my stun gun, wondering whether or not I should wait or risk walking by. My mind is made up for me as a group of Scrubs approaches from behind. I tug the defibrillator out of my pocket and power it on, acting preoccupied. It begins to gently whine. Then as the group passes me I slip onto the end, my face bent over the readout.

The Scrubs, who had been talking quietly, fall silent as we pass Hitch, Sarlow, and two Xeri boys. I glance at their faces, and names come to mind: Caleb and Namir. Seeing Caleb's brow taut with anger draws a memory of his aggression. I see him seizing the front of my jumpsuit and throwing me back into a wall. It isn't my memory. Someone else's.

I focus on the defibrillator, on keeping my posture natural as I pass.

At the end of the corridor, the Scrubs peel off toward their biome. Outside the kitchen door is a colony transport cart. I've always thought they looked creepy. Like plastic coffins on wheels. I step past it into the long hall of the kitchen.

Just as I hoped, Chloe is the first one here. Today her hair is woven into an elaborate braid that twists around her head like a crown. Maybe it's the French in her blood, but Chloe has always harbored a love of fashion. Of course, the colony has certain rules about dress code, but as long as hair is kept healthy and neat, it's generally considered fair game.

As I draw closer, I lower my head. I can almost hear the uncertain smile in her voice.

"Hello," she calls. *Ello.* "Can I help you?"

"Maybe."

I raise my head and pull down my surgical mask so she can see my face. Her look of shock and wonder makes me laugh in relief. I know at once, she remembers me. She hurries forward and grabs my hand as if to be sure I'm real.

"Lizzy! How did you—"

"Shh, not so loud."

I lead her away from the door, toward the mound of corn she must have just unloaded from the transport. In case someone steps in on us, I keep the mask pulled just below my chin.

"Are you all right?" she asks urgently. "When Shiffrin followed you out of the cafeteria—"

"I'm fine," I reply, probably less than convincingly. My voice sounds like gravel over my dry throat. "Could use some water, though."

"Of course!"

She hastily fills a plastic water bottle. Then, as if reading my mind, she retrieves a sealed packet of almonds and a banana from the pantry. I take the water sip by sip, feeling I might be ill if I drink too quickly. Between mouthfuls, I ask, "What happened, Chloe? I overheard Dosset say they were going to talk to you. They didn't alter your memory, did they?"

Chloe shakes her head.

"No. I don't think so. But you were right, Lizzy. It's like they think of you as a terrorist or something. They asked some really weird questions."

I peel the banana and take a bite.

"What kinds of questions?"

"About Doctor Atkinson mostly. Whether or not I'd seen him around you. They wanted to know if you'd been acting weird. Or if you had given me anything recently. I thought that was strange. And then they asked me if you'd made any predictions."

"Predictions?" I repeat, mystified.

"Weird, right? Then they searched my sleeping pod and told me not to repeat anything they'd said. They told me to keep an eye out for you."

An eye. My chewing slows as I realize I haven't checked the room for cameras. But my fear is needless—a quick glance proves we're safe.

Still, I pull the hat lower.

"What'd you tell them?" I ask quietly.

"That you'd seemed kind of delirious yesterday, like you had a fever. And that you kept talking about your mom and dad, and how you missed Earth."

I nod.

"Do you think they believed you?"

"I guess. They didn't fry my brain, so that seems like a good sign." This makes me smile again, but her expression is tense. "I'm just glad you're okay," she says.

I realize she isn't joking. No doubt she's been worried sick about me this entire time. As footsteps shuffle past the door, she grabs an ear of corn and begins nervously tearing off strips of the husk.

"Thanks for covering for me," I say, sipping water again. My stomach is beginning to settle, and my headache has finally eased a bit. "You did great."

"What are you going to do now?" she asks.

"I'm still figuring that out. Noah thinks we should rescue Atkinson."

At this, she drops the ear of corn, which bounces off the counter and thuds on the floor. Her eyes are wide.

"Noah Hartmann?"

I'm instantly reminded of Chloe's feelings about Noah. Which reminds me of his feelings about me. Two things I hadn't even considered when I decided to stay the night in his pod.

The decision suddenly seems selfish. How could I have forgotten so quickly? I know the answer. Because I was only thinking of myself. Certainly not of the danger it might put Noah in. Or how Chloe's feelings might be hurt. But what was I supposed to do? I had nowhere else to go. And it's not as if anything happened between us.

The opposite, really.

"I ran into him last night," I reply lamely, grabbing my own ear of corn to distract myself from her penetrating gaze. "We talked. I told him what was going on."

"And he... he believed you?"

"I used some of his memories to convince him, like I did with you," I say. I need to tread carefully if I don't want this whole thing blowing up in my face, and I know it. "Before I bumped into him, I overheard Shiffrin and Dosset talking. It turns out Atkinson was the one who gave me the Memory Bank. They think he had a plan to overthrow the whole system or something."

"Oh, uh... that's incredible." She stoops to pick up the fallen corn. "Do you have any idea where they might be keeping him?"

"Somewhere in the Helix, I think." I focus on stripping the corn husk, but I can't shake the hollow feeling that's growing in my chest. Chloe is my best friend—my only friend—and I'm lying to her. What is wrong with me? Telling her that I spent the night in Noah's pod might be hurtful, but it'll be far worse if I wait and let her find out from him. I can't bear to take that risk.

I set down the half-peeled ear of corn and face her.

"Chloe, I don't know how to tell you this, so I'm just going to say it plainly. Obviously, I know how you feel about Noah. And I think it's great. But he and I don't get along very well. He kind of makes me... uncomfortable."

She arches that single quizzical eyebrow at me, a half-smile on her lips.

"Is this one of those times when you're being sarcastic and I don't get it?"

"I wish," I mutter. "Last night, I needed somewhere to hide. And since Dosset expected me to go to you or to someone else I trusted, I did the opposite. I went to Noah. I told him what was going on and stayed the night in his pod."

She blushes. Merely the thought of being in a boy's sleeping pod is enough to make her self-conscious. I guess I might feel that way too, if I liked him. Before she can let her imagination get too far, I hurry on.

"Nothing happened. I only knew I could go to him because, well, I had all your memories. And I knew you couldn't feel that way about a boy who wasn't trustworthy."

It's a small lie. Much smaller than keeping it from her altogether. And there's no way she can find out it isn't true, unless I tell her.

Still, it makes my insides twist. How can I possibly tell her the other half—the way Noah feels about me? That I went to him, put him in danger, without really giving it a second thought? Because some part of me must've known, even in the airlock, that he would want to listen. That his feelings would cloud his judgment in my favor, while Terra's would lead her to betray me.

Again I feel a swell of shame for my actions.

"I just want you to know that I don't have any feelings for him, and I didn't want to keep anything from you," I say quietly, pushing my guilt down into the swirling pool of emotions.

Chloe is still blushing, clutching the ear of corn in her delicate hands.

"Thank you for telling me."

"Sure." The voice begins on the overhead, announcing seventeen hundred hours. Time for me to leave. "We're going to make a plan tonight, to try to pull this thing off before Dosset catches us. Can you meet me in the Xeri domes during free time? In Noah's pod?"

"Oh, um... which one is his?"

"End of the hall. Just check the nameplates."

"Okay."

She hesitates.

"Hey, Lizzy?"

"Yeah?"

"Be careful, okay?"

I nod, though I'm not sure exactly what she means. Be careful to not get caught? Or be careful with the power I have, knowing what I know?

As I turn to go, Chloe disappears into the washroom, maybe to rinse her hands or maybe to hide her true reaction to my words. At that same moment, the door to the hall opens and Terra pushes inside, a sweeping grin on her face.

"I'm not sure I got all that," she says with evident glee. "Exactly what're you two trying to pull off before Dosset catches you?"

Chapter Seven

Just like in Noah's panic attack, my mind goes blank.

Not her.

Anyone but her.

Icy dread races from the top of my head to the tips of my toes, gooseflesh turning me to stone. Blame what happens next on lack of sleep. Blame dehydration or emotional trauma. But there's isn't any time to think, so I don't—I just step up next to her, pull out the patches of the defibrillator, and slap them onto her forearms.

Confusion registers in her eyes as I place my fingers on the shock button.

"What are you—?"

A strangled yelp escapes her lungs. Her body spasms, then lurches forward. I barely catch her before she hits the floor.

My heart is racing. I can't believe I just did that. Rather than feeling proud, I feel horrified.

What *have* I done? I check her pulse to make sure the alteration worked, and I feel a giddy rush of relief. She's still alive.

Thinking fast, I hoist her up into a fireman's carry. Chloe still hasn't returned from the washroom. Setting my teeth, I poke my head out the door and see that the transport cart is still there, lid hanging open.

Aware that I'm only about a half-meter or so outside of the nearest camera's view, I stagger forward and dump Terra's body into the space. It's a near-perfect fit. Making sure I don't crush any fingers, I close the lid and snap the surgical mask back over my mouth just as a pair of Clovers round the corner.

So much for being careful.

The whole trip back to the Xeri pods, I'm just waiting for someone to catch me. Cadets shuffle past in droves, headed to dinner. But I make it all the way back. And then I realize that if I hope to get her into Noah's pod, I'm going to have to carry her up the stairs.

In my current exhausted state, carrying is optimistic. The adrenaline that aided me in tossing her into the cart is long gone, leaving an empty fatigue in my limbs. So instead, I do my best to ease her onto the floor, then seize her by the wrists.

For the record, to say dragging a limp body up a staircase is difficult is a bit like saying a marathon is kind of long. Lucky for me, the entire population is feasting on corn on the cob right now, or someone would surely see me panting, sweating, and wrestling with the lifeless body.

I'm just glad there aren't any cameras on the stairs. And that she isn't awake. When Terra comes to, she'll have more dents than the surface of the moon.

Now we're here, sitting across from one another on the floor of the pod. I've used rope to tie her to the chair, and tape to cover her mouth. So what next?

Of course, it would be her. Of course, of any cadet on the planet, Terra would be the one to overhear our conversation.

It's over. Once she's missing for longer than a meal or two, the doctors will come looking. The plan is already ruined. There'll be no convincing her to stay quiet. Terra hates me.

I pause.

Terra hates me. But why?

I've never given it much thought. To be honest, I've never really cared. But there has to be a reason for her to be like this. And if there is, I should know what it is, shouldn't I? Even if *she* doesn't remember.

By now I've realized that a memory is usually triggered by

something—the sight of a defibrillator, the sound of Noah's voice, the smell of Italian pine. I haven't pulled up any of Terra's memories yet, so I'm not really sure where to start. In fact, I'm not sure I know anything about Terra other than that she detests me.

So far, deep breaths seem to help me focus. And closing my eyes. So I shut out the pod, the voices, the rest of the world. Then I fold my legs beneath me and try to relax. Bit by bit, little by little, I remember...

Nothing.

I ball my fists and scrunch up my face, but all I feel is blood swelling in my curled fingers. The problem is, it's not just that Terra doesn't like me. It's that I don't like her either.

In every interaction I can recall, Terra has been unkind to me. So at some point, I decided I didn't care. I pushed her side of the story, her thoughts and feelings, entirely out of my head. To go against that now, to tolerate her perspective when I've rejected it for so long, is like trying to tear down an invisible wall. I'm not sure I could break it if I tried.

And really, I'm not sure I want to.

But I don't have much of an option. There's a lot more at stake here than me and Terra. If I can't find a way to keep her quiet, the memories of the entire colony will disappear overnight—and I'll likely vanish with them, like the other missing cadets.

Just relax, I tell myself. Then I try to imagine our first meeting. Was it at Mars Academy before the spacecraft even launched? Did I somehow insult her by mistake?

It was a joke.

The memory grabs me, and I catch my breath at how vivid it is. I'm not at Mars Academy. I'm on Mars, our third day here. Terra and I haven't spoken yet, because the Polar domes are so far from the Scrubs. But Terra has seen me running during fitness hour and wanted to meet me. Chloe is introducing us, and I'm watching Lizzy—watching myself—from Terra's eyes, just like I did in Noah's memory. However, the way she sees me is totally different.

To her, I'm not pretty. At least, not as pretty as she is. Her gaze skims me over, evaluating the way my jumpsuit hangs on my body, gauging how fit I look compared to her. It's weird, but I've never noticed how alike we look. Not the way she does. To her, we could be sisters. Ivory skin, thin lips—even our eyes are a similar shade of blue.

But she doesn't simply notice our similarities. She also makes note of the scar on my chin, the dotted pimples at my hairline. Every little imperfection.

She rolls back her shoulders, aware of how this highlights her figure. Smiles, knowing how it brings out her dimples.

"This is Lizzy," Chloe says. "Lizzy, this is Terry."

"Terra," she says immediately. I can tell the mistake irritates her. For some reason it makes her feel embarrassed. I absently recall how her brother would call her Terry when he wanted to make her angry.

"*Je m'excuse*," Chloe murmurs with a blush. "I've been meeting so many new people." She turns to other-Lizzy and says, "Terra is a Clover."

"You can't get anything right, can you?" Terra says, and I can feel her annoyance spike. But she quickly smiles again because she knows her tone is cutting. "I'm a Polar, silly."

Chloe's face turns a deeper shade of red. The comment landed.

Good, Terra thinks. She hates being embarrassed. She hates when people make her look stupid. And of course, the blunders of others are an opportunity to shine by comparison. Gracefully she turns to other-Lizzy. "Does she always give you this much trouble?"

But other-Lizzy's face has become closed off. I can see a muscle tighten in her jaw as she returns a cold smile.

"No."

That's the only word she says. Just "No," and then she takes Chloe by the arm and heads off down the hallway toward the cafeteria.

Being inside Terra's thoughts, I'm instantly reminded of her mother. A one-word answer dripping with intent, just because Terra said something she didn't like. Is that why Terra hates me? Because I remind her of her mother?

Terra turns away, grinding her teeth.

Immediately a new memory blooms. I'm in a house. It's Terra's house, the one she grew up in. The ceilings are so high they almost remind me of the domes—all white, shining, and new. We've just gotten home from recital. Mother drops the keys in a ceramic bowl and opens the refrigerator. A bottle of chardonnay is placed on the counter with a *clink* as she retrieves a glass from the rack. Whenever Terra makes a mistake, Mother starts drinking early.

"It was almost perfect," Terra is saying. The kitchen is big too—granite countertops and silver everything. Mother finishes pouring the rest of the bottle into her glass. Picks up the stem and swirls the liquid impatiently, whipping it around the glass in a practiced arc.

"Almost," she says. One word. It's more a challenge than an agreement. She promised that if Terra did well, they'd go shopping. But there's no thought of that now. Terra was outscored by the girl from Springfield, the one whose parents can't afford private school. How close it was doesn't really matter.

"Sorry," Terra mutters. I feel her shame. How wrong she feels, as if she went out there and admitted that she wasn't really her mother's daughter. Because she knows—has been told—just how much her parents spent to make her as smart, beautiful, and healthy as she is. Genetically enhanced, even as an embryo, to be better than everyone else. But instead of perfect, they got *almost*.

"For?" Mother intones, lifting the glass to her lips. This one is like a threat. That if Terra doesn't answer the right way, she'll drink it all in one swallow and then start complaining about how her children ruined her figure.

Her size used to be double zero, she likes to say. Like Terra's is now.

The memories continue. Overhearing her mother at practice, pointing out her missteps. Comments dropped about her diet, how tight her clothes are looking. And on, and on, and on.

When the mission to Mars is announced, her mother suggests that Terra's brother apply. And Terra sees a chance to prove herself. To prove her worth—her superiority. She doesn't tell her parents she submitted the application. Her brother's rejection and Terra's acceptance letters come the very same afternoon.

No one knows what to say.

Her father grunts, "Just don't get pregnant. I hear they plan to deliver babies in the airlock." He chuckles and heads off to his study. Terra's brother goes upstairs without a word. For a long period, her mother only stares at her. Then she abruptly smiles with the detached edge of a scalpel.

"So," she says. "When will you be leaving?"

At last the memories fade and I'm back inside the pod. Terra's golden hair has fallen around her shoulders in silky waves, concealing her birthmark.

What must it have been like, I wonder, to be measured at every step? To be compared and judged by your own family? There's some part of me that feels sorry for her. But I can't excuse her completely. Just because she had a terrible mother doesn't mean she can abuse others. Like Chloe. Terra would probably treat me just as badly if she weren't so intimidated.

It's a little gratifying to know she's afraid of me.

"Wake up."

I nudge her with my foot, but she doesn't respond. Who am I kidding? If dragging her up a dozen stairs didn't wake her, it'll take more than that.

Going through a few drawers, I find a water bottle. I bring it over and splash a bit in her face. She inhales sharply through her nose, and suddenly she's thrashing, slamming the chair up and down.

"Don't move," I warn, shifting my hand to the defibrillator. The patches are still on her arms, now moved closer to her elbows. Ugly red welts show where I placed them the first time. Seeing the threat, she grows still, eyes wide.

Once I'm convinced she isn't going to start flailing again, I lean in close to her face, trying for a menacing tone.

"You and I need to have a talk. Got it?"

A timid nod.

"Good. In a second, I'm going to take off the tape. And if you don't keep quiet, I'm going to zap you. I don't know how bad that hurt the first time, but I'm betting round two will be even less fun now that you're all wet."

No response.

"Okay. Are you going to be quiet?"

Another nod. I reach forward and tug the tape off of her mouth as swiftly as I can. It still leaves a blotchy rectangle on her skin.

I open my mouth to begin telling her the same things I told Noah and Chloe, but words fail me this time. Am I really going to trust her? Can I hope that someone like Terra will believe me? And that if she does, she won't turn me in as soon as I let her out of my sight? I can't help but feel like that's exactly what she'll do.

Yet as I already figured out, I don't really have a choice. I wish I could just lock her away in a Helix of my own, to silence her the way Dosset has silenced Atkinson. It'd be so much safer.

But I have no Helix, no Stitch to erase what she already knows. Time passes as we stare at each other. I'm searching for the right way to begin, to make her see reason. No doubt she's hating every centimeter of my guts right now.

"You really don't like me, do you?" I finally say, more aggressively than I'd intended.

It's not what she expected, I can tell. Not point blank like that. Her eyes flit to the floor, then dance around the pod before coming back to mine. "Why do you say that?" she rasps, a bitter smile on her lips.

"Because in all your memories, you hate me."

She blinks, uncomprehending.

"I've got a story to tell you. And you're going to believe it, because if you don't, every cadet on the colony is going to lose something important. Including you."

"Making threats?" She says it with a sneer. "No wonder the doctors are after you."

"Just listen," I snap, placing a hand on the defibrillator again. My anger is a fuse, I realize. A spark to the fire that propels me, making me bold. Or determined, at least. Stopping, thinking, planning—those are my weak points.

The sneer vanishes and her lips draw into a thin white line.

"Go on."

And so I tell her. Once I get going it's actually pretty easy, having already been through this twice before. Plus, I literally have a captive audience.

Her face remains expressionless for most of what I say. When I start relaying memories of her life on Earth or our various encounters, she stops clenching her jaw and just listens.

Even if she doesn't believe me, maybe that's okay. Maybe, like Noah, she'll just choose to accept what I'm saying rather than wholeheartedly believe it. There's no getting past the fact that I attacked her, abducted her, threatened her. Trust may no longer be an option.

"None of that makes sense," Terra says once I'm finished. "What could they possibly be hiding that would cause them to alter our memories?"

"That's what we need to find out."

"Who's 'we'?"

"Noah, Chloe, and I." Then I carefully add, "And you."

She pauses. "Oh, so this is part of the recruiting process? You actually want my help?"

I've already got a barbed answer on my lips, but I manage to swallow it. She's testing me. Trying to get the best of me. Isn't that what she was after in each of her memories—to prove that she was better, stronger, prettier?

"I won't say you were my first choice," I say. "But unless you want the doctors deciding which memories you get to keep, you're going to have to trust me. Or at least help me."

At that point I hear footsteps, and I instinctually put my hand back over the defibrillator. Terra sees the move and tenses.

We both sit in absolute silence as the steps grow closer and closer. A combination is punched outside the door and it opens, revealing three people: Noah, Chloe, and one other.

It's Romesh, the boy who imagined my stun gun.

Chapter Eight

The trio enters the room, takes in the sight of Terra's captivity, and gawks. With her arms wired up to the defibrillator, I must look like a torturer at work.

"Hi," I say awkwardly.

"What's going on?" Noah closes the door, a hand wrapped in white gauze from where I bit him earlier. "What's she doing here? Are we taking hostages?"

"Seems that way," says Terra in a pained voice.

Chloe's mouth is hanging open.

"We bumped into each other," I say, feeling suddenly defensive. "She threatened to turn me in, so I zapped her. What's *he* doing here?" I shoot a look at Romesh.

"Just observing," he says with a small, nervous wave. "I'm Romie."

"I know who you are. This is one of your ideas." I tap the defibrillator. "Modified stun gun. Ring any bells?"

He scratches his head.

"Well, not exactly. But it's very creative."

"Lizzy," Chloe interrupts, following the wires up to Terra's burned arms. "Did you... did you tell her about—"

"The doctors? Yeah, I told her."

"Seems like she's taking it well," says Noah quietly. He's recovering from his shock. I can almost see his reticence settling back in— the slope of his shoulders, the way he leans back against the door bent like a palm tree, away from the others. "Is she going to help us?"

"I didn't say that," Terra says, frowning. She seems to be enjoying all the attention. "It sounds like a lot of work."

This actually makes me laugh.

"You have more important things to do?"

"Not me. I mean the doctors. Like I said, none of this makes sense. It must take forever to go through all our memories and erase them one by one. Have you thought about that? The kind of time it would take?"

"Of course."

But I haven't. Not really. Up until now, I'd just assumed they were hiding a really dark secret, and that it was worth whatever it took. And maybe I'm right. Only maybe the secret is darker than I had even imagined, for it to merit such meticulous labor.

"You still didn't tell me why Romie is here," I say, changing the subject.

"I told him," says Noah, face flushing. "I... wanted to be sure I wasn't going crazy."

"You thought I was lying," I say.

It isn't meant to be an accusation, but it comes out that way. Because clearly I've underestimated him. Or misunderstood him at least. He doesn't just blindly trust me after all. I find that I feel a little betrayed—which surprises me.

I should have expected this, shouldn't I? If I were him, I'd probably think I was going crazy too. Undoubtedly I'd confide in Chloe.

My head is already muddy with digging into Terra's memories, but I reach back for any of Romie's other thoughts. Inventions float through my mind: the assembly for a solar panel lining, the schematics for a more efficient water reclaimer. The effort makes the room spin, so I stop.

It's a little late to be screening him anyway. He already knows.

"It's not that I didn't trust you," Noah is saying. "I just..."

"He wanted proof," Romie volunteers. When I turn on him, he

pales a bit. "S-so, we conducted a search. And we found supporting evidence."

From the pocket of his jumpsuit, he produces a small white tube. It's an inoculator, just like the one Shiffrin used to knock me out before each Revision. Like all the doctors used on all the cadets.

I take my hand from the defibrillator and hold it out, and he drops the cylinder into my palm. The numerous fine needles are concealed beneath a plastic cap.

"Verced," I murmur. "You stole it?"

"From Doctor Conrad's suite. One of his lab coats was hanging on the back of the door. It was in the front pocket."

Not surprising. Conrad is usually a bit absentminded. Unlike Dosset, who seems to be calculated in everything he does.

"How did you know what it was?" I ask suspiciously. I've got no reason to be so skeptical of him, but I'm still bothered that Noah didn't believe me on his own.

"You said they used a drug to knock us out," Noah says. "What else would it be?"

"Insulin?" Terra says.

"He doesn't have diabetes," I reply.

"Okay, so a booster," she sneers. "Just because he carries an inoculator, that doesn't mean he's out to brainwash all the poor, helpless cadets."

I'm strongly considering another jolt from the defibrillator when Romie interrupts.

"As I said, the inoculator isn't proof," he says. "It's supporting evidence. Lizzy's theory isn't so unrealistic. It's not hard to change a person's mind about something, even without the use of an apparatus."

"A Stitch," I say.

"Um, yes. Whatever that is. Doctor Atkinson was telling me about this kind of thing just days before he disappeared."

"You knew Atkinson?" I say, dropping the inoculator into my pocket as I finally let go of my misgivings.

"He was the Clover psychologist and therefore my therapist," Romie replies. "A kind, sensitive man. We had many meaningful conversations. He was also a chemist and a highly serviceable engineer."

"Did he say anything about me?" I ask impatiently. "Or the Memory Bank?"

"No, not that. But in a way, yes. We talked about memories often. How we tend to think about them as files in a database, to be called forth whenever we like. In reality, the process is more like repainting a memory from scratch each time we recall it. The accuracy fades. And perhaps more importantly, since we essentially recreate our memories, they're susceptible to distortion. Small details, like whether or not it was raining outside, can be easily confused. Even just a pointed question, or casting doubt on an account of an incident can do the trick. You might ask someone if they're *sure* someone's eyes are green and not blue, and it would be enough to make them change their memory... or at least doubt the truth of it. The thing is, memories aren't nearly as reliable as we make them out to be. And we usually see them very one-sided."

He says all of this very swiftly, then pulls his glasses from his nose and begins polishing them on his jumpsuit. The rest of us trade blank faces.

Suddenly I think I know why the idea for his stun gun was so detailed.

Noah clears his throat.

"I think what Romie's saying is that suggestion is a powerful tool," he translates.

"Exactly," says Romie. "And if you have technology that could amplify it, say, by a few multiples of ten, it'd be tough to resist. Or even tell the difference." He shrugs. "I find the whole concept incredibly fascinating."

"But we're not talking about suggestion," says Chloe. "Lizzy has our memories. Ones that were taken from us."

"Okay, so reverse it," says Romie. "Use that technology to capture the memory in some format, and then burn out the neurons in a subject's brain. It's not that dangerous. We kill brain cells constantly. Just with simple things, such as stress or dehydration. With the right hardware, you'd simply target precise areas of the mind. Then you'd do the suggestion method to implant those memories in the new surrogate's head. Easy as three point one-four."

Again, we're all quiet.

"You mean... pi?" Chloe says slowly.

Romie smiles again, bobbing his head so that his curly hair bounces. "Yes. Easy as pi. It's an expression."

"But why?" asks Noah slowly. "That's the question. We still don't know why they would be doing this in the first place."

They all look at me.

"Whatever the reason, Atkinson had other ideas, and apparently I was part of them. But he got caught. If we can get him back, we might be able to finish what he started," I say.

"That's a pretty weak plan," says Terra.

"It's all we've got so far," I growl, temper rising again. "Do you have a better idea?"

"I might," says Romie. Everyone turns. "Well, maybe a different theory at least. It's possible that Atkinson wasn't looking to overthrow Doctor Dosset at all. Maybe he was looking for answers that he thought were inside the Memory Bank. To gauge an uncertainty, such as whether or not a person's eyes were green. Er, so to speak."

The thought is so unexpected, yet so plausible, that I can't even think of a reply. If Atkinson didn't have some kind of strategy, then no one can help us.

I suddenly realize just how important it is that someone out there has an answer. That it doesn't all come down to me.

"But then why would he give the Memory Bank to Lizzy?" Chloe asks. "If he wasn't trying to help us, he could have left her out of it."

"Maybe he couldn't read the memories unless they were in someone's head," Romie suggests. He looks at me. "You called the device a Stitch?"

"Yeah."

Silence fills the room. For being so filled with thoughts the past twenty-four hours, my brain has gone suddenly quiet.

I'd thought I was picked for a reason. I'd thought there was a plan. Now I see how foolish I was, believing it could all be so easy. But the notion that I'm alone out in this swirling darkness with no one to step in and make sense of it all…

I close my eyes.

It's just like my nightmare, the one about being crushed. I can feel the way I do when I wake up standing in the hall or alone in the kitchen, not knowing where I've wandered in my fretful sleep. Mother used to blame my dad for encouraging my imagination. And who knows? Maybe it was his fault for all the wild stories he'd tell me before bed. But the terror was nothing to how good it felt when he came running.

Even now, I remember the beating of his heart as he wrapped me in a hug so strong that nothing could tear me away. He'd whisper in my ear that everything was fine, that it was going to be okay. I'd try to tell him about what I'd seen, how scared I'd been, but he'd say, "You're safe, Dizzy. It doesn't matter. Nothing can hurt you now that I'm here."

And I believed him. His deep, gentle voice, the special name that only he used, his way of being there the second I needed him—it was all proof that nothing could hurt me as long as he was around, and he was never far.

But that was before the colony. Before my parents had different ideas about what they wanted for their future.

About what they wanted for me.

Standing in the middle of Noah's pod, alone in my head with the voices of over two hundred strangers, I know with certainty that the monsters are real this time. No one will come running or make them go away. Though I long to feel someone wrap their arms around me and tell me that I'm safe, it isn't going to happen. It's just us out here.

"I don't believe that," Chloe says.

My eyes open, bringing the room back into focus.

"You don't believe what?" asks Terra. "That Atkinson was only thinking about himself? It's human nature, kids. People do what it takes to survive."

"But he wasn't just thinking about himself," Noah argues. "He didn't run. He tried to fight. You saw Conrad's eye, didn't you?"

"Yes," Chloe agrees. "And… and I don't think he would do that to Lizzy. He wouldn't have just chosen a random cadet to dump these memories on and then given up. He could've at least erased them afterward if he really felt it didn't matter. Right?"

"In theory," says Romie.

"On top of which, as Noah said, he gave Doctor Conrad a black eye," Chloe continues. "Why would he resist if it was hopeless? He must've been trying to get away, to fight back. He wouldn't have done that if he didn't think he could win. He would've just let them erase his mind." She folds her arms, revealing the scar on her wrist. "If he's as kind as you say he is, Romie, then he'd probably help us if he could. But right now he needs *our* help."

And this is why everyone likes Chloe. Because she believes the best about people, even the ones she's never met. I wonder how it's possible for someone to be so full of hope while others can only assume the worst. Like Terra.

Like me.

"Good thinking," Noah tells her.

Chloe blushes and tucks a loose strand of hair behind her ear.

"Also, he let me keep the memories of our talks," Romie adds. "Maybe he was trying to subtly tell me what was going on. I don't know. I just think we should consider all the angles."

One by one, they all look at me again. I know they're expecting some kind of direction. But I'm not like my dad or Chloe. I have no comfort, no reassurance to give. So for the first time in a long time, I decide to just be honest about what I'm thinking.

"Look," I say quietly. "I didn't ask for this. If I'd found out Atkinson was going to give me these memories, I would've told him to pick someone else. But now that I know what I know, I can't go back. Because I think in some way, even if we don't remember our past, we still feel its effects. And if we aren't given the chance to deal with things, to understand them and put them to rest... we may never grow beyond them."

I look at the floor, thinking of Noah's panic. Terra's insecurity. Chloe's denial. But now my boldness has burned out in a trail of smoke. I risk a glance and find that Chloe is smiling at me.

"So it's a long shot," Romie says abruptly. "Beyond a long shot—a *moon* shot. But perhaps we can do it if we integrate our strengths." He almost sounds excited. "I mean, if Atkinson was able to outwit Doctor Dosset once, he might be able to do it again."

The others take a moment longer.

"How do we get him back?" Noah finally asks. "We need a plan."

"I think that might have to wait until tomorrow," murmurs Chloe.

It's true. Green letters on the clock read ten minutes until end-of-day Briefing. After that, the others will have to meet with their psychologists and return to their pods for power down.

All at once a kind of burning terror settles in my throat, almost choking me. I've just entrusted myself to four people... which is four more than usual.

I look at Terra and see that she's still watching me. Again she's got that look in her eye. The one I always get from her when she's thinking something she isn't saying. I can't tell if I've won her over or not. But in about an hour she'll have the perfect opportunity to get her revenge, to beat me. All she has to do is tell her therapist where I am.

I force myself to hold her gaze.

"So, are you going to help us?" I ask.

A coy smile plays at the corners of her mouth, still slightly red from the tape.

"Well, I don't really have a choice, do I?" When I glare at her, her smile widens. "I'm kidding, Lizzy, god. Of course I'm in."

"Fine, you're in," I mutter.

"It doesn't look like it much," Romie says. "I mean, she's still restrained to the chair."

Stiffly I nod. If we're going to be allies, I have to at least *act* like I trust her. I kneel and unbind her ankles and wrists, keenly aware of how vulnerable I am in this position. The defibrillator patches come off last. I retract the wires with the push of a button.

"I hope those weren't too tight," I say awkwardly.

No reply. Instead she stands, cracks her neck, and begins massaging the imprint of the rope on her skin.

"The Sick Bay should have something for those burns on your arms," Chloe says, as if sensing the tension between us. "Right, Noah?"

"Oh, yeah. Definitely."

Terra eyes them up.

"Sure," she says. A one-word answer.

For some reason, I recall what Meng said in Group before this all started. About how if we work together, humanity can accomplish anything. The question is, will we be able to put aside our differences long enough to get Atkinson back?

I honestly doubt it.

"Lizzy, why don't you spend tomorrow with me in the Clover domes?" Romie asks. "I want to hear about the inventions I made up that I no longer remember." He grins, somehow reminding me of a boy in a sandbox. "Maybe one of them will assist with our rescue attempt. Then tomorrow night we can all meet in my quarters to discuss our plan in detail."

"Okay," I say, surprised. And also grateful for his support. At least he's on my side.

"We're sure we want to do this, right?" Chloe suddenly asks. "I mean, I know they've been altering our memories, but it doesn't seem like they're out to hurt us. Maybe whatever they're hiding... maybe we're better off not knowing."

"But is that something you want them to decide?" I ask.

"Well, no."

"If we fail it won't matter much," says Noah. "They'll just erase our memories and we'll forget we even had this conversation."

"Or we'll become Atkinson's new neighbors," Terra replies.

I don't bother arguing. Because as everyone shuffles out of the room, I have a feeling Terra's right. Only, I don't think they'll make us all disappear. Because in order to change my mind, they'd have to erase everything. For the others, the doctors can make it all go back to normal by erasing only a single person.

Me.

Chapter Nine

The next morning, after Noah goes to breakfast, I sit on his bed and prepare myself for whatever the day will bring.

My back aches from sleeping on the floor again, even though he offered me the mattress. As I drifted off, I could see his golden eyes watching me in the near-darkness. Almost as if they were glowing. I guess in some weird way it was nice to know that someone was looking out for me.

But he still makes me uncomfortable.

Since that first night I've been careful not to stumble into any of his memories. It just feels wrong, like I'm reading his diary or something. And knowing how Chloe feels... it's a big mess.

At the moment we have much bigger problems than hormones and high school drama.

While I wait for Romie to arrive, I wrap myself up in a blanket and make a meal out of what rations Chloe smuggled to me the night before.

Cadets aren't allowed to take food out of the kitchens, but the doctors aren't exactly fascists about it. You've just got to be sneaky.

It seems Chloe is sneakier than I realized, because she somehow managed to pocket three tangerines and a few handfuls of almonds and raisins, plus two vegan banana pancakes rolled up and tucked into her sleeve. The pancakes are cold and a little dry, but my appetite has long outweighed my pickiness.

At this point I think I'd be willing to lick rice pudding off the floor.

It's funny, thinking back to when I first learned about the mission to Mars. Never in a million years would I have expected what it is... what it's now become.

When it began, there were candidates from all over the country. The idea was to put brilliant people on the planet to monitor and care for the biomes while Mars was gradually terraformed.

But when training began, a study on interplanetary travel made an unexpected finding: teenagers were better equipped to endure the rigors of cryosleep than adults. They were also better at handling the pressures of living inside the colony.

Test domes were built on Earth to further explore the idea, and after a three-month trial, it was decided that young astronauts were a healthier choice for the prolonged, isolated journey. Soon, students were recruited, a five-to-one ratio of cadets to adults.

At my private school alone there were dozens of applicants. Some came from families like Terra's, with parents who wanted their children to excel for their own benefit. For me it was different. My parents were hardly involved. After the divorce, I lost myself in academics because I *wanted* to get lost.

I guess my running was a piece of that—a world I could get lost in. Coming to Mars was just the next logical step in that direction.

So now we're here doing the grunt work. Shepherded from one duty to the next while doctors take notes. Notes that go to who—Dosset?

The thought makes my blood boil. It also terrifies me. If all my memories are just floating around out there, does that mean Dosset knows everything about me? About all of us?

It must. After all, he felt he knew me well enough to predict my actions that first night in the airlock—even if he did get it wrong.

I think about how Conrad called me predictable in the biome, and how Hitch was able to head Caleb off before a fight could even ensue. Does having access to our personal memories mean Dosset knows us so well that he can anticipate what we'll do next?

And if it does, and I've got those same memories... do I have the power to draw the same conclusions?

That could explain why the doctors asked Chloe if I'd made any "predictions."

So early in the morning, this is a lot to take in. But there's another question still waiting to be asked. One I've already skirted, and likely the most important question of all: Do I have any of the doctors' memories?

I've suspected all along that I don't. None have surfaced, anyway. Yet if I do have them, that insight could make the difference between overcoming Dosset or not.

Since Shiffrin is the doctor I'm most familiar with, I feel that she's my best candidate. Of course, I'll need the right trigger to bring her memories to mind. But as I think about it, I realize that I don't really know anything about her. Not her personal life.

With Noah, I had myself as a point of reference. With Shiffrin, every conversation we've ever had revolved around my week. Nothing about her.

I decide on a different approach. One by one, I recall the items from her Wellness Suite. The warm, comforting scent of mandarin from the oil diffuser. The snow globe on her desk from Juneau, Alaska. The reading glasses that were always pushed up into her tangled hair—

Nothing comes to mind.

"Didn't think so," I mutter. Why would the doctors have brainwashed each other? It just doesn't make sense.

And yet I still have this feeling tingling in the back of my head. As if something is asking to be brought forward. Maybe I should try another doctor.

Why not Atkinson? He's the one who gave me the memories, after all.

However, this will be even harder. Atkinson is little more than a stranger. The only thing I know about him is that he was assigned to the Clover cadets. I can't even picture his face. What had Dosset called him?

Marcus.

With the name, a tiny memory pops. It's shadowy and vague, as if I'm viewing it through smeary glass. We must have landed only a day or two ago, because I find myself standing in cryonics, watching as Dosset oversees the waking of the cadets: the crack and hiss of the cryobeds as they split like carbon eggshells; the pale bodies held in vacuum-sealed bags, submerged in azure blue liquid; the tubes in their noses; the corpse-like stillness.

Dosset begins talking about how this generation will carry on the legacy of humankind as we span the cosmic canvas, and Atkinson feels a swell of pride—and then I'm right back in Noah's pod, watching a beam of light inch across the wall.

And, yes. My headache is back with a vengeance.

Still, I can't help but smile. This is some kind of clue. Maybe about what Atkinson was after. Certainly about what Dosset is capable of doing.

If I've got memories from one doctor, I probably have memories from others—and if I can recall those memories, I might be able to use them to my advantage. Just as long as I don't split my skull in half while doing it.

Since my head has again become a drop forge, I decide to lie down for a while. But by ten hundred hours, the rest of the colony is attending Group and I'm beginning to grow restless.

Is Dosset looking for me? I wonder. By now he must assume I fell into a crater. That, or he realizes I never left the colony in the first place. Maybe the doctors are already patrolling the halls, checking rooms.

All it would take is a simple sweep of the pods, and I'd be found right here, huddled under a blanket, eating raisins.

The endless thinking isn't helping my headache. I have to stop this. Honestly, I could probably use a therapist right about now.

Just, you know, not the brainwashing type.

I do some stretches until ten thirty. Stare at the wall until eleven. Go through Noah's drawers and refold his shirts, even though I hate doing laundry. Then I try to braid my hair like Chloe's and then unbraid it because it's no good. Hum to myself. Shoot surgical masks across the room by their straps.

By thirteen hundred hours, I'm hungry again and considering doing strides down the hallway. Then there's a knock on the door. I pull it open so fast that Romie actually flinches.

"Oh," he says.

"Ready?"

"Yes." He examines the way I've tucked my hair up under my hat and how the surgical mask hides my face. "Is that how you've been getting around? The cap is suitable. But I don't think the mask is necessary."

"But what about cameras?" I ask in surprise. "And the other cadets?"

He adjusts his glasses and smooths his dark hair to one side.

"Facial recognition software isn't as good as you think. Really, it comes down to vantage point and face occlusion. By wearing the hat and surgical mask, yes, you are occluding much of your face, which would throw off a camera. After all, cameras need to glimpse a minimum of fifty percent to make a positive identification. But what happens when you pass a suspicious doctor? You're going to look very peculiar."

I snap the surgical mask off an ear, frowning. "Better peculiar than like myself, right? All it takes is one person to recognize me and we're toast."

"True," Romie admits. "But I'll wager the mask will stand out even more than your facial features. To our benefit, whoever designed our surveillance system did a poor job. Because the cameras are so high on the wall, they don't get a good look unless you're facing straight ahead. By simply tilting your head at the proper angle, you should be able to elude them."

For talking so much more than Noah, he consistently makes less sense. I find myself wishing that Noah were here now to translate.

"So you're saying...?"

"Just look at your feet," he says.

"My feet."

"It's as good as a mask but less conspicuous."

I can't tell if he's joking.

"Uh, no offense, Romie, but aren't we taking a big risk, just walking around without a disguise? I mean, shouldn't we be more cautious?"

"According to Noah, the priority is for us to remain unpredictable, correct?" He smiles. "This is unpredictable. It's the hiding-in-plain-sight strategy."

I take a deep breath to soothe my fraying nerves. He could be right. But what if he's wrong? This whole "trusting others" thing is going to be even harder than I'd imagined.

We take to the halls. I feel almost naked, strolling around like this. But I keep a steady gaze on my shoelaces as Romie instructed, and no doctors come running. And then it hits me. No doctors have come running. That must mean Terra didn't turn me in after all.

Maybe there really is a chance we'll pull this thing off.

The corridors are predictably thick with shoulders and elbows. As cadets hurry past, going about their daily duties, I again hear voices that I recognize. But this time something different happens.

Rather than simply recalling details about the cadets, I begin to remember the way they *move*. I can't describe it any other way. As Julia Mazer passes on my right, talking briskly about a forecasted hailstorm, I instinctively recall the way she cracks her knuckles when she's lost in thought. How Lars Bone will bob his head as he walks, or how Valeska Jones will often take short, timid steps.

Even being hunched over like this, eyes on the floor, my loping posture reminds me of Noah's diffident stride.

It's almost as if, little by little, I'm learning the words to their body language.

"You see?" Romie asks.

"See?" I repeat thickly. Lost in my recollections, I hardly notice the headache until it begins to make me nauseous again. "I'm staring at the floor, Romie."

"We just passed Doctor Samar. He didn't notice you."

I glance up at him then swiftly remember to keep my head down. I don't know what to say. Belatedly I realize I've begun cracking my knuckles and stop myself at once.

"That's... that's great, Romie," I mutter.

This Memory Bank thing is getting weirder all the time.

Still avoiding the tight security of the Helix, we make the trek across the desert habitat. I don't say much, mostly because my throat is sucked dry as a bone before we're even halfway across. As if immune to the heat, Romie whistles to himself as we wind down the switchbacks into the valley, stopping here and there to remark about the plant growth.

"It's the first thing that tipped me off that you were telling the truth," he says. "Even with genetic enhancements, the vegetation is too advanced to make rational sense. We must have been here for many months for it to be this far developed. Is that right?"

"Yes. Months at least," I tell him, squinting. "I guess it could be as long as a year."

"Really?" He stoops to look at a prickly bush. "Astonishing!"

Has it really been that long? According to the memories, I guess it has. And if that's true, we've missed a lot. Like my birthday. Could I really be eighteen?

Carefully I sneak a look at the flourishing cacti around us and realize how obvious it is. Why didn't any of us notice how quickly the plants were growing? I guess we just didn't think about it in that way.

So the question is—what else haven't we noticed?

"The terraforming could nearly be halfway finished," Romie concludes, whistling again.

Once we're inside the Clover domes, he leads me to the Workshop. Each dome subset has its own specialty. Scrubs have the Fitness Center. Xeris have the Sick Bay. Polars have the Wellness Suites, and Bolos have the Laboratory. Here in the Clover domes, they handle mechanical repairs and most of the 3D printing—really, all of it but the food.

This is where my running shoes come from, along with most of my tools and clothing.

"What is all this stuff?" I ask quietly as Romie leads me through a maze of tables, tools, and boxes, all made of shiny chrome or white plastic. Cadets are busy fiddling with various contraptions—coating pipes with sealant, soldering circuit boards, typing on flat, holographic keyboards projected from a glass iris.

"Anything and everything," he replies over the hum of their work. "Today we're preparing for maintenance on one of the water reclaimers. But our supplies were dropped before we arrived on Mars. Essentially, NASA sent crates of whatever they thought we might need. All of them stored in here."

He hooks a thumb at row upon row of sleek boxes stacked on a network of shelves that nearly reaches the ceiling.

"They had to plan for any possible scenario between our landing and the arrival of the next settlers," he tells me. "Three and a half years is a relatively long time."

I've heard all this before, of course. The way I understand it, the process of terraforming Mars began long before I volunteered—even before Aster began her work.

First, we had to find a way to kick-start the planet's core, to create a geomagnetic layer that would fend off radiation from space. Then, we had to actually build the domes. That took years of sending materials and Mechs to assemble it all before we even left Earth. Cotton swabs, seeds, shower heads—anything we use on a regular basis had to be ready.

I've heard cadets say we have enough extra materials to last up to five years, which is much longer than we need. The planet will be terraformed in three, and the next spacecraft will arrive four months after that.

Since we've already been on the planet for a year or so, settlers for that ship are probably being chosen right now.

A ripple of nerves runs through me. Relations of the cadets get top priority. But will my parents be accepted?

Will they even audition?

"This is my corner."

Near the dome wall, a privacy fence of foldable plastic panels has been erected around one of the desks. The desktop is strewn with wires, microchips, and various other strange items—mostly half-built inventions.

I cautiously lift my gaze to take it in.

"There are no cameras back here," Romie assures me, "so you can look around all you like." He pushes aside a stack of aluminum casings and hoists himself onto the desk. "Well, what do you think?" he asks a little shyly.

"I think NASA overplanned," I say.

He laughs.

"Maybe. Not all of this stuff is from the crates. Some of it came from probes and landers we sent before Mars Colony One. Just scrap, you know. Outdated at this point. Sarlow brings it in to be recycled, if we can use it."

"I had no idea we sent so many." I pick up a robotic arm. "Was this part of a Mech?"

He nods.

"Just one of the little ones. The larger versions have been retired since the biomes were completed. Too much energy usage." He hops back down with a squeak of his shoes. "Come over here. I want to show you something."

At the very back of the area, beside the dome wall, a plastic sheet has been pulled over a lumpy heap. Romie gently tugs it back, revealing a flat disc with a series of knobs and buttons.

"What on earth is that?"

"Not on Earth, on Rusty!" he replies with a grin. When I don't react, he quickly adds, "That's what Noah and I nicknamed Mars, because the planet's red color comes from all the rusted iron dust. Do you get it? Rusty?"

I reward him with a patient smile.

"I get it. You were showing me—?"

"Oh, right. Allow me to present my latest creation: an EMP device."

"As in, electromagnetic pulse?" I say skeptically. I may not be as gifted as Romie, but I know what an EMP is. When detonated, it'll shut down any nearby electronics. "Won't that turn off all the machines that are, you know, keeping us alive?"

"See, that's the thing," he says, hefting the disc. I step back warily. "You don't need to worry, Elizabeth. I easily control the blast radius with this dial here. And as you can see, it is currently set to zero. Perfectly safe."

I carefully lean in for a closer look. It's as big as a waffle iron, welded together from various alloys like pieces of a metallic quilt. Or maybe some kind of robotic Frankenstein.

"Seems like you have a lot of dangerous ideas, Romie," I tell him. "First a stun gun, now this? You might want to talk to your therapist."

He laughs again, high and bubbly.

"That's funny. I suppose Dosset *has* seen all of my ideas." Romie's eyes glaze slightly. "Do you think he'd actually use any of them? I had an idea yesterday for speeding up bacteria growth outside the airlock. The concept is to use microwaves, which would be difficult on Rusty. Back on Earth, the atmosphere created a greenhouse effect. Here, I'd have to figure out—"

"Romie."

"Hm?"

I point at the EMP. "Focus."

"Oh, right. Sorry. Well, I was thinking this morning, and here's my idea. If the water reclamation system breaks, who repairs it?"

"We do," I say.

"No," he corrects me. "I do. And as a result, I know how to break it in ways that are not so easy to repair." He waits for me to respond. "Do you understand?"

"Uh... no, sorry," I say. "Why do we want the water broken?"

"Well, we don't. Not necessarily. But we control their attention for as long as it *is* broken. Do you see now?"

I shake my head. Either he's being cryptic on purpose or he still doesn't realize how confusing his explanations can be. He certainly fits the "best and brightest" criteria for a Martian cadet. In fact, he sort of makes the rest of us look like toddlers, the way he grasps complicated technologies just by glancing at them.

Whatever the case, he has a knack for making me feel stupid.

"Okay, okay. So let's say I walk around with this EMP and turn up the blast radius just a little bit." He demonstrates. "When I activate it near certain pieces of electronic equipment, what happens? As you said, I shut them down. Think of it like sabotage. The doctors will see that their system is malfunctioning and have us repair it for them. And if we're unable to repair it for some reason, then they'll—"

"—just have to leave it broken," I cut in. "Or fix it themselves."

"Right. Either way, it's a distraction. And if the equipment that keeps breaking is, say, their security cameras..."

Now I really do laugh. Suddenly the EMP seems a lot less frightening.

"Romie, that's brilliant. When did you start working on this?"

"Monday," he replies, blushing slightly. "I had intended for it to do the reverse, actually. Wirelessly charge electronic devices from a distance. It kind of took a different turn, though."

"Well, it's perfect for us. You'll have the whole surveillance system down in a few hours."

"Not exactly," he says, scratching his head. "For one thing, the Helix, the cryobeds, the domes, they're all built to deflect radiation—which is what an EMP is. So we can only shut down a single dome at a time. The other thing is, it doesn't work yet. I mean, it works. But so far 'working' just means it shuts itself down."

"Oh."

"It will work the way I want it to," he assures me quickly, "in time.

I'm still working out the kinks, that's all."

We spend the next few hours discussing all the ideas that Romie forgot, weighing their usefulness. Most of them can't really be applied as weapons, but a few are promising. Like a sonic cannon that knocks someone off their feet, or reprogrammed LED lights to make them sick. Romie even messes around with the blueprints for a kind of hyper-realistic holographic imager, in the hopes of projecting a decoy.

In the end, we decide that the EMP will be our best bet for a rescue attempt, partly because it's nearest to completion.

Other Clover cadets interrupt throughout the afternoon, seeking Romie's help with one problem or another.

Each time it happens, panic surges through me and I swiftly turn away. But the cadets are apparently too engrossed in their work to really notice. Lost in their own worlds.

And I find I envy them for that... that *escape*. Because I've experienced it so many times in my own way, running on the holotrek for an hour at a time. And though it's only been two days since my last run, I already feel hungry for it. To feel that the world is empty, the trail is mine, and no one can take it from me.

Truly, deeply, I *miss* running.

While Romie goes to dinner I wait in his pod alone, stomach growling insistently. Back on Earth, there were times I'd miss dinner when we drove straight to my dad's house. Or when Mother had eaten at the office and forgot to bring anything home.

Still, it was nothing like this. I haven't had a proper meal since Sunday night.

At this point, the lack of food is beginning to show. In my reflection in the chrome bed frame, Noah's jumpsuit hangs even looser than before. My eyes have taken on a sunken quality as well, ringed with dark half-moons. It makes me look older. But then again, if we've been here for over a year, I guess I *am* older.

The time crawls, and I begin daydreaming about flatbread, cheeseburgers, and French fries—not the Martian version, but the deep-fried Earth kind. I distract myself by taking inventory of Romie's pod.

Like his lab space, the room has been heavily customized. Gadgets clutter the shelves and floor. He's also managed to fashion a kind of hammock out of two clothes hooks and extra netting from the Bolo Biome.

I wonder if he'll be allowed to keep any of it now that Atkinson is gone. It doesn't seem like the doctors are in favor of cadets having personal items. Likely because they bring on too many memories. I bet they'll empty the whole pod after the next Revision.

No. There won't *be* a next Revision. If there is, that means we failed—and we'll lose a lot more than just Romie's toys.

At last, I hear the tack, tack, tack of the keypad. The door opens and Romie enters.

"Food?" I ask blankly, staring at his empty hands. But then Chloe steps in behind him.

The first thing I register is that her cheeks look red, which briefly puzzles me. They didn't allow makeup to be brought to the colony, mostly because there wasn't any weight to spare on the ship from Earth. But I know a few of the girls borrow a compound from the Laboratory that works as well as any blush.

So is that what I'm seeing? Or is she simply out of breath from carrying the lump I've just noticed in her jumpsuit?

"Is that—?"

"Veggie hash," she says, producing the bundle. "I thought you might be hungry after a long day in hiding. How was the Workshop?"

"Fine," I say, snatching it from her hands. "Chloe, you're a goddess."

Truly I've underestimated Chloe's career as a food smuggler. While I wolf down a bowl of polenta, peppers, and caramelized onions with a sweet, spicy drizzle that tastes of habanero, Noah shows up with a hunk of bread to add to the meal.

I'm so transported by my feast, I hardly even notice when Terra shows up.

"Okay," says Romie once the door is shut. He perches on the hammock, gently swinging his legs. Chloe and I take the bed, while Terra claims the chair. Noah leans against the wall on the far side of the pod. "Now that we've had a day to think it over, I suggest we all present our plans for rescuing Atkinson. Any idea is a good idea. No judgment. Let's just open the floor and see where we arrive."

And so the talks begin.

We can all agree that a prisoner would be held in the Helix. It's the only place cadets aren't allowed to go. Also, cryonics is there. Without any sort of jail on Mars, I feel almost certain they'd use cryosleep to keep him quiet. But I don't dwell on that. Even though we used the cryobeds to get here, the idea of being locked in one of those capsules against my will is horrifying. Like being buried alive.

But even knowing where he is, the problem is getting *inside* the Helix. Without a doctor's thumbprint, we won't be able to get through the door. That's not counting the abundant security cameras, or the doctors coming and going all the time. We'll need to fool the reader and create some kind of a distraction if we hope to slip in unnoticed.

The first option comes from Noah. He suggests we tell the other cadets the truth and stir up some kind of rebellion.

Though it's not a bad idea, a rebellion relies heavily on others. Sure, they might believe us. But they might not. Even if I were able to relay memories from everyone's past in one sitting, they could just decide I'm crazy. It's not as if we can tie them to a chair and *make* them trust us.

Plus, I wouldn't exactly call any of us the "rebel leader" type. Except maybe Terra. And I'm definitely not about to put her in charge of an angry mob.

Chloe briefly proposes that we appeal to a doctor like Bauer, trying to bring them over to our side. This gets almost no consideration.

First, it again hinges on other people. Second, it would mean trusting someone who's been lying to us for months. I feel bad, but I have to agree with the others. Getting help from a doctor just isn't an option—at least not until we've ruled out every other possibility.

Since the EMP still isn't ready, Romie presents a different approach: stealing a Stitch and kidnapping a doctor. We could use the device to scan their memories and find out where they're holding Atkinson, without their cooperation. The problem is, we'd need to understand how to use a Stitch. And though I've grown increasingly confident in Romie's genius, taking hostages seems like an awfully big risk. Even he can admit that.

Only a half hour before free time ends, we still don't have a plan.

"The problem is, we don't even know what's inside the Helix," says Chloe uncertainly. "If Atkinson is in cryosleep, he's going to be groggy when he wakes up. That means he'll probably be unable to walk. We should scout the place out before we attempt a rescue, so we know the shortest way in and out. Right?"

It gets quiet. I look at Terra. Since arriving, she's hardly said a word.

"What do you think?" I ask.

"I think you're all making it too complicated," she says, examining her nails. "Rebellions, kidnappings, scouting? It's way too much. I assume you've all heard of Occam's Razor?"

Noah frowns. "No. What is that?"

"It's a theoretical principle," puts in Romie. "It states that the most plausible theory is also the most probable. Essentially, it argues against overcomplication."

"Exactly," says Terra sweetly. "Thank you, Romesh."

"Okay, so make it easy for us," I say. "What's the most plausible answer?"

"Just use the front door."

"But there are dozens of security cameras surrounding the Helix." Chloe reminds her. "How will we get inside without being seen?"

"Again, simplify. We won't *all* be going," says Terra, looking at me. "Just one of us."

Her meaning is obvious. And I guess it makes sense to just send one of us rather than the whole group. I'm faster than the others. Probably the fastest on the planet. Also, I know the colony better than anyone else, with my memory roadmap. If I get into trouble, I'm sure I could get away again. Assuming they don't jab me with an inoculator.

"Okay," I allow. "So how does *one* of us get past the cameras? Walking up and knocking doesn't exactly scream 'surprise.'"

"That's why you won't be walking up," says Terra coolly. "I'll be wheeling a transport cart up to the door, and you'll be inside it."

"And how will you persuade them to take the cart?" Romie asks.

"Like Lizzy said. By knocking on the front door."

Everyone exchanges a look.

"You're not making any sense," I say impatiently.

"I've delivered dozens of transports to the Helix," Terra replies, flashing me one of her infuriating smiles. "Didn't you know? I'm a floater. I fill in where I'm needed. And when I'm not stuck helping the Scrubs, sometimes that means restocking supplies."

"Why didn't you tell us this sooner?" says Noah in disbelief.

She shrugs.

"No one asked."

"Why don't I already know all this?" I ask warily. "I don't have memories of delivering transports to the Helix."

"Probably because they didn't erase them from my mind," she replies. "Isn't that how it works? You only got the memories they removed?"

But something isn't adding up. I narrow my eyes.

"What's inside the carts you deliver?"

"I don't know."

"You don't check?" I ask.

"Of course not. They're locked," she retorts.

"And they just trust you to deliver them, no questions asked?"

"For someone who talks so much about trust, you don't seem to have very much," she snaps, suddenly fierce. "What exactly are *you* hiding, Elizabeth? Why don't we get to peer into *your* deepest secrets?"

My face gets hot as they all consider this.

"I don't have any secrets."

"Well, I guess we'll just have to trust you on that," she says sarcastically. Then, glaring at the others, "Whether you like it or not, my plan is the best you've got. And I think you all know it. Don't you?"

Again my instinct is to fire back something harsh, something cutting, like she would. But I restrain myself. I still need her as an ally—especially if she can get me into the Helix. And though I hate to admit it, she's right. Her plan *is* the best we've got.

But she's right about something else too. I don't trust her. Not even for a second.

"Okay, so you can get me in," I say, fighting to remain civil. "How do I get back out?"

"Find the room where they watch the cameras and pull the plug. Or use that stun gun of yours to knock out the doctor on duty, tie him to a chair, and then blackmail him into doing what you want. Seems like you're pretty good at that."

I'm about to lose it when, to my surprise, Noah speaks.

"That doesn't help."

Awkward silence expands, filling the room. His face reddens as he hesitantly continues.

"You're right to be mad. It was wrong for Lizzy to put you in that position. Just like it was wrong for Atkinson to put Lizzy in this one, and for Dosset to start the whole thing. But we're all just doing our best. Taking it out on others won't make it easier. It just continues the cycle."

The effect these words have on Terra is profound. She glares at him, then shrugs and looks away as if she, too, is embarrassed.

Maybe they're right about Noah. Maybe his silence does hide

some kind of maturity.

"Well, it's time for Briefing," Chloe says at length, glancing between Terra and me. "We'd better be going. I'll come along tomorrow to help with the cart. Okay?"

"Great," I say.

"Fine," says Terra. Then she slips out the door without another word.

Chloe gives me a hug and then leaves as well. When Noah opens the door I move to follow, to head back to his pod for the night. He hesitates.

"Aren't you staying here?" he asks.

"Huh?"

His question blindsides me. But it makes sense, doesn't it? Of course I'd stay. The less I'm out wandering the halls, the better my odds of staying hidden.

Yet for some reason, I waver.

"You're more than welcome to stay here, Elizabeth," Romie volunteers. "You can sleep in my bed while I take the hammock, if you like."

My next decision doesn't really make sense to me. I don't have a logical reason to make it. But right now, in this moment, knowing that someone is watching over me, that they're staying awake to be sure that I'm safe, sounds like something I need. So I shake my head.

"No thanks," I tell Romie. "Noah and I have... gotten used to me sleeping there."

This announcement does little for Romie, but for Noah the change is immediate. His whole face brightens. As if his eyes are shining.

"Really?"

"Sure," I say awkwardly.

As he opens the door, I see Chloe only a few steps down the hall and hurrying swiftly away. Like she's trying to run away from something.

My heart turns to ice.

I'm no moron. She heard us, I know it. Through the crack in the door, while she waited to walk back with Noah and steal a precious few moments with him, moments she surely imagined when she put on her stolen makeup, hoping to catch his attention...

I take it back. I *am* a moron. The worst kind of moron and the worst kind of friend. For every kindness Chloe has done me, I've only thought of myself. Terra was right about that as well: I don't know anything about trust. And certainly, no one should trust me.

"Never mind," I say as Chloe disappears down the stairs, out of sight. "I'll stay here."

Confusion registers in Noah's features, making me feel even worse. But I'm past the point of protecting anyone's feelings now.

I turn away, allowing Romie to step into the hall and follow the others to Briefing. Then I close the door and turn out the light, casting myself into darkness. Kicking off my boots, I climb into the hammock and curl into a ball. With nothing to weigh me down, it feels like I'm floating. Like I'm drifting away.

This is why I don't let people in, I remind myself. This is why I'm not vulnerable. Because then people can hurt you.

Hanging in my little web, I try my best to get some sleep. But instead, I stare out into the unfeeling void, searching for the eyes that are no longer staring back.

Chapter Ten

No rest comes to me, though the hammock turns out to be pretty comfortable. Instead, I lie awake, contemplating a serious problem.

Her name is Elizabeth.

Just how long have I gone through life like this, not thinking about other people? Even the ones who claim to be my friends?

I guess before the Memory Bank was dumped on my unwitting shoulders, I didn't give much thought to what others might be feeling. Not really. I mean, sure, if someone was clearly hurt, I wouldn't ignore them. But these kinds of things, like with Chloe and Noah... I just looked past them, I guess. Didn't think too hard about how they might be affected by my actions.

It's a little hard to ignore now that I can simply walk through Chloe's memories and see exactly how I've hurt her.

But there's a twist. I've got Noah's memories too. So I know what he *doesn't* feel for her and what he *does* feel for me. That puts me in kind of a lose-lose situation. I can't make her happy without crushing his hopes. And I can't make him happy without breaking her heart.

These are not the thoughts I want filling my head before I sneak into the Helix and risk everything. So while I wait, after Romie wakes and heads down to fitness hour, I allow my mind to wander. It takes me home. To Earth.

My mother and father.

Bubbling in my head, the memories take over, tugging me down, down, out of the room, into another time. I can feel the heat of the deck burning my bare feet when I climb out of the pool. Glimpse the badminton net, and the bats flying out to savage the birdie whenever we play after dusk. Smell the woods behind the house, dense, dark, and mysterious, and treacherous in the winter months when it rains without end.

In the glimmering years that filled my young life, we explored it all together. Shared each joy, every new discovery. It seems wrong that they're not here with me now. As if in some way they abandoned me.

And that's the question that suddenly invades my mind: Did they abandon me?

Or did I abandon them?

I feel I must have the answer locked in a tangle of memories at the back of my head. But there is something keeping me from it. Maybe guilt... or fear.

Footsteps outside the pod, and a tap on the door. Hunger, which has been my constant companion, deserts me as I'm drawn back into the present, into the problems that require my attention. I put on Noah's hat and oversized jumpsuit. My hands are slick with nervous sweat.

Opening the door, I find Terra in the hallway, alone.

"Where's Chloe?"

"Couldn't make it," she replies flatly. "You ready?"

Guilt creeps over me afresh. Maybe she's lying. Maybe she bullied Chloe into staying behind. More likely, Chloe cried herself to sleep and didn't want to face me. I don't blame her.

At the moment, I don't feel like facing myself.

"Ready," I mutter.

The transport cart is waiting at the bottom of the spiral staircase, lid propped open. Terra checks to be sure that nobody is around. Right now it's time for Group. The colony should be all but empty.

"In you go," she says with mock enthusiasm.

For a second I'm struck by the irony of the cart's coffin-like shape and what it very well might signify for me. I realize in a way I never have before just how much I hate being confined. To be able to keep moving, to distract myself, to have an escape from my thoughts—that's how I stay balanced. As I climb into the padded box, my whole body goes cold.

I manage to give Terra a thumbs-up before she slams the lid, roughly shoving the cart down the hallway.

It comes as a surprise that the box is so cushioned. And the perfect size to fit a cadet—almost as if it were designed for the task.

Maybe it was. I wonder if this is how they haul us around after a Revision. The thought strokes a shiver up my spine as I imagine the doctors shuffling about the halls in white coats, pulling lifeless bodies from plastic caskets, and tucking them into beds. I try to distract myself by going over the plan again in my head, the one Romie worked out before he fell asleep and relayed to me just after dawn.

While the cadets are going about their morning duties, Terra will wheel me over to the Helix and have the cart sent to cryonics. Once I find Atkinson, I'll use that same cart to transport him back to the Xeri domes.

Meanwhile, Noah will gather medicine to neutralize the drugs that kept him in cryosleep. Chloe and Romie will gather supplies for his period in hiding, such as food and water. Once I'm finished, Terra will be waiting outside the Helix at the juncture to the Xeri domes.

If I'm followed, she'll take the cart. That'll leave me free to focus on my escape.

While Atkinson stabilizes, the rest of us will regroup in the Bolo Biome, by the tool shed that borders the avocado trees. There will be no risk of cameras. And there are plenty of tangled nooks in case we need to lose pursuers.

"One other thing," Romie had told me, still rubbing the sleep from his eyes. "To be sure you get away, we need to do something about the surveillance cameras."

"You said the EMP isn't ready."

"It isn't. But even if we can't turn the cameras off, we might be able to get around them. I need you to locate a port, to access their system."

"A port," I said, still fighting my own groggy senses.

"Yes. You'll take my splicer, here, to do a TCP/IP scan—"

"—and get a signal upload for the password," I finished, following his train of thought. "I can remove myself from the database then leave a backdoor for you to access their feed." He stared at me as I reached up to adjust my glasses, then realized I was mimicking his own quirk. With a blush, I dropped my hand. "Um, is that... is that what you were thinking?"

"Yes, exactly," was his reply. "Exactly what I was thinking."

I waited until he left to collapse into the chair, trying to stop my hands from trembling.

Another rattle shakes me from the memory as the cart goes over a seam. Even with the padding, it feels like I'm getting bruises. I wonder if Terra is doing it on purpose. I can hear her humming through the plastic. Then, abruptly, we stop.

Moments pass, and dread begins to pool in my stomach. What am I doing? Why did I agree to this? I was a fool to think I could trust her. Ever since I abducted her, she's probably been waiting for just the right moment to turn me in. Probably she wanted to be there when it happened. It burns me to think how easy I've made it for her.

Breathe slowly, I tell myself. I know I don't have much air in here. But the claustrophobia is like an itch, growing worse with every second in captivity.

We begin moving again, another jarring bump. To my bewilderment, the cart begins to slant as if we're going up a ramp, my body sliding down until blood rushes to my head. I clench my teeth, straining to ease the pressure, but my arms are pinned at my sides. What is going on out there?

Abruptly we level off, and then we come to a halt.

Nothing. No movement, no sounds. I can tell my air is getting low because my lungs have started that trickly burning sensation again, just as in the airlock.

I try to lie still, running my fingers over a hard plastic tube in my jumpsuit pocket, along the back, the smooth wings, the cap... It's the Verced inoculator that Romie found in Conrad's coat. I'd forgotten about it. Has it been used, I wonder?

In my other pocket, the cumbersome stun gun is all charged up and ready to go. Still, even with both weapons, I feel drastically underprepared for what comes next.

Will someone open the lid? Will they leave the cart for later? If I'm found, my best chance will be to catch them off their guard.

Hopefully, it won't be Sarlow or McCallum.

I hear feet shuffling. Then the latch pops and my whole body goes rigid. The lid is thrown back, but it's not one of the maintenance directors staring down at me. It's an angular face, stubbly and aged. The doctor's eyes go wide as they meet mine.

"How—?"

Without thinking, I lurch up like a cobra from under a bowl and jab the inoculator into his neck. He cries out and recoils.

My feet slap on the tile floor as I swiftly uncoil my stun gun. But I can already tell it isn't needed, because his knees have begun to buckle, and the next thing I know he's falling into my arms, dead weight.

I ease him down as gently as I can, but he's much heavier than Terra. It's like wrestling a sack of mulch. He slips, and his head thuds on the tile as I grapple with his arms. After several pathetic attempts to pick him back up, I end up dragging him into a corner and leaving him in a heap.

It takes me a few seconds to catch my breath.

That's when I take in my surroundings. I made it to cryonics. Along the walls, stacked like angled bunks, are giant capsules. Small, darkened windows show that most are empty. Except a few.

My heart begins to thump harder and harder, until I can feel it pounding against my ribcage. I don't know why I'm so nervous. This is why I'm here, to bring Atkinson back with me. But for some reason I find myself terrified of what else I might find. I look around once more to be sure I'm alone.

No cameras in here.

Sensing that time is short, I approach the first bed. Through tempered glass, I see a girl about my age. Sealed tightly in a clear bag, blue liquid fringing her face.

My first thought is that she's dead. But no, panels beside her give some sort of readout, and a pulse is one of them. Instead, I choose to think of her as looking peaceful. The idea of a still lake comes to mind, no ripples to disturb it. It's less creepy, anyway. Her features are bony, her hair pulled into a dark ponytail. I realize I know her face.

She was one of the cadets who disappeared, who came to mind back in Noah's pod.

How long has she been sleeping here? And what could she possibly have done to deserve such a prison?

Maybe she found out what they were up to, like me. Maybe it was too great a risk to erase all her memories, and this was the best way to keep her quiet.

Didn't the doctors say Atkinson could have killed me by uploading so many memories at once? The same could be true of erasing them.

In the next bed, I find the Bolo boy with freckles on his nose. There are five more that I hadn't remembered, but upon seeing their faces I know exactly who they are.

One, a girl with pale skin and coppery hair like Noah's, used to sleep in the pod at the end of my hall. Her name is Hannah.

Soon I've checked the whole lab, but there's no sign of Atkinson. I don't know how long the Verced will last, but I want to put a lot of distance between me and that doctor before he wakes up. Slinking to the door, I crack it open.

Now I understand why it felt like a ramp from inside the cart. To my left, the floor of the Helix rises gradually, while to my right it slopes back downward, curving around an enormous cylindrical terrarium to suggest the spiral shape for which the ship was named. Inside the glass, vines and ivy hang in a loose knot of vegetation.

And again, no security cameras. I guess they don't want a recording of what happens behind these walls.

I return to the cart for my hat, which fell off when I sprang pward. Do I take the cart with me? I'd expected Atkinson to be groggy from the sleeping drugs. Now I feel like it'll just slow me down. I resolve to leave it.

Before I go, I decide to take the unconscious doctor's lab coat as an extra precaution. The fit is closer to my size than Noah's jumpsuit. Maybe, if the doctors don't look too hard, I'll have a better shot at blending in.

It's just too bad there isn't more Verced in the pockets.

Feeling a bit better disguised, I cast one final glance at the imprisoned cadets then slip into the hall and get moving.

It's amazing how vulnerable you can feel, walking along a brightly lit corridor. Every little sound, a hint of pursuit. Every alcove, a place for an attacker to hide. Except no one is hiding or pursuing. Only the thriving plants inside the glass show signs of life. Beyond that, the Helix is as barren as a morgue.

I pass several doors on the outer edge of the spiral: Telemetry, Astrometrics, Operations. Then I see a label that catches my attention.

Comm Room.

Quick thinking says that if the doctors were going to set up a surveillance center, it'd be in here. I test the handle. Incredibly, it's unlocked.

As I step into the darkened room I hear the dull murmur of voices. I freeze—but only for a second. Instinct kicks in, and I dive for cover under the nearest desk, curling into a ball. Behind me, the door clicks shut.

I cower in absolute stillness, waiting for a sign that my entrance was noticed. But the voices continue in undertones, their owners apparently too distracted to notice me or the door. Rallying my courage, I sneak a glance and count five doctors at the end of the room, their bodies silhouetted by glowing screens.

Just as I'd predicted, the displays show the security feeds from various domes and corridors around the colony. And I see the thick, blinking towers of the surveillance network forming a few short aisles along a wall.

At my back the door opens again, and for a second I think I've been followed. But no, the figure walks past me toward the others, pulling something on wheels. I hear the click and drag of a respirator.

"Good morning, doctors." That voice is unmistakable.

Dosset.

Icy sweat breaks over my body, driving the breath from my lungs. Other than his first meeting with each cadet, I have no memory of being near Dosset in person. Never, not once have I seen him roaming the halls.

Being in the same room with him now, I'm petrified. Like having one of Noah's panic attacks all over again.

The others have given some kind of response. To my mingled horror and surprise, they're beginning to leave. One by one, they pass in silence. The door has hardly shut before Dosset himself starts to move. From under the desk, I can see his spotless white shoes headed directly toward my hiding spot.

Does he know I'm here? How could he? There were no security cameras in the hall—I would have seen them!

I make myself smaller, as small as I can, huddling in fear as he draws nearer. Then he stops right above me. So close, I could reach out and touch the wheel of his oxygen tank.

An endless moment passes. I hear a soft drumming. It takes a second to realize he's typing on a projected keyboard. Abruptly he steps past me, clicks the deadbolt on the door, then heads back over to the displays.

Though I can hardly stop myself from shaking, I slip from under the desk and peek over. Unexpectedly, the screens have gone blank.

"Flag Mercer," he says.

"Calling Doctor Mercer," replies the same female voice that announces the time stamp. "One moment, please."

A short period of silence passes, then a pop and a crackle. In the middle of the room, a glowing blue hologram takes shape, projected from a hidden lens in the ceiling.

The man is wearing a lab coat, just like every other doctor. His face looks pocked, as if riddled by tiny craters.

"Hello, Adam. Checking in?" asks the projection.

"Just wondering about the readouts," Dosset says. "Do you have an update?"

"I do," Mercer replies. He sounds out of breath. "Naturally, things are pretty much exactly as you predicted."

"Of course they are," Dosset says dryly. "Have you shut down Aster, then?"

"Not... quite. You're sure you want to go ahead with this? We could wait and see if—"

"There is no reason to wait."

"But the plant life—"

"Trust me, Andrew. Wrong as it may feel, there is little use in keeping her online any longer. I take personal responsibility."

"Understood."

In the following silence, I feel their words like an anchor catching in the base of my stomach. Is this it? Could this be their terrible secret? That they've halted the terraforming, allowing Mars to return to dust?

"About that missing cadet... Engram, I believe?" Mercer ventures.

Dosset absently reaches over and presses a button on one of the consoles. The giant screens blink back to life with a feed of the colony. "There was no sign of her?" he guesses.

"Um, no. There was not."

"I'm not surprised," Dosset says.

Mercer frowns, his forehead wrinkling like a walnut.

"You're not."

"No," replies Dosset with a chuckle. "To be honest, I don't believe she ever left the colony in the first place."

"How is that possible?"

"She did the same thing I do, Andrew. She anticipated our move, then made her own. I'm impressed at how quickly she has acclimated to the memories. But if I had to guess, I'd say the longer she goes on like this, the more calculated she'll become."

"Then... what can we do to stop her?"

In the flickering light of the screen, I see an eerie smile cross Dosset's face. He reminds me of a wolf again. The thought makes the hair stand up on the back of my neck.

"Consider more drastic measures," he says. "Though, as always, we must exercise strict caution. We cannot afford a panic. More than anything else, our primary concern is keeping the cadets in good health mentally, emotionally, and physically."

The projection distorts as Mercer tilts his head, revealing a film of sweat on his brow.

"What do you plan to tell the others?" he asks haltingly. "About Aster?"

"Nothing at the moment. I'm afraid information like this will only confuse them." Dosset turns his back on the hologram. "Why don't you come up to the Bridge when you're finished? We'll have a proper debriefing."

"Understood."

The hologram disappears and I slink back into my hiding place. As Dosset shuffles past me, I hold my breath. Then he's gone.

As soon as I'm alone the sobs come. The fear, the dread, the horror of the moment is a vise on my chest, and I can't catch my breath. Anyone could walk in and find me. But right now it doesn't seem to matter. My hands tremble as I hold them over my mouth, telling myself it will be okay, *willing* it to be okay. Forcing myself to believe it.

The gasping eases at length, and I finally begin to breathe normally again, icy sweat shrouding me in a crystalline shell. I'm severely tempted to turn back now. To tell the others what I've learned before I'm silenced like the cadets in cryonics.

But I can't. The news about Aster only makes our mission that much more important. More than ever, we need Atkinson's help to bring down Dosset.

So, against my better judgment—against every fiber in my body—I wriggle out from under the desk and continue with the plan.

Locating a port isn't difficult. By the time I'm tucking the splicer back into my pocket, a doctor has returned to keep watch over the surveillance feed. I crouch between the rows of servers for a good fifteen minutes, waiting for him to settle. Then I dart out into the sloping hallway, not risking a backward glance.

Where are they keeping Atkinson? I have no idea. We'd been so sure he was in cryonics, we didn't even discuss an alternative. But at this rate, I could end up checking every room in the Helix.

Not that I have a better plan. So I keep trudging up the curve until I reach a new door, this one labeled Sick Bay.

I almost decide to keep going, but a memory gives me pause. Something in Noah's head about the risks of sedating trauma patients. If Atkinson was injured, the doctors might be waiting until he's stable before they put him into cryosleep.

Really, it can't hurt to look. I've got no other leads and no other ideas.

As I push through the door, I know at once that the Sick Bay is no longer being used for patients. The beds have all been replaced by tables spread with beakers, burners, and trays of an electric blue powder. Doctors bend over the various pieces of equipment, everyone wearing a surgical mask.

Rather than hide, my instinct is now to flee. But I've only just stepped into the room, and a sudden move like that will surely draw attention. Instead, I turn my back to the doctors, digging my own mask out of my pocket and slipping it over my ears. My hands occupy themselves with a rack of test tubes as I watch the white figures through a reflection in the cabinetry.

No one speaks. They seem fixated on their work, checking this and weighing that. What are they doing? I half wonder. But my curiosity is swiftly buckling under the weight of my nerves. Trying to act natural, I risk a move toward the door. But then my eye catches on the end of the nearest table, where the product of their work is amassing on small plastic trays—inoculators, the drug funneled into a tiny reservoir. At once I know what they're making.

Verced.

After seeing how useful the drug can be, I yearn to grab one. Or maybe ten. Because I'm painfully aware of how vulnerable I am, outnumbered and unarmed. Verced is a way to defend myself without just running away. But to steal them, I'll need to get very close to the doctors.

Paralyzed with indecision, I face the door, lingering. At any moment they could notice me and demand to know who I am, why I'm here. Yet I find myself edging back to the table anyway, my face still turned. I scoop up one, then two of the small tubes.

"Carver," says a voice. "Do you have that backlog?"

I freeze, certain the question is intended for me. But I compel my knees to bend, stiffly obeying the only impulse that seems to be firing in my brain:

Run away. Run away.

"Hey—Carver!"

But I don't stop, because I now recognize Meng's curt tone. As soon as I'm out the door I take off at a trot, no longer able to make myself move at a walking pace.

Stupid. It was so stupid to steal the Verced. If I could've just found Atkinson, I might not have even needed it. Now I'm going to have the entire Helix hunting for me, as soon as they realize they've got an intruder—which won't take very long.

I've only just started down the spiral when voices echo up at me, urgent and thin. I spin and dash back up the curve, past the Sick Bay and onto a new level of the Helix. Here, the glass terrarium is capped off by a hallway of uniform doors. Breath short, hands trembling, I pick one at random and pull the handle.

Locked.

The voices behind me are growing louder. Footsteps picking up speed. I see a door at the end of the hall, ajar. My legs propel me forward and I reach it, swinging the door closed as quiet as a whisper.

Inside is some kind of atrium, bare except for an empty desk. There are three rooms that split off from here—two appear empty, their windows dim. The third has a light on. I choose one of the darkened rooms.

There I hover in the shadows, waiting. Through the wall I hear the atrium door opening, footsteps stepping through, and I know that any second they'll find me here. Any moment they'll crash into the room and drag me away, kicking and screaming.

But they don't.

When enough time has passed for me to realize I've actually eluded my pursuers, I can't believe it. But my relief wavers as I look around and see that the only way out of this room is the way I came in.

Peering through the window, I see that a familiar doctor has taken up his post at the desk. McCallum. He sips a cup slowly, reading something on his tablet.

I lean against the door and ball my fists, trying desperately to remain calm. It feels as if I'm trapped in the coffin-cart all over again. The surgical mask is making it hard to breathe, so I rip it from my face.

But I haven't even recognized the room yet, because it's so dim. Slowly my eyes adjust, and it dawns on me:

This is the interrogation room. This is where Dosset and Shiffrin cornered me, asking the questions that would chart the memories for my first Revision. A long metal table. Cold, sterile air that smells of rubbing alcohol. Nameless tools suspended on twisted arms hanging stiffly around the chamber.

I think about the other two rooms that connect to the atrium.

The one that was occupied.

Could Atkinson be locked in there? The doctors captured him almost four days ago. Surely Dosset would've extracted any valuable information from him by now. What logical reason could they have to keep interrogating him?

Not that logic has played much into Dosset's recent decisions.

Whatever the case, I'm not going anywhere until McCallum leaves. I take a deep breath and prepare myself to wait.

And wait...

And wait.

Time crawls. No voices announce the hour. Judging by my hunger, I'm stuck in the room until long past lunch. Maybe even dinner. McCallum doesn't budge, though at one point another doctor brings him food.

Hollow aches come and go, rumbling up through my abdomen. And again, dehydration sets in. Every time I stand up to stretch, black spots dance across my vision. I eventually end up sitting cross-legged under the table to conserve energy, and to keep hidden in case anyone enters suddenly.

Part of me wishes I knew how late it is. Another part is thankful I don't. At least this way I can't listen to the hours dwindle by. I wonder if this is how it feels to grow old. Knowing that time is still passing but you're no longer a part of it. Weak and forgotten by the ones you loved.

"Getting pretty grim, Liz," I mutter to myself, shivering. "Think happy thoughts. Ones that don't involve food."

Finally, I hear movement outside the door. When I scramble to the window, I just catch sight of McCallum as he exits the room, two other doctors on his heels.

Am I alone now? I can't be entirely sure. But if I'm going to make it out alive, I have a feeling that this is my chance.

After tiptoeing out of the interrogation chamber, I hesitate, staring at the window that's still lit.

What waits behind this door? For some reason, the same dread that settled on me in cryonics has returned. Could it really be Atkinson? Or am I about to come face to face with yet another secret—one even darker than before?

Bracing myself for another run, I close shaky fingers around the handle and pull.

Chapter Eleven

The room is the same as the first, though this one is thick with the smell of sweat, urine, and the sour hint of blood. And seated on the other side of the table, a man with ragged brown hair, pale skin, and heavy bags under his eyes fixes me with a bloodshot gaze.

There is only one man on the planet this can be. Even without Romie's memories to confirm it, I simply know.

"You must be Lizzy," Atkinson says hoarsely.

If I was tongue-tied before in the Verced lab, now I'm positively speechless. He looks as if he's been awake for days. Tortured, maybe. Though I can't understand why. If it's information they're after, couldn't they just use a Stitch to extract it?

"Doctor Atkinson."

My voice isn't much more than a squeak, under the circumstances. I hurry across the room. His arms and legs have been tied down by synthetic straps. Bandages crisscross his forearms, covering what... wounds?

The sight reminds me unpleasantly of the way I restrained Terra.

"Can you get me out of here?" He's growing frantic. "They could be back any moment."

"I'll try," I promise. The weight of the Verced in my pocket is reassuring at least. "Are you able to walk?"

"I'll try," he echoes.

I smile, but he doesn't return the gesture.

With the straps free, he's able to lean forward and stagger to his feet, but he leans on me heavily. I wish I hadn't removed the surgical mask. His acrid stench makes bile climb into the back of my throat. What have they been doing to him?

Together we manage to reach the door, though we're both perspiring by the time we do. Ignoring the smell and dizziness, I peer through the window. Still no sign of the doctors. But if we really hope to get out of here, I'll need the cart I left back in cryonics. He'll never reach the exit in his current state.

"Can you wait here?" I ask him, digging the surgical mask out of my pocket.

His eyes widen in terror.

"We need to leave," he tells me. "Now!"

"Not so loud," I say, trying to use the soothing voice that Chloe is so good at.

This isn't at all what I'd expected, a trauma victim on the verge of a breakdown. But then, none of this is what I expected. I notice the dilation of his eyes, the way he keeps twitching and jumping at small noises, and realize there's no chance of leaving him alone. He'll just follow me anyway, or wander off and get caught.

"Come on," I tell him reluctantly. "We'll just have to go quick, all right?"

He nods.

"We need to leave," he says.

"I know."

We start forward, me pulling him along, him groaning with every step. He moves like a creaky old man, as if his joints are made of wood. Fortunately, we only have to move down the spiral, which is much easier than going up. We make it past the converted Sick Bay and Comm Room. I start to believe we might actually make it.

"There," he huffs, pointing a finger.

I look up as a silver door comes into view at the bottom of the slope, a thumbprint reader beside it. Just a dozen more meters and we're free.

"Hang in there," I say.

No response now, just heavy breathing. He reaches out a hand as we near, scanning his thumb over the glossy surface. Green lights flash and the door clicks.

If they didn't know he'd escaped his room before, they do now.

We lumber down the short hallway and around the Wheel, then enter the access point to the Xeri domes. This is where Terra was supposed to meet us. But there's no sign of her. In fact, there's no sign of anyone.

Atkinson is practically heaving.

"We need to leave," he says in a slurred voice.

"One second," I say, glancing at his shaky hands and pasty skin. Now that I've recovered from my initial surprise, it's easy to recognize the signs of dehydration. He needs water before anything else. I know there's a bottle in Noah's pod, but I don't think Atkinson will make it that far. The Xeri kitchen is much closer.

And yet the kitchen is so exposed. Anyone could just walk in and catch us.

I'm too weary to linger but too fatigued to choose. Then all at once the overheads click off and my decision is made for me.

"This way."

We stagger onward, following green runners along the path. Is it power down already? I was in the interrogation room longer than I thought.

In a way, this has worked in my favor. The shadows will help shield us from the cameras, and with the hallways empty, we should be able to stick to the walls and mostly avoid their gaze.

Then as we enter the kitchen I hear them—footfalls—echoing all around us. My heart is in my throat before I realize that the noise is just Atkinson's heavy steps bouncing off the flat metal cabinetry. He's still gasping for breath. I drag him to a water station and, since I don't have a water bottle, fill a small saucepan to use as a cup.

Half of the first panful goes down the front of his lab coat, but he doesn't even seem to notice. The next one is better. After four pans he leans back and wipes his mouth with his hand, now a little steadier, the frantic gleam in his eye a bit diminished.

While he hiccups, I fill a fresh pan and slake my own thirst. By the time I'm done, I'm so full that the liquid sloshes around my stomach like a wave pool.

"How are you feeling?" I say, turning my attention back to Atkinson.

He squints at me in the gloom.

"You're Lizzy?"

I nod.

"Lizzy Engram?"

"Yes. Yes, I'm Lizzy."

He blinks at me as if he's confused.

"What happened, doctor?" I ask hesitantly, unable to help myself. "What did they do to you back there?"

I immediately regret the question. From the way he reacts, the words are like a trigger. He begins to quiver, scratching his finger-nails over the bandages on his forearms as if whatever lies beneath has begun to itch uncontrollably.

"My memories," he says. "He took my... my memories."

I feel a coldness begin in my toes and work upward through my body. A suspicion I don't want confirmed. But I have to know.

"You mean Dosset?" When he nods, I ask, "Which memories? Which ones did he take?"

"All of them," he whispers. "One by one. He asked me questions and... I tried not to, but he made me think about them. About everything. My family, my... my son." His face crumples and his lips tremble. "I think he was my son. My child. But I... I can't remember. Not his name, not his face." He fixes me with a gaze so full of agony, I have to look away. "He told me I stole the Memory Bank and gave it to you. Is that true?"

His words are almost an accusation. As if I forced him to steal the bank against his will. And then their meaning sinks in and I realize how foolish I've been.

131

Dosset would never have taken the risk that Atkinson might somehow escape. Not when he had me on the loose with a conceivable plan to overthrow the system. Isn't that basically what Dosset told the others in the airlock? *Let's have no more talk about Atkinson.* Because Atkinson no longer exists.

When they discover him missing they'll probably laugh. And what a joke it is, my thinking I could outwit these doctors who have so fully controlled us. They're likely on their way to collect us right now.

I glance at the door apprehensively, but it remains closed.

His next words take me by surprise.

"It was the Verced, I think. The drug we use to sedate our cadets. It produces retrograde amnesia. Do you know what that means?" Before I can answer, he explains, "It means it erases your short-term memory. Everything from the past few hours. Apparently, I took two doses when they captured me. As a result, I almost didn't wake up... and when I did, I no longer recalled anything about that night."

He scratches harder and a bandage comes loose, revealing jagged scabs where his fingernails have torn zig-zag lines in his skin. Two begin to bleed.

"Dosset has been *encouraging* me to think down the same neuron pathways I did when I stole the memories," he continues. "To imagine what I must have thought the first time—to reformulate the plan, to recreate the lost memories. As if, given enough time, my brain will produce the same result as before. But... it won't. It just won't."

I force my eyes to turn away again, this time from the grotesque sight of his wounds. Drinking all that water so quickly was a bad idea. I feel like I might throw up.

"So you don't even remember stealing the Memory Bank?" I finally ask, yet clinging to hope that he might be able to help us. "Or... or why you gave it to me?"

"Why?" He looks up as if bewildered by the question. "No, I

don't know why. Although, more than anything, I wish I did."

My mind is reeling. I want to keep him talking, but I feel so exposed. And overwhelmed. I don't know what to think or do. But even if scanning Atkinson's thumb didn't alert the doctors to his escape, they must have discovered his empty cell.

They'll be coming after him—and soon.

As if he's reading my thoughts, Atkinson says, "We can't stay here."

"Yes," I quickly agree. Right now I don't want to think. I just want to get somewhere safe, where we can figure out what to do next. "Are you ready to go?"

He nods. Having rehydrated a little, he looks as if he'll be able to walk on his own. That's a step in the right direction, at least.

"This way, then," I say. "And stay close."

Relieved to be moving again, I peer into the hall. Still empty. But the familiar passages, ever so ordered and clean, have become something else to me now. Something haunting and disturbed. A facade to hide the nightmares under the surface.

I think about how it must feel to know that your world is being deconstructed. That the things and people you love most are slipping away and there's nothing you can do about it. Then, as I turn the corner toward the Bolo domes, my thoughts are halted by a figure heading toward us. By her lumbering stride, I immediately know who it is.

Sarlow.

My pulse quickens. Is she looking for us? She must be.

"Get back," I whisper.

As I turn around to push Atkinson back up the hall, I find it empty.

"Doctor?"

No reply.

Panicked, I dash into the previous corridor and glance around. At the end, I can just hear the echoing sound of heavy footfalls.

I almost shout for him to stop but catch myself before I bring

Sarlow down upon me. Instead, I race after him, running on the tips of my feet for a furtive stride. By the time I catch him, he's already reached the airlock.

"What are you doing?" I hiss fiercely.

He gasps, almost falling over in surprise. He must have already typed the access code because I can hear the gears turning behind the bay door.

"We can't stay here," he insists. "We need to get off the colony."

"There's nothing out there," I tell him. "They've... shut Aster down. I think—" And then I give voice to a suspicion that I had yet to admit to myself. "I think he might be trying to prevent the next wave of colonists from coming, to hide what's happening here."

He stares at me blankly.

"If the planet isn't terraformed, more settlers won't be sent from Earth," I explain slowly, to help him understand.

"You don't know why he does it," Atkinson murmurs. "Why he changes your memories."

I swallow, unnerved by the way the shadows hide his face.

"Because of a secret," I say.

"Yes," Atkinson says. "He let me keep it. He wanted me to remember the... the reason."

Again, he starts to shake. When I reach out to steady him, he stumbles into the airlock as if afraid I might hurt him. He reminds me more of a wounded animal than a doctor. All I can think about is not scaring him away. Not before he tells me what he knows.

I waver in the archway, chest tight, one eye on the button that will seal the room and push him out onto Mars.

"Tell me."

Atkinson falters.

"He does it because... because they're dead."

"Who's dead?"

"All of them. Just months after we arrived. Everyone on Earth. Dead." He shrinks further away, fiddling with the strap of the nearest spacesuit. It occurs to me that maybe he hasn't just had pieces of his mind erased.

Maybe he's lost it entirely.

"They can't be dead," I say as carefully as I can. "I talked to my dad last week."

"Did you? Are you certain it was last week?" he asks.

I hesitate. When I think about it, talking with my dad seems like it was only a week ago. But I realize that my sense of time is still skewed by the memories that were erased.

How long has it really been? If we've been on the colony for over a year, maybe... I think back frantically. My knees grow unsteady as I remember week after week, the doctors telling us that a geomagnetic storm was blocking the signal to Earth.

"A nuclear holocaust," Atkinson says distractedly. He begins to scratch again, drawing fresh blood in streaks over his ragged flesh. "It destroyed the planet. And we were two hundred and twenty-five million kilometers away."

"That doesn't make any sense," I throw back at him, suddenly angry. "There are billions of people on Earth. Even... even if there was a war, people would've survived!"

I might as well have struck him with my fists, the way my words affect him. He stumbles toward the button that will cycle the airlock, a hand reaching out, twitching. I freeze.

"You see?" he says desperately. "When the cadets were told, they became inconsolable. Depressed. Aggressive. Dosset said that if we could erase what happened and give you a fresh start, it would give you a chance to move on." He licks his lips, the cadence of his words picking up with every syllable. "And of course that's very important. You're the future of mankind now. Your health... is the most important thing of all."

He smiles at me, his face contorted. As if an earthquake has damaged the surface yet beneath is where the true damage lies.

"All that remains of Earth is our memories," he says weakly. "I won't let him take what few I have left."

Before I can react, he punches the button. I stumble back as the door closes rapidly between us. Then the alarm, the red lights swirling on the walls as I stand there motionless, unable to grasp what just happened.

It's like day one, when I first put the pieces together about the Revisions. Numbness spreads like freezing smoke in my lungs. But the alarm is loud, so loud that it gradually stirs me from my daze. The doctors will be coming. I need to get out of here, and fast. I begin to move, slowly at first, then breaking into a disjointed run.

But where do I go? I'm so rattled that I can't even remember. It's all too much to get my head around, so I don't even try. I just focus on the next step.

We were supposed to meet in the Bolo Biome. By now, Noah and the others will have assumed that I failed. That I got caught and stuffed in a cryobed. More than anything I want to go after them, to tell them I'm okay—but this time I think I should ignore what I want. Dosset will have concluded I must have allies in order to get in and out of the Helix unnoticed. He's probably watching the sleeping pods right now, just waiting for us to regroup.

Which means the safest and least-expected option will be to spend the night in a biome, where the cameras won't be watching. I can figure out how to contact the others in the morning.

Rather than risk the Wheel again, I decide to make the long trek through the Xeri Biome, followed by Polar. From there I can loop back into the tropical habitat, well out of the path of any doctors. The rainforest climate should be comfortable enough.

And this way I'll be able to check if the others left me any kind of message.

Stepping through the portal into the Xeri Biome, I'm briefly startled to find that with the coming of evening, the usual heat has been replaced with a senseless chill. I pull my hands into my sleeves as I work my way down to the valley floor, the spines of cracked plants poking up at me like monster teeth. Then the questions start to break free.

Was Atkinson telling the truth? Are we like Voyager 1, the last chronicle of Earth floating out here in the exile of space?

My home, gone. My mother and father, gone. Everything lost forever in a burst of flame and ash. I feel a burning ache form in the back of my throat. If it's true, maybe Chloe was right. Maybe it is better not to know. But I swallow the emotion, silencing it with the very obvious truth:

Atkinson was deceived.

Obviously, he was tortured. If what Romie said is true, Dosset could have made him believe anything, could have manufactured whole new memories to make Atkinson think all was lost.

If Dosset is willing to alter our minds, to erase Atkinson's family, nothing that comes from him can be trusted. Not until I see proof.

But I'm still shaken up. Because really, how do I account for the length of time since I last spoke with my parents? Is there another archive somewhere containing a year's worth of messages from home?

And if there is… what do they think, our families? Has NASA given them similar lies to keep them from guessing the truth?

I spend the trip through the tundra habitat trying to call up memories about Earth being destroyed. It's too cold to focus well, and nothing is forthcoming. Eventually, I let myself break into an easy sprint, burning what's left of my energy reserves, sweating in spite of the frigid temperature as I make my way around the frosted hill.

Blue archway markers for the Bolo domes come into view at last. Just a little further. Just a bit further and I can finally rest.

Inside the rainforest climate, the air hangs heavy. After so much cold, it's a bit like being wrapped in a warm, wet blanket. I carefully weave between the trunks of smooth, springy trees, over a floor of tangled vines that pop with colorful wildflowers. I'm just beginning to relax a little when I hear voices.

More doctors? I catch a glimpse of something gold rendered nearly gray in the faded light. It moves, and I recognize Terra's bright blond hair.

For a full minute, I just watch her, uncomprehending. It's after power down. How can she still be out here? Is she waiting up for me?

Unexpected anger swells inside my chest, gaining a speed and ferocity I can't control. If she'd been waiting like she promised, Atkinson wouldn't have escaped. We could've gotten answers. But instead, she let this stupid rivalry get in the way, just like she always does.

"Where were you?" I demand as I burst out of the trees.

Her head whips around. For a second her eyes are so wide I can see the whites. Then they narrow as Romie steps up beside her.

"Me?" she snaps. "Where were *you*?"

"What happened?" Romie asks, stepping between us and holding up his hands as if trying to create a barrier. "Are you hurt?"

"I'm fine. No thanks to her."

"What did I do?" she demands.

"You said you'd be waiting outside the Helix," I say, shoving Romie out of the way. "You know, just in case I needed help. Just in case I was being followed."

Terra laughs, which only fuels my rage.

"Hours ago, Elizabeth. You were supposed to be back hours ago. Do you have any idea how long you've been gone?"

"Long enough, apparently," I say. A part of me is aware I'm overreacting. That I'm taking out my fear and frustration on her. But at the moment I can't seem to care.

"What is that supposed to mean?"

"I think you know."

"No, I don't know," she growls. "I waited until Shiffrin came by *twice* to ask what I was doing. Seemed like I needed to move on if I didn't want to be joining you in cryonics. So I left. What did you expect me to do?"

"Lie," I snarl. "Like you're doing now."

She slaps me so hard I see stars. When my vision clears, I find myself sitting in the dirt, holding the side of my face as she leans down.

"Call me a liar again."

I hear scuffling, and Terra leaves my field of view. Beyond, the tool shed opens and Noah appears, Chloe on his heels.

"What's going on?" Chloe asks, a note of panic in her voice. "Why are you—" Her eyes find me and she lets out a moan of relief, kneeling beside me, examining my cheek. It's selfish of me, but her concern is immediately comforting.

Maybe she doesn't hate me after all.

"Lizzy, what happened?" she asks.

"She slapped me," I mutter. I can already feel my cheek swelling.

"Next time I'll just electrocute you and tie you to a chair," Terra spits, Romie holding her at bay.

"We're being too loud," says Noah nervously. "Come on."

Allowing myself to be hauled to my feet, I join the others inside the small plastic building. Rows of tools have been sorted in their proper blocks and buckets. Shovels, spades, rakes, and hoses. All of it ordered and accounted for. Out of habit I check for cameras, knowing I'll find none.

"How come you're still out here?" I ask, wincing. If only we were still in the Polar Biome. I could use some packed snow for my jaw, which is starting to throb.

"Waiting for you," says Chloe. "We thought you must've been caught. What happened? Did they chase you?"

"No," I murmur. "I had to hide, and it... took awhile."

Noah nods.

"We were forming a rescue plan to come in after you," he says softly.

"Yes. We were just discussing our options," Romie agrees. "I saw you managed to find a port, by the way. Excellent work."

"So did you find Atkinson?" Terra asks, arms folded. "Because I'm guessing you didn't."

Everyone gets quiet. So I tell them. About reaching cryonics and discovering the frozen cadets. The Comm Room. Mercer shutting down Aster. The Verced lab. As I talk, I notice how close Chloe stands to Noah. I suddenly wonder why the two of them were alone in the tool shed while Romie and Terra kept watch.

Is that why she's being nice to me? Because she snuck off with him? The idea bothers me. Not that I'm jealous. It's just, I know Noah doesn't feel that way about her. And the thought that he might be stringing her along makes me defensive.

But now is not the time, so I shove that down too.

Finally, I reach the part about finding the interrogation rooms and Atkinson. The others immediately look around as if expecting him to crawl out from under the terra cotta pots and throw confetti in the air.

"So where is he?" Romie asks.

"Gone," I say. "I got him some water and tried to lead him back here, but he went nuts. Stumbled off to the airlock and left the colony."

Chloe gasps.

"He left?"

I nod.

"Did he at least say something?" asks Noah. "Like, about his plan? Or how we might overthrow Dosset?"

I open my mouth to tell them about the nuclear holocaust, about Earth being destroyed and our colony being the very last fragment of humanity. But as I do, my anger slips. An unexpected sob rises in my throat. I catch it, feeling it burn like salt in a wound. I have to keep it together. What Atkinson said probably isn't even true.

But what if it is? I've already seen how learning the truth about the doctors impacted Chloe. After a loss like this, I don't know if she'd ever be the same. And Noah, he'd probably just shut down, crippled by anxiety. I don't even take time to consider what the news might do to Romie or Terra, because everyone is still staring at me, hanging on my every word. Whether or not I believe it's true doesn't matter. Because if it is, if there's any chance that it is...

"He told me that Dosset erased his memories one by one, as a way to torture him," I say evasively. "I guess he had a son, but Atkinson doesn't remember a thing about him. So he told me... he told me that he wouldn't let Dosset take the memories he had left. Then he closed me out of the airlock."

And that's how it happens—another lie to protect those I care about.

I suddenly wonder, is this how Dosset justifies his actions? By believing them to be some kind of mercy? The thought makes me want to scream, to tell them everything I know. And yet I can see the logic in it. If I didn't, I'd have already told them the truth.

"But... I can't believe it. I can't believe he would just abandon us like that," says Chloe.

"He seemed pretty delirious," I say quietly.

"If the terraforming isn't completed, no one from Earth will come to Mars," Romie says blankly. "Our families will never arrive. We'll be stranded here."

"Living the same week over and over," Terra says. It's the first time since I met her that she seems sincere. No trace of the sarcasm I've grown accustomed to.

Outside the shed, the sprinkler system clicks on.

"I don't get it," says Noah. "That still doesn't answer the question."

"What question?"

"Why is Dosset doing this?"

No one has an immediate reply. Because it's true: The big question still hasn't been answered. In fact, it's gotten more complicated. Even if Earth was destroyed and the knowledge was too much for us to handle, Dosset has been altering our memories to keep us healthy. So, why stop the terraforming?

There must be something we missed, something Atkinson didn't know about.

"I believe there is yet a way to get an answer," says Romie at length. "A way to end the Revisions and get Aster back online."

"How?"

Frowning, he removes his glasses and begins polishing them on his sleeve. "Well... I propose that we move forward with our original plans."

As usual, his words are met with silence. Chloe leans back against a shelf, arching an eyebrow at him. "What original plans, Romie?"

"The complicated ones. You know—stage an uprising, steal a Stitch, kidnap a doctor."

"How would that work?" asks Noah.

"And which doctor would we kidnap?" asks Terra.

"The one with all the answers, of course," says Romie.

Slowly I begin to nod. Because I think I know what he's getting at. And as much as I don't want to admit it, I think he's right.

"We're going after Dosset."

Chapter Twelve

That's where the conversation ends.

We all agree it's best to get some sleep and sort things out in the morning. Especially now that Dosset is considering "more drastic measures," I feel we'd better not push our luck. A sweep of the sleeping pods is in no way outside of his capabilities. Empty pods will draw more suspicion than we can afford.

As a result, I now sit alone in the tool shed, sucking on the core of an apple from Chloe. Having no Atkinson to share with, I ended up with a feast of stuffed poblano peppers and pearly printed grain topped with a mango chutney.

It took a small argument to convince Noah to leave me by myself, but this time I insisted. For Chloe. And, really, for myself. I need some time. To think, and to sort out what could possibly come next, now that our first plan has failed so completely.

I'm surprised to find that it's actually kind of nice to be alone. Listening to the hiss of the sprinklers, the dribbling of water on the roof as I probe my tender jaw. I feel stupid for the way I acted with Terra. It's just... I didn't know what to do. I *still* don't know what to do.

Everything is different. At least for me.

Because now I know the secret. That the people of Earth are dead... and also, that Aster has been abandoned. The problem is, I don't know if either one is true. Or what it will mean for the future if we fail to bring Dosset down.

Dosset.

I wish I had a window into his memories, to fully understand what it takes to turn a man into a monster. Poisoning the minds of others, stealing away their pasts. It goes beyond cruelty and arrives at a place entirely more chilling.

Unlike me, with my anger that ignites so suddenly, Dosset makes his calculations coldly. Then he takes what we love most and somehow he believes it'll help us.

Revisions, he calls them. Simple adjustments to the truth to cloud the way we see the world. Now that I think of it, the procedure is named appropriately. He has changed our vision, skewed the way we see life. The way we see each other, and ourselves.

And what twisted logic could have led him to this? It must be very elaborate. I crack the door open and toss my apple into a compost bin. If we manage to defeat him, I guess I'll know the answer in a few days.

If not, I guess it doesn't really matter.

Fatigue finally takes over, and I crawl beneath a table to nestle amongst plastic pots and bags. I'm grateful for the extra fabric of the lab coat. I also manage to find a thick blue tarp on one of the shelves. I crinkle it up around me, which helps reflect some body heat. Although my stomach already feels empty again, somehow I manage to get comfortable.

But when I close my eyes, I don't begin to wander the secluded avenues of sleep as I'd hoped. Instead, I see the horrific scenes of the day play out on the backs of my eyelids.

The coffin cart. Running out of air. Cadets frozen in cryosleep. Mercer's shiny, pocked face. Dosset's eerie smile.

Atkinson.

His bloody arms, his haunted eyes. And, finally, Chloe and Noah stepping out of the shed together. The way she stood so close to him, and how he didn't move away.

Heat flares in my face, making my bruise ache. Why does it bother me so much? If Noah and Chloe have become friends, or even something more, I should be happy for them. It means things can go back to being a little more normal.

But even though I've held them in shadow, I can't shake off his memories. All the times he went out of his way to talk to me despite his clouds of anxiety. I may not be an authority on friendship, but I know him well enough to know that he loves me.

Correction: that he *thinks* he loves me. I'm sure a lot of girls would swoon over the whole pining-boy scenario, but sappy displays of affection have always made me sick. Yet even here in the seclusion of the shed those very feelings are trying to surface, to play out in my head like some tragic, pathetic movie.

I scowl, feeling irritated all over again. If he's so head over heels for me, why doesn't he tell Chloe the truth? Why haven't *I* told Chloe the truth? I push the questions, the memories—all of it—to the back of my head, where I relegate everything else I don't want to think about. It's become increasingly easy to do, even if it does make the headaches worse.

Sleepless, I lie in the gauzy light, feeling my head pound in time with my heart. It'd be nice to forget, wouldn't it? To make it all just go away. At first I wished it would. Now I realize how awful it would be if one of us actually got caught.

If they hauled Noah away.

Read his mind.

Erased his memories.

Despite my annoyance, the idea of being erased from Noah's mind makes me suddenly afraid. Like Atkinson, losing the ones he loved. I don't want to find out what Noah would become if that happened to him.

Or what I'd become, knowing that I'm the one responsible.

I roll over and try to get some rest, but sleep remains elusive. I'm plagued with the worry that I'll get caught. That I'll end up losing everything and everyone I care about, and no one will even know it happened.

When I do sleep, I have terrible dreams of being locked in a cryobed. The ship is twirling through space, off course, but everyone else is asleep. Over and over I scream at them to wake up, but we just keep floating, floating, aimlessly drifting toward the black hole that yawns before us, like the hole left by all the things we forgot, all the people who were crushed beneath the weight of things too big for us to outrun.

It's with a gasp that I wake this time, not a scream. I'm shivering, covered in the sweat that never seems to evaporate in the tropical heat. The pink glow of morning fills the air like the ghost of an exotic flower. It feels too early for duties to have begun. Probably a little after seven. The colony won't rise until eight. Then it'll be fitness hour, shower, breakfast, and Group.

What I wouldn't give to slip into the cafeteria and eat a warm breakfast with the others. The meal from last night has only awakened my appetite, causing my stomach to tighten in a painful fist. Too uncomfortable to lie still any longer, I fold up my tarp and carefully put it back where I found it. Then I stretch and absently peruse the shelves for useful items.

My findings are mostly what you'd expect in the way of jungle tools: ropes, synthetic netting, and, of course, bolo knives—the flat hacking blades for which the biome was named. I always thought they were machetes, but I guess there's a difference in the width. For a fleeting moment I consider taking one, but decide I'd better not. I still have Verced, and the knives are too conspicuous. Even if I did need to attack anyone.

At this point there's no getting around the fact that, having not showered in days, I'm beginning to stink. If I hope to blend in while walking the halls, I can't go on like this. Plus, the thought of clean clothes is almost more appealing than food. I resolve that it's worth the risk. The cameras won't recognize my face anymore, and it's not as if they have surveillance in the bathrooms.

The very instant eight hundred hours is announced, I head out, trotting down the path toward the Bolo domes then exiting back into Scrubs. It's the first time I've returned since talking to Chloe in the kitchen three days ago.

Has it only been three days? And just four since I got the Memory Bank. It seems unbelievable that such a short period has passed.

Somehow it feels like a lifetime or two.

When I enter my old hallway, an eerie sense of foreboding fills me. I haven't been back to my pod since that very first day, when the memories began unfolding in my mind. Have they removed my things yet? Probably left plenty of extra cameras and microphones lying around, just in case I was dumb enough to return.

Playing it safe, I punch the code to Chloe's pod instead. She's not here, of course; she's in the Fitness Center, exercising with the other cadets. Everything is perfectly in order, undergarments and spare jumpsuits neatly folded and tucked in their drawers.

I take what I need and hurry off to the showers, hoping to beat the stream of sweaty cadets that will soon be forming.

Heavenly. That's how the water feels. Like being reborn. As if I'm not just washing my skin but receiving an entirely new version of it. The foams and gels rinse off days of sweat and grime, and with it, much of my worry. It's incredible how a simple thing like water can change your whole perspective.

I towel my skin until it's pink, and even blow-dry my hair with the wall unit since no one is around to notice. Then I clean my teeth and step into fresh clothes for the first time in days.

Noah's jumpsuit is more rumpled than dirty. After zipping into it, I shove the lab coat down the laundry collector, taking the Verced and stun gun with me.

At this point, I'm supposed to return to Noah's pod to meet up with the others. That was the agreement. So I start the walk toward the Xeri domes. Along the way it occurs to me that it's Friday. That gives us today, tomorrow, and Sunday to find a Stitch, form a rebellion, and corner Dosset. Only three days to pull off three daunting tasks.

Of course, I did manage to rescue Atkinson in a single afternoon. But now we've ruined the element of surprise. I hope Romie has finished that EMP.

We're going to need it.

I'm stirred out of my thoughts by the sound of my name.

"Lizzy Engram, the Scrub," says a girl. Her name is Samantha, I recall.

"Since when?" her friend asks. Jessica Berkley. Both girls are Bolos. They don't notice me, so I fall into step a little ways behind them.

"Kayla said she hasn't seen her since Monday."

"Weird," Samantha yawns. "Do you talk to Lizzy much?"

"Not really," Jessica says. Then, more quietly, "She's kind of... stuck up. She never laughs, and she's always on that stupid treadmill."

"I know."

"Also, Michael said she can be kind of a bitch."

Their words sting. But the experience is more strange than hurtful. These girls don't even know me. It's bizarre to hear them judge my actions and intentions so openly. I realize I haven't used my memories to learn what the other cadets think about me. Well, besides Terra.

And speaking of Terra...

As I break away from the girls and mount the stairs to the Xeri pods, I hear someone approaching. A slender arm encircles mine. Before I can resist, I hear Terra's sickly-sweet voice in my ear. "Ready for your performance?"

"What're you talking about?" I say, annoyed at once.

"Our little rebellion," she croons as she leads me to Noah's pod and punches the code. Inside, I'm surprised to find Romie already waiting in the chair. No one was supposed to show up until after breakfast.

"Don't you two eat?" I ask, pulling my arm free.

"Three days until the Revision," replies Romie. Dark rings hang beneath his eyes, as if he hardly slept. Which doesn't surprise me. From his memories, I know he has a hard time resting when a problem remains unsolved. "The next stage of the plan must begin at once."

"Sit down, Lizzy," Terra instructs me.

"I'd rather stand."

I don't even bother hiding my irritation, because again I'm sick of her making everything a competition. As far as I'm concerned, my bruised cheek says we're even.

"Fine," she shrugs. "But you'll need your energy in a couple hours."

"What's she talking about?" I ask, turning on Romie.

"During fitness hour we talked with some of the cadets," he says, almost guiltily. As if we're back in front of the tool shed with him caught in the middle. "We invited ten from each dome subset. Only those we were sure we could reasonably trust."

My whole body tenses with foreboding.

"Invited them to what?"

"A performance," says Terra.

"A private meeting," Romie amends. "Including us, there should be around forty-five cadets. That makes up around twenty percent of the cadet population. At its essence, the plan is for Terra to lead the group in distracting the doctors, while a smaller team covertly enters the Helix. We'll corner Dosset with the help of my EMP, which is nearly complete. We just need to get our hands on a Stitch."

"Hold on, back up," I say, my emotions trying to catch up with what I'm hearing. "Nearly complete? We didn't even talk about this."

"Yes, we did," says Terra. "Romie came up with the plan last night while we were waiting for you to get back from the Helix. Well, really it was mostly *my* plan, but he helped me iron out the kinks. Didn't you, Romie?"

"Ah... well, it was mostly a hypothesis then," Romie mumbles.

It might be petty, but this angers me. Up until now, they've been looking to me for some kind of direction. Or at least including me on the big decisions. Now they're all keeping secrets, skulking around behind my back, not even asking my opinion.

What if I thought this was a bad plan? Because if I'm honest, I still maintain that putting Terra in charge of a rebellion is a mistake. She can barely be trusted to show up when she's supposed to. But at least I expect her to try something like this. As for Romie and the others... yet again, I think of Chloe and Noah alone in the shed.

My fists tighten in my pockets.

"Just for starters, what if the cadets refuse?" I direct my question at Terra, struggling to keep the edge out of my voice. "What happens when you tell them about the evil doctors and they think you're lying?"

"Well, um... strictly speaking, she won't be addressing them," Romie replies, "You will."

"Oh, I see. And I'll just recite all their memories to them while I'm at it, right?"

"Is that a problem?" Terra asks, arching her back in a stretch.

"Yes. It's a problem," I snap. "I can't do that. I already told you—"

"It'll be too hard for you, I know," says Terra dismissively, pivoting to Romie. "See? I told you she couldn't do it. And since I'll be the one leading the rebellion, it only makes sense that I address them. They trust me, not *her.*"

"Perhaps," says Romie, his expression pained. "But we're asking these cadets to take a very big risk. They'll need more than trust. They'll need proof." He turns to me, and his sincerity catches me off guard. "I've been contemplating it since you told us that Atkinson abandoned us, and I don't really see another option. Our window of opportunity is closing. By Sunday night the memories will be lost. Our only hope is for you to convince the cadets to help us unseat Dosset. And personally, I believe that will be achieved best with their own memories."

I hear what he's saying. And regardless of my desire to spite Terra, I know he's right. Some piece of me already came to the same conclusion. But I can't get around the idea of standing up in front of everyone, trying to call up memories on command.

Part of it is that I'm nervous. I've tried this before and failed. But the bigger part is the risk we're taking. *Forty-five cadets?* We don't know the first thing about running a rebellion. What if they turn on us?

What if someone gets seriously hurt?

And then the last part... okay, I'll admit it. I feel uncomfortable. Because I'll be asking all of them to trust me. These cadets, who apparently think such negative things about Elizabeth Engram. I don't deserve their trust. And they know it.

It's going to be a disaster.

My gaze finds Terra, who seems to be drinking in my discomfort. Strangely, her open antagonism is what snaps things into perspective.

I won't change anyone's mind by avoiding them. If I want the others to think of me as some kind of leader, I need to start thinking of myself that way.

"Fine," I say through gritted teeth. "Who'll be there?"

"Huh?"

"The cadets. Which ones are coming?"

"You want their names?" Romie asks.

"Yes. I want to know which memories to get familiar with."

"Let's see," says Terra, holding up one finger at a time. "Dylan, he's a Clover. Nalika is a Polar. Keegan is also a Polar, and Danielle is a Xeri. Phillip—"

"Okay, just... stop," I say wearily. There's no way I'll be able to conjure the memories of forty-five cadets in time. I'm going to have to wing it. "Just give me some room, okay?"

"Whatever you want, Elizabeth," Terra replies. "But you'd better not screw this up too." And she saunters out of the pod.

Romie lingers until after the door is closed.

"I wanted to give you this," he says quietly, holding out a white plastic device. It's about the size of a thumb drive. Surprised, I accept it.

"A token of your affection?" I joke.

He only gives me half a smile.

"It's a beacon. I stole it from a scrapped probe and converted it to shortwave. I've got a few trackers back in the Workshop, which should pick up the signal. You know, just in case you ever get... separated from us again."

This brings me up short. I look at him closely and suddenly realize why Romie spent all night thinking about the plan. Why he's sticking up for me now, with Terra and the rebellion. He wasn't trying to keep secrets from me.

He feels guilty.

At once, my anger cools.

"Now that you've patched me into the security system, I can always keep an eye on the cameras too," he continues awkwardly. "But in case something *else* happens and—"

"Romie, what happened last night wasn't your fault," I say, pulling an encouraging tone from Chloe's mannerisms. "Atkinson running away, the fight with Terra... those things had nothing to do with you."

He falters into an awkward shrug.

"Perhaps," he begins. "But if the EMP had been ready—"

"It wasn't. You can't blame yourself for things other people do, Romie. And you know what? Now we can use the EMP when it really counts."

"Sure," he says. Though he smiles, I can tell I haven't changed his mind. He points at a switch on the beacon. "Just flip that to turn it on. I'll make sure everyone gets a tracker so that at least one of us is able to find you quickly." He glances at the clock. "Okay. Well, we'd better get set up. Good luck, Elizabeth."

"No need for luck," I tell him. "It's all talent."

The moment he's gone, my facade of confidence drops. I begin pacing the short span of the pod, my heart fluttering like a tiny sparrow.

I'm more nervous than I expected. Even more than when I entered the Helix. Because it's true. Time is almost up. If we're going to stop the Revisions, we need to do it soon. And we'll need help.

So when the headaches start, I'll just have to keep going—no matter how painful it gets.

I decide that for now, the best plan is to relax. Once I'm in the moment, I can use the cues of their faces, voices, and expressions to help me remember.

Finding a water bottle on the desk, I drink it all in one pull. Then I sit in the middle of the floor, cross my legs, and slow my breathing. Empty my mind of worry and thought, focusing on each swell of my lungs. I imagine that I'm breathing in the color blue, refreshing as an autumn wind, and breathing out all the hurt, anger, and stress in a glaring red.

Some period of time passes this way, and then there's a knock at the door. The illusion of calm pops and fear rushes back in, closing around my chest. When I reach for the handle, I expect to find Terra's jeering face on the other side.

But instead, I find Chloe.

"Hey," she says softly. "Are you ready?"

I'm so nervous that I can only manage a nod.

As we reach the bottom of the stairs, the hour is announced. Any other day I'd be headed to lunch. Now I feel like I'm heading to an execution. I stare at the floor, allowing Chloe to guide me through the crowded halls, hearing voices discuss things that no longer matter. Not to me, at least.

It seems incredible that our worlds have become poles apart in the course of only a few days. Their concerns are already so different from mine. They have no idea the pressure I'm under, the kind of responsibility I feel for their memories.

How can they not even suspect what's happening behind these artificial walls? Was I ever so oblivious? I know that I was. But my blissful ignorance is long dead.

I doubt even a Revision could change that.

To save time we take the Wheel, then head into the Bolo domes. Chloe is silent beside me. I can't think of what to say. Back on Earth, the old Lizzy would've just withdrawn. But that's not good enough anymore.

I wronged my friend. I should be apologizing for what happened in Romie's pod, when I was so careless with her feelings. I should do what I can to explain and try to make it up to her.

The conviction builds and I gather my courage, but when I finally manage to speak, all I'm able to get out is, "Are you still mad at me?"

My voice is hardly more than a whisper. I can't see her reaction because I'm doing my best to mimic someone else's body language, keeping my gaze locked downward to avoid the eyes of strangers. Trying in so many ways to be anyone but me.

It takes her a minute to reply.

"Mad at you for what?" she finally asks.

"For being stupid. For not thinking about your feelings that night."

She lets out a long breath.

"You're not stupid, Lizzy," she says. "But... yes, at first I was hurt. I couldn't understand why you wanted to sleep in his pod again. But then I remembered that the first time, you came right out and told me what was going on. You said there was nothing between you two. And, well, I realized that I wasn't trusting you. I wasn't thinking about how hard this must all be for you. I was only thinking about myself."

"Chloe—" I begin, but she isn't finished.

"And you know what? Right now, it's not about me. It's about all of us. And if we're going to get through it, I *need* to trust you. I think you've earned that much."

Now I'm glad I'm looking down, because she can't see my face. What did I ever do to earn such a friend? I feel sure that I'll never deserve her.

As we enter the Clover Biome, my lungs are greeted by fresh, heady air. It strikes me again how much more pleasant this climate is than the chill of Polar, the heat of Xeri, and the humidity of Bolo.

Pollen fans on the west curve of the dome create a soft wind, rippling leaves and lifting stray hairs off my forehead.

"They're all waiting in the glade," Chloe tells me.

I nod. As usual, the swelling verdancy of this habitat makes my own herb beds feel like a trifling backyard garden.

Nearing the trees that fence in the flower beds, I begin to catch glimpses of pink camellia, red rose, and the full midnight of bluebell. I can also sense the traces of memories stirred up by the perfumed air. Evening walks between these trees, soft discussions of home. Even stolen kisses. The remembrance brings heat to my chest, so I focus instead on the sprays of color.

It really is like a glade, if you can overlook the plastic divider blocks.

As we emerge into the glade, I'm a little relieved to see that there are fewer than forty-five cadets. Fifteen, tops. They stand in an awkward circle, fidgeting and stealing glances back toward the path as if afraid they might get caught skipping lunch.

When they see me, a ripple of surprise moves through the group. Then their murmuring ceases.

"Hey, Lizzy," Terra says, her tone unnaturally friendly. She waves me into the center to stand beside her. "We're all waiting for you."

"Thanks," I say flatly. I try to draw on my earlier irritation for confidence. But as I step up and survey the group, the feeling evaporates. What if I don't know what to say? What if the headache is too strong and I can't remember a thing?

My throat has turned to chalk.

"Glad everyone made it," Terra begins. "So sorry for all the mystery. We've got some things to tell you, and we couldn't risk being overheard."

I almost snort at the irony of this coming from her but manage to restrain myself. She's being uncharacteristically bubbly. But then I recall her many ballet performances on Earth, when her whole personality was so carefully poised to please judges. It must be second nature to her.

"Like what?" asks Stephanie, a Scrub. She's all angles, with sharp elbows and a pointed chin. We've never really gotten along.

"You said if I came you'd take me in your gathering crew," says a boy named Ian. "That you'd make sure I could drive the rover."

Still smiling, Terra nods.

"And I will. But first, we need to talk. About the doctors and that virus they keep going on about. If you know Lizzy, you know she hasn't been around lately. A lot of you probably thought she was in quarantine. The real reason is much harder to believe. And much more important."

Now she's just being theatric. Some of the cadets are raising skeptical eyebrows. A few shuffle uneasily or frown. I take a deep breath.

Whatever happens next, I need to stay calm and keep talking.

"Yes," I say. "I wasn't in quarantine."

"Louder," says Matthew—a Bolo, I think. "I can't hear you."

"I wasn't in quarantine," I repeat, flustered. "I was... in hiding. I've been hiding from the doctors because of what they were trying to do to me."

Everyone is staring. I can feel my face getting hot. As if Noah's anxiety is creeping through my veins and up my neck.

"What were they trying to do to you, Elizabeth?" Terra prompts me through her teeth. I look at her, standing with her hands on her hips, and I'm struck by how assured she seems. And it occurs to me that if *she* can be so confident, so can I.

Deliberately I push aside my misgivings and pull from her body language—her charisma, her bravado, her sense of importance.

"Doctor Dosset and the others have been erasing our memories," I say, raising my chin and turning to meet their gazes. "They do it every Sunday night. It's called a Revision. Dosset has been storing them in a kind of Memory Bank. And last Monday, I woke up with that whole bank inside my head."

I take another breath of blue, expelling red. Relax my shoulders. Allow my hands to become expressive as I speak instead of just hanging at my sides.

"Recently I learned that Doctor Atkinson was the one who gave me the Memory Bank and that he had a plan to stop the Revisions for good. So yesterday I broke into the Helix to rescue him. Dosset had him locked up and was slowly erasing his memories as a way to torture him. Unfortunately, he was too traumatized to help us, and he fled the colony. Now we're looking for support from you, to help us stop the next Revision—which will happen in two days."

The glade goes quiet as a gentle wind strokes the tresses of a willow at my back, trickling through the leaves. It's just like it was with Noah, everyone stunned into silence. I play with an inoculator in my pocket, absently popping the cap off and on, off and on. Finally, a slow smirk appears on Stephanie's face.

"This... is a joke, right?"

"I think I should go to lunch," a girl named Julia speaks up. She takes a step backward.

Terra elbows me in the ribs, hard.

"I can prove it," I say quickly. At least for a second, this stops them. "I can tell you about the memories they erased."

I feel a little like the hokey magician my mother got for my fourth birthday party, who was about as convincing as his curly black wig. Every year after that, my dad would do a "birthday trick" in his honor. Now I almost pity the guy.

The cadets hesitate at the edge of the glade.

"Like what?" Julia asks.

This is it. I edge closer and attempt to clear my head, to think about her face, her name, trying to allow dormant memories forward.

But the second I do, my headache reaches a fever pitch. It's as if a white-hot iron has been placed behind my eyes, strobing daggers to the back of my skull. I stop at once, feeling dizzy. Drawing on Terra's persona while digging around in the Memory Bank is obviously too much for me to handle.

So I break my focus.

It feels as if I'm deflating. As the cold, grasping fingers of anxiety wrap around my lungs, I turn to Julia. Her eyes are wide as she stares into mine.

Can she sense my fear? I wonder what she must think of me; what this must look like to her. What would I think in her shoes?

I'd think she was insane.

Or at least sick with the rumored mind-warping virus. How could I not, after hearing such wild accusations thrown at the doctors I'd have every reason to trust?

And a rebellion—now, there's a ludicrous suggestion. A laughable idea. What would compel me to trust a stranger to the point of a mutinous uprising? Really, I'm no better than a tacky magician pulling memories from a hat. None of these cadets will trust me. I wouldn't even trust myself.

Seconds pass as these thoughts cycle through my head and I remain frozen. Julia takes another step backward.

"What's she doing?" Ian says uncomfortably.

"Say something," Terra growls.

I force myself to open my mouth.

"W-when you were little, you were in a friend's basement and the lights went off," I say, clumsily drawing a memory at random. The effort sends a stab of pain through my head. Ignoring it, I scrunch my brow in concentration. "You were terrified, bumping into things, trying to find a way out. For years after that, you were scared of going into the basement. That's why you're afraid of the dark."

Everyone looks at Julia, who glances around at the probing eyes.

"I don't remember that," she says.

"Well, it was erased," says Chloe gently. "Does it seem familiar?"

"Not really. I mean, I'm not sure."

I lick my lips, barely keeping it together. This won't help. But how can I just quit, with everyone watching?

"Try another memory," Romie urges from nearby.

"What about—" I dig deep, but the recollections are growing jagged with the pain, like pieces of wood being slowly ground to splinters. Blindly I lay hold of another memory. "Um, you used to hide under the kitchen table when your parents would fight. You memorized the spiral of the rug, because you'd trace the creases with your fingers to distract yourself when they yelled."

Her eyes go wide and then her face flares red. Some part of me recognizes that I've said the wrong thing. I'm again reminded of my first talk with Noah, the way I fumbled, pulling up embarrassing memories.

These are experiences she doesn't want to recall.

"You're making that up," Julia stammers, shaking her head. "That didn't happen."

"Something *else*," Terra says.

"All right, fine," I snap, my anger finally returning. It's the boost I need. I clench my teeth so hard my jaw aches. But still, the memories flutter away from me like startled moths.

I stubbornly fix my gaze on Ian.

"You had a younger brother. He was more like your mom, so she liked him better, which made you jealous. Sometimes you'd bully him to make yourself feel better." I turn on Stephanie as the headache ratchets higher. "You stole money from your brother and he got in trouble for losing it. You never told anyone." Next is Lauren, a Xeri girl. "You didn't say goodbye to your father when you left for Mars because of a stupid fight. You regretted it every day until they erased the memory. " A noxious substance is burning at the back of my mouth. I look at Matthew as my eyes begin to water. "When you left, you had hardly anyone to say goodbye to—"

"Lizzy," A voice says.

The trees are spinning, but I keep going anyway.

"—felt like no one cared—"

"*Lizzy.*"

Someone is at my arm, keeping me stable in a world that has turned upside down. For a few moments, I just blink at Noah, at his gaze filled with worry. I focus on his face, his deep, gentle eyes. Slowly, balance returns. I look out and I see that the cadets are watching me with stunned expressions.

"What's wrong with her?" Stephanie asks.

"The memories give her headaches," Chloe explains.

"I didn't do that," Ian interrupts. He's turned pale. "I wouldn't do that."

"Me neither," Lauren agrees defensively. "I love my dad."

There's a beat of silence while the glade wobbles around me. I feel as if I should say more, but I have a feeling I've already said too much.

Anyway, I'm afraid that if I open my mouth again I'll vomit.

"So... what?" Matthew asks at length. "You expect us to believe we're all being brainwashed or something?"

"Exactly," says Terra, straining for her winning smile. "And we need your help to stop them. Because in two days, they're going to do it again."

Her words are met with another span of incredulous silence.

And that's when the alarm goes off.

Chapter Thirteen

From the overhead, echoing around the biome, a sharp beeping fills the air. It's the same alarm I heard that morning in Group, right before Dosset appeared in Meng's class.

"All cadets, report to your theater," the female voice commands above the drone. "All cadets, report to your theater. All cadets, report..."

I look at the others. The shock I see on their faces is no doubt mirrored in my own. Then, as one, the cadets scatter out of the glade like startled deer.

"No, wait!" Terra begins, but it's too late. In no time we're left alone. She wheels on me. "What the *hell* was that, Elizabeth?"

"They wouldn't have believed me," I say, but I know an explanation is pointless at the moment. "Anyway, we don't have time to get mad at each other. That alarm is about us."

"We're not getting mad at each other," Terra snarls. "I'm getting mad at *you*."

"Please, Terra," Romie intervenes. "Elizabeth is correct. We don't have time for an argument. Dosset must be retaliating for Atkinson's escape."

"Couldn't it be anything else?" Chloe asks hopefully. "An emergency drill?"

"If it is, we can be pleasantly surprised." Romie turns to me. "For now, it's essential that you get as far from here as possible."

"What about you?" I ask, looking at Noah. He's still supporting me on his arm. "Those cadets could turn you in. If they tell a doctor you were involved..."

"I guess that's the risk we took," he says quietly. "Don't worry. We'll figure it out."

Romie nods.

"Find somewhere safe. Alert us when you get there."

The beacon. I instinctively reach for it, feeling the tiny lump in my pocket. Then I look at each of them and know there's no point resisting. For now, I have to run. We can think through our next step when it's safe again.

And just like that, I'm off.

The ground pitches beneath my feet, legs still shaky from the trauma of the headache. It's not until I'm out of view of the glade that I realize: The next time I see my friends, they may not know me. Any one of those fifteen cadets could decide I'm crazy or sick and turn us all in. All it takes is one.

Jogging down the path, I wonder who it will be.

Hysteria fills the Clover halls like poison gas. Bodies choke the tight passages, rushing for their theater as I push deliberately through, slipping the surgical mask over my ears and tugging the hat lower. It almost makes me manic, walking in a crowd like this. Even with the majority of my face hidden, anyone could potentially spot me.

Ahead I see my route, the portal into the Scrub domes. If I can reach it, I'll lose myself in the biome—perhaps in the swamp, in a dense pocket of reeds that reach to my shoulders.

I'm halfway there when a group of Xeris crosses my path. I try to shoulder by, but the boy in front stops me.

"This way, cadet," he says gruffly.

His voice is familiar. I think his name is Maxwell. Domineering. Stern. One of the oldest cadets on the colony.

"I need to speak with Doctor Shiffrin," I say, not meeting his gaze. "It's an emergency."

"So is this broadcast," is his reply. "It'll have to wait."

"Fine. I'll just go to my theater, then." As tactfully as possible, I try to step past him. But again he stops me.

"The Xeri theater is this way," he says, a bite of annoyance in his voice.

For a second I'm confused. Then I remember: I'm wearing Noah's jumpsuit. With a clear orange badge that designates me as a Xeri.

As I'm trying to piece together a more convincing excuse, I catch sight of McCallum just up the hallway, moving toward us.

"Right," I say, allowing myself to be directed the other way.

I try to keep calm, but I can't seem to slow my breathing. How am I going to get out of this? If I try to run, McCallum will notice. If I get trapped in a theater, I'm sure to be discovered. Somehow, between here and there I need to slip away unnoticed.

But there's no opportunity. More Xeris join us at the Wheel, and I'm boxed into the middle of the group. I've nearly reached the Xeri theater when a flash of red catches my eye; Noah, his bright hair easily noticeable from the other end of the room. For a split second our eyes meet. A moment later he's at my side.

"What are you doing?" he whispers in my ear, tugging me away from the group. "You were supposed to hide."

"I couldn't get away," I say. "McCallum—"

But another white coat is approaching.

"You two," says Doctor Hitch impatiently. "What do you think you're doing? Emergency meeting. That means stop talking and start walking."

"Sure," Noah replies.

With no other choice, we're corralled back into line, slowly filling out the tiered seats. I'm wedged between Noah and John, a Polar with sallow skin. Around us, the room is burning with panicked whispers. Speculation about the virus. Skittish laughter. Hitch jogs down the stairs to the front, circling the holographic imager.

When he turns, his sharp eyes scan the room in a predatory way. Nervously I slump lower in my seat.

"You have to get out of here," Noah breathes, sitting rigidly beside me.

"Good idea. How?"

Suddenly the alarm stops and the room goes quiet.

"All right, everyone," says Hitch. "We've got word from the colony director, Doctor Dosset. It turns out that yes, the virus we informed you about on Monday is still spreading. And it gets worse." He sucks in a tight breath. "Apparently the virus is more contagious than we initially thought—and if left untreated, it can be deadly."

Murmurs break out around the room again, volume and tension escalating.

"We're on the lookout for a cadet," Doctor Hitch continues. As he speaks, my face blinks to life on the holographic imager, a plain photograph like a mugshot. I'm tempted to sink further, wishing I could vanish into the chair, but I realize this will only make me look more conspicuous. I settle for pulling my hat so low that I can't see past my knees. "Her name is Elizabeth Engram, a greenskeeper. She has presented symptoms of the virus, including aggression, delirium, and paranoia. If you see her, you're to report to a doctor immediately—not just for our safety, but for hers as well. The longer she goes without treatment, the less likely we can save her."

Hitch goes on about the virus, assuring everyone that they've nearly perfected an antidote, that as long as I'm caught they'll all be safe, but I've stopped listening. Because whatever chance we had, it's over. I don't give Dosset marks for creativity, but he got the job done. No one will believe me now.

And surely, if our "rebels" had intended to keep quiet, this will break their silence. The longer I sit here, the sooner I'll be found.

I sneak a sidelong look at the aisle. I need to run. But to reach the exit I'll have to leap over Noah and another cadet, which will be tricky. And there's the question of where I'll go. I guess I'll just have to work that out along the way.

My heart is pounding in my ears, but my legs feel rooted to the floor. It's just like a race. Once the gun goes off, there'll be no stopping. They know I'm here. And Dosset has made it clear that he will hunt me across the colony, room by room, until he has me back under the glowing lights of a Stitch.

"This virus is crazy," says John, fidgeting. I keep my eyes on my knees, hoping he isn't talking to me. But I can feel his gaze like a gun in my face. "What if they can't find her before she infects the rest of us?"

"Mm," I mutter.

"I'd just like them to tell us what it is. Some of us are medically trained. Maybe we could help them with the antidote or something." He pauses, shifting in his seat. "Hey, are you okay?"

I want to scream *Shut up, moron, you're going to give me away.* But instead, I manage to quietly say, "Yeah, I just don't feel great."

And now he's looking at me closer.

I really need to stop using that excuse.

"Maybe you've got the virus," he says. It sounds like he meant it as a joke, but his voice comes out flat.

"Okamoto," Hitch snaps. "If you don't stop—"

He halts mid-sentence. With mounting panic, I realize just how quiet the room has grown. I look up and lock eyes with Hitch, who is staring right at me.

"It's her!" someone gasps.

Noah bolts upright and yanks the cadet beside him out of his seat, pushing him into the aisle. Startled cries fill the air. But Noah is still moving; he reaches back and pulls me up by the arm, propelling me toward the exit.

"Run!" he yells at me. "Lizzy, run!"

It's pandemonium. Everyone starts rising and shoving as I launch up the stairs. But no one tries to stop me—in fact, cadets stumble over each other, some falling over the tiered seats in an effort to avoid me. I blast through the door, voices shouting, noises of a scuffle at my back, and then there's Noah, abruptly at my side with a burst of speed that can only be adrenaline.

I look up just in time to see Sarlow looming in my path.

But somehow Noah out-sprints me. He throws himself into her, going over a plastic bench, fists and legs flying.

"Go!" he shouts. "Don't stop for—"

His voice is cut off and I almost *do* stop, wondering what happened, but manage to resist. My last sight of him is with his arm pinned behind his back and blood gushing from his nose. Sarlow's face is scarlet with anger as she holds him down and glares after me. Then I'm gone.

I head for the Polar Biome's archway but shift course at the last second, realizing I'll only end up trapped in the habitat. Now that the cameras won't track me automatically, my best shot is to put as much distance between me and my pursuers as I can. Then I'll slip away from the cameras altogether, leaving the trail cold, and find a corner far from prying eyes.

My mind is blank as my body surges, arms pumping, feet soaring on instinct. Survival drives me like a cornered animal. Underlying everything, all I know is that if they catch me, the memories of the world go with me.

I turn a corner and find myself in the Clover domes. Not so very far from the bioreactors. If I'm going to disappear, this is as good a place as any.

Hoping that Sarlow and the others are still far behind, I dance clear of four cameras in a row—at least as far as I can tell—and reach the access door. With my last shred of focus, I evoke the key code and turn the handle, tumbling inside.

Light sensors power on as I totter between the giant cylinders like massive silver kilns. As part of the reclamation cycle, these reactors convert human waste into pure oxygen, water, and compost. They even produce electricity. At the moment, my only concern is that they offer a wide enough shadow to hide in.

I slide down between a pair of them, gasping as much out of horror as from the effort of running here. And that's where it catches up with me.

They've got Noah. Dosset will put him straight into an interrogation room. Pull apart his brain, piece by piece. Learn who was involved and what we were planning. We've taken too many risks. The cadets know. The doctors know. Everyone is against us.

And Noah is gone.

The thought tries to suffocate me, but I shove it away. *Think*, I command myself. This isn't the time for sorting out my feelings. It's the time for taking action. We can stop this, can't we? Get to Dosset before he can cripple Noah's mind?

But no, the rebellion isn't even started yet—and now it seems it never will be. We don't have a Stitch. And even if we managed to get one, Dosset will never leave the Helix willingly.

For a long time, I just sit here, trying to get a handle on my emotions. No longer sensing any movement, the lights slowly dim until I'm in darkness, only the winking orange lights of the bioreactors to keep me company. I click on the beacon and wait.

But for what? The blackness strips away the distractions, and just like in the coffin cart, I'm left with nothing but my thoughts. I see Noah's face, the blood gushing from his nose. Feel the numbness trickle down my arms and legs, moving out from a hole in my chest as, again, reality overwhelms me.

He's gone.

I try to shove it down, to focus. But I can't. Not this time. It's too much, and like a seam under pressure the canvas of my heart has torn at last, squeezing the tears from my eyes.

Somehow I knew. I knew this would happen—or something like it. That they'd take one of them and erase their memories. And it would all be my fault.

But they didn't take just anyone. They took Noah. For some reason, that feels different.

"Why?" I whisper.

Why is he different from the others? And why did he sacrifice himself for me? I know he thinks he loves me, but that isn't an answer—it's only another question.

Why is he *so sure* he loves me that he's willing to risk everything, even his own identity?

At the back of my head, inside a twisted knot of ignored memories, I know the answer is waiting. It's where I've hidden everything I don't want to admit to myself, everything I'm unwilling to face. And now, after everything that's happened, I can't seem to stop myself from tugging at the threads. Pulling them loose one by one until the knot slips.

The memories come in a torrent. They transport me out of the chamber, away from the bioreactors, back into the buried past. But these aren't the memories of another cadet.

These belong to me.

I'm in the Sick Bay. It's one of our first weeks on Mars, maybe the very first. I've been feeling groggy, with a persistent headache. Since Zonogal has just been called away, Noah is alone on duty. I tell him I need a diagnostic. He stares at me.

"You want me to do it?" he asks, a mumble.

At the time I think he's being lazy. I scowl and say, "Who else?"

So he leads me back into the small alcove where the diagnostics are run. Has me sit on the stool and takes my pulse. He seems distracted. I swear he counts for at least two minutes, just staring at his watch. Maybe he isn't only lazy, but incompetent too.

I bite my lip impatiently.

"Okay," he says at last. "You seem good. I just need to look in your mouth and ears and eyes, and take a swab of your mouth."

"Fine."

We don't say another word as he gently examines me with his medi-scope. His hands feel strange. Not like a doctor's hands. Like... something else. I'm not used to being touched, especially not by boys. I've never been kissed. Never even held hands or gone on a date.

The fact that I'm thinking about these things makes me more uncomfortable, so I bite my lip harder and wait rigidly for him to finish.

But that's just my side of the story.

The memory flips, as if the shadows have become deeper, the light more intense. Now I relive the experience through his eyes.

When I enter the Sick Bay, his hands go cold. He's seen me around the colony, noticed me in the mornings when I run on the holotrek. But he hasn't yet had the courage to say hello. I approach and tell him how I'm feeling, but he hardly hears me—he's listening to the cadence of my voice, not the words I'm saying—until I ask for a diagnostic.

"You want me to do it?" he stammers.

All he can think about is having to sit right next to me, touch my skin, look into my eyes while mere centimeters from my face. As he leads me into the alcove, he's keenly aware of each time his fingers brush my skin, sending electric currents up his arms, as if I'm made of lightning.

Trying to count my pulse is almost impossible because all he can think about is how delicate my wrist is. How like gravity I am, making his heartbeat swell the closer I get, like the tide.

Finally, he stops counting because he knows he'll never focus long enough to get it right.

"Okay," he chokes out. "You seem good. I just need to look in your mouth and ears and eyes, and take a swab of your mouth."

For the next five minutes he wages war in his head, fighting to concentrate, but he can't stop sweating. It's a good thing I wasn't seriously ill, because other than the swab of my mouth, he barely does anything correctly.

Later I learn that my symptoms were a lingering effect of the drugs from cryosleep still making their way out of my system.

But the memories don't stop there. Week after week they go on. Awkward encounters. Fumbled greetings. Then one night Chloe drags me to the Polar recreation room for a ping pong tournament with some other girls. I'm usually very competitive, but tonight I'm tired from an eight-mile run and get knocked out by the second round. Meanwhile, Chloe makes it all the way to the final four. Noah is there, playing cards with Romie and Logan, a Polar.

When I decide to leave early, Noah offers to walk me back.

"Don't worry about it," I tell him.

"It's not a problem," he shrugs.

At the time I don't notice his blush. As we walk down the stairs, I catch a glimpse of Chloe staring after us.

"Let's go this way," Noah says, pointing toward the Bolo Biome. It's the long way back, and my feet already ache. But for some reason, I don't say no. I've always liked the rainforest habitat at night when the sprinklers kick on.

We ascend to the canopy walkway just as the soft hissing begins, passing other cadets and doctors out for an evening stroll.

For the first kilometer, we walk in silence.

"Chloe goes bananas for this climate," I say as the path winds through the banana trees, their bunches growing upside down like strange, alien chandeliers. Ironically, I never knew the fruit grew that way until I came to Mars.

Noah blinks at me.

"Huh?"

"Nothing."

We fall back into uncomfortable silence. Noah seems fixated on the gray slats that pass beneath our feet. "Do you... ever miss home?" he abruptly asks.

"You mean Earth?"

"Earth, yeah."

"Not really," I say. And I realize it's true. I don't miss Earth. But I guess I feel like I should. "Why, do you?"

"I think so," he says slowly. "But I guess I don't know." He looks up, eyes now wandering the canvas of the dome far above. I'm just thinking he won't say more when he continues. "I guess it feels like I left home behind, but it's also like home disappeared."

"Disappeared?" I say skeptically.

"Yeah. Like I want to go back, but I feel like I can't. I feel as if when I get there, it won't be there anymore. Do you know what I mean?"

"I guess so..."

He seems flustered, searching for the words.

"It's like... okay... when I was growing up, everything seemed so big and stable. But after coming out here, you see that we're really just on these planets spinning through all this space. No one is steering the ship. And that's kind of scary, isn't it?"

By far, this is the most I've ever heard Noah Hartmann speak. He seems so sincere. As if he's almost desperate for me to understand him. And truthfully, there's a part of me that knows exactly what he's talking about. I, too, fear the chaos of life. But then, there's a much bigger part of me that dreads admitting that fear.

"Does it make any difference?" I ask, oddly irritated by the conversation. "We've always been spinning through space, right? We just didn't know."

He glances at me in surprise.

"Uh, sure. I mean, you're right. But..." His neck flushes, the red creeping up into his freckled cheeks. "I've been thinking about how it's all disconnected. And yet it all works together in each moment, making life." He points at my chest. "It's like a heartbeat, right? Everything collapsing, then everything exploding outward. Like the big bang. It just happens. And it couldn't be more unstable, yet we rely on it day after day."

"Like ordered chaos," I say.

His face lights up as we start down the stairs toward the ground floor.

"Right, exactly. But when you're a kid, it isn't chaos. It's just a heartbeat. Your house isn't floating through space, it sits on the ground. Once you get old enough you start to see that color is just paint and doors are just wood. Then, at some point, that feeling of home vanishes entirely. And... that's what I fear. That nothing will ever make me feel like I'm safe again. That once you leave home, you never get it back."

I have no idea what to say. It's the first moment I realize that I've never seen him before. Yes, I've seen his height and his red hair.

But I've never seen the person he is underneath. He just shared something deeply personal. Noah Hartmann, the boy who never speaks.

Yet for some reason, the exchange leaves me feeling as if I'm the one who opened up, not him.

We've reached the end of the biome.

"Um... thanks for the walk," I say.

I hurry off. Behind me, he feels awkward. Almost wishes he hadn't said a word.

But our conversation stays with me. It reminds me of something I *do* miss from home—having someone to talk to. Someone to share my own intimate thoughts with, who truly understands me. Like my dad used to be, before things changed.

Two days later during fitness hour, I see Noah stretching between workouts. As I walk toward the holotrek, I pass him and say, "You know, the one thing I hate about the Fitness Center is all the waiting."

Surprised, he looks up.

"What?"

I crack a smile, feeling self-conscious as I step up onto the treads. "Weighting, waiting. They're homonyms. It's wordplay, Noah. Lighten up."

For a second I think he doesn't get it. Then I hear him laugh behind me, a kind of guilty snicker that reminds me of a little kid.

"That's bananas," he says.

I laugh too, but quickly stop when I see Terra Donahue staring at me. Sobering, I quickly choose a path for my workout and start running. It's stupid, but it feels like a first step. Toward a new kind of friendship.

And so it is. Over the next two weeks, little by little, we begin talking in the hallways. Taking walks during free time. Because in a lot of ways, just like that first night, he surprises me. The way he won't push me when I don't feel like talking. The way he'll be silent for half an hour, just staring into an unseen world, and then suddenly he won't shut up. Mostly, how he sees life in a way I don't expect, a way I'd never see it myself.

Where I'm a volcano, erupting when the pressure becomes too great, Noah is an ocean, endless and deep. Something about the way he quietly observes, it soothes me. And the more time we spend together, the more I see his depth—and the height of the waves that paralyze him when stirred by winds of uncertainty.

Every day grows more natural, each conversation easier. The weeks turn into months.

Until one Sunday afternoon.

That day, Chloe and I are assigned the task of pruning ivy in the cafeterias. Ivy is like a weed, growing almost anywhere, surviving almost anything. I'm up on a ladder, clipping off long tendrils and letting them fall into Chloe's bin.

"I know it's impossible," I tell her as I work. "Because you'd burn through your oxygen too fast. But think about it. I could be the first person to run a marathon on Mars. I mean, technically I've already come close. But I'm talking about out there, on actual *dirt*."

Chloe nods absently. Then she asks, "Um... are you and Noah dating?"

I'm so blindsided, I nearly drop my shears.

"What?"

"Noah Hartmann," Chloe says, not looking up at me. "Everyone says you're dating now."

"No. We're not."

"Do you want to be?" she asks.

"That... you don't... that doesn't matter," I splutter. "We can't date. It's one of the rules. And anyway, that's no one's business. Who told you that?"

I attack the ivy plant and lop off a giant strip. When I realize she hasn't answered, I look down and find that she's crying.

"Hey, what's going on?"

I slide down the ladder to face her. And immediately I know.

"You like him," I say.

"No," she says. "I don't... it doesn't matter."

"It does," I say quietly.

I don't know what to do. Chloe is the only friend I've made since coming to Mars. I don't want to hurt her. And yet, the last two months with Noah... in a strange way, it's felt almost like having a home again. But it hasn't been anything more than a friendship.

Has it?

After giving Chloe vague assurances about the situation, I finish my duties. But I can't help feeling nervous. Because now that I'm considering it, I realize how much Noah frightens me. Just being around him makes me want to share things that I would normally keep buried. Things I haven't shared since the divorce. It feels like a nerve being reattached, painful and sensitive. But it's also *hungry*. This desire to know and be known has grown wild in its long captivity. And the longer I deny it, the more desperate it seems to become.

When I see him that night during free time, I'm guarded. I find myself watching his lips when he talks, how his eyebrows go up when he listens. Though I don't know what any of it means, I know I've entered an uncharted world. And I begin to realize that, even more than hurting Chloe, I'm terrified of getting hurt myself.

But I don't get hurt. Because that night the doctors Revise our friendship.

Maybe they see heartbreak coming for one, or all of us. Maybe they see it as mercy. Whatever the reason, the next morning I've forgotten the past few weeks. It's just as if they never happened. Chloe and I have nothing wedged between us. Noah and I are strangers.

Yet there is a trace of a feeling that remains. A tension I can't identify, circling around him in an orbit. My confusion, my discomfort, all the uncertainties and hopes that were never answered, they cloud the way I see him. So I avoid him.

But week after week he watches me, feelings simmering under the surface. Wishing he could find words to express what he no longer understands.

Finally, the memories fade and I come back to myself in the darkness, tears still brimming in my eyes. Our friendship was stolen from us.

And I never knew.

Yet despite his memories being erased, it never changed what Noah felt for me. Did it change what I felt for him? If the doctors hadn't intervened, would I have risked trusting him fully? When given the chance, I chose to stay the night in his pod—even knowing it would wound my dearest friend. Which means, my tendency was still to be close to him. Right?

How close would he get if I allowed him?

I'm brought to my senses by the lights clicking on around me. I have no time to react. No presence of mind to ready my Verced. Swift footfalls move toward me, and then their owner rounds the side of the cylinder.

Chapter Fourteen

"What are you doing?"

Terra scowls at me as she pauses beside a bioreactor. She clicks off a tiny blinking device in her hand. I stare at her in a daze.

"Huh?"

"I said, what—are—you—doing?" she repeats each word deliberately, as if I'm a child. "You're supposed to be hiding, not out in plain sight." Her eyes narrow. "God, Lizzy. What, are you crying?"

"No," I say, wiping my nose on my jumpsuit. Reliving these memories so soon after the glade should make me nauseated. But as I struggle to my feet, I'm surprised to find that I actually feel a little better. The weight of the knot has eased.

"Liar," Terra sneers. She adopts a mocking tone. "Oh, what happened, Lizzy? Did you finally realize you're not very popular around here? Is that why you're sad?"

"This isn't about the glade," I mutter.

"No? Then why are you sitting in here blubbering?"

I hesitate.

"None of your business."

This sets her off. She closes the gap between us in two steps, and for a second I think she's going to hit me again.

"Give me one good reason why I shouldn't turn you in right now," she says acidly. "One good reason."

"Why don't you?" I yell back at her. Suddenly I don't care if the doctors hear me. All of the tension, the fear, the lies, the sadness, the loss of Noah and his memories, it's broken free, and I don't care to contain it anymore. "Isn't that what you've wanted all along? To prove you're better? Why did you even help me in the first place?"

For a second her features are stiff as iron. Then a cold smile curls her lips.

"None of your business."

We just glare, each daring the other to take it further. But we don't. Slowly the tension bleeds out of the room like oxygen sucked from an airlock.

"They took him," I say, averting my gaze.

"Who?"

"Noah," I say bitterly. "They're probably scanning his mind right now, trying to figure out who I've been working with. Assuming your rebels haven't already told."

"They haven't," she says. "I've been working on some of them for a couple days. Even if they think you're crazy, they know *I'm* not."

Beside me, one of the bioreactors beeps and starts whirring.

"We need to get him back," I say.

"Noah?"

"Yes, Noah. Who else?"

Now her smile isn't cold but triumphant.

"So there *is* something going on between you. I told Chloe. She practically bit my head off, saying your 'sleeping arrangements' were innocent, but I told her—"

"There's nothing between us," I snap, and this time I'm in her face. She just laughs.

"Yeah, okay. Whatever. But like you said, they've probably got a Stitch on him by now."

"Then we need to act," I say, lowering my voice. "We go for Dosset—now. It's our only chance of stopping him before Noah's memories are gone." I don't say it, but that old fear is growing in the back of my head, that rather than erase every troublesome memory, they'll simply erase me from Noah's mind entirely.

I'm the root of the problem, after all.

"No, we need to think," Terra replies. "This is your problem, Elizabeth. You think that because you've got all the memories, your feelings are more important than the rest of ours. Well, they're not. Noah is gone. Blindly rushing after him will just put the rest of us in danger."

"Then what do you suggest?" I demand.

"Well, you said it took them days to break Atkinson. Why should Noah be different?"

"Because with Atkinson, they had obstacles. Noah didn't take a double dose of Verced right before they caught him."

"Okay, fine. Then we've got, what—a couple hours? We'll just have to rush the plan."

I grind my teeth in frustration. My thoughts keep racing down the corridor, through the Helix, and up into the room where Dosset is interrogating Noah. Torturing him, even. But gradually, stubbornly, I realize that Terra is right. If I want to help him, I can't just react on emotion. I have to use my head. If anyone can outsmart Dosset, it's me.

If later I find that Noah doesn't remember me, well... I'll just use a Stitch to put the memories back into his head.

"Fine," I mutter.

A grin twists her pretty features, as if she thinks she's won the conversation.

"See, was that so bad? If you'd just listen to me more often, we wouldn't have so many problems together."

"The rebellion won't work, Terra," I say resignedly. "They're never going to believe me."

"I know. That's why *you'll* be sitting in here hiding, while *I'll* be winning them over. Chloe can get the Stitch while Romie finishes the EMP." Her smile widens. "We all have a part to play, Elizabeth. Yours is staying out of my way."

"You're not—"

"No, I *am*. I think we've all had enough of you throwing our memories in our faces, acting like you know something about us.

This time I'm not going to let you ruin things for me."

We regard each other evenly. Whatever pleasure she took from pushing me around has dried up. Now she's turned cold and fierce, a vein of bitterness running beneath her words.

And if I'm honest, I don't know that I blame her. To her, it probably seems as if I've only been thinking about myself. Because in many ways, I have.

Maybe if I could get out of the way, things would start working for once.

"Okay," I say. "Go for it."

"You're not going to fight me?" she says skeptically.

"No."

"Why not?"

"Because you're probably right."

This draws her up short, but only for a second.

"Of course I'm right. While I locate our rebels, I'll send Chloe to the Wellness Suites for a Stitch. We'll meet in the ice cave in two hours. Think you can get yourself over there in time?"

"I'm sure I'll manage."

She smiles again, more sweetly.

"I'm sure you will."

Turning on her heel, she slinks out of sight. I lean against a bioreactor and listen to the door closing. Again the question surfaces in my mind, nagging me. I have to wonder: Why *is* Terra helping us?

Clearly, it has nothing to do with her liking me as a person. She can hardly stand me. And it doesn't seem like her past is something she cherishes, either. At first, I felt certain she'd turn me in. Now, even more than Chloe and Romie, she seems determined to be sure we don't fail. So again—why?

I can't think of a good enough reason.

Every muscle aches as I ease back down to the floor, this time taking care to squeeze myself between a bioreactor and the wall. Five minutes pass, then ten. The lights slowly dim again, leaving me alone with myself.

Myself.

What *is* my part to play in all of this? Does it even matter? It's funny how, even when I'm trying to help other people, I still end up thinking about myself. Meanwhile, those people end up falling through the cracks.

Like Noah. I wasn't thinking about him. Not until he turned himself into a human shield for me. Certainly, I haven't been thinking about Romie. Even after all he's done. And of course Chloe. How many times have I–

Abruptly I sit up. The movement catches the motion sensors, triggering the lights to snap back on.

Chloe!

She still doesn't know about Noah. More than most cadets, she has a direct tie to him. And to me. And when I first went missing, didn't they send doctors to question her immediately? I'm sure they'll do it again. Or maybe this time they'll just drag her straight into the Helix.

The same could probably be said of Romie, but I have a feeling he's already taken precautions. He's likely been keeping an eye on the hacked security feed to alert him of any coming danger.

But I know Chloe. She won't suspect a thing.

She'll be totally defenseless.

I've already lost one friend today. I can't just abandon another. Wriggling painfully out into the open, I push to my feet and jog toward the door, leaving my agreement with Terra forgotten among the shadows.

The time stamp announces sixteen hundred hours as I step back into the hallway. By the look of things, the colony has returned to some kind of normal. Maybe taking Noah prisoner has momentarily sated the doctors, who know that his mind holds the details they need to track me down.

The thought reminds me just how little time we have left.

So where is Chloe? I'll bet Terra went straight to find her, to be sure Chloe had enough time to complete her task. Owing to the good fifteen minutes head start she had on me, they've probably already spoken—which means my best shot is to go straight to the Polar domes. Hopefully, I can intercept Chloe before Dosset does.

It's nerve-racking, walking these halls. Since the announcement of my "sickness," every cadet I encounter will be as good as a doctor. I cling to the sides of the corridors, slipping into service domes at the sound of approaching footsteps.

The effort is painstaking—and too time-consuming. With each disruption, I feel more convinced that I'll be too late to help her.

By some miracle, I manage to reach the Wheel. I've just stepped into the Polar domes when I see her, Chloe, being led away by a pair of doctors. One on either side.

Just as when I stunned Terra, I don't have time to think. I slip a hand into my pocket and retrieve my precious inoculators. Pop the caps. Move toward them with a determined stride. Lift my arm to strike—

I hit the first doctor in the neck, planting the tube with my fist. He cries out in surprise as I release the inoculator and turn to Doctor Varma, who has spun to face me. Disbelief is written across her features as I seize her wrist and pull it toward me, jabbing the other inoculator into the flesh of her forearm.

"Engram?" she mumbles.

The drugs don't kick in immediately, and I cringe as the doctors attempt to shout for help. But they only stumble a few meters before they crumple to the ground.

My whole body tingles. Chloe's eyes look as if they might fall out of her head.

"Lizzy, what are you doing?" she gasps, finally finding her voice. "You're supposed to be in hiding! If the doctors catch you... they made an announcement—"

"I know," I reply. "I just... I knew they'd come for you, and I couldn't let them get—" I stop myself short. *I couldn't let them get you too.*

If it's possible, her eyes have grown even wider.

"You knew they'd come for me?"

"I don't have time to explain," I tell her. "Just follow me, okay?"

With that I turn on my heel, heading toward the Wellness Suites. Chloe scurries to catch up.

One hall, two halls. Into the next dome. A security camera catches my eye, and I hiss at Chloe to keep her head down, but it doesn't matter—I can already hear voices shouting behind us. Doubtless, they saw my attack on the fallen doctors.

We enter a wide hall with an arched cathedral ceiling, patterned silhouettes of bonsai trees along the glowing roof. I'm about to suggest we make a run for it and double back later when the lights abruptly flicker and go out.

It's pitch black. I can't even see Chloe right beside me.

"Lizzy," she breathes. "What happened?"

At first, I don't answer, my mind racing. Are they trying to trap us? Did the solar panels malfunction? I reject the thoughts as the voices grow louder, knowing we have precious little time. By feel, I pull Chloe along the wall, groping until I find a door handle.

Locked.

Confused shouting echoes around us. I can also hear a humming—the emergency runners trying to kick in. Any second, they'll come to life and reveal us.

I conjure a mental image of the hallway just before the lights died. If we're as far down the hall as I think we are, we should be in front of Shiffrin's suite. And if so... I start pulling up memories at random, blindly dragging them out of the fog of my mind, searching for the key code, the key code... I can sense it, but the numbers are jumbled.

What was it?

"Lizzy," Chloe insists.

"I know. Just give me a second." I begin pressing the numbers by feel. But the lock sticks. I try again, switching the first two numbers. Still, nothing.

"What happened to the lights?" someone demands. Just

meters behind us.

One more time I punch the numbers, this time swapping the last two digits. The handle finally turns. I've only just pulled Chloe inside and shut the door when the hallway comes to life in a green glow that buzzes along the doorjamb.

The shouting ceases. We hover motionless, listening as feet shuffle nearer.

A door rattles loudly and we both jump, a small squeak escaping Chloe's lips. I grab her hand to steady her. She's trembling. A second later another door rattles, and I realize someone is checking handles. Quietly, carefully, I reach out and press the lock button—

Our own door shivers in its frame as someone pulls on it violently. Chloe has stopped trembling—and by the look of her, stopped breathing.

Through the barrier, a gravelly voice swears.

"Did they run?"

"Must have," replies another. "The suites are locked tight."

Another series of curses, then— "All right, I'll go after them. Help Patterson and Varma to the Sick Bay before we have a panic on our hands."

Footsteps disperse in opposite directions. Once the sounds have gone I collapse against the wall, my whole body suddenly limp. That blackout just saved our lives. Did Romie finish the EMP? I wonder if he's responsible. At least we know the cameras will be down for a little while.

For a time the room is disturbed only by our gasping. I squint at the lumpy shapes, an eerie sense of aversion tugging at me.

Once, this room felt safe to me. In spite of the pressure to share my thoughts, despite my discomfort, it represented a space where someone cared. Now I see it for what it really is—a pretty interrogation chamber designed to draw out secrets and manipulate minds. The very opposite of what therapy should be.

Chloe is eyeing the room as well, looking troubled.

"This is Shiffrin's suite," she says.

"Yeah."

She seems to fight off a shiver.

"That was close," she whispers. "Way too close."

"I'm just glad I caught up with you, or it could have been a whole lot worse," I say.

To my surprise, this seems to agitate her. She grabs my arm.

"Lizzy, you shouldn't have come out of hiding. *Everyone* is looking for you. Doctor Meng made an announcement. He told everyone you had that virus they made up and everyone went nuts, scared they might have it. He said the virus could be deadly if left untreated." She takes a breath and lets it out slowly. I can sense the same fear she felt for me the first time I was nearly captured. "Of course, Meng was quick to calm everyone down, making promises of an antidote. But I'm glad you weren't in the theater. You would've been trampled."

The room seems to crystalize as I remember the wild fear, the way cadets were almost violent in their attempt to get away from me. And those memories lead me back to Noah.

I realize I have to tell her. Right here and now. Because if I don't do it before we regroup with others, Terra will. Because when we enter the Helix and corner Dosset, we'll find Noah too. And he might not remember who we are. I can't let her walk into that blind. After everything I've already put her through, everything I've kept from her. This is the least I can do.

"They didn't trample me," I say slowly. "Actually, they all seemed pretty desperate to get away from me."

"What?" She turns to look at me in the soft, emerald light. "What are you talking about?"

"A group of Xeris picked me up and dumped me in the theater with Noah. Doctor Hitch made that same announcement. One of the cadets noticed me."

I watch as my words work their effect, creasing her features in confusion. Suddenly I can't bear to do it. My eyes begin vainly searching for a Stitch, but Chloe steps in front of me.

"Okay, well, obviously you got away..." Her voice wavers.

"Noah fought Sarlow," I whisper. "And I got away. Barely."

"He... he fought–?"

"They got him, Chloe." My voice catches. "They took him into the Helix."

It's in that moment I know I was right to hide things from her. To keep secret the possibility of Earth's fate, to hide Noah's feelings. Because just this bit of information is almost enough to break her.

I can see it in her eyes; I watch the mirror of her spirit crack as she quickly makes the same calculations I made. Grasps what it means that Dosset has him. I hurry to tell her about the plan to move forward, but it's not enough. Chloe can hardly breathe.

Her feet give out from under her as I guide her into a chair.

"We... we have to go now," she stammers. The look on her face is chilling. It reminds me of Atkinson when he told me his memories had been taken. "They'll erase his... his memories."

"I know," I say. "We're going to break into the Helix in an hour. We'll get him out, and if they erased anything, we'll use a Stitch to put it right back."

But I can't calm her down. She's always been the soothing one, the one to disarm even the worst situations. And I'm not her. Even though here, in this moment, I have to be.

She's practically hyperventilating.

"What if they erase it all, Liz? Like Atkinson. Or what if it kills him like it could have done to you? Or what if they put him into cryosleep, and we fail, and I never see him again? We have to get him back before it's too late!"

"Look at me." I take her gently by the face, pulling from her own caring nature. "Chloe, hey. Look at me."

Finally, she turns her dilated pupils to meet mine.

"We won't lose him. If we bring Dosset down and give back everyone's memories, we'll get him back. Noah is too strong to end up like Atkinson. Okay? We need to make sure our plan succeeds. We'll see him again in just a few hours, and we'll make it all go back to normal."

"But—"

"Trust me. It's going to be fine."

It's strange, telling her that. Because it's a lie. It might not be fine. But I guess I've gotten used to lying. I guess I've learned that sometimes the truth is simply too much. And right now I have to believe that it'll all work out in the end.

I'm saying it for both of us.

It takes several swallows for the lump in her throat to go down.

"What do we do first?" she breathes.

"I'm thinking that somewhere in this room is a Stitch. You and I need to find it."

I begin opening drawers at random. I find a first-aid kit, a plastic cylinder of mint tea, an empty box with a latch. For some reason, I have the general sense that it once held Verced.

Chloe starts moving too, checking mostly bare shelves. One carries a picture of a young man with brooding features, another holds a model of Earth. But before long she grows listless, chewing at her nails with a worried expression. If we had time, I might have her sit and make some tea. But we don't.

I pull open another empty drawer. Does Shiffrin even leave the Stitch in here? Maybe not. Maybe she has to remove it, so she can download new memories into the bank. I'm not willing to accept that. Because if it's true, the Stitch could be inside the Helix. Could even be on Noah's head, right now.

When I reach the final cabinet, it sticks. But there's no keyhole. I run my fingers beneath it and they scuttle over the buttons of a numeric keypad.

I allow myself a small, brief smile.

"Think I've got it," I say to Chloe, trying to sound encouraging. "I just need to remember the code and we'll be out of here."

She doesn't answer. I turn my attention back to the cabinet.

Okay. Just one more code.

It's doubtful that Shiffrin would've shared access to something like this with one of her cadets. Which means if I know the code at all, it'll be coming from the doctor's own memories. The problem is, the only memory I've ever pulled from a doctor was Atkinson's, and that was almost nothing. Still, I have to try.

I hold my breath in an attempt to focus, aware as always of the dim throbbing at the back of my head. Then I sink into the memories, diving toward where it's cold and dark. I reach out for something to grasp, for anything that might help me. But I come up empty-handed.

Again, harder this time, I push lower, deeper. Yet my mind has gone as quiet as one of the Martian moons, immobilized by the trauma of the day. The suite whirls in muted colors, making me dizzy. I slump into Shiffrin's chair.

"On second thought, let's rest a minute," I pant. "My head is mush."

To stop the room from spinning, I close my eyes. Last time I was brainwashed, Shiffrin gave me Verced before she typed the code. I think back through previous memories. Each session, she would dose me before pulling out the Stitch. The memories are murky, like—

Tick, tack, tack, tick.

My eyes fly open. Chloe is at the cabinet, typing a code. Before I can even react, the latch gives a soft click.

I'm vaguely aware of my jaw dropping.

"How did you—?"

"It's the date of our last day on Earth," Chloe says faintly. She looks almost bewildered, as if she just woke up. "Shiffrin told me about it once. It was the last day she talked to her son. Sometimes... sometimes during therapy, she tells me about her life and what she misses. She said her son doesn't talk to her anymore."

"And she let you keep those memories?" I say in disbelief, struggling from my chair.

"Maybe... maybe she wanted someone else to know about him. Maybe she didn't have anyone else she thought she could trust."

I nod vaguely. Leave it to Chloe to psychoanalyze her own therapist.

As I open the cabinet door, the pearl-like diodes of the Stitch catch like fish eggs in the dull light, an alien cocoon of glistening webs. And there's something else. A glass square. Shiffrin's tablet. Carefully, I lift them both from their hiding place.

"Is that—?"

"Yeah."

When I press the power button, I find that the tablet is dead. I guess whatever killed the lights drained it too.

"Come on," I say. "We've got to meet up with the others in the ice cave."

We head out for the Polar domes, warily making our way through the gloomy halls. This time I lead Chloe by the hand, staying sharp. The news about Noah has given her a shock, and she floats along like a person underwater.

Luckily, though I hear footsteps twice, we manage to slip away before a threat can present itself.

The time stamp announces eighteen hundred hours—dinner time—just as the fragrant smell of roasting lentils reaches my nose. Stomach growling, I tug Chloe past the chattering doors of the Polar cafeteria.

Again, I'm struck by how strange it is for things to feel so normal after the panic of the morning. Truthfully, the panic of the entire day.

I remind myself yet again that most cadets don't know what's really going on. We hurry toward the biome archway.

The tundra habitat is so hushed, it feels like an empty shell. We stop at the tool shed for a pair of the heavy coats that Polar cadets wear, insulated with a wonderful microfiber mesh. Then we round the craggy hill and make for the ice cave, the coldest part of the entire colony.

It'll be miserable inside the enclosure, but I suppose it is our best bet for a meetup point. No one goes there unless they absolutely have to.

Once we're inside, the temperature drops another ten degrees. The rock walls are patterned with lichen in glowing shades of orange, blue, and neon red. We huddle near the entrance and, since Terra and Romie haven't shown up yet, we make a meal out of what food we have left.

Chloe was smart about what she chose when she gathered food for Atkinson's time in hiding: carrots, broccoli, beets, radishes. Roots and vegetables that don't spoil fast. We each have a banana for dessert, smeared with a rare packet of almond butter.

When we've finished I begin fiddling with the Stitch. Chloe hasn't said a word since the Wellness Suite. She sits beside me, staring at the swirls of vegetation, her gaze in another world. Now that I've remembered everything, the posture reminds me unsettlingly of Noah.

"What're you thinking about?" I ask, hoping for a casual tone.

"Lizzy, do you ever wonder what people think of you? Like, what they *really* think?" She glances at me and blushes. "Oh, n-never mind. I forgot you already know everything."

"Not everything," I say, running my fingers along a diode of the Stitch. It lights up as if sensing my touch, and I quickly withdraw.

Chloe stares at the wall again, but nods.

"Did he ever think about me?" she says hesitantly—almost pleadingly. "Noah, I mean."

I look at her, then turn away. Now it's my turn to be silent. It's worse than before, having the knowledge of all the history between Noah and me. This isn't the first time I've caused Chloe pain. It feels inevitable that it won't be the last.

And maybe that's true. But right now, minutes before we're going to invade the Helix and it could all come to an end—it just isn't the time.

"Chloe," I fumble. "That's... I don't..."

Outside, a boot crunches on gravel. Before I can even move, a cadet ducks into the cave, a metal disk slung over his shoulder on a strap. Relief floods through me as I catch Romie's face beneath the navy blue hood.

"You made it," I say, standing.

"Oh, thank goodness," he replies breathlessly. "I was afraid the EMP wouldn't be enough. When I picked Chloe up on the cameras and saw the doctors—"

"So it *was* you. Did Terra tell you what was going on?"

"Yes, she did. But I'd already managed to finish the EMP before she reached me." He pauses, his eyes wandering to the Stitch. "Is that it?"

I nod, holding it out to him. Curious, he stoops until his glasses slide down his nose. "Fascinating. I wonder what it's made of?"

"Evil," Chloe mutters.

"Where's Terra?" I ask.

"I don't know. I haven't seen her since she informed me of Noah's capture."

A silent moment passes. I feel grateful I decided to tell Chloe when I did.

Standing, Chloe brushes off her coat and voices the obvious next question. "Do you think they caught her?"

"No," says a voice, and Terra enters the cave, wrapped in a coat of her own. She glowers at us all. "But it wouldn't have mattered if they did."

"What do you mean?" Chloe asks.

"I mean, congratulations, Elizabeth. You wasted our only shot. Now the colony is on high alert, the cadets are on the verge of a meltdown, and the doctors are watching us all like hawks. Great job, really. It's impressive how you not only failed to inspire a rebellion, you actually made sure we'd never get another chance at forming one."

"Those cadets would never have believed me," I tell her again, growing impatient. "And just for the record, I didn't put anyone on high alert. Dosset did. This isn't an accident. He intentionally made sure no one would trust me once they knew I had some deadly virus."

"At this point, it doesn't matter, does it?" she mutters. "Dosset probably knows that Romie and I are involved by now. Hiding one person was bad enough. Trying to hide all four of us just isn't going to happen."

For a moment the cave is filled only with the white, puffy air of our breathing.

"I'm sorry," Romie says quietly. "If I could've just—"

"What are you apologizing for?" Terra snaps. "It's Lizzy's fault."

"No, it isn't," Chloe says defensively. "She was doing her best. We all were. Remember what Noah said? Blaming others won't help."

I want to agree with her. But now I don't think I can. Noah was wrong.

This isn't about our best. It's about *them*. Even before the virus, no matter what words I used, the cadets have had every good reason to think I'm lying. Because the truth is, they *want* me to be lying.

Why shouldn't they? If I'm telling the truth and the doctors are as conniving as I say, everything changes. It's so much easier to just believe the world is fine. Who wouldn't want that? I know I would.

The thought makes me pause.

Yet again, this is my problem. I've been thinking about *myself*. How I'd view me—what I'd have to do to win myself over. But what about *them*?

What do the cadets really want? In an instant, I know.

More than anything, they want life to just go back to normal. That's why the virus is so frightening. It threatens their world, just like my accusations. And what has Dosset repeatedly said that he wants to avoid at all costs? For that normal to be disturbed. For the colony to dissolve into a panic.

A shiver runs through me, though it isn't the cold. Because suddenly I know what to do.

"We don't need the rebellion to believe us."

"Actually, we do," Terra says sharply. "If they don't believe us, they won't help us. And in case you haven't noticed, we can't do this on our own."

"You're right, we can't. But we don't need a rebellion to cause a distraction. All we need is the distraction itself. And Dosset has given us the perfect tool to make one."

"What tool? What are you talking about?"

"This virus I supposedly have," I say. "When I was in the Xeri theater, just the sight of me was enough to send the cadets into hysterics. If I were to show up somewhere crowded, like one of the cafeterias..."

"It would be anarchy," says Chloe, her eyes wide.

"Okay, sure," says Terra slowly. "But if you just walk in there, the doctors will catch you. There's no way they're going to let you pull a stunt like that and just slip away again."

"That's true," says Romie. "And we need you to guide us in the Helix. None of us have been inside other than you."

"Then after I start the riot, I'll need to be sure they're chasing someone else," I say. My thoughts are moving so rapidly that I can hardly say them fast enough. But the framework of a plan is already taking shape in my mind.

As if sensing where I'm headed, Terra narrows her eyes.

"And just who do you think they'll be chasing, Elizabeth?"

"That depends, Terra. How fast do you think you can run?"

Chapter Fifteen

"Twenty minutes," I say, trudging back through the cold rows of plants toward the main path. My thoughts are flying a kilometer a second. "I'd say we've got about twenty minutes before dinner ends. Which means if we're going to do this, we have to do it now."

"Um, can we back up a moment?" Romie asks. "You're planning to just walk into one of the cafeterias and... and expect some kind of riot?"

"No," I reply, considering a new angle. "No, that'll be too localized. We want the whole colony in a panic. So, we'll use the same method as Dosset. The overhead."

"How will you do that? The Comm Room is inside the Helix, and—"

"—we'll never get to it, I know. But I'll bet I can reverse-engineer a broadcast from one of the holographic imagers. Don't you think?"

Romie is silent, so lost in his calculations that he doesn't even notice the cabbages he's trampling. "That could work," he finally concludes.

"Can we slow down?" Chloe asks, almost jogging to keep up. "We need to think about this, Lizzy. What if someone gets hurt in the riot?"

"Unfortunately, it's a risk we'll have to take," I say grimly. "Dosset hasn't given us any other options, has he?"

Like most of what I'm saying, I don't stop to consider my words until they've already left my mouth. But I'm right, aren't I? Dosset is the one who forced us into this position. No one can argue with that. Not even Terra.

"So we'll use the EMP to bypass the door, is that it? I suppose that would get us inside quietly, without too much trouble," Romie says.

But I'm already shaking my head as another idea forms. "No, we'll save it. I think I have a better way to get through the door."

"You... you do?"

Now I allow myself a full-on grin. "Trust me."

For the first time in days, it feels like my mind is working. *Really* working. Maybe at a level it never has before. It's as if all the thoughts that were once so painful are suddenly lining up, connecting the dots in the darkness, forming shapes and constellations where before there was only empty space.

Not that it isn't painful. The telltale pulsing has already begun to gouge at the back of my head. But right now I hardly care. We finally have a plan that I think could really work.

We just have to put it into action.

The Workshop is deserted when we arrive, which doesn't come as a surprise. I head directly for the 3D printers—some of their glass cubes large enough to print an entire table, while others are equipped with crane-like arms no bigger than my fingers.

Beside them, a storage bin contains bottles of printer filament. Everything from syrups to pastes to pigments.

One by one I begin pulling the bottles free, checking labels as I go. I soon find the bottle I need, a tiny one filled with bubbly orange syrup.

"Over here," I say, leading the others to a nearby work desk.

I push a space clear and then set down Shiffrin's tablet, tilting its reflective surface back and forth to catch the light. It takes me a few minutes while Romie fidgets beside me, and then I see it—the rippled impression of a fingerprint.

"There," I murmur, holding it up for him to see. Chloe leans over his shoulder. "A perfect impression left by the oil in her finger. See it?"

"I... think so." Romie takes off his glasses and squints. "Ah, yes... yes, I see it."

"Perfect. Now we make dessert."

He frowns as I hold up the bottle, revealing the label. It strikes me as funny that only a few days ago he would've said something mystifying like that to me—and I would've been the one confused.

Oh, how the tables have turned.

"Gummy syrup?" Chloe asks in surprise.

"Yep."

Romie stares at me, and then a flicker of understanding lights his face.

"One might use it to create a template of something," he says slowly. "Say, the debris on the tablet. It could form a mold around the debris... and, in so doing, create a replica of the original fingerprint."

"And because the membrane is so thin, it'll carry my body heat, which should make it read like normal skin," I add.

"That's brilliant," Chloe says blankly.

"It's all thanks to Romie," I reply. "I just copied what he did with the defibrillator. I took apart a fingerprint and put it back together in a different way. Now, if we add just a bit of this—" I squeeze a dollop onto the glass and it slowly spreads, like molasses. We wait while it begins to dry, then I hand Romie the bottle. "Now we form a sleeve around my finger." As I speak, I press my thumb onto the congealed resin. He takes his cue, expelling more syrup around my knuckle. It feels like cold wax.

"Should we try it out on the tablet?" he asks as it begins to bond.

"Can't. Your EMP killed it."

"Oh." Suddenly he looks alarmed. "What about the Stitch?"

"It seems okay. I'm not sure how the batteries work, but the design seems to avoid any coiled wire components, which would have prevented an EMP from—"

"—increasing the voltage to a point of damage," Romie finishes. "I was just going to say the same thing."

He snaps the lid onto the bottle.

"So, now what?" Chloe asks hesitantly. "Terra needs a surgical mask, so she can pass as your double?"

I nod as I carefully slide the gummy sleeve off my thumb. "Right. We might as well just print a new one rather than risk a trip back to the Xeri pods."

"Delightful," Terra says, arms folded. I hadn't noticed, but she's standing across the aisle from us, leaning against a battery reserve. "But just so we're clear, I haven't agreed to *be* your double." She pushes off the cylinder, glaring. "You realize this is suicide for me, right? If I pretend to be you, they'll catch me within minutes."

My temper spikes and, as usual, my instinct is to lash out at her. We don't have time for another argument. So rather than argue, I decide to apply my newer method—to ask myself what she wants and use that knowledge against her. "Only if you let them," I say aloud.

She stares at me.

"Let them what?"

"Catch you. I've been running for days, and they haven't yet."

"That was different. At least you had somewhere to run. Now, you're basically going to scream 'come get me,' and then let me take the fall."

"They had me cornered earlier today, and I managed to get away. I don't see why you can't do the same."

"Maybe I could, if I had Noah to protect me."

The room gets quiet. Chloe has gone as white as her jumpsuit. I clench my fists, my calm evaporating in the fire beneath my skin.

"But I don't, do I?" she purrs, sensing she's hit a nerve. "Because you already got him caught. And now you need someone else to sacrifice."

"Stop it," Chloe whispers. "That isn't what's happening."

"I think it is."

"Well, you're wrong," I say, somehow managing to redirect my anger into my curled fists. My fingernails sting as they bite my palms. "By now they've read Noah's mind. Which means if we don't do something fast, they're going to catch us. All of us. Probably within the next hour. If you want to stand around picking fights, go for it. But this is the best plan we've got, and I think you know it. Don't you?"

They're the same words she threw in my face, back when we were first planning to enter the Helix. And they're as true now as they were then.

"You all think this is the right thing to do?" she says, turning to the others. "Romie. Look me in the eye and tell me you still trust her after the glade."

His ashen skin pales a little.

"I'll be honest, it... sounds risky. But I actually think it has the potential to work. And really, it's the only option we have, isn't it?"

Chloe nods.

"What other choice do we have?" she says to no one in particular.

"It won't work," says Terra defiantly. "We're wasting our last chance on her when she's already wasted all the others!"

"What's your plan then, Terra?" I ask. "Tell me what you would do."

She shakes her head in disgust.

"I would've raised a rebellion. But you already made sure that isn't going to happen."

"There's no use arguing about what already happened," I say shortly. "We have a very short window to pull this off. Either you're with us or you're against us."

A long moment passes, and I realize that I don't know how she's going to respond. I've wondered so many times what compels her to keep helping me. I wonder if, right now, she'll decide she's had enough.

"So I just need to dress up as you?" she finally asks.

"That's right. And—"

"Just look like you and act like you and do whatever you say? I guess if I really want to get into character, I need to be sure I save myself. But if I'm going to do that, I should probably rethink this whole plan of yours. It only works for one."

In that moment, I hit my limit. All my general fear and frustration suddenly comes to a point like a needle, all of it directed at her.

"You know what, Terra? It's kind of funny how your whole big problem with me is that I remind you of your mother, when really, looking back through your memories, it is so painfully clear that *you're* the one who's like her. Just as cutting and self-absorbed and cruel. No one liked her, and no one likes you. They just put up with you because they have to. Because when they try to ignore you, all you do is make everyone miserable. They *fear* what you'll do to them. None of them would miss you for a second if you vanished. They'd forget about you and move on—and they'd be happier."

All the color bleeds from her face. I know I've gone too far. Her hatred for her mother is the very thing that brought her to Mars in the first place.

It takes her a second to find her voice.

"You're right, Lizzy," she says hoarsely, stepping backward. "You're exactly right. Why am I not jumping at the chance to be perfect for a little while? Because obviously you don't have any problems. None that anyone knows about. And even when you make a mistake, it seems like everyone is happy to blame it on someone else."

I open my mouth to say something, but I don't know what to say. In this war between us, it's clear I've had a victory—a terrible, bloody victory.

She turns away, not quite concealing the trembling of her lip. With her back turned, I just barely hear her.

"Oh, and for the record? They won't miss you either."

And then she's gone.

Time seems frozen in her absence, as if the world is caught in some kind of transition. At length, Chloe speaks and breaks the spell.

"Lizzy," she says.

A single astonished word.

I stare into blank space, not daring to look at her. I don't have the courage. I know what I've done. And with that, I recognize that I've crossed a kind of boundary. Used my knowledge, my intimate knowledge, to tear her down. I've treated her as Dosset does—as a subject to be manipulated.

Now I'm no better than he is.

Anger flares white hot, stoked by shame and denial. I catch my breath as it burns me.

"Oh, well," I mutter, shoving the gummy into my pocket. "We didn't need her anyway. I can cause a riot without a decoy. I'll just have to be faster."

"Elizabeth, that... you shouldn't have..."

Romie can't find the words either. His confused disappointment is like helium in my lungs, fueling the fire of my guilt. I roll it into anger, clenching my teeth as I glower at them.

"She forced it," I snap. "Okay? She pushed me and she pushed me, and what was I supposed to do? Just let her say whatever the hell she wanted?"

They glance at each other, then stare at the floor. It feels as if I'm watching from across the room, unable to stop myself.

"Forget it," I growl. "I'm going to finish this. After my announcement, they'll be looking for me in the theaters. I'll sneak back here to meet up with you, and then we'll head into the Helix together. Got it?"

"Sure," Romie mutters.

"Good."

I hurry out into the halls without stopping, trying to outpace my humiliation.

Focus, I tell myself. *Just focus.* Dinner should be ending at any minute. I don't have time for this.

As I enter the Clover theater and make my way down to the holographic imager, the lens is black and lifeless. It doesn't take long to recalibrate the feed. Then my finger hovers above the button. And again it hits me that this is it. Our one last chance. I take a final deep breath, which does nothing to calm my frazzled nerves.

I press the button down.

Blue light shines from the lens like an aurora, cascading over my face and shoulders. Above, I hear the telltale *ding-dong* of the overheads clicking on. Then, only quiet. I clear my throat and the sound echoes around me. Time seems to stop again.

What happens if they don't believe me? What if, as in the glade, the colony sees through the act and disregards my words?

I feel my chest growing tight as arguments shift inside my head, each rehearsed thought as flimsy as the last. The pressure of how much rests on these moments, of deciding whether or not I see Noah again, has me shaking.

But before I was asking them to trust me. To take a stand for something I thought they wanted. This time I'll be using their fear against them.

And, as I'm beginning to realize, fear is a powerful weapon.

"Hello," I say, my voice cracking. In spite of myself, I reach deep into my memories and pull up every last shred of confidence from Terra that I can. "Hello," I repeat with greater force. "This is Elizabeth Engram. And I have something to tell you."

I pause, letting my words register.

"Doctor Dosset is a liar. He's told you I have a virus that could kill you. But I don't. And now I'm going to prove it to you." I clear my throat again, trying to still my trembling nerves. "Over the past few days, I haven't been in quarantine. I've been walking the same halls as you, touching the same handles and keypads. And now, using tools from the Laboratory, I've added a pint of my own blood to the humidifiers. Which means the air you're breathing is now laden with my supposed virus." Again I pause, but this time the silence has a jagged quality to it. Brittle, like glass about to shatter. "So if I'm sick, you're sick. Go ask your 'doctors' for a cure."

Quickly I cut the feed, my breathing shallow. There's another *ding-dong*, and then again, silence. A cold, pervasive calm settles over me. Though I feel almost certain that throughout the rest of the colony, there is anything but calm or silence.

I glance up and notice that a camera has a clear shot of my face. Even if the software doesn't know my features, all it takes is a manual sweep for a doctor to find me standing here. It's time to start running.

Looping the mask over my ears, I bolt to the top of the stairs and throw open the door.

The halls are empty, but only for a second. I've hardly cleared the first corridor when the shouting begins. Then the flood comes, cadets surging from a hall to my left where I know the cafeteria is located.

It's a human stampede. Cries fill my ears. Screams of distress. No one is thinking about me or anyone else as they stumble over each other's bodies.

Each one is only trying to save themselves.

But from what? It's the very air that they fear. I shrink into an alcove as Caleb breaks free from the group and barrels past me into a biome. Others are going that way too. They probably think the plants will shield them from my contagion.

The doctors haven't mobilized yet, so I use the mob to my advantage, ducking down as I edge back the way I came, jostled, shoved, struck with careless limbs. By some miracle, I reach the giant arch of the Workshop. As I scuttle inside, the white coats appear, whipping past me as they shout orders, doses of Verced clutched in their fists.

I catch my breath in the shadow of a shelving unit. Belatedly I look around and see no sign of Romie or Chloe. An iron fear grips my throat, fear that they too have abandoned me.

"Hello?" I say as loudly as I dare. "Romie? Chloe?"

Eyes peek out from behind a wall of boxes, and then Romie's

face appears. "Were you successful?" he asks. Chloe tiptoes out behind him.

"If you mean 'Is the colony in the midst of a meltdown?' then the answer is yes," I say, almost shaky with relief. "We... we should get going."

"Sure," Chloe says in a small voice. "Romie?"

"This way."

I reenter the halls between Romie and Chloe, this time moving with the crowd as we're funneled back toward the Wheel.

I'm jittery. Not only because I thought I'd again been deserted, but for the thousands of ways this could all go wrong.

And yet I also feel a kind of resignation. This is the end. In the next hour, whether we succeed or not, the struggle will be over. Either Dosset wins or we do. And if we win, we'll have answers. About how we can reach our families and why the doctors began their experiments in the first place. Or confirmation that Earth is really gone and they've simply been hiding the truth.

After that, well, I guess it's up to us. To decide what to do next, how to get back home—or how to preserve the human race. And, ultimately, what to do with our freedom.

We shrug off a group of Clovers as we step into the Wheel, more doctors pouring out like wasps from an angry nest. The alarms begin as we make our way around to the silver door.

Half a dozen cameras observe our approach. Though I'm sure Dosset's attention is diverted elsewhere at the moment, I can't help feeling a dire sense of exposure as I slip the gummy-print onto my thumb and press it atop the reader.

Two beeps and green lights.

It works.

We push the door open, and then we're stepping through, one by one, and gathering in the curved passageway. Behind us, the door takes a moment to seal. When it's finished, Romie puts his finger to the scanner on the other side. It flashes red.

"What are you doing?" I say in disbelief. "They'll know we're here."

"One moment," he says, putting his finger to the reader again.

Red lights. He does it one last time and the lights stay red. I hear a clunk, a lock sliding into place. He turns and lets out a heavy sigh.

"Okay. Now it won't open for half an hour. Or until the power gets reset." He glances at our stunned faces. "It's a safety protocol. We've had a couple of incidents here and there, and I had to reprogram the software so that if an unauthorized person tried to access the Helix three times, it would automatically—"

"—seal itself. That buys us time. Good thinking, Romie."

Together, we turn to face the upward slope. After the panicky tension of the colony, the quiet presses down on us like a physical weight.

"Where do you think we'll find Dosset?" Chloe asks quietly.

"At the top," I say. "That's where the Bridge will be. Where he can monitor everything from the safety of his private tower, alone."

"Then that's where we're headed," says Romie. "Lead on, Elizabeth."

With determination, I begin the climb. I no longer take the steps of a victim, watching for signs of danger, ready to flee at a moment's notice. I have friends with me now. Not to mention the EMP.

If anyone should be afraid, it's Dosset.

One at a time we pass doors on the outside of the curve. I half-expect one of them to open, but I have a feeling we're alone in the Helix. Dosset's fear of a colony-wide panic, coupled with his desire to capture me, will make him overconfident. Just like in the airlock, when he sent Sarlow and McCallum out into the storm rather than consider all the angles.

This time I'll use that arrogance against him.

When we reach the Verced lab, I decide it's worth the extra time to replenish my supply. But when I pull the handle, it holds firm. No keypad in sight. Not that I'd know the combination even if there was one. Still, the missed opportunity irks me.

About halfway up the spiral, we reach the hall of interrogation rooms. I pause, my eyes flitting from door to door, wondering which holds Noah.

"He's in one of those," Chloe says in a hushed voice. "Isn't he?"

"Yeah."

All of us pause, and in that moment I have a sudden, fleeting sense of what Noah means to each of us. Friendship. Trust. Love. For different reasons, each of us feels compelled to go to him now, before letting more of him slip away. But we can't. If we truly want to save him, our fight lies with Dosset. We won't get a second chance.

Resisting the tugging on my heart, I turn away and start up the slope just as Chloe pulls away from my side.

"Chloe?" Romie asks uncertainly.

"I have to help him," she whispers, wringing her hands. "I can't just leave him here, with whatever they're doing—"

"You *can't* help him," I say, reaching out for her. But she manages to twist out of reach. "Chloe, stop. We have to get Dosset first, or none of this matters. Noah won't be of any use to us until it's over."

"It's not about use," she says, and her voice catches. "I can't leave him like this."

I can see that arguing is pointless. Because I know what she's thinking—and I know that if I were her I'd probably do the exact same thing.

For half a second I consider trying to dig deeper into her thoughts, to find a way to use them against her like I did with the colony and the virus. Like I did with Terra. But I repel the idea at once, my shame returning in a swell of heat.

I'm not going to be like Dosset. That is a bridge I refuse to cross again—no matter how desperate I become.

"Okay," I tell her tightly. "Just be careful."

Romie clears his throat behind me.

"Should we really be splitting up?" he asks carefully. "It seems to me that, now more than ever, solidarity should be our highest priority. If Dosset doesn't—"

"It's fine," I say.

"Are you sure?"

I glance back at Chloe, who regards me hesitantly. Almost fearfully.

"We'll be fine," I tell her.

She gives me a quick, grateful nod. Then she's hurrying down the hallway, reaching for the first handle. I don't stick around to see what she finds.

Further up the coil, the ship begins to change. Instead of the clean lines and smooth paneling of the rest of the colony, I see wires curling out from a myriad of plugs in the walls, sleek computers suspended on metallic arms, a line of barometric gauges. It's chaotic by comparison, and it makes me feel claustrophobic. It wouldn't be difficult to hide up here.

The doors grow fewer and fewer, and then we reach a final landing with a single door at the end. Silver, like the one at the bottom. Yet, just as with the entrance to the Verced lab, there's no keypad or thumb reader here. Nothing but a camera watching me. I look straight into it.

"This is it, Romie."

"I'm with you," he replies, his voice betraying a quaver.

Behind this door are all my answers. It's funny—I've spent all this time thinking about how to get to Dosset, but I never really considered what I'd say to him once I did.

Then again, maybe I won't say anything.

Isn't that what the Stitch is for?

First, I dial the blast radius of my EMP up to full. Then I reach for the handle and find it surprisingly unlocked. I follow my momentum, pushing it open and sweeping inside with Romie on my heels, one finger on the trigger of my weapon.

The domed room has two levels. The area beneath us is filled with rows of desks and chairs, all of them lightweight carbon, while the upper bridge spans the center of the room, looking down on everything else. One wall is made entirely of glass. From here you can see the whole valley, which is now cast into shadow by the rapid approach of another storm.

Along the other walls are the screens. They show security feeds from around the colony: cadets being rounded up, the panic now mostly subsided. And directly ahead of Romie and me, perched on the bridge and leaning against the railing, is Dosset.

The ghost of a smile crinkles his face.

"Well," he says warmly, straightening up. "Here we are at last. I'm curious to see what you'll do next, Elizabeth."

Chapter Sixteen

My body is electric. I've envisioned this moment at least a dozen times. Anticipated how it would look, how I'd feel. I saw myself powerful and him cowering. I saw myself making threats and him asking for mercy, begging forgiveness for the things he's done. But just like so many times before, I don't see what's coming until it's too late.

Behind me, I hear the door click open.

I don't have time to register the threat. What save me are my instincts—sensing the confidence in Dosset's posture, the heavy feet moving behind me, I duck and stumble down the stairs to the lower level. At the bottom, I pivot, gaining my balance in time to see Romie clamped in McCallum's thick arms.

Sarlow halts at the top of the stairs, leering at me.

"Just the two of you?" Dosset asks, his calm unruffled. "I imagine Chloe must have gone after Noah then."

"How do you know that?" I demand as I backpedal, knocking chairs out of my way. I put a desk or two between us, expecting Sarlow to charge. But she doesn't. She remains very still, watching me with open hostility.

What holds her back? I follow her gaze and realize she's looking at the EMP. Of course—she doesn't know what the device is.

As far as she's concerned, it could be a bomb.

"Call it an educated guess," Dosset says. "Why don't you set down the device, and we can have a talk, you and I?"

"Let Romie go first," I say with as much ferocity as I can gather.

"Relax, Elizabeth. We're not going to hurt anyone."

"No, you'll just put us to sleep, right?" I'm grateful my voice is sharp—almost raving. It makes me sound determined even if my hands are shaking. "Tell them to let Romie go, or I'll detonate this thing."

Dosset's expression is impassive as a blast of lightning cuts the room in a camera flash, long shadows splayed across the walls. I don't take my eyes off the doctors, but I can tell the storm is nearly upon us. The light from the window is swiftly fading, leaving the chamber an ominous, sterile gray.

"Patrick, give Romesh a little room to breathe, please."

Obediently McCallum shoves Romie into a chair, placing a big hand on his shoulder, near his neck. Sarlow remains close to Dosset. Really, it's kind of amazing to watch the two hulking scientists obey such a feeble man. Just as before, I can't decide whether the doctors respect Dosset or fear him.

Maybe it's both.

Dosset presses a button and a shield begins to lower behind me, covering the glass wall like an eyelid. Then he walks toward the stairs with his oxygen cart, the wheels giving a faint screech. I heft the EMP, keeping a thumb on the button.

"Stop," I say. "Don't come any closer."

"What are you going to do, my dear? Set off your EMP and make us all root around in the dark for awhile?"

My face burns at having the gambit exposed so quickly.

"I could fry your Memory Bank. That'd be a terrible loss."

"You needn't worry," he replies. "The Memory Bank is not only stored here. There is a copy. Though you are quite right—the loss of the cadets' data would be most regrettable."

The cadets' data. His words breathe fresh life onto the dying embers of my anger. I lean into it, slipping it on like armor.

I just hope it's enough to carry me through this.

"Before you drug us and erase all our memories, I'd like to know a few things," I tell him. "About the whole 'nuclear war' story you fed

Atkinson."

I can feel Romie looking at me, but I don't return his gaze. I stare Dosset down as he raises snowy eyebrows.

"Fed him?"

"It was a lie."

Dosset frowns. "Why would I lie about that?"

"To torture him. Twist his thoughts. That's what you do, isn't it? Why else would you have kept us from our families?"

In response, he starts down the stairs toward me. When I raise the EMP threateningly, he sighs. "Have a seat, Elizabeth. It's time we had a talk."

"I don't trust you."

"Well, that's understandable. But I—"

"Stop moving!" I scream as he reaches the bottom of the stairs, a note of hysteria in my voice. I back into a chair, nearly knocking it over. "I don't trust you. Just stay where you are."

"Very well," he says patiently, easing down at a desk.

Silence fills the gap between us, broken only by the raspy hiss and click of his oxygen tank. I wonder if there are any electronic components involved. I don't think so. But if anything was reliant on power, I could kill him easily. Just the push of a button.

I stare at the tank for so long that I forget he's watching me. Clearly waiting for me to speak. Just like Shiffrin used to do.

"I asked you a question," I say coldly, allowing my temper to carry me forward.

"Yes," he says. "But I think you've known the answer, haven't you? Denial is the first step in grieving. You know that, at least."

I swallow the lump in my throat. Searching his dark eyes like black holes, like the lenses of the cameras, I don't find the malice I'm looking for. I find something else. Something that makes me hate him even more than I knew I could, choking my fury and leaving only a cold vacancy where the fire once burned.

Pity.

"They're dead," I say, testing the toxic words.

"Yes."

"Why don't I remember that?"

"Because those memories were not stored in the Memory Bank," he says without even hesitating. "They were discarded."

"That doesn't make any—"

"It was a cataclysm," Dosset interrupts. "As I'm sure Marcus told you, the bombs claimed millions. However, a nuclear warhead had never been detonated in a modern city. The result was firestorms like the world had never seen. The fires drew in air, as fires will do, creating vortexes, pushing ash up into the stratosphere. In turn, the ash superheated the ozone, burning it off. Higher ultraviolet radiation meant mutation, diminished plant life, diminished marine life… diminished life in general. Global famine for anyone who survived—not to mention cancer from that same radiation. Tumors developed, people went blind, and then they died. All while we were building the place that could have saved them, in theory. But time was not on our side."

The whole image is so horrific, I can hardly take it. I look away and find Romie staring at me. The shock is written all over his face. But even without it, I can guess at what he's thinking. That I betrayed them by keeping secrets? That I should have told them sooner? Well, I didn't. I tried to be selfless, to protect them. But all of that is over with.

"Not really on our side now, either," I say as I turn back to Dosset. "Since you've stopped terraforming the planet."

His eyes widen and I know I've surprised him. So he didn't think I knew about that. He takes a moment before he answers.

"When I volunteered for Mars Colony One, I was chosen to be the colony director. But that's not why I pursued the mission. By occupation, I'm a neuroscientist. My primary interest was to understand humanity and how our surroundings affect us." He pauses, as if weighing his next words. "Tell me, what was it like seeing the thoughts of your fellow cadets for the first time? Did it change your opinion of them, to know their most formative memories? I imagine it must have been quite the adjustment, balancing their feelings and desires with your own."

His words take me off guard. Yet my surprise is quickly drowned in a flood of indignation.

It's none of his business how I felt. Now that I've finally got him out of my head, I'm not about to let Dosset back in so easily.

"Why did you shut down Aster?" I ask again.

He eyes me steadily.

"Sit down, Elizabeth."

"I'd rather stand."

Dosset turns in his chair.

"Take Romesh to interrogation room three, please," he says.

"No!" I shout, stumbling forward. But Sarlow blocks my path, and McCallum is already pulling Romie from the room. The last I see of him is his eyes, wide with fear, as he's roughly dragged out the door.

I long to detonate the EMP, to do something, *anything*, but I can't. Because who would it even help? Not Romie or the others. Even in the dark, they'd catch me. And I have nowhere left to run even if I did get away. I'm powerless.

Dosset watches me, as if reading my thoughts.

"I admire your resilience," he says. "Undoubtedly, it's what equipped you to withstand the burden of the Memory Bank. But now you must realize that resisting won't help. Not if you want answers. So I wonder: Will you choose to give up your weapon and hear what I have to say? Or will you continue to make threats and fight a battle you can't win?"

His gaze has taken on a new quality. He regards me steadily. Probingly. Like a scientist observing a test subject.

In a fresh wave, I feel the puncturing frustration of my helplessness. If he isn't lying—and I have no way of being sure—he's offering me a final chance to learn the truth, which is more than I could have asked for.

But to give up the EMP would be giving up my very last hope.

I'd be accepting that I've seen Noah for the last time. That if I ever reunite with my friends, they won't know who I am. And quite possibly neither will I.

Words fail me. In the mere seconds that follow, my mind works numbly through the steps that brought me to this defeat.

Because it *is* a defeat. I can't make Dosset talk. Even if he's bluffing and the EMP could destroy the Memory Bank right now, I'd never do it on purpose. I couldn't make that sacrifice for the other cadets. And Dosset knows it.

Yet for some reason, he's carrying on with the ruse that I have a choice.

Why?

My finger works in tiny circles over the trigger. From the iron grip that Sarlow is exerting on the railing, I can tell her patience is wearing thin. But Dosset remains as placid as ever.

I can't see any other option. He outsmarted me. Yet as I carry the EMP to the desk, set it down, and slide it across the surface, I feel strangely detached from the experience. I can't rid myself of the idea that I missed something.

Dosset smiles.

"Jackie?"

Instantly Sarlow lumbers down the stairs to retrieve the device. But as her hands close around the strap, Dosset says, "You may go."

She straightens up in shock, the EMP swinging like a pendulum off her shoulder.

"Go? But she—"

"I'd like to speak with Elizabeth alone," he says firmly.

Her jaw tightens, and she flicks her gaze at me, as if somehow I'm responsible for the order. But her reply is neutral as she says, "I'll be right outside the door."

As soon as she's gone, Dosset calmly turns his gaze back to me. No longer sure what to do with my hands, I cautiously slide into a seat on the other side of the table.

Now it's my turn to wait for him to speak—and in only a moment, he does.

"First, I must apologize for the pressure that Atkinson has placed on you. His quarrel was with me, and his decision to involve you was carelessly unfair."

I snort.

"I don't think you're in a position to comment on what is or isn't fair."

"Perhaps," he says with a mild shrug. "But consider that you have only heard Atkinson's half of the story. You may feel differently once you know mine."

Again I wait for him to go on.

"When the nuclear war began, we'd only been here a month," he says at length. "At the time, all of the cadets were allowed to speak with their parents weekly by sending video logs. When the nuclear attack happened, return messages ceased."

He takes a long pull from his tank, as if burdened by the weight of the memories.

"Upon receiving word of the cataclysm, the doctors were divided. Some thought the cadets should be told the truth. Others thought we should wait and shield them from the news. Eventually, it was decided that they should know."

Again he pauses. When he goes on, his voice is pained.

"Despite intensive therapy, many cadets became despondent. Others were hostile. Some developed high anxiety, suffering episodes of panic, while a few even tried to harm themselves. Yet this sort of emotional trauma was natural, for they had likely lost their families. We held out hope that Earth would recover. So we awaited a message from the survivors."

"Did it come?" I ask in spite of myself.

"Yes, it did. We learned that the planet's atmosphere was failing. We were forced to contend with reality. Unless survivors could reach us, we were to be the last of humanity."

I can feel my anger ebbing as I imagine how it must have felt to be placed in leadership during the worst calamity in human history. Then I remind myself of everything he's done and attempt to rekindle the blaze.

"So you started lying," I say.

"We were faced with a stark truth," Dosset replies. "People die quickly if they can't sustain themselves. If we did not succeed in keeping the cadets of Mars Colony One alive, our entire race would go extinct. Your health became our top priority." He leans back heavily. "The first Revision was a success, though difficult. Such exhaustive memory alteration left many cadets disoriented. Yet the progress we saw was truly remarkable. Disagreements between cadets became almost non-existent. Psychologists reported an increase in general coping abilities as related to weekly stressors. Our main obstacle to contend with was body memories."

"Body memories?"

"It's when one is confronted with the feeling that surrounds a past experience but can't link it to a specific memory. For instance, you might see the face of an acquaintance from many years prior and have a sense of recognition. Yet until you're able to uncover the tie you share, you'll have difficulty anchoring that person to a name. Think of it as the ghost of a memory."

"Like déjà vu," I say in surprise.

"Yes," he agrees. He's begun to take on a new tone, that of a doctor discussing faraway patients, clinical and flat. "Sometimes a body memory can be something as simple as a sound or smell. Though we Revised the experiences these triggers engaged, we couldn't erase the body memories themselves."

"Then why keep doing it?" I demand, growing angry again.

"Because you were happier without them," Dosset says simply. He removes his glasses and polishes a lens on his sleeve, just like Romie. "After a week or two, the cadets again grew agitated, and we saw a resurgence in emotional unrest. So we administered a new Revision. This time we kept the memories and studied them. Eventually, we found consistently positive results by doing a Revision at the end of each week, guided by the memories of the previous one. Of course, we had to rethink other difficulties. With their memories reset so often, we had to give the cadets things to look forward to. That's where First Expedition originated. It became their focus. It's important to have goals. Psychologically speaking."

I push away from the desk, feeling sick. So this is it. This is the big secret. If Dosset is trying to save the human race, why would he shut down Aster and keep us from leaving the domes?

For the same reason we tend the biomes. To him, we're just plants to be trimmed. Nurtured. Preserved. And we're so much easier to manage in a block.

All he has to do is think of us as something other than human.

"You're insane," I say, unsteadily getting to my feet. "You didn't save the human race. You enslaved it. The whole colony believes their families are out there waiting for them, and they're not! They're dead. And we deserve to know that."

But Dosset doesn't lash back. In fact, he seems to consider my words.

"Judging by his reaction, Romie was surprised to hear about the nuclear war," he says. "Why didn't you tell him what Marcus said?"

"I... because... because I didn't," I say, flustered.

"And when you went to Noah for help, what about then? Did you tell him the truth? Or did you keep things from him?"

"That was different."

"Why?" he presses. "Because you knew you could manipulate him and use his feelings to your advantage?"

"That's not what happened."

"No? Then why did you seek him out as an ally? How did you overcome your extreme aversion to him?"

"I didn't!" I snarl. "I went to him because I knew it'd outsmart you."

"Ah," Dosset says, standing as well. "No doubt that's why you used the fears of your fellow cadets against them to cause a panic.

It wasn't manipulation, was it? Just strategy."

His sarcasm is biting, and I have no words to defend myself. But to my surprise, his tone doesn't remain sharp. In fact, his next words are almost gentle.

"You were faced with the same dilemma I was," he says. "On one hand was an instinct for self-preservation, and on the other, the ability to see how your decisions would affect your friends. After all, you have their memories. They're a part of you now." He squints at me as if assessing me under a microscope. "So what should you do? Make others suffer, knowing you could make them happy? Or sacrifice your own happiness to help others heal? How does one determine which feelings are most important?" He holds out his palm as if weighing the hopes and desires of the colony in his weathered hand. "How do you balance Noah and Chloe, with your own happiness caught in the middle?"

It's as if he's still inside my head, the way he's so accurately pinned down my struggle. To use my knowledge to control what others do, to twist them and mold them, for better or for worse—it isn't a dilemma. It's a black hole. And I've been trying to escape it ever since I first woke up with a head full of memories.

How can I choose between the people I love? How do I know what's best for them, especially when it goes against what they want?

Against what I want?

My whole body is trembling.

"That's not how people work," I say, taking a shaky step backward. "You can't just control them. They have to be free to make mistakes and learn from them on their own. That's how we grow. That's... that's what makes us human."

He looks at me now, placing the full weight of his gaze on me as if for the first time.

"Is it?"

And his voice is so grave, his words filled with such conviction, that I go cold.

"Some of us are too slow to learn," he says. "Some of us won't consider the impact our choices have on the rest of us. I'm afraid we simply don't have time for those people anymore."

He turns and walks back up the stairs toward the bridge. I sense that our conversation is over, that doctors will soon be returning to lock me away in cryosleep. But I don't feel like I got any answers. I want to run after him, to shake him, to make him tell me what the point is and where it all ends.

But what would it even matter? Sarlow is waiting outside, and my friends have already been captured.

"So you're just going to brainwash them, then?" I choke into the silence. "Just change whatever you don't like?"

And it's then that I feel truly afraid, because I know that's exactly what he'll do. The fear fills my body like lead, and I almost collapse back into the chair. I try to remember—was I happy before, when I didn't know? It feels like, in some way, I was.

But how deep could that happiness have gone, when it was without the people and memories I cared about most?

"Why even tell me any of this?" I shout after him.

At the railing, Dosset faces me.

"To satisfy a curiosity," he says. "When I realized that Atkinson had given you the entire Memory Bank and that you'd survived, I knew that for the first time I had an equal. A person unlike the other cadets, or even the other doctors. Did you guess it?" He taps his temple. "I have all their memories as well. So tell me, Elizabeth. Knowing what you know now, would you have done differently? Would you have told your friends that everyone they loved was dead? Or would you have hidden what you knew to protect them?"

Even as I open my mouth, I know my next words will be only partly true. Because I didn't lie to my friends. But I didn't tell the truth, either. I just left out the parts that were most painful.

"I wouldn't have lied," I say faintly.

A small, sad smile crosses his face.

"And yet if you can't tell the truth, you have to ask yourself—

what version of it will make the most people happy?"

"Most people?" I blurt out. "Or just you?"

But he's already turned away.

As he opens the door, Sarlow enters, followed by McCallum. No Romie this time. I can feel my pulse quicken, fluttering in every vein. The EMP still dangles off Sarlow's shoulder as the pair creeps forward. I back away, the familiar animal instinct to survive rising again inside me. But there can be no escape from this. No outrunning the inevitable.

Even if I could evade them, where would I possibly go?

Unless... unless...

Now it hits me. My only hope—my very last hope—is to leave the colony altogether.

And that's how I come to it, my most terrifying conclusion yet. The same conclusion that Atkinson arrived at and eventually acted upon. If I truly hope to get away, I have to leave. Here, Dosset is in control. Out there is all that's left.

"Nice and easy," says McCallum as they creep nearer.

I scramble between the chairs, keeping as much furniture between us as possible. But I've already strayed too far, and like a wedge, McCallum has isolated me from either stairwell, working me toward the glass wall. Sarlow plants herself on the bridge, preventing me from somehow slipping by and outrunning them again.

There has to be some way out of this. I just need to pull it apart, like Romie would, and put it back together in a different way.

Now shoving chairs to the ground to block McCallum's path, I reach the far wall. A deep terror settles in my ribcage, a swell like a scream. But I manage to stay focused.

One thing at a time. Start small. First, I need to get past McCallum.

So how?

An idea registers. A long shot—a moon shot, as Romie once said—but at the moment, it's all I've got. I reach down and unclip the buckles of my weighted boots just as McCallum reaches the table in front of me. Floating up like a feather, I take a shaky step onto the tabletop, lean into a tipping angle, and push off.

It's such a quick decision, I don't process what I'm doing until I'm airborne. I go up and up, adrenaline giving me greater height than I imagined—I soar upward one meter, two meters, three—while beneath me McCallum shrinks. Though he strains to grasp my ankle, his weight is too much. With a roar, he stumbles over a table and falls away.

The arc of my jump takes me halfway to the bridge. I awkwardly land on another table, nearly skidding off the edge as I coil my legs for another leap, exhilarated and terrified by the sheer height as I waver into the air again. Then I've cleared the railing, landing on the bridge directly at its center.

I don't have time to feel amazed by the success of my plan. McCallum is shouting, cursing, hurtling through the chairs to reach me, and there's still about a hundred meters between me and Sarlow. Not exactly what I'm built for. This kind of sprint is about explosive speed, the kind that makes your whole body surge and the wind whistle in your ears. And Sarlow is waiting at the end of that sprint, smiling. Knowing I'll never slip past her.

So I have another crazy thought. My instinct is to run—and she'll know that, having failed to catch me twice already. So what if I didn't run away?

What if I ran *toward* her?

My eyes flit to the EMP. When she took it, the blast radius was set to full. All I need is to engage the trigger and the whole Helix will be on blackout. With the pair of them blundering in the shadows, I might be able to make it down the spiral and disappear.

Yet reaching the device will be no small feat. I don't stand a chance of overpowering Sarlow. It doesn't take much to remind me of what happened when Noah got in her way: the blood pouring from his nose, Sarlow twisting his arm behind his back, immobilizing him so swiftly. Why would I be any different?

She must have at least sixty pounds on me. I can't contend with that.

But I'm out of time. McCallum has nearly reached the stairs at my back. I launch into a sprint as best I can, heading straight for Sarlow. Yet my stride is painfully languid, each step lifting me more than a dozen centimeters off the ground.

Sarlow's jaw tightens as she crouches, knees bent, ready to pivot. I think she's saying something, but I don't hear it. I'm focused on every step, on the shrinking distance. She rises to the tips of her toes, off balance, expecting me to adjust course at any moment. But I don't. Her eyes widen and then—

We collide.

Again, I've risen higher than I expected. My knee slams into her shoulder; I flail, catching the strap of the EMP. There's a half second that it bobbles toward me. Then Sarlow has seized me around the waist and my momentum changes. I'm driven toward the ground in a rush.

Impact. The kind that echoes in your bones, pushing you outside of your body, forcing you to watch from across the room. Then oxygen rushes back into my lungs at the same time I return to my body, and Sarlow comes down on top of me, her steel grip clamping on my arm.

But I'm still clutching the strap. With willful movements that still feel somehow disconnected from my consciousness, my fingers follow it to the device.

Finding the button, I press it.

A high-pitched whine fills my ears. The air seems to bubble outward, and then at once the lights go black in a seething wave, leaving us in total darkness.

There's a delay, and then the pain. My whole body is paralyzed with it. I can't breathe. I can't move. My lungs convulse, straining for oxygen, but I'm struggling beneath the heavy knee on my chest, planted atop my ribs. I begin to squirm and push, but a fist knocks my hands aside, banging my head back into the floor.

My teeth clack. White dots flood the darkness. A thick arm is shoved against my throat, and in that moment I know that Sarlow means to kill me.

Or maybe instead of Verced, this is how she'll put me under. Her violent payback for all the hell I've put her through these past few days. The thoughts evaporate with my failing air; I feel a tingly chill beginning in my toes like frostbite, sensation growing fuzzy and indifferent.

A voice is shouting somewhere far off. It feels as if my lungs are filled with acid, a burn in my mouth and nose. I grope around for something, anything, and my fingers brush wire and plastic. I'm vaguely aware that this shape is familiar.

But what is it?

Rubber and plastic. Square patches at their ends. Confusion flickers a dim bulb, my last shred of focus beginning to fade. My stun gun. Did it fall out of my pocket during the fall?

Desperate understanding rockets through me, buzzing with a remembrance of the unit's internal casing. It should have shielded the battery from the EMP.

With what little strength I have left, I tug the patches free and lay them one by one on Sarlow's arm as she barks for assistance.

Spiders of light dance over her, and she goes rigid with a jagged gasp. Then the black folds back in and she collapses on top of me, compressing my ribcage even further. With her arm no longer pressing into my throat, I have just enough energy to shift her weight to the side and wriggle free.

Coughing, panting, I allow myself five seconds, just five seconds to gather my wits. Not far off, McCallum is calling for his fallen partner.

That's it—time's up—I stagger to my feet. I'm so weak I can hardly stand. But somehow I find the railing and let it guide me, limping, carrying my feeble body, grateful to have less mass with my boots gone.

When the railing ends, I paw darkness until I find the door, then the handle. It swings open, and I stagger out into the profound blackness, willing my body to *move*, knowing my pursuer will be close behind.

It's the strangest, most surreal feeling, walking blind. Never knowing whether your next step will carry you through the void or propel you into a solid wall.

I try to anticipate the curve, but I can't get the hang of my newly diminished weight. Each movement ends up as a leap, and every few meters I collide with something, bruising my knees, my shins, fingers, and face. At one point my foot catches and I sprawl, slamming into something sharp—a knife-like edge that slices my shoulder, deep.

The wound is bad, and I know it. But I can already hear the clumsy pursuit of McCallum at the top of the incline. I clap a hand to the cut, tears stinging my eyes, and pull myself back to my feet. My fingers are slippery with blood.

A hum begins, and green runners ignite as I near the interrogation rooms. The Helix is far smaller than a dome, so the power is returning much quicker. I squint down the hallway of doors and again feel tempted to stop and help my friends. But I have no help to offer them anymore. I'll be lucky if even I make it out of here.

I focus on staying upright. Just moving forward, no matter what. One step at a time.

Finally, I see the exit. I nearly collapse as I reach it, cramming the gummy onto my finger. I'm about to press it against the reader when I see that the interface is still dead.

Without power, I have no way out.

The footfalls above me are growing louder, now thundering as McCallum pounds down the spiral. Panic suffuses my limbs. He'll be upon me any second. If the power doesn't come back on, I'll have to hide. I'll have to—

Light abruptly floods over me, painfully splintering in my eyes. But I squint and manage to engage the reader.

Green lights.

Yanking the door open, I slip through and slam it shut behind me. I've just ripped off the gummy and am about to take off running when I catch myself. Turn back to the reader. Flatten my bare, bloody thumb against it. Red lights.

I repeat the process, hands shaking.

"Come on, come on..."

One last time the lights flash red, then stay frozen. The lock begins aligning. I step back, relief cascading over me in a waterfall that pools in my gut.

SLAM.

The impact of McCallum throwing his weight into the door makes me recoil so sharply that I almost fall over. Even through the metal, I can hear him shout in frustration. His fist slams the door, and for an irrational moment, I fear he'll break right through and seize me.

But of course, he doesn't.

Don't rest yet, Lizzy, I tell myself. I don't have time for relief. I still have to get off the colony. Turning, I see a brightly lit hallway leading back to the Wheel.

Now, in the blinding light, I am most vulnerable.

I begin a careful trot, my floating steps making it hard to gain any speed. As I move around the Wheel, the corridors blur. It feels as if I'm running underwater. The breath, the step, the momentum, the weightlessness, all carrying me to a decision I can't possibly be making, though it's the only decision I have left.

To leave is death. I know that. But now I think I understand what drove Atkinson to this moment. To be willing to die rather than give up the reasons I'm living. If I let Dosset take my memories, he'll take away my parents, Chloe, and Noah... only empty space will remain.

And I really believe that would be worse than dying.

I round the bend and see the airlock. Limp to the keypad. Type the code and smear blood over the numbers.

Red lights.

Taking a shuddering breath, I slump against the wall and try it again, more slowly. But it still doesn't work.

"Elizabeth?"

Spinning, I see Doctor Bauer coming up the hall behind me. She looks exhausted. "What are you doing?"

"The code changed," I say numbly.

"Yes." She looks me over, and the color drains from her face. "Oh my god, Lizzy, you're hurt. We need to get you to the Sick Bay immediately." She starts toward me, but I shrink away. "Lizzy," she implores. "I'm going to help you."

"Help me forget?" I say with evident hostility. I'm surprised to see shock and hurt flicker across her features. "If you really want to help me, prove it. Open the airlock and let me go."

"There's nothing out there," she says gently. "The terraforming isn't finished."

I can sense that other doctors won't be far. What amount of arguing will change her mind? Bauer really thinks she's doing the right thing, to keep me safe.

I'm too weary to conjure a strategy out of this. I'm out of friends, out of tools and ideas. Short of threatening to hurt myself, what can I possibly do?

Maybe nothing. If all the doctors care about is keeping us alive and healthy, Bauer won't allow me to hurt myself. Will she?

I decide to take the gamble. Ragged with desperation, I dig into my pockets and retrieve the three empty Verced inoculators. Then I hold them to my neck.

"One of these knocks you out, right?" I say. "Atkinson took two and he almost died. With these, I'll overdose for sure. Right?"

She swallows, her expression now turned to clay.

"Elizabeth, you don't understand—"

"Open the door," I say.

For a second I expect her to call my bluff. After all, I've never been very good at lying. But then I hear another voice behind me.

"Let her go, Olivia."

I whirl to find Shiffrin up the hall, maybe six meters away. Her hair is matted, and deep bags are slung beneath her eyes. For an endless moment, we just stare at one another. Then I hear Bauer's fingers typing, and the airlock begins to twist and click.

As soon as it opens I retreat into the cave-like room, paranoid they'll still try to stop me. But they both stand as still as statues. I suddenly wonder if maybe I was wrong about the doctors. If maybe, like the cadets, some of them were manipulated into doing things they never wanted to do. But if that's the truth, it seems far too late to matter.

I punch the button, and the door begins to close.

The empty inoculators hit the floor, and I stumble to the nearest spacesuit, fumbling with the straps, fingers sticky with my own blood. My only hope is to get the suit on before the airlock begins to depressurize. If I don't, I'll be dead in less than a minute.

Thirty seconds. I release the bottom half of a spacesuit, hands shaking, as the vents begin to fluctuate. I squirm up into the top half, then released the clamps to stagger forward, stooping awkwardly to pull up the bottom half and clip the suit together.

Fifteen. As I straighten, my vision swims, red lights swooping around me, the added weight pulling me down again like an anchor.

Ten. I go down to a knee, fingers working the clamps of my boots.

Five.

I click on my air as light floods the room.

The door is open. A bleak, tumbling desert swirls before me, clouds momentarily parting to show a brilliant sun setting over the Red Planet. But I don't stop to take it in. Stumbling out of the airlock, I make my way off into the wasteland of Mars, moving as quickly as I can.

Like an omen of what awaits if I continue on this journey, the clouds swallow up the sun, stealing the light from the surrounding world.

Faintly, I hear the airlock close behind me.

Chapter Seventeen

I am going to die on Mars.

That's my only thought as I plod further away from the colony, kicking up dust with every step. My adrenaline is gone, my panic is gone—everything is replaced by the weight of my suit, of being awake and bruised and bloody, of knowing that every breath I take is a ticking clock.

Already my mind is straying down dark corridors, wondering how far I'll get before I collapse into the rusty dirt that will surely be my grave.

I can't allow myself to think like this. Not yet. Instead, I focus on my steps. *Just one foot in front of the other, Lizzy.*

Just one foot in front of the other.

Because the colony is in a valley, no matter which way I go I'll have to climb. I can make out tire treads half-buried in drifts of dirt as they wind up over the nearest hill. A rover must've driven this way. How long ago was that? Hours? Days?

I'll bet Aster is in that direction. And if that's the case, I'd say my best chance of survival is to head that way too.

Maybe that's where Atkinson went before his oxygen ran out. Assuming he made it out of the airlock. Last I saw, he didn't even have a suit on.

The colony slowly shrinks behind me as I trudge along. Since I've seen Mars only through portholes, it feels profoundly alien to be wandering among rocks the size of domes, cliff faces chiseled by winds for millennia. Again I'm struck by the wild reality that life existed here.

And that if Dosset hadn't pulled the plug, it would have existed here once more.

How far did Aster get before Dosset shut her down? Back when we arrived on Mars, the atmosphere was very thin. Less than one percent of what we had on Earth. I wonder how thick it is now, if plants are able to eke out an existence from this dirt.

I wonder when it became too thin to breathe on Earth and everyone began to suffocate.

"Stop... thinking," I mutter, the words coming out one at a time, punctuating each exhale. Already I feel nauseous, but I don't think it's simply related to my breathing. It's everything I've put my body through over the past several days. I take care not to stumble. If I do, I'm afraid I might not have the strength to get back up again.

Finally, the incline tapers and I begin to crest the hill. At the top, I turn to take in the valley and the colony once more. It'll be the last time I see it—though technically it's the first time I've seen it from the outside.

Shining white domes form a ring of pearls around the Helix, the surrounding fields of solar panels winking like fish scales in the fading sun. It reminds me of a Stitch, in a way. All interconnected diodes and gossamer ties. I shiver deeply at the thought.

On the other side of the hill, the road snakes down a rugged slope before disappearing into a valley far vaster than ours. And out there... out there...

I stand motionless, staring over the plain. For maybe a full minute I watch and blink, teetering as the wind rises up and tries to topple me.

It's not like Earth.

It doesn't even look like a planet.

The soil is cracked and broken into sharp, zigzagging fissures. An emerald smoke curls upward in surges, as if the very ground is breathing.

As if the very ground is dying.

There are more of those scrubby bushes, much more, dotting the landscape with progressive intensity the farther they get from the colony. In the distance, I can make out spindly trees too, like tiny people lost out on the plain. To my left are hundreds of saw-toothed caves in a titanic canyon wall, the plateau rising in a dizzying climb up from the valley floor, with ivy-like creepers forming esoteric designs in the rock. And there, cradled in the middle of the expanse, is a single ivory bead.

Aster's dome.

Whatever I expected a terraformed Mars to look like, I guess my mental image wasn't all that different from Earth. Despite my discouraging words to Noah so many days ago, I never really thought it could be so foreign.

We were bringing plants from home, weren't we? Plants to inhabit this rock, to create a familiar ecosystem.

What's happened here doesn't feel familiar—or even *right*. It feels violent, harsh, savage, and uncertain. It makes me want to turn and run back to the simplicity of the biomes, where I know I'll be safe. Even if it means living in a bubble.

But I can't. I know that. So instead, I find myself stumbling down the hill, only just keeping my balance as I gather speed in a clumsy, tromping gait.

Is this what Aster was intended to do? Could it all be part of the process? Or did things go terribly wrong at some point, and Dosset decided to pull the plug before it got any worse?

"There is little use in keeping her online any longer," he said. Maybe the world Aster was building was so far off track that there could be no correcting it. From the look of things, the problem wasn't the terraformer's effectiveness.

Yet another mystery to be considered, just as lopsided and strange as the rest.

My head has begun pounding again, making the dizziness worse, my movements more sluggish. I've gained too much speed in my distraction. I attempt to slow, but the decline has steepened, and the red world swirls around me in alarming shapes. Skidding, I hit a patch of loose gravel and my left boot catches in a hole.

I fall.

There's a moment before impact when I envision my faceplate shattering, slivered glass thrown into my eyes, air sucked into the vacuum. My hands go up instinctively, and then I crash into loose rocks and dirt—I flip over and around, tumbling down, unsure which way is up until I come to an abrupt stop on the hillside.

Gasping, too terrified to move, I stare up into a tattered sky just as the sun breaks through. It washes everything a candle-lit orange as dusk settles, kindling the frayed clouds with a soft halo. Now that I can see the atmosphere, I realize how chaotic it is. The tufts of white and gray are carried off like sails in a high wind, the needle-like points of stars only just poking through, or winking between gaps in the canvas.

For a moment I feel like I'm twelve again, staring into the heavens with wonder.

But I've been careless—and it almost cost me. That fall could have been deadly.

Yet there are no alarms. Nothing feels broken. I register that I'm still taking giant, panicked gulps, and I attempt to calm my heartbeat. At this rate, I'll plow through my oxygen in no time. I will myself to relax.

It's not a race, I tell myself. *If you don't slow down, you'll die even sooner.*

That thought sobers me.

Gingerly I drag my body into a sitting position then ease back to my feet. My suit seems to have absorbed most of the fall. My shoulder is throbbing, though. I faintly wonder whether my wound is still bleeding. After a fall like that, it must be.

Now that I'm righted, I continue more carefully, focusing on maneuvering around the rifts in the ground, which are half-obscured by the billows of green smoke. The sun is again drowned in clouds, this time inky and menacing. Such dim light makes it difficult to see.

Still, here and there I make out the formation of striated yellow moss. It reminds me of the ice cave. I take care not to step on the tiny bulbs that poke up where the dirt has grown firm.

Yet, whether from the fall or the memories that preceded it, I'm struggling to keep my mind from straying. I concentrate on just reaching the dome, ignoring the pounding in my head, the painful pulsing of my shoulder, the surreal feeling that I'm not even moving as I drag myself over the rocky landscape.

Gradually the kilometers pass. Light continues to fade until it's almost completely smothered by the swift, heavy clouds.

Then the lightning begins again.

Out here, I can hear it. It's grating, sharp, and atomic. The flashes splay over the world in angry bolts, scattering monstrous shadows. It occurs to me that the reason I've never heard the thunder before is because the atmosphere is too thin.

I check my oxygen readout and find I've already used more than half of my supply. The knowledge makes my pulse quicken. But I take slow breaths, compelling myself to calm down. As long as I make it to the dome, I'll be fine.

For me, the problem isn't technically a lack of oxygen in my suit. It's the carbon dioxide. Once the filters in my suit become saturated, the carbon dioxide levels will begin to rise. First I'll grow drowsy. Then disoriented, having real trouble staying awake. These symptoms will worsen until eventually, I'll just pass out. Then I'll die in my sleep.

Ironically, the same kind of fate Dosset had planned for me. A peaceful sleep that ends in a peaceful death.

But that isn't going to happen. Not to me. I can handle a little carbon dioxide poisoning. It'll work itself out of my system once I'm in the safety of Aster's dome.

Never mind what I'm going to do after that.

"One problem at a time," I mutter to myself. "Just keep moving, you'll be fine."

I press on, and the wind turns vengeful. It cuts low, whipping the smoke into ragged streaks, forcing me to stand my ground. Above me, the sky turns black as coal. It feels the way it did when a thunderstorm rolled in back on Earth. When the world tensed in anticipation, and you could taste electric pressure on your tongue.

Come on, Lizzy.

Returning to a state of survival once more, I hurdle over a giant rock, part of a landslide from the upper plateau. I'm just lumbering down a sharp decline when something strikes my faceplate, making me cry out.

I whirl back and forth, fists clenched, looking for what hit me. But there's nothing.

Then I see the tiny white stone beside my boot. A second later, a stone the size of my fist bounces off a boulder to my left.

Hail.

Without hesitation I throw myself down the slope, running as fast as my suit will allow—which isn't fast enough. More stones strike the landscape, skittering like golf balls into gaping cracks. I hold up a hand to ward off any more direct hits to my faceplate, afraid a big enough stone could rupture the glass.

Ahead, a thin wedge of stone forms a bridge over a rift in the ground. Swells of livid smoke churn around it, shuddering the air like a mirage.

"Come on, come on..."

I charge across the gap and keep running, right past a yawning pit big enough to swallow a dome. This close to the rim, I can see glowing soil deep below, pulsing with an eerily verdant light. Whatever Aster has done to the planet, one thing is certain: It can support life of some kind now.

The hail continues to intensify, each clanking blow sending an echo of pain through my body. I've just made it away from the worst of the chasms when I look up—

And a giant chunk of ice hits my faceplate.

Instantly the alarm goes off, shrieking in my ears, making me recoil. I fall to my knees, pressing my hands against the glass, searching for the hole. But I can't find it.

It takes me nearly a minute to realize that the beeping isn't a fracture. It's my low-oxygen reader warning me I've hit critical. I swear and jab the button to make it stop.

Weak with panic, I take a moment to regain my nerve, wincing under the deluge of ice. Then I force my battered legs to bend.

Somehow my suit feels twice as heavy as before.

Fatigue sets in. Despite ordering myself to run, I've reduced my pace to a weary trot. I'm gasping again, but I can't help it. My air is becoming less breathable by the minute.

Though the hail has shifted to smaller stones, the downpour has grown even thicker. I can hardly see three meters in front of me. I could walk right into a pit and not see it coming.

My thoughts wander to Noah. He's probably forgotten me by now. Maybe Chloe has as well. It almost pulls a bitter laugh out of me, the realization that Terra will be last to forget. But I don't have the energy for laughter. My thoughts are thick, like a freezing river. Each wavering step takes all the strength that I have.

Only vaguely am I aware that another alarm has begun, this one more insistent than the first, though I don't bother turning it off. I'm walking now, my steps slow and languid. I don't even notice when the hail abruptly stops as if someone turned off a faucet. I teeter, stumble, and just raise my head in time to see white canvas a few meters away.

A dome.

Have I come back to the colony? My thoughts are having trouble connecting the dots. I was trying to get away from here. Or at least I thought I was. But now it doesn't sound so bad, lying down in a cryobed. It actually sounds nice.

I could sleep forever and not really mind at all. I think I'd find that pleasant.

Shuffling, I work my way around the dome, only just managing to keep my balance. It feels as if my legs and arms are fifty meters long. I find an airlock. Fumble for the keypad. But I don't know the code. I try to conjure a guess, anything, but my mind is blank. My mind is blank. My mind is blank.

I collapse against the door. Eyes so heavy... I can barely keep them open. I just sit there gasping, idly focusing on the way my chest rises and falls so quickly. Funny how important air has become recently. It seems as if I'm always just catching my breath when something else tries to squeeze it out of me.

Will these breaths be my last? I suddenly wonder if this is how my mother and father felt. If they survived long enough to be among the last. If they died gasping too.

If they were together, or alone.

Like I am now.

I slide down onto my side, helmet in the dirt. I know that this is the end. My lashes flutter. I've just closed my eyes when light hits them, a subtle crimson at the corners of my lids.

Light? Where is it coming from? I squint, groggy, barely able to tilt my head up. I see an open airlock. A figure silhouetted against it. He or she is stooping over me, tugging at my arm, dragging me inside.

Some part of me feels as if I might want to resist. But I can't bring myself to do it. The light changes places as I blink at an oil stain on the floor. Is it oil? Or dirt?

Again I look up, and now find myself gazing into an entirely new dome. One I've never seen before, filled with all kinds of plants. Familiar plants. Plants that produce a great deal of oxygen, such as sansevieria, and...

Oxygen!

Suddenly the alarm in my helmet arrests my attention. With the last of my willpower, I reach up and disengage the seal.

There's a pop, and warm, heady air floods in like a rush of healing water. I simply lie there gasping and coughing, trying to get a grip, but I can't. It's as if my lungs have been soaked in an oppressive wax. I close my eyes, just trying to find a normal pace.

Eventually, the heaving stops. Though I truthfully feel like I could fall asleep right here in the airlock, I coerce my bone-weary body into a sitting position and more thoroughly take in my surroundings.

It's a lot like the Helix. In the center of the dome, a giant cylindrical terrarium—this one much larger than its twin at the colony—holds an Eden of vegetation, the monstrous vines and leaves and needles pushing so thickly against the glass that it seems almost ready to crack.

Moss and algae have spread creeping blankets over every surface, leaving a Rorschach test of woolly patterns. To the left of the cylinder I see stairs leading up to an elevated room; to the right, the path snakes out of view behind a patch of furry lichen.

And standing directly in front of me is a figure. He's wearing a lab coat rolled tightly at the sleeves, a bolo knife in one hand, bandages on his forearms stained with brown blotches. Numbly, I realize I know his face.

"Lizzy?" Atkinson asks.

Somehow it's him. It doesn't make any sense, but it's him.

After everything that's happened, for some reason it's the sight of this doctor, this man returned from the dead who still remembers my name, that pushes me over the edge.

I begin to tremble. Shock takes what's left of my strength—and perhaps my sanity—as I sink back against the bay door. Then he's kneeling beside me, checking me over with concern.

"What happened? Are you hurt?" Atkinson leans closer. "Did he send you?"

Without asking, I know who he means. I try to shake my head, but even that proves too much for me. The weariness from my journey, compounded by near-asphyxiation twice in the span of a few hours, has left me hollow.

He leaves, then returns with a water bottle. With his help I'm able to sit up enough to drink, alternating between gulps of liquid and gasps of air. I realize we've done this before.

Only he was in my shoes, and I was in his.

"Better?" he asks.

A few more seconds pass before I can answer.

"Yes, thank you," I say.

"Good." He seems jittery, glancing over his shoulder and bobbing on his heels. "How... how did you get here?"

"I ran."

"Ran?" He leans back, eyes widening. "You came through the valley? Over the pits?"

"Didn't you?" I ask uncertainly.

"N-no."

I wait for him to elaborate, but he doesn't. Then I hear the hail begin again, just as before—a single strike on the roof, followed belatedly by another, and another, then a sudden, urgent downpour. He stands and pulls a lever. At my back, I hear the bay door's manual lock thunk into place.

"I was just preparing for dinner. Are you hungry? I'll... I'll make us some food."

Before I can object, he hurries off to the right.

For some time I don't even try to move, reveling in the fact that I'm still alive—and so is Atkinson. I listen to the clank of carbon utensils, the beep of a 3D printer, the murmur of throaty air as it pours through the vent beside me, nuzzling my cheeks. The blank sensations slowly begin to take shape as questions.

How did he get out here?

Why hasn't Dosset sent someone after him?

At length, the questions outweigh my exhaustion. I compel myself to stand, groaning, my jumpsuit sticking to my skin along my shoulder and back, as tacky as undried paint. As I come fully upright, darkness squeezes my vision and I'm forced to lean into the wall for support.

I must've bled more than I realized.

Once the dizziness passes, I uncouple the halves of my spacesuit and dump them into the corner. Feeling blessedly insubstantial without my weighted boots, I limp-hop after my host.

On the other side of the cylinder is a kitchen. Empty bottles of protein and fiber filament are scattered along the counter, flecks of sucrose like tiny coins. Atkinson is cueing up a dish from one of two 3D printers. It occurs to me that for a kitchen to be out here, there must be someone to use it.

Someone like Mercer.

But if Mercer was here, he must have given up his post after shutting down Aster. No chance he would have simply let Atkinson inside.

The printer comes to life, clicking and spinning as Atkinson lays out a pair of plates. Food begins to appear in complex layers—chicken patties out of protein, followed by chopped carrots and blobs of mashed potatoes. He selects a bottle of gravy, pouring a generous dollop over both plates without saying a word.

While he finishes, I sink onto one of the stools at the counter.

"Eat quick," he says as he slides a plate in front of me. "We can't stay long."

I stare at the food.

"Atkinson," I begin. "How did—"

"Marcus."

"Okay. Marcus. How did you get out here? And why hasn't Dosset come after you?"

"I imagine he's had other things on his mind," Atkinson says evasively, picking up a fork and digging into his chicken. He chews loudly. "What about you? How did you get away? Did Dosset send you?"

"No," I say. "I came on my own."

He considers this for a moment and then chuckles. I notice his eyes still have a glassy quality to them. Like they did just before he fled the colony.

"Excellent," he says. "This is excellent. Just the twist we needed, to flip things around on him. You'll help me, won't you?"

"Help you what?" I ask warily.

"Get back at him," says Atkinson. "Free the others."

My fork wavers above the mashed potatoes.

"I think it might be too late for that. When you left, we tried to stop him. It just blew up in our faces. He saw it all coming."

"Yes," he says. "But you didn't know what I know."

"What do you mean?" He stuffs his mouth with more food, and I realize how frustrated I feel. At how casual he's being, at how nothing is making any sense. "What is this? Why hasn't Dosset sent anyone after you, Marcus?"

"As I said, I'm certain he's had more pressing things on his mind. Also, he probably assumes that I'm dead. It isn't easy to get here without a rover, as you must have noticed."

"I noticed," I say. "So you took a rover?"

"No. I took a detour to avoid the crags, following a pair of tread marks through a ravine. Along the way, a rover passed me. When I arrived here, the dome was empty."

"Right," I mutter. I should've had the sense to pay more attention to the path. If I had, I might have avoided my own perilous journey.

"Well, I'm glad you made it," says Atkinson. "Those pits are volatile."

I grunt in assent. "I'm not sure what Aster was doing to the planet, but it seems like she made a pretty big mess of it."

He glances at me sharply and then he laughs—high, sudden, and startling.

"Mess? This is no mess. It's life, Lizzy. This is what life is, in its purest form. Chaotic, untamed. Everything doing what it must in order to survive."

"So this is what we expected?" I ask in disbelief. Despite nearly a week of poor eating, I find that my appetite is gone. "The smoke and the hailstorms... you're saying that's normal?"

"Those aren't even the worst of it," he says almost proudly. "But no, this isn't what we expected. Creating life, you can't know what to expect. It's always different. And things have moved at an incredible pace. So much faster than Dosset, or anyone, could have predicted."

Above us, the drum of hail grows stronger.

"Until Dosset shut it down," I say, unnerved. "He stopped the terraforming. Unless..." A suspicion takes shape. "Unless you started it up again."

But he's already shaking his head.

"Lizzy, you don't understand. I have no reason to put Aster back online. Her job is already finished." He looks me dead in the eyes. "The planet has been habitable for weeks. From this point, we just need to let nature do her work."

I grip the edge of the counter, as if by holding onto something physical I can force it all to make sense. Finished? How can it be finished? No one could live out there.

Atkinson sets down his fork and pushes back his empty plate, standing.

"Come along, Lizzy. I will show you."

Chapter Eighteen

Atkinson leads me out of the kitchen, past the exterior airlock, beneath the stairs, and around the perimeter of the glass cylinder. We reach a door with rubber seals and he tugs it open, ushering me into the hive of plants. Cold air swirls against my body, chilling me to the bone, rippling my sticky jumpsuit, whipping stray hairs around my head.

The door has hardly closed before my chest grows tight. I try to catch my breath, but again I can't. No matter how deep I suck the air, it still feels shallow and quick.

My heart begins to race.

"It's just low air pressure," Atkinson tells me, seeing my struggle. "Like being at high altitude. There isn't enough oxygen in the air. Your lungs are just trying to keep up with the levels your body is accustomed to."

Rather than waste my breath on a reply, I nod.

There's no clear path, so we just walk right into the underbrush, feathery plants slapping at our arms and faces. When we reach the center, it's like the eye of a storm: Mesh trellises loop in an exaggerated circle, forming a tower of empty space from the ceiling to the floor.

And right at the center is a device throbbing softly like a sleeping animal.

It's about the size of an automobile—round and squat, with a thousand tiny vents that remind me of gills on a fish, the panels idly fluctuating. The whole sphere is choked with moss, standing upon four convex legs, like a hunched beetle. Even though the indicator light is set to "Dormant," I still feel warmth radiating off of it in a ghost of dry heat.

Looking up, I see that the normal thermoplastic roof has been replaced with the same tight mesh, likely working as a shield against the persistent hail. Inky clouds roll swiftly along. But for now, the hail has stopped again.

Understanding funnels through me.

"Is this...?"

"Aster," confirms Atkinson. He leans against a carbon railing, the final barrier between us and the terraformer. Still short of breath, I lean against it too. "You may not know this, but every doctor who came to Mars had dual specialties, in case anyone got hurt. Mine were psychology and engineering." He stretches his hands over the waves of heat. "Seeing Aster in person is... truly inspiring. She really is a technological wonder."

Following his gaze, I'm again struck by the feeling that the machine didn't just produce life—the engine itself is living. Like the heart of the dome, beating even as it sleeps.

"I was very surprised, and a little disappointed, to find she had indeed been put to rest," he murmurs. "But then I saw the readouts and knew why."

"There was no use in keeping her online," I say, again recalling Dosset's words. "Her job was already finished."

"Well, yes," says Atkinson, fidgeting. "It was."

He lapses into silence, staring wistfully at the machine. I fold my arms. Maybe it's my difficulty breathing, but I'm growing impatient again.

"So you spent nearly a day getting here. What was next? You were going to steal some food and then live off the fertile new land?"

He stops flexing his hands.

"I... I don't know," he says. "I was still forming a plan when you arrived. But your arrival changes everything."

"Does it," I mutter. "And how does it do that, exactly?"

"You... you are the key to getting back at Dosset for what he did to me. For what he did to you!" He runs a hand through his filthy hair, lank with the dust of Mars. "If not for him, the rest of the doctors would know that Mars is habitable. They could leave the domes. They could be free to inhabit a new world! But his obsession with control has led him to push us into these positions. That's why you're such a fortunate asset. You can change things. Can't you? You know what everyone is thinking. You have the same tools he has."

His words are like gasoline poured on the fire of my anger. Because this all feels too familiar, reminding me of the exact way Dosset thinks about me. I'm not about to be used for someone else's purposes. Not anymore.

"I don't think so," I say hotly.

He blinks at me.

"W-what?"

"I'm not an asset. I'm a person. And even if we were able to work out a plan to bring Dosset down—which I'm not convinced we are—I want some answers before we even think about going back there."

"Oh." He stands a little straighter. "Um, of course. What do you want to know?"

"First, I'm not following this whole 'Aster is finished' idea. That"—I jab a finger at the sky—"is not habitable. At least not by my standards."

"It is by ours," he says simply. "According to science, I mean. For example, think of the deciduous forests in the biomes. They must be weeded and watered often in their infancy. But after a time they become self-sustaining. When leaves are shed, they simply become part of the fertilizing ecosystem of the forest floor and help the plants to grow further. So it is with Aster. Her job was to get the planet started, beginning here." He gestures at a snarl of vines held back by the mesh. "Now that Mars has reached a certain maturity, her own weather will carry bacteria and moisture around the globe."

"But the plants in the biomes—"

"Will preserve the species of Earth," says Atkinson. "But new species will grow too, be it from seeds and bacteria hidden beneath the crust or simply because of evolution."

It's hard to wrap my head around. The idea that we could live out here is appalling—and revolutionary to our strategy against Dosset. All we'd have to do is find a way to free the cadets, and we could start a new life out here. Just as Atkinson said.

But as he also pointed out, the planet is chaotic. How would we grow crops in this new soil, or raise a forest in this valley of smoke and hail? Even with all of my memories and all of the ideas and solutions that come with them, it seems like an impossible task.

Again I have an inkling that this was why Dosset wasn't in a hurry to leave the domes. Which makes me even angrier as I realize that, yet again, I might agree with him.

"Let's back up," I say, massaging my forehead, "to why I'm an asset."

"Well, you have the Memory Bank."

"Yes. Tell me why."

"Why?"

"What made you pick me?" I ask. "Even better, what made you steal the Memory Bank in the first place?"

"I... I already told you, I don't remember why I picked you," he murmurs, reaching for his bandages again. But I grab his wrist, stopping him.

"You said you don't remember that night because of the amnesia from the Verced," I say sternly. "But people don't just up and do things like that. There's a pattern. Something motivated you. So let's back up to the part where you decided you had a reason to steal the Memory Bank and go from there."

He half-shrugs, the gesture oddly reminiscent of a guilty child.

"It was during a therapy session. One of my cadets, Romesh, asked me a question in regard to Earth. About something he couldn't remember. It made me question the Revisions, as I do from time to time. Whether or not we should be doing them."

I release his hand.

"And?"

"And when I thought about how we began this format, this weekly memory alteration, I realized I couldn't recall. I think there was a vote at one time. But when I think about it, all the memories are warped. It's not like when he stole my... my family." His expression becomes tight. "These memories aren't missing. They're skewed. And I began to wonder if Dosset had changed the minds of the doctors as well. Maybe not just changed them by simply altering memories, but maybe he... he..."

"He what?" I press.

"Maybe he created them," Atkinson finishes.

In my mind, everything Romie told us about memories and suggestion comes floating back. How easy would it be for Dosset to not only erase our memories but create entirely new ones? In a way, isn't that precisely what Atkinson did when he gave me the Memory Bank? He created new memories in my mind—even if they were real, once.

"He created them," I repeat, trying to make sense of what he's telling me.

"Maybe," Atkinson says, now scraping at his bandages. "Maybe he was covering up another one of his secrets."

"What secret?" I demand. I'm tired of all the secrets, all the lies. "That he rigged the vote? That Aster was way ahead of schedule? What else could he possibly have to hide?"

"That's what—what I wanted to know," says Atkinson, almost a whine. "So I began digging around, listening in on conversations. And I learned things."

"Like what?"

"Well, that... that some cadets have disappeared. That they

were given the Memory Bank, like you, and as a result, they went brain dead. As if their minds were light bulbs, or fuses, blown by too great a charge. They're kept in cryonics. I saw them myself."

My mouth has gone suddenly dry.

"Why were they given the Memory Bank?"

"I don't know. M-maybe to... to succeed Dosset?"

He's growing more and more agitated; one bandage has come loose again, displaying his horrible wounds. My impulse is to stop him, but his words have given me pause.

Why would Dosset be seeking a replacement? And more importantly, if Atkinson knew that Dosset was looking for a successor and that the search had already resulted in a number of casualties, why would he risk giving the Memory Bank to me? Because whether he recalls why he did it or not, that's exactly what he did.

An oily nausea crawls through me.

"So you decided to gamble with my life, since Dosset had already stooped so low."

"No!" he cries in alarm. "Lizzy, I never... I must have had better reason than that. I must have somehow known that you'd be resilient. Perhaps..." His face brightens. "Perhaps this was my plan all along. Not for you to help with my plan, but for you to make one of your own. A... a plan that I could help *you* with." He licks his lips. "That's what Dosset kept saying, isn't it? That I must have had a p-plan? Why else would I have taken such a risk? Only my plan wasn't really a plan at all. It was you!"

I glower at him, uncertain what to think. Knowing that my friends won't remember me is its own kind of torment. But the idea that Dosset might destroy their minds just to find someone as resilient as I am?

The thought is enough to make me sick.

Around me, the terrarium is abruptly bathed in gray light. I tilt my head and see that the clouds have parted like a curtain, revealing an ocean of cosmic jewels. Stars so tightly woven that they could be part of the same seashell, the same geode, one dazzling formation that laughs and blinks and whispers.

The sight is so peaceful and apart from everything I'm feeling, for a second I can do nothing but stare.

And that's when I see it—a pale blue planet like a sapphire, a twinkling ember almost snuffed, fighting for enough air to keep burning.

Earth.

I'm transfixed, momentarily forgetting everything else. And suddenly I feel a chill as I realize my parents are no longer on that planet. Not on any planet. Everyone and everything I knew from Earth is dead and gone.

The overwhelming reality of this is followed by the eerie sense that I've known. All along I've known. Ever since Atkinson first told me. I just didn't want to believe it. I've simply been running from the truth. Repressing it all at the back of my head, sealed away in the shadows, bound in a knot that I loop tighter every day. Like my history with Noah.

Even now, in the turmoil of the last several hours, certain memories are trying to edge into the light. But I shove them away.

"So that's it," I say around the tightness in my throat. "I'm the one who didn't go brain dead, so I'm the one who has to stop him. Is that right?"

He looks at me uncertainly. Because that's exactly what he thinks. And I know it.

"Don't you *want* to stop him?" he asks.

I want to scream at him, to tell him *of course* I do but it's not that simple. I'm tired of being the one caught in the middle. Between Chloe and Noah, between Terra and the others, between Dosset and everyone else.

But it's obvious now that if Dosset thinks of me as a subject to be studied or a plant to be tended or even a replacement to be groomed, I'm something equally reduced in Atkinson's eyes. Certainly not a person with thoughts and feelings and desires of my own. To him, I'm simply an asset to be used. A tool to inflict damage on the one who damaged him.

And that, too, reminds me of my parents.

"We're *going* to stop him. But you can't... you can't just *use* people like that," I say, and my voice catches. My breath is coming shorter every second.

He just blinks at me, still not getting it.

"Lizzy, we need to act swiftly. You're the reason Dosset hasn't sent anyone after me. Now that you're no longer there to distract him, he'll have every doctor in the colony coming after us. If we linger, he'll—"

"We'll stay as long as I feel like it," I snarl. My words drip with malice, but I know they aren't meant for him. Still, it feels good to vent my bitterness, so I do. "Either give me some time to think or go figure it out yourself."

And I storm back through the terrarium, not even bothering to deflect the branches.

I return to the kitchen and order up a feast. Two pizzas and an entire bowl of broccoli-cheddar soup. Then I slam the plates down on the counter and begin to eat.

Some part of me is aware that he's right to be cautious. That at any moment, Sarlow and McCallum could burst into the dome and drag us away. It'd be easy, considering my current state. But at the moment I'm so tired and angry, I don't even care.

Let them come. Let them fall into a smoking pit along the way or get buried in hail or fried by a blast of silent lightning. Two fewer obstacles for me to worry about.

I'm halfway through the first pizza when I hear Atkinson return from the terrarium. He slinks up the stairs to whatever is inside the upper chamber. Obviously, he knows how angry I am with him. Though I'll bet he doesn't have the first clue as to why. He's just as bad as Dosset and Shiffrin and Bauer and the rest of them.

Worse, maybe, for risking my life on an impulse.

But if I'm honest with myself, I know it's not that simple. This is just like what happened with Terra in the rainforest habitat.

Yes, I'm mad at Atkinson. But the truth is, the entire situation feels far too familiar. Two selfish people making selfish decisions, never considering the people who'll get hurt. Not thinking about me at all while I stand in the center, slowly pulled apart from the inside.

Suddenly I feel cold all over, the food turning to ash in my mouth. I get up and stumble away from the counter, back out into the hallway, to the stairs and past them, around the glass of the terrarium.

I don't know where I'm headed until I find the room of supplies. I close the door, and since there's no lock, I wedge a trowel through the handle to bar it shut. Turn on the light and slide the dimmer until it feels like dusk. I'm shuffling toward a pile of folded burlap bags, ready to fling myself down and block out the world entirely, when I catch movement from the corner of my eye.

Freezing, I turn. Shovels hang blade-up in a row against the wall—one of them unused. Its shiny surface mirrors my reflection.

But the girl I see is a stranger. The right side of my face is a mask of dried blood from a cut near my eyebrow I hadn't noticed. When I blink, my eyelid moves slowly, still sticky from the clotting. I reach up and gently tug at a clump of matted hair then run a fingernail along flakes of salt on my cheeks, left by evaporated sweat. Lines cut through the grimy crust, probably left by tears that ran from my eyes as I nearly suffocated.

Who is this person?

Not me. Not the girl I was.

Slowly I unzip my jumpsuit. The cold rushes in, whispering down my neck. I examine the once-white fabric now stained red by my blood. At one end of the room, I notice the basin of a water reclaimer. I pick up a sack, wet the fibers, and scrape away the stipple on my cheek and temple. Repeat the process on my neck, using a fresh portion of the burlap.

When I reach the wound on my shoulder, I prod the inflamed skin, finding it tight and angry, and only thinly clotted. On the wall is a med cabinet. Surely I need stitches, but I'll have to make do with a temporary sealant for now. I pull a tube of Kog from its slot.

The glutinous purple liquid is cold, but as I smear it along the cut it begins to bond, numbing the skin and appending it in a glossy line. It's not intended for a gash like this, but it's certainly better than nothing.

Following the trail of gore, I scrub my body clean. When I'm finished, I ball up the coarse material and toss it into a corner.

There I stand in my undergarments, shivering as I examine my reflection. Just like the blood and grime, my old life has been wiped away. There's nothing left. Not of my old self. Not of my home. Not of my family.

It feels as if I've lost so many pieces of my identity. All of the stories, the quirks, the little things that only my parents knew about me. Every inside joke with my father, gone. Every conversation with my mother, gone. They've been swept away like footprints in the dust.

Now all I have left are the memories.

And this is where they find me. All this time, all of my running and neglect, all of my attempts to bury what happened, have led me to this place. Now that I'm alone with nowhere left to run, the memories come to me at last.

My throat tightens again, and a painful ache squeezes my chest, this time not from lack of oxygen but from deep, inexpressible sadness. The room swims as the tears form, turning white shapes into chalky swirls. For no reason at all, I still try to keep the memories at bay. But it's just like before, with Noah. They won't stay out.

So they come.

I'm back in Michigan, where it all began. Or at least, where I once thought it began. After we moved, everything got so much worse.

But now I think I understand that when we left our life in Oregon, we simply removed the distractions. The habits, the supports. And when you strip away all that noise, you're forced to face what's right in front of you.

Even though you might want to pretend it isn't.

The memories start with my fifteenth birthday. Dad insisted on making it special since I hadn't really made any friends yet. He suggested camping, something we'd often done with my cousins, aunts, and uncles. But mother didn't want to go. She said she'd never liked camping—not before, when they were dating, or later, when "his family" went every year. Anyway, she had a big presentation with an investor coming up, and she needed good sleep.

"This isn't about you, Kris," Dad said quietly, the way he did. He'd face away, not meeting her eyes because he knew his words would mean a fight. "It's about Lizzy."

"No, it's not," I'd quickly said. "I don't even want to go, really." Just hoping it would drop. But I could tell by my mother's face that it was already too late.

"See?" she said sharply. "She hates it too. If you'd stop and think just for a second, you'd realize you're doing it again."

"What am I doing, Kristen?" he demanded. And now he was facing her. "What exactly am I doing other than thinking about our daughter?"

"Oh, I get it. Because I'm not?"

I went to my room to let them fight it out. They didn't even seem to notice.

That night I heard them shouting again. Like they did so frequently since we moved. It went on for hours while I blocked it out, blasting music against my eardrums. Then came the slamming doors. Pounding footsteps. Dad's car pulling out of the driveway so he could cool off. I thought about how I hated it here, how I wished we'd never moved.

Two months later they told me. About their plans to separate. That word—divorce. It didn't mean anything at first. But quickly it became the world I lived in. Mother got an apartment. Dad kept the house. Said it would provide "stability" for me.

"Sure," I told him. Shoving down what I really felt, I told him it was fine. I was fine.

I started living out of a backpack. Carrying anything I might need, everything I cared about. Because one night I'd be at the apartment. The next, back at the house.

Over time I began to realize they didn't really know me. Not anymore. Not what I was becoming, deep down. It wasn't mean or malicious. It was neglect. And as the distance grew, I gradually came to understand that I didn't know them either. Really, I wasn't sure I knew myself.

No one knew what I was going through. Sure, a lot of my friends at school had divorced parents, and I guess they'd gone through similar turmoil. But somehow it didn't feel the same. They talked about it like it was normal. Or they made it sound as if they'd always had terrible parents. As if they hated them. And I didn't hate mine at all.

I missed them.

Who they'd been. What they'd represented. The warmth, the feeling that I was safe. I missed it so bad, I physically ached. As if my heart had been surgically removed and replaced with an icy tumor.

It was the strangest thing, to miss people who were still in my life. It sounded too dramatic, too predictable. And I refused to be the girl with emotional baggage.

So I focused on my grades and shoved it down deep.

But they brought it right back up.

"Go for a walk, Dizzy?" my dad would ask. That was his signal. That whatever he wanted to rant about, whatever Mother had done, had pushed him over the edge.

I guess sometimes you're too mad to whisper. Too hurt to keep it down. So I'd put on my coat and trudge out into Michigan winter, so cold your eyes throb and your breath stabs and the wind is as fierce as your anger.

We'd tromp through the woods behind the house—a swamp in summer, reduced to barren sticks in January. He'd growl about how unfair it was. Spit cutting things about her worst qualities. He hated the way things were. Blamed mother for not working things out. Exactly the way my mother did about him.

Sometimes she'd take me out to dinner. Or we'd rent a movie. Whatever it was, the conversation would find a way to work around to my dad. And then she, too, would put me in the middle.

I began to see the ways they were using me to get back at each other. Poisoning my opinion of what had *really* happened—or at least trying to—and telling me what I should say to the other parent.

Not that I ever did. But I knew what they were trying to do.

The worst part? They kept me on the outside. Even though they put me right in the center of it all, they still didn't trust me.

Yes, they talked to me. But they never told me what was really going on. It was the petty stuff. My mother's comments. His stubbornness. Symptoms of the bigger problems. I never got to the roots. Not after it was over or back when I might've been able to help them work it out.

I guess they thought I couldn't handle it. As if a divorce with no explanation was in some way better than letting your child hear the truth. And the deep, mysterious reason that I finally put together on my own?

My parents were only thinking about themselves.

They were too buried in their own hurt—or pride. They each refused to see the other point of view. Decided it was better to focus on their personal wants rather than on the needs of others—even those of their own child. They tore apart my world. And they didn't even notice.

Over time I adjusted to the new normal. It wasn't all miserable. Dad still made me laugh sometimes, though it wasn't like before. And Mother was smart. Cold, but smart. We had that in common. Only, underneath my layer of ice was a fire waiting to burn. Beneath hers were bones as unyielding as iron.

My only escape was running. I'd leave my problems on the line or in the woods, where I could rely on my own strength of will. Out there, no one could let me down but myself. Which I guess was my thinking when dad decided to move back to Oregon. By then, things had gotten so bad between them, I could hardly stand it. So rather than pick which parent to side with, I jumped at the chance to leave it all behind.

Mars Colony One.

As far as escape goes, there's not much farther you can go than to another planet. Six months. That's all I had to wait. Six months until I went to the Academy to begin preparations for leaving. And I'd never be coming back.

I don't know what I expected from them. Maybe I thought they'd try to stop me. That if I could make them realize what they'd done and how hurt I was—if I could make them see that they were driving me away—maybe they'd finally wake up. But when I sat them down and told them my plans, told them I'd been accepted, they didn't care.

We support you, they said. *It's your decision.*

In some abstract way, I could tell that the idea of my leaving made them sad. But it wasn't because they saw that they were responsible. It was just that they saw their daughter growing up. It was still about them and their feelings.

And that was it. A month with my dad, and then he moved. Since I still had school, I was forced to stay with my mother until the end.

I fixated on running. Others liked me for what I could do on the track but not for who I was on the inside. They didn't know me, because I didn't let them. On the inside I was frozen, the fire almost entirely gone out.

Dad came back to say goodbye and see me off at the airport. But even then the drive was either silent or interrupted by brittle conversation. Each of them still too bitter to be civil to the other, even in the midst of our goodbye.

I never told them that I blamed them for everything. That I hated who they were. That I was leaving because I didn't want them in my life anymore. And when they said they loved me at the gate,

I said it too. Even though I knew we were lying.

Because it doesn't count. You can't ignore me and mistreat me and use me, and then turn around and call it love. I don't care if I'm biologically your daughter. Not then, and not now. It doesn't atone for years of mistreatment. It isn't an excuse to abuse me and neglect me, and then tell me it's an unbreakable bond.

At first, I'm not aware that the images have faded. Then a small, choked sound escapes my throat. I stand alone, shivering, feeling as hollow as a broken promise. The grief swells until it suffocates me. A shackle in my throat that can't be set free.

Staring at my metallic reflection, I realize that what Noah said all those weeks ago was truer than he ever could've known.

You can't go home. Not ever. Even if you want to. Once it's been torn down, it can never be built again. Not the same as before.

I miss them so much. Who I thought they were when I was small. Who they should have been when I grew up. And I'll always wish they could've been more. There will always be a hole in my life that should have been filled with loving parents.

But that isn't the story I got. Instead, all of these longings are overshadowed by my hatred of who they turned out to be and what my life turned out to be as a result. And in this moment, with all that's happened on this desolate planet, I realize something else I hate.

Myself.

Because I'm just like my parents, aren't I? Maybe because of them. Maybe because of my choices. Either way, I've managed to pick up their worst qualities.

Haven't I treated Chloe the same way they treated me? Haven't I refused to see things from her perspective—from every cadet's perspective—all this time? Rather than understand them, I've used my intimate knowledge of their lives as a tool for reaching my personal goals.

Without meaning to, I've become the very thing that I abhor.

"But you don't have to be that way," I whisper longingly to my reflection.

I'm reminded of what I said to the others back in Noah's pod that first night. I told them the reason we needed to remember the past was so we didn't repeat it. So that we could grow beyond it.

Only, I was the one who wasn't listening. I was blinded by my own thin perspective, consumed by my fears.

Well, I'm listening now.

The world grows still as the voices fall silent inside my head. I realize how quiet it is in this room. As if the whole world stopped talking at once. And I'm listening.

I feel a tension start to lift off me. As if the knot at the back of my head has finally come free and all the threads are tumbling down in a wave. Tears well at my eyelids. Just like in the ice cave, when I realized how I could use the virus to my advantage, I have a surreal moment of clarity as everything fits together.

All this time I've been mourning my parents. But I don't have to mourn them anymore. There are others who do love me, who care for me, who see the Lizzy I could be. Like Noah.

From the beginning, hasn't he seen my potential? Hasn't he tried to pry beneath my rocky surface and nurture what he found there?

I can be that girl.

I don't have to let anyone use me. I don't have to bend the truth. Even if I'm not ready to forgive just yet, I don't have to be tied to my scars, to the people who wounded me, or to the anger and fear that grew out of it. I can be myself and be honest and not be afraid. Not of getting hurt or of hurting others.

And that's when I realize that I know how to save my friends. How to save everyone, even the doctors, and finally put an end to the Revisions.

Yes, I have a plan after all. And it begins with Atkinson.

Chapter Nineteen

"There're two parts to the plan," I say. I'm back in the kitchen, having roused Atkinson from a doze. The coffee machine spits thin, black liquid into a carbon mug. "Well, three, I guess. The first part is getting back into the colony undetected."

"I can manage that," Atkinson says. When I knocked he'd only just nodded off, apparently overcome by fatigue. He still seems jarred by my sudden willingness to help. "I was able to bypass Aster's security without much trouble. Once we return to the colony, we should be able to simply enter through one of the airlocks."

"Great," I nod. "After that, we need to make a few bombs."

His eyes widen.

"Bombs?"

"When Dosset wanted to flush me out, he decided to use 'more drastic measures.' I'm simply returning the favor."

"So we're going to... to threaten him?" Atkinson asks uncertainly.

"No," I reply. "We're going to destroy the biomes."

He stares at me while I retrieve the mug and take a careful sip. It's awful. But the caffeine should keep me awake for this.

"I'm not sure I follow," he says.

"Dosset cares about keeping the cadets healthy more than anything, right? So our best shot at stopping him is to threaten that health."

"With bombs."

"With food," I correct him. "If we remove the biomes, the colony won't be able to make enough food to support itself. Dosset knows this. All we need to do is blow a few holes in the canvas and he'll be forced to make a decision: either watch everyone starve or come clean. Even if he wanted to erase what happened, it wouldn't fix the ruined domes." I blow steam off my mug. "Certain plants should be able to survive, even with a wall breach. Once Dosset surrenders, we'll gather seeds from the ones that can't and begin cultivating the new land. That's part three. Or four. I've probably missed a step or two."

I slurp more coffee while Atkinson blinks at the floor, digesting my words. Gradually, an eerie grin lights his face.

"Yes," he says. "I get it. We would be doing exactly what he did to me." He looks up. Written all over his face is what I knew I'd find—hunger. Desperation for revenge. "We'll be taking what he cares about most."

"Right," I reply, trying not to show my uneasiness.

It took some time to pull myself back together and to formulate the details of the plan. Knowing that he risked my life, I don't trust him. At least not fully. But I need him for these next steps, there's no way around it.

"We can probably get most of the materials we need from the Workshop," I continue. "Once we've made the bombs, it's simply a matter of splitting up and detonating them in each biome. Then, when the dust settles, Dosset will have no choice but to cooperate."

"I know just the bombs," Atkinson says. His gaze has gone a little glassy again. "Simple pipe construction. Very powerful."

It's late, but we stay up talking, going over every scenario. More than anything I'd like to slip away and give in to my fatigue. But these next hours, before the doctors show up to drag us away, will be the most critical of all.

Dawn is breaking when the conversation finally ends. Despite our exhaustion, Atkinson seems almost chipper. While I drink my fourth cup of sludge, he prints up breakfast, humming softly as he bustles around the kitchen. The whole scene reminds me bizarrely of someone's father preparing for a family outing. A trip to the zoo.

One where the animals don't wear lab coats and try to steal your memories.

"How many pancakes?" he asks.

"Twelve," I say, rubbing the fire from my eyes. "And there'd better be syrup."

"At least a ration," he says, delivering the first batch in a steamy heap. "Bon appétit."

Now he reminds me of Chloe with her tiny French interjections. To ignore this, I shovel down the stacked cakes until I can't stomach another bite.

Once we're finished, there's nothing to do but put our ideas into motion. While I swap my suit's carbon dioxide filters in the airlock, Atkinson steps inside the terrarium. He hasn't been gone long when the lights begin to dim and flicker, the whole dome swelling as Aster churns back into an active state, sending ripples over the glass in acoustic waves.

Atkinson returns and gives me a sharp nod. We both step into our spacesuits and cycle the airlock. A moment later we emerge back onto Mars.

The sun is white and hazy in the sky above us, bleaching the dirt a terra cotta orange. I've left my helmet off for now, tucked under an arm. A high wind tugs at my ponytail, and I catch the foul smell of sulfur as, again, my breathing grows rapid.

Will my body get used to this kind of atmosphere? Running will certainly be a challenge. Though if I ever get the opportunity to run again for pleasure, I can't say that I'll mind much.

Gesturing for me to follow, Atkinson trudges around the dome wall. On the other side, I catch sight of the trail he took, a slivered canyon that cuts right through the plateau. It must've been carved by eons of wind—or more likely an ancient, long-evaporated river.

As we make our way toward the cliff face, I begin to grow light-headed. Finally, I give in, sealing my helmet and getting the suit's oxygen flowing.

But Atkinson doesn't seem to mind the thin air. He doggedly traces a path between a graveyard of sun-baked rocks as, behind us, a billow of gray rises from Aster's dome. It's a mixture of aerosols, the compounds that so rapidly converted the planet's atmosphere into something livable. Clearly visible in the violet sky.

It takes us a quarter of an hour to reach the nearest cave. As we climb over the lip and down among the shadows, I have the irrational fear that creatures are hidden here. Of course, there are no animals on Mars. But there's a sense of something sinister keeping watch.

Above, meter-long icicles hang like teeth around the mouth of the cave. Atkinson's breath forms ghastly puffs in the air until, with lips tinged blue, he secures his helmet at last.

Now we wait.

Centimeter by centimeter the shadows crawl across the valley floor, etched by the path of the sun. My stomach squirms—from nerves, from lack of sleep, from my several cups of coffee. I begin to worry that I was wrong.

Did Dosset anticipate our plan? Has he decided to just seal the colony and allow us to starve out here?

I run a dry tongue over my teeth, growing antsy. If anyone is out searching for us, they'll surely be drawn to Aster's dome first, especially with her murky plume visible a few kilometers high. Won't they?

So what's taking so long?

Another half hour trickles by and I begin to fidget like Atkinson, trying unsuccessfully to stretch in the restrictive suit. I'm about to suggest we go back to the dome and have lunch when I hear it: a vague rumble.

The resonance grows louder, and then a rover appears out of the canyon, crunching over loose rocks as it winds into the valley, headed straight for the dome.

"Finally." Atkinson's whisper is barely audible.

I crouch down beside him, afraid the white of my suit will give me away. But the rover doesn't stop until it reaches Aster's dome. Two figures get out, carefully approaching the airlock.

Sarlow and McCallum. It must be. I squint, only just able to discern them as the astronauts step into the airlock. The bay door shuts, and I leap to my feet.

"Let's go."

Atkinson scrambles down the slope after me, and we take off at a lumbering jog. I keep my eyes fixed on the rover, making every step count. Willing our pursuers to remain distracted. If Atkinson did his job correctly, the pair should have difficulty getting inside the terrarium. Which will hopefully buy us enough time to hot-wire the rover and escape.

Unless they sense a ploy and one of them returns to the rover, just in case.

I pick up the pace.

The return journey is perilous, maneuvering the uneven ground in our clunky suits. But the dome is still quiet when we arrive.

Atkinson sidles up to the rover's entrance, an extended airlock that juts out the back of the vehicle like the socket of a giant vacuum. While he fiddles with an access panel, I bounce my weight from foot to foot, eyes glued to Aster's bay door.

"How's it going?" I ask, unable to contain myself.

No answer. Then I hear the telltale click of a lock shifting, and the rover's airlock opens with a pneumatic hiss.

Only room enough for one.

"Me first," he says simply, and he climbs inside.

The door shuts behind him, humming with the cycling of atmospheric pressure. I'm practically shivering, both from nerves and an excess of caffeine. So exposed, only meters from Aster's dome, I have to remind myself that this was a necessary risk. That another journey across the entire valley would've taken too long, and we likely would've been spotted.

But it's no consolation for the fact that if Sarlow or McCallum were to return right now, I'd have no means of getting away.

And suddenly, that's exactly what they do.

The bay door opens and both figures emerge. I know with certainty now that it's the two hefty doctors. The way they shuffle. Freeze. Cock their heads in disbelief. Break into a clumsy sprint, charging toward me with powerful, bitter rage.

I'm hardly aware of the rover's airlock opening. One second I'm watching in terror as they race toward me, the next I'm stumbling inside, slamming my fist against the button, and the feeble carbon door closes just in time. An atmospheric readout spins from red to green; I stumble back into a bubble-like cabin as the rover leaps forward.

"Sit!" Atkinson barks, jabbing buttons in a frenzy.

Unsteadily I fall into a padded chair, my legs trembling.

The rover isn't accelerating fast enough. In the rearview mirror, I can see the doctors tottering after us. But we pick up speed by degrees, and then they grow smaller and smaller, until finally, they disappear in a cloud of thick ruby dust.

"Too close," I whisper. I can't shake the oppressive fear that took hold of me at being stranded outside the airlock. "That was way too close."

Atkinson nods sharply.

"It's going to be bumpy," he says, gloves clamped on the wheel. We pass a spear-like boulder. "You should buckle."

We roll into a deep crater, gaining speed as we go. On the other side, I see the canyon already looming as if stretching out to swallow us. I have the paralyzing sensation that the world is folding in, and I consciously remind myself to breathe.

So far, the plan is working. The best thing I can do now is relax and conserve my energy.

But how can I? Last time, all of our plans failed. Last time, I barely escaped with my life. Now I'm going back. And when I get there, I may find that no one remembers me.

I bite my lip, eyes drifting over the time-worn rocks, cacti struggling for a drop of sun, needles like waxed chrome. If they don't know who I am, I'll just have to remind them. And really, what's more memorable than homemade explosives?

I'm sure they'll be very impressed, I think morbidly.

Considering the mania my announcement about the virus caused, this should be apocalyptic.

Neither Atkinson nor I speak, each surely feeling the strain of what's to come. The rover makes good time. Soon the canyon walls are falling away, the Red Planet expanding around us.

I can see the hill I climbed yesterday, maybe two kilometers off. We accelerate into the low valley, gaining momentum for the uphill climb. At the slope, we grind and stutter, tires briefly shifting for traction. Then as we near the top I have the sudden, irrational fear that we're too late. That when we crest the ridge the colony will be gone. Everyone will have disappeared.

We reach the peak, and I glimpse the basin below.

Of course, the colony is still there.

And they're waiting for us.

Spacesuits are clustered around the nearest airlock, at least four of them, stark white against the ruddy ground. Another rover is already halfway up the hill, headed toward us.

"Marcus," I begin, my voice tight. But he's already accelerating and we're tilting over the edge, gaining gut-dropping speed as we tip forward.

"Hold on!" he cries.

Within seconds we're on top of the other rover. We almost clip its side, but the other driver manages to spin clear at the last second.

The whole cabin shakes as we fly down the slope. Atkinson banks clear of the airlock, throwing me into my seat as he whirls away, heading out and around the domes. We pass a biome, seemingly even more massive from the outside.

On we go until another airlock comes into view. This one is guarded as well.

"Dosset was ready for us," I shout above the rattling din.

He looks at me then, eyes wild. We circle wide again, kicking up gravel as the doctors wave for us to stop. Out and around more domes, another biome towers into view. The sun is eclipsed as we enter the rim of its shadow. We're headed straight for the geodesic wall.

"Atkinson?" I call. My heart is in my throat.

His face is drawn, arms locked.

"Hold on!"

The last detail I see is a bead of sweat frozen on his brow. Then there's the crash, like thunder inside the rover. My world becomes noise and madness.

Awareness returns in pieces: white dust, an acrid burning, a deep pain in my ribs, my shoulder, my knee, and racking coughs that radiate knives into my lungs. Vaguely I'm conscious of hands tugging at the restraints that keep me in my seat. Then I'm dragged into startlingly cold air, both a terror and a relief.

My vision stutters, and I see the wreckage of the rover, its front end smashed and folded, protruding through an enormous gash in a hexagonal wall; a rift that stretches up and up like a tear in an immense sheet of paper.

I'm shoved into the dirt. Then Atkinson leans down, his face warbling.

"D-did we crash?" I try to ask, but I'm overcome with coughing again.

"Are you hurt?" he yells in reply. But my ears are ringing, and it's hard to make sense of anything. It feels like I've been drugged.

He's pointing at the wreckage, then out across the biome. I realize we're inside Polar. To my left is the ice cave, and directly ahead of us, the snowy hill. There's wind too, a chilling wind that calms my burning lungs.

But this feels wrong. There isn't ever wind in this habitat. I glance back and realize that air is escaping through the hole in the canvas, rushing out into the vacuum.

"...before they realize what happened," I hear Atkinson say.

The world is still coming back together, misshapen pieces of a sensory puzzle. Atkinson pulls me to my feet and shoves me out over the frozen ground.

But the second I put weight on my left knee, the joint erupts in pain. I grit my teeth, eyes watering. It takes me a second to get a grip. I'm coherent enough now to realize how dire our situation is. So I force myself to tough it out, limping after Atkinson as he hurries over the wintery fields. There's simply no alternative.

It feels like an eternity that I stumble along, knee screaming, nearly falling again and again. Yet the pain clears my head, a tempest that overwhelms everything else.

By the time we reach the portal, I can hardly bend my knee at all. Atkinson has already set to work, removing a maintenance panel just like he did with the rover.

"Any luck?" I say, collapsing against the wall as he tugs at a coil of wires. In response, the portal miraculously opens.

"Done," he says curtly.

He ducks inside, and I hobble after him.

As soon as I'm through, the portal seals behind me, silencing the great, moaning roar of the punctured dome. My eyes take a moment to adjust to the dark.

The lights have been cut, but instead of green, the runners are the noxious red of an emergency lockdown. A kind of underlying dread seems to rise from the quiet, a haze broken only by the rhythmic sequence on the overheads.

"Dome breach," declares a stern yet calming tone. "Cadets, report immediately to your sleeping pods. Dome breach..."

We linger briefly, listening for the scurry of unseen feet—cadets rushing down hallways to do as they're told. But we're far from the sleeping pods, and it's early. Cadets will likely have just finished up with their showers. A simple trip upstairs, rather than a panicked rush from every corner of the colony. For that I'm grateful.

One less thing to worry about.

My suit is making far too much noise, and anyway, my knee

can't support the weight any longer. I detach the halves and carefully ease them into an alcove. Risking a glance, I find that the fabric of my jumpsuit is still intact. Whatever damage was done to my knee, it's concussive. Which is actually not a very comforting thought.

Atkinson has also shed his suit, picking at his forearms as he trudges deeper into the colony. Without the extra load, I'm again able to establish a sort of hop-step pattern that mostly shields my knee.

Yet by degrees, new pains begin to reveal themselves, and my shoulder is throbbing with renewed sharpness. When I reach beneath my jumpsuit and down along my collarbone, I have to bite my cheek to keep from crying out. The flesh is torn anew. My fingers come back slick with fresh blood.

Focus, Lizzy, I tell myself firmly. We have an entire colony of doctors looking for us. After the bombs are in place, I can lapse into a coma for all I care. But until then I need to remain alert.

We continue on with sharp vigilance until I split off at the Xeri domes, headed for the Sick Bay to gather the explosive compounds—and for Kog, to seal my newest wounds. With a cursory nod, Atkinson continues on to the Workshop alone.

I've just reached the Sick Bay when I hear approaching footsteps. As I duck out of sight, a team of doctors rushes past in a flurry of reddish white.

I hold my breath until they're gone, then glance at the frosted doors of the operating room. The nitroglycerin—medically used to improve blood flow but a potent explosive in liquid form—will be in there. And sutures for my shoulder, if I'm feeling adventurous.

Kog hasn't proven sufficient to the demands of my recent lifestyle.

Caution—or maybe fatigue—keeps me grounded longer than necessary. I finally suck in a breath and swing my arms, pitching to my feet, incidentally bending my knee.

Pain spirals up my left side, pushing bile to the back of my throat. But I clench my jaw and stumble toward the doors. I'm on the point of turning the handles when I hear a crash on the other side.

I totter backward, almost knocking into a shelf of gauze as adrenaline floods my body. Someone is in there—possibly a doctor. But who? And why? I have no weapons now, no means of defending myself in close quarters. I can't even run away.

Heart throbbing like a hammer, I wait and listen, hoping for some kind of clue. But nothing is audible over the drone of the alarm.

At length, I lay out my options. I can either wait or try to surprise them. I might be able to get ahold of a scalpel and use it as a knife. But just as before, the notion of deliberately harming someone—of cutting them and watching them bleed—makes me queasy. And that's assuming I'd even be quick enough in my current state.

When I don't hear anything for another full minute, I slink forward and press my ear against the glass.

Strained breathing, thick and guttural. Almost animal. Whoever's in there, they must be hurt—or worse.

I suddenly have a horrible image of the doctors turning to new kinds of torture, surgically altering my friends to make them cooperate. But no, Dosset would never risk the health of his cadets.

Or would he? Apparently, he already burned out several of my peers in his furtive search for a replacement.

But I'm taking too long. Atkinson will have already reached the Workshop and begun assembling the bombs. So, bracing myself, I tug on the handle. Cold air rushes over me in an antiseptic swell.

The operating room is divided into two halves—one for surgery, one for recovery. Plastic sheets hang between them, fluttering in the metered flow of the oxygenators.

It isn't hard to tell where the breathing is coming from, it's so loud. I glance at the far wall, a mosaic of cabinets and drawers. Each holds surgical implements, disinfectants, and, of course, the more potent medicines and painkillers. Perhaps even Verced, it now occurs to me.

But to reach them, I'll have to pass the recovery beds and the source of those horrific gasps. My hands are shaky as I step forward and come to a decision. I reach up and yank aside the curtain—

And my heart stops.

"Noah!"

I stand paralyzed—dumbfounded—and abruptly, very weak. My fist tightens on the white fabric to keep me from collapsing.

He's tied to the bed by the wrists. Microfiber straps, just like they used on Atkinson. But that's hardly the worst of it.

The familiar, gentle face is now bloated in purple and green smudges, dark crescents underscoring his eyes, a thick white bandage covering his nose. He must have kicked over a side table, because it's lying on the floor, silver instruments scattered at my feet. When he sees me, he squints. A strange expression crosses his features.

And in that moment, I know. I'm too late. He doesn't recognize me anymore.

"Noah," I say again, more softly this time. Tears prick my eyes. "I'm so sorry. If I could have stopped them… but I didn't think—"

"Lizzy?" he asks. Again my heart stops.

He remembers.

And suddenly I'm crying. I don't even know why. I close the distance between us and wrap my arms around him fiercely.

Because I thought I'd lost him. Because I thought I'd lost everyone. But here he is, right in front of me, and he remembers.

He tries to reach out to me, but his wrists catch on the restraints.

"Sorry," I choke into his shirt. "I'm sorry. I—"

"It's okay," he says awkwardly. "You didn't do anything."

For a minute I let myself cry, just allowing myself to be close to him. To someone I can trust. But then, at last, I have to pull away.

"I'm sorry," I say again, swiping at my eyes. "I just—"

"You thought they'd erased my mind?" he asks.

But that's not it entirely. If I'm honest, I'm not sure what it is. Now that I've remembered our friendship and everything it could've been, things feel different between us. But how? All of that is still just in my head.

He doesn't know.

"Why didn't they?" I ask, fumbling with the straps to free him. "Erase your mind, I mean."

"They wanted to, I think," he says. "But they couldn't. See, the thing about sedation is, you've got to be able to keep a patient breathing while they're under. And breathing has been a bit challenging since Sarlow broke my nose. Well, that's not completely accurate. Since I broke my own nose when I tackled her into a bench."

I shake my head regretfully.

"Dumb move. All for a girl who was just going to run away."

"Looks like she came back."

"Yeah, well I think she came back a little late," I say. Even with a broken nose, his gaze is penetrating. I pull the first strap free. "You look horrible, Noah. What were you thinking?"

"Lots of silly things," he says, a rueful smile tugging his lips. "It's not true what they say, you know. You should never follow your nose. At least, not with your body weight."

"I could've told you that," I say, pulling the second strap loose. "I took a nosedive down the side of a mountain earlier. Wasn't pretty."

"A mountain? Like, a *mountain* mountain?"

"Rocks and everything."

He stares at me.

"You went out on Mars?"

"Long story," I say evasively. "Can you walk?"

"I think so." He stands and immediately loses his balance, grabbing my arm for support. My knee groans, and I swallow a grimace of pain. "Sorry," he says. "What I think and what's real don't seem to be in agreement just yet."

Even through the pain, I'm keenly aware of his touch. The real-ness of him. Because it doesn't seem possible that he could be here right now, leaning on me. I don't exactly know what to think, but I know how I feel. Relieved. Or maybe grateful?

Or maybe something I've never felt before. The bloom of a seed that's yet to be named.

As he regains his balance, he releases my arm, and this time I can't help but gasp. He looks at me in alarm, and it's then that he notices the red blotches on my jumpsuit.

His face pales, freckles sharp by contrast.

"You're bleeding?"

"It's just a cut," I say, trying to sound dismissive.

Unzipping my jumpsuit, I make an effort to keep my face straight as I peel back the fabric, revealing the tattered skin. The Kog at least disinfected the wound, but the purple adhesive has since ripped free, leaving an uneven line of bloody flesh.

I kind of expect Noah to panic or be stunned or even disgusted. Instead, I watch a change come over him. It's as if he's flipped some kind of switch. Steady and calm, he leads me to the other side of the room, allowing me to lean on him for support. Without my boots to weigh me down, he nearly carries me.

As I settle onto the operating table, he retrieves supplies.

"This might burn a little," he warns, and then he's wiping away the blood with a mud-brown cotton swab, dissolving the last of the Kog. It does hurt, but only for a second. Then the flesh goes numb and cold, and he begins sliding a tiny hooked needle through my skin, looping black string, pulling the wound closed with practiced movements.

His hands don't tremble, I realize. Not the way they would have when we first met. And it occurs to me that since I found him here, he's been talking to me like he used to. Casual and easy. As if we're friends.

I watch him closely, feeling how gently he touches my skin, not-ing the way his hair hangs near his eyebrows, as soft as brushstrokes, the radiant orange of a Martian sunset. He glances up and catches me staring. Unnerved, I look away while he finishes tying the last knot, a ribbing of shiny threads.

"Anything else?"

"I smashed up my knee a bit." I zip my jumpsuit back up to my throat, covering a shiver. "But I think I'll live."

"Can you bend it?"

"Uh, kind of."

He pushes off the bed, crinkling the paper top-sheet.

"Well, you don't have to show me, but you should at least take an anti-inflammatory. And something for the pain, if it's bad."

"Do I need to sign for them?"

"Is that supposed to be a *joke*?" he asks in feigned astonishment. "Lizzy Engram, the most serious girl on the planet, making jokes?"

I almost remind him of all the stupid puns we've exchanged, but I'm again stung by the reality that he doesn't remember them. He vanishes behind the curtain then returns carrying two cups—one with water, one with pills.

"Here," he says. "Take these and let me know if they help. I don't want to give you anything too strong or you'll get loopy on me."

"Thanks," I say. Once I've taken them I sit back, considering how to tell him about the plan with Atkinson. "Hey, do you remember last Monday when I snuck into your pod?"

"Rings a bell."

"I said I had some heavy things to tell you."

"That's right." He looks at me suspiciously. "And now you've got a few more?"

"Well, I was out there. On Mars, like you said. And it isn't what we thought. The planet is... habitable. It's chaotic. And dangerous. But we could live out there if we had to."

He watches me closely as he puts the tools away.

"And... you think we have to?"

"Yes." I take a deep breath. "Atkinson was out there too. And he came back with me, with a plan to destroy the biomes."

"Destroy the—?"

"It'll prevent Dosset from lying anymore," I hurry on. "If the biomes can't produce food, he'll have to tell the truth. To us, and the doctors. We can save the seeds of whichever plants don't make it, then rebuild on Mars. Just like we were always meant to do. Dosset is keeping us here to be sure we're under his control. Out there, he won't have control anymore."

Noah swallows as he leans against the table. I'm tempted to say more. To tell him about what happened on Earth and what's at stake. But it still isn't the time. The last thing he, or any of us needs, is that kind of emotional blow. We can sort it out when we're no longer vulnerable to Dosset.

When there are no more dangers to run from.

"This is pretty drastic, Lizzy," Noah says at length.

"I know. But I can't see another way. We've tried the rebellion and cornering Dosset, and nothing seems to work. Maybe there's a better option out there, but I can't think of it. Apparently, since I've got everyone's thoughts, no one can. This is just the way it is."

For a time he just stares at the wall, and I wonder if he's wrestling with his anxiety again. But then he takes a deep breath and nods.

"Okay," he says.

"What does 'okay' mean?"

"It means okay. If you say there's no other way, I trust you."

The proclamation takes me off guard.

"You trust me," I repeat.

"Yeah. If you say this has to happen, then I trust you. Only, can I ask what you plan to do after the bombs go off?"

"Do?" I say, confused. "Dosset will be finished. We'll do whatever we want. Start over."

"I get that. But what I mean is, who's going to lead the colony after Dosset? When the bombs go off, everyone will panic. They'll look for someone to make them feel safe again. If we set off the bombs, that puts Dosset in a position to step in and be the hero. To catch us, make an example of us. Demonstrate why he needs to stay in control rather than give it up. He can just play it off like he didn't know Mars was habitable yet. And who could argue with him? The cadets don't know anything. We'd have to trust the doctors."

As usual, he's cut right to the heart of the issue. I've been so fixated on the task at hand, I couldn't see the bigger picture. This is the reason Dosset knew I'd try to corner him during the riot. Why all the airlocks were guarded when I returned this very morning.

"So what do we do?" I ask. "Who's going to lead them?" And I narrow my eyes because, though I don't say it, that leader can't be me. I've already proven that.

"It has to be you, doesn't it?" Noah says as if hearing my thoughts and rejecting them. "You've got the memories."

"But they don't trust me," I say in exasperation. "They think I'm just trying to *convince* them of something. I don't really know them."

"Then don't try to convince them. Just be honest. Tell them exactly what's going on."

I bite my lip. *Just be honest.*

Isn't that what brought me back? The realization that my parents might have worked things out if they'd simply been honest with each other? That if I could strip away the veneer of the domes, Dosset would be forced to tell the truth and set us free?

That I could be a different sort of person if I stopped hiding behind my fears?

Still, it was one thing to consider these changes in the solitude of Aster's dome. Putting them into practice feels like an entirely different matter.

Can I really hope to change people without being manipulative like Dosset? Or selfish like my parents or cutting like Terra?

My thoughts linger on Terra and the way we've never really spoken without tearing each other down. How I've never trusted her with what's really going on inside my head.

How I've never trusted her at all.

That's when it dawns on me. All along, Terra insisted that the rebellion would've worked if she'd only been allowed to lead it. Because the cadets trusted her. Didn't they show up in the glade, skipping duties to follow her?

And all along I stood in the way, refusing to let her do her part. Even though she was probably right.

So what if she's still right? If I could somehow win her over, would the cadets still follow her?

It seems now that she was always the one to convince. More than anyone, the cadet who had every reason to doubt me. If I could make amends, maybe—just maybe—we could put the past behind us. She could be the leader we need.

Or our best option, anyway.

"Okay," I say. "I'll... give it a shot."

Noah smiles, then winces and gingerly presses at his bandage.

I suddenly hear voices outside the glass, and my sense of safety evaporates. We both freeze, staring at the curtain while muted tones deliberate. I realize that the alarm has stopped. The moment carries, and then I hear footsteps hurrying away, taking the voices with them. We both exhale slowly.

"So what's our first move?" Noah whispers.

"Well, our first priority is getting Atkinson the nitroglycerin. After that, we'll get started on recruiting our fearless leader."

"Wait, what?" he says, frowning. "I thought you just said you'd give it a shot."

"I did. And I will. Just... trust me, okay? I think Terra is the leader we need."

My casual tone sounds flimsy, and I know it. All I can hear are the terrible things I said to her during our last exchange. But Noah wasn't there for any of that. He hesitates only a moment before he says, "Okay, sure. Terra it is. Where's Atkinson?"

"In the Workshop, hopefully."

"That's on the other end of the colony from the Polar pods." Noah's frown deepens. "If you're sure we need Terra, you should go after her while I take Atkinson the nitro."

His words pull me up short. "Wait, you think we should split up?"

"Don't you?"

"Why would I?"

"Your knee for one," he says slowly. "You said it was bad."

"I'm great at limping."

He cocks his head at me. "Um, sure, but there's a good forty-some doctors out there looking for you. Hopping around on one leg seems like kind of an unnecessary risk, don't you think?"

"Too bad," I say dismissively. "I've got meds. I'll be fine."

"Lizzy..."

Defiantly, I get to my feet. My knee almost buckles, and I can't quite hide the way I shift my weight, grimacing.

"I'm not going to risk you getting caught," I growl before he can say another word. "Not again. All right?"

He looks as surprised by my words as I am. Where is this coming from? He obviously has a point: I'm in no shape to be trudging around the colony, and speed is critical to our plan. So what is my problem?

"Look, I might have a busted-up nose, but you can hardly stand," he says tolerantly. "I'm just saying, you won't be able to run if you're spotted. So let me help."

"I've gotten away every other time, haven't I?" I say, unable to stop myself. "And last time you tried to 'help,' look what happened."

I gesture at his nose, and his eyes widen.

"It happened because of you!" he snaps, finally out of patience. "Do you remember what happened when you got stuck in the Helix and we thought you'd been captured?"

"That doesn't—"

"We spent the whole time making plans for how to save you, but there was nothing we could do. Only wait. I swore if you somehow made it back, I'd never get into that position again. That's what was going through my head when I tackled Sarlow. That's what I was thinking the entire time I sat here waiting for them to decide I was ready for the procedure."

"Noah—"

"No," he says, and I'm surprised by his intensity. "If I'm going to trust you, you've got to trust me too. This works two ways."

He isn't asking for anything outrageous. But I don't want to let it go. What if something goes wrong and he needs me? I can't risk losing him again. And yet, is it really my decision to make?

You're being selfish, I tell myself bitterly. *You're already doing it again.*

"Do you trust me?" he insists.

"Okay," I say in frustration. Even now, using my anger for confidence. "Yes, okay, I trust you. I just... I don't want anything to happen to you. All right?"

"I'll be fine, I promise."

I give him a flat look. "You can't promise me that."

"Fine. That's true. But we're still splitting up."

"Yes, you win. Are you happy now?"

"I'd be smiling if it didn't hurt so much," he says, but then he smiles anyway. "Ow. Really, seriously, never do this. It's the absolute worst."

"Come on."

We exit the Sick Bay, our levity vanishing in the cold, lifeless halls.

It's immediately obvious how dumb it was for me to argue with him. My knee has stiffened, reducing me to a stilted hobble. I hang onto his arm and he guides me, carefully steering my tiny, weightless leaps.

Every few meters we pause to listen for doctors, but none are forthcoming. Thankfully, Noah's breathing has grown less ragged now that he isn't thrashing against the restraints.

Too soon it's time to part. Noah lingers at my side. I can tell he doesn't want to leave me. I linger too. Because, despite his promise, we both know there's a chance that, again, this could be the last time we see each other. And neither of us knows how to say that kind of goodbye.

"See?" he finally whispers, pointing at my leg. "You really didn't have a leg to stand on."

I can't help but smile.

"No one *nose* better than you, bandage boy."

He snorts, then swiftly quiets himself, scrunching his face in pain.

And suddenly I feel a compulsion to do something I don't entirely understand. Like when I chose to stay the night in his sleeping pod just to feel his eyes watching me sleep. It's odd, but in some way, it seems like the most natural thing I've ever done.

Because he saw me for who I could be, before I saw it myself. Because he trusted me when no one else did. Because even without the memories to fall back on, he never gave up on loving me—whatever that might mean.

So in case we fail and I never see him again, I want him to know that I'm thankful. For his friendship. For his trust. For being the boy that he is. And since I don't have the time or the words to say all these things, I reach up on the tips of my toes and brush my lips against his cheek instead.

I don't give Noah time to reply. I just whip away, letting my momentum carry me into the Polar halls, which are throbbing red, just like my body. I'm so distracted by the buzzing in my limbs that I almost don't see Doctor Meng bouncing a flashlight in a wide arc and headed right toward me.

Somehow I manage to bend myself into the shadow of a doorway as he mutters into his watch, then hurries on.

From there it doesn't take long to reach the sleeping pods. Terra's room is halfway down on the right. I let my pace slow, wondering what sort of conversation is about to unfold. It won't be easy. But somehow, in my bones, I feel like it could be my first real step as a new Lizzy.

Rather than reach into my memories for a code, I simply tap my knuckles against the plastic and wait for her to answer.

Chapter Twenty

"What—?"

I watch the tremor of disbelief roll through her at the sight of me standing in her doorway. Who knows what she assumed happened to me after she abandoned us in the Workshop. Judging by her expression, she at least felt sure she'd never see me again.

And yet, here I am.

"Can I come in?" I ask.

Still, she's speechless. I gently push into her pod and close the door behind us. After several failed attempts, she finally shakes off her astonishment.

"H-how did you—?"

"Just barely," I finish, sinking into her chair. "We need to talk, Terra."

"We have nothing to talk about," she retorts. Coldness swallows her surprise like a morning frost. "Get out."

"Just listen—"

"I said, get out!" she snaps. "Get out before I call the doctors and you—"

"Apologize?" I interject. This is so unexpected that she falters again. I sigh, my energy dwindling. "Sit down, Terra."

"I'd rather stand."

"Déjà vu," I say with a humorless smile. I suddenly feel like this week will never end. "You and me, we need to get some things straight. Not like before, when I tied you to a chair and made threats. We need to have a real talk. In which we trust each other."

"You expect me to trust you?" she sneers. "Trust starts with respect, Elizabeth. Of which I have none for you, and you so clearly have none for me."

"You're right. These past few days, I haven't. So let me start by respecting you enough to say I'm sorry."

She narrows her eyes, looking for the blade she expects to find hidden in my words. "No, you're not."

"Yes, I am."

"No. You expect me to believe you're *sorry*?"

"That's right. For writing you off so quickly when we met. For bullying you at times. For losing my patience so fast, and for taking out my frustration on you in the Bolo Biome. But most of all I'm sorry for not listening to you about the rebellion. It might've actually worked if I hadn't let my pride get in the way."

As I'm talking, each occurrence flashes through my mind in graphic detail. But this time they don't come with the painful headaches. Rather than feeling hindered by the memories, I feel somehow free of them. Rather than burdened, empowered.

Terra just stares at me. Eventually, she does sit.

"I once asked why you were helping me," I go on hesitantly. "But now I think I might get it. Because we both had parents who damaged us, growing up. Right? And we both ended up with a lot of problems because of it. And the worst part is, a piece of the damage they did was that we ended up being like them in certain ways. Didn't we?"

"You only know that because of those stupid memories," she mutters. "And *sorry*, but you don't get to come in here and ask questions like that. You didn't earn the right."

I bite my tongue. *Just be honest*, I remind myself. No versions of the truth. Just the truth itself, as well as I can manage.

"Okay," I say patiently. "Let me give you some answers instead. My parents had a messy divorce when I was fifteen. And they put me in the middle of it. They treated me like a burden to be shuffled around or a weapon to be used against each other. The biggest reason I came to Mars was to get away from them."

"A lot of people have bad parents, Lizzy. So what?"

"So, it wasn't until yesterday that I realized I hated not just them but myself too. Because in a lot of ways I've acted like them. I only think about myself, and I shut everyone else out to keep myself from getting hurt. And who cares who I neglect in the meantime, just as long as I can be sure I'm safe, right?"

She shifts on the mattress, bunching the microfiber sheets in her fists then smoothing them out again. "Yeah, that sounds like you," she says at length.

The comment is meant to bother me, and as usual, it does. I try my best to remain calm. My being ready to trust her doesn't mean she's anywhere near ready to reciprocate. It took me almost a week to admit these things to myself—and that was with the aid of the entire Memory Bank. This could take awhile.

Of course, we don't have awhile. In fact, our time is very short. Atkinson and Noah could detonate the bombs at any moment.

"That's why you helped me, isn't it?" I say, pressing forward. "Because of your past and your mother. Because you knew if Dosset made you forget—"

"I'd just keep being awful, like her?" she finishes sweetly. Then she shakes her head, a bitter smile on her lips. "Oh, Elizabeth, you still haven't put it together, have you? I don't remember my mother. Not even a little. Instead, I just have you."

"Me."

"Yeah, you. Every time I see you, or you do certain things, I get this sense of someone else. Someone that I hated. And it sets me off. Like I'm possessed or something. I just want to rip you apart."

"It's called a body memory," I say. "It's a learned aversion to—"

"Great. Well, I have a lot of those, I guess." Her nostrils flare as she breathes sharply through her nose. "So, yeah. When you tied me to a chair and told me about her, it all kind of fit. I had this image in my head of a faceless woman that I would see sometimes.

And then other times I'd hear her voice. Not a real voice. But a judgment. Like, I'd want to eat something and then the voice would say, 'You're disgusting.' It'd tell me all kinds of things. About how I'm useless and clumsy and not good enough."

She pauses, lip trembling in a flash of vulnerability. I feel like maybe I should say something. But instead, I just listen.

"When you told me about her, I knew it was the truth. I just knew. And then later that night, when you told us that if we couldn't remember the past we wouldn't grow beyond it? I knew you were right about that too. I hated that you said that. Because I knew if we failed, I'd just go on being like her. A young, miserable version of a woman I don't even remember. And do you know *why* I don't remember her?"

"Why?"

"The reason. Isn't it obvious?"

"I don't—"

"The doctors erased all my memories of her. *All* of them. Because apparently, she was such a terrible person, Dosset didn't even want to leave a trace. Like a cancer. And yet with or without the memories, she won't go away. She's still ruining my life. Even from back on Earth."

Her eyes, always cunning and sharp, now seem like open windows. The look is oddly intimate. I avert my gaze.

"So... when I told you, right before the riot, that you were just like her—"

"It was the worst thing you could've said," she replies.

I nod. Because of course, it was. Even then I knew it was. Why else would I have said it?

"For what it's worth, I'm sorry for that too," I say quietly.

"You shouldn't be," she shrugs, the edge returning. "It was true, wasn't it?"

I vaguely nod again, because I'm not sure what else to do. It was true—but it was harsh. And it feels like maybe a harsh truth can be as hurtful as a lie.

"Terra, there's... a way we can still beat Dosset," I say after a moment. "If you're willing to help me, that is."

"Still trying, huh?" she snorts. "What's the plan this time? Release a real virus?"

"Actually something a little more drastic," I say. "Atkinson is back. We're going to plant bombs around the colony and destroy the biomes. It'll force Dosset to let us leave."

"What?"

"Mars is habitable, Terra."

I watch the thoughts chase each other around her head for a full minute. It's not hard to guess what she's feeling. Disbelief, followed by hope, followed by cynicism. Considering all the reasons I must be wrong, then all the reasons I might be right. Finally, she just says, "*What?*"

So I back up. And I tell her as much as I can, as fast as possible. About my plan to stop Dosset and why it's so important that when the smoke clears, the cadets have someone to follow. Someone who won't use their secrets against them but will rather set them free.

"And who will that be?" she asks, her expression unreadable. "You?"

"Us," I correct her.

A peculiar smile touches her lips.

"Oh, so this is part of the recruiting process?"

This actually makes me laugh.

"Well, I'm not going to say you're my first choice."

It feels strange to be talking to her this way. Like friends—as if we really are friends and not just relying on each other to overcome a common enemy.

"So what do you want me to do?" she asks. "Line everyone up in the hall and tell them I'm in charge?"

"If you think it'll work," I say wryly. "For now I just need you to be ready. They trust you. And when the bombs go off and the world starts falling out from under them, they'll be looking for someone to trust."

"When are the bombs going off?"

I look at the clock. It's probably been half an hour since Noah and I parted ways. Really, the first bomb could go off at any time.

"Soon," I say.

"We just wait then."

"Yes. We wait."

But as the minutes continue to crawl, electric numbers counting upward, a suspicion worms into my mind. A fear like swirling wind, eroding the edges of my calm, whispering that Noah was cornered. Or that something went wrong with the bombs. After ten, then twenty minutes pass in silence, I can't wait any longer.

"I'm going to see what's taking so long," I say. "Stay here until you hear an explosion."

"What happens if I don't?" she asks flatly.

"Then... you might need to whip up that rebellion on your own."

Clicking the door behind me, I start back down the hall, my whole leg now stiff from the pain in my knee.

Where do I begin? It shouldn't have taken long to build the bombs. Still, I decide to go to the Workshop, just in case they got held up. If they aren't there, they must've run into trouble in one of the biomes.

The corridors are disturbingly lifeless as I shuffle along. There are no alarms, not even footfalls to stir the air. Only me, limping through the crimson halls as if I'm the only girl on the planet. I shake off the unsettling feeling as I duck inside the Workshop.

Empty. I don't find any sign of their work until I reach Romie's desk, where a space has been recently cleared.

Well, the problem wasn't with the bombs. They must have hit a snag in the biomes. But which one?

For the sake of time, I'll bet Noah and Atkinson split up. The Clover and Scrub habitats are closest to the Workshop, which makes them obvious first targets. Knowing Noah, he likely volunteered for woodland, simply because of its connection to me. I decide to start there as well.

However, I've taken only a few hop-steps down the hallway when I hear something. Pulse spiking, I come to a halt.

That's when I see the white lab coats moving steadily toward me like ghosts appearing from a fog, rendered monstrous by the blood-red light. At my back, ahead of me—I'm cornered. And, in their hands, Verced at the ready.

They move with clinical calm.

"Elizabeth," calls a familiar voice. It's Shiffrin. "Don't be alarmed, dear," she says in her gentle, motherly way. "You're scared and confused, I know. We can help you."

I've crouched on instinct, legs coiled like springs, ready to flee. But this time, there's no chance of escape. They're knotted in threes and fours, shoulders forming a blockade across every path.

Anyway, my knee will never allow me to move fast enough. No amount of adrenaline will change that.

"Just relax," Shiffrin croons. "Everything is going to be fine."

And then I see her, leading one of the groups. She looks as if she's trying to calm a startled kitten, creeping forward, arms extended. Unlike the others, she doesn't carry Verced.

My eyes dart, seeking an exit, thoughts vainly racing to find a solution. But I can't see any way out of this. I want to scream. How did they find me?

"That's it."

I almost feel faint as Shiffrin reaches me, gently taking me by the shoulders as Meng reaches forward with an inoculator.

"No," I hiss, and I try to jerk away. But other hands have joined Shiffrin's, and this time I know that it's over.

Whatever becomes of Noah and Atkinson, even if the bombs go off, I'm not likely to find out about it.

Ding-dong.

The overhead clicks on and there's a crackle. Then a voice speaks.

"Hello, Adam. It's Marcus," Atkinson says in his usual twitchy tone. Everyone freezes. "I surprised you this time, didn't I? Or m-maybe you knew I was here. After all, you seem to know everything. Don't you?"

He gives a throaty, humorless chuckle.

"I want you to know that I've placed bombs around the colony, one in each biome. I've wired them to detonate if anyone tampers with them. And I'll... I'll detonate them myself in just twenty minutes. Unless..." He hesitates. "Unless we can strike a deal. You destroyed something important to me. And now I'll destroy something that's important to you—unless you meet me in the glade with my missing memories. You've got twenty minutes. Come alone. If you don't, well... we'll just have to learn to survive outside the domes."

I can't believe what I'm hearing. Judging by their expressions, neither can the doctors. We all listen for more—perhaps a response from Dosset—but dead air meets his words. Then there's a pop and the feed goes out.

Meng has just turned back to me when I hear a beeping on Shiffrin's wrist. Seconds later, Dosset's hologram appears. He looks exhausted. But when he takes in the group and sees me, he brightens a little.

"You found her after all," he says. "Hold onto her. I want her to accompany me into the biome for my meeting with Marcus."

"But I thought he said to come alone?" says Conrad in surprise.

A swift look from Dosset silences him. "I'll be there in a moment," he tells Shiffrin. Then he's gone.

More hands tighten on my arms as the doctors crowd around, as if afraid I'll somehow vanish into smoke. But I'm no longer thinking about escape. I'm too stunned, my insides too numb, like my skin when Noah sewed the stitches.

Did I misjudge Atkinson so entirely? Does he really plan to make a deal with Dosset? Or is this some kind of ruse we didn't plan?

Once the bombs go off, Dosset will be at our mercy. We can make him do whatever we want—and I feel certain that returning the memories to their original owners will be among our first priorities.

So why stop now, when we're so close?

These thoughts orbit my mind while we wait in strained silence. The doctors seem to be looking to Shiffrin, but Shiffrin only stares into the shadows, her soft features tense. And then, gradually, we hear the hiss, click. Hiss, click. And like an apparition, Dosset emerges from the darkness, rawboned and pale as ever.

"There she is," he says warmly. As if we're old friends. Family, even. "I'll admit, I did expect to see you again, Elizabeth. But not like this."

"Walking and talking, you mean?" I shoot back.

His smile is jarringly easy.

"I suppose the bombs were your idea?" When I hesitate, he says, "Come, Elizabeth. We must take responsibility for our ideas and our actions."

"Ironic, coming from you."

"And that, my dear, is the point. After all, Atkinson is a monster that I created and you unleashed." He glances at the doctors. Their faces are blank with dread, a sharp contrast to his levity. "I only hope we can stop him before he dooms us all."

"The bombs aren't going to doom anyone," I say, temper rising. His words are a sliver under the nail of my calm. "Mars is habitable. And you know it."

"Do I?" he asks, bushy eyebrows rising. "Do you? Are you *sure* you know what you're committing your friends to, living out there with the brutality of Mars? Are you absolutely sure that Marcus told you everything?"

"He told me the truth," I say, glowering.

The old doctor clicks his tongue.

"Don't be so superior, Elizabeth. If you and I can agree on anything, it's that there are always versions of the truth. I only wonder—which one did he give you?"

I tighten my jaw, realizing that he's trying to rile me on purpose. To get me to question what I already know.

He watches me, eyes twinkling, then glances at his watch. "Well, I suppose I'll just have to trust in your good judgment. Shall we?"

My captors release me. With the lack of support, my knee falters again, and it's Shiffrin who steadies me. As I regain my balance she squeezes my arm, and I feel a small weight fall into the pocket of my jumpsuit.

I look up sharply and she smiles.

"Like I've always said," she murmurs. "I'm here to help you. Remember that."

Bewildered, I can only nod as I turn away. I casually slide my hand into my pocket and discover the familiar shape of an inoculator.

Lightning angles down my spine. Does she expect me to use it on Dosset or on Atkinson?

Before I can puzzle it out, Dosset moves forward, leisurely swallowed by the shadows. I limp after him as quickly as I can, the rest of the doctors trailing behind.

I half expect to see Sarlow or McCallum materialize out of the gloom and join us, but then I remember they're still stranded somewhere between here and Aster's dome. Dosset leads me to the entrance of the grassland habitat, and we part from the other doctors, heading out across rippling fields that sprawl like a rumpled blanket.

Behind us I hear the passage seal, and—do I imagine it?—the subtle click of a turning lock.

Since the glade is in the center of the dome, Dosset and I have some ground to cover. Neither of us is well-suited to travel. We move slowly, my fingers tight around the inoculator.

I could dose him right now. It'd all be over. When we don't show up, Atkinson will have no choice but to detonate the bombs.

So what stops me?

It's doubt. Immediately I recognize the black, slippery feeling. Even in Aster's dome, before Dosset so bluntly framed the question, I've wondered if destroying the biomes would be an indelible mistake. It's that uncertainty that keeps me lurching along in my reduced gravity until the trees of the glade embrace us, reaching for a sky they've never touched.

Bursts of color begin to show through gaps as we pass from tree to tree. Then around a tall oak, I lay eyes on the glade itself, and the exterior wall of the biome just beyond. It all looks idyllic and undisturbed, exactly as we left it after our meeting with the rebels.

How silly that plan seems to me now. How silly, all of our plans. Even Dosset's.

And then I see it—the bomb. It looks strangely out of place here in this garden sanctum.

The design is simple enough: a copper cylinder with frayed, shiny threads of wire poking out at one end, all wound into a small gray box. The construction feels familiar, maybe one of Romie's designs—which would make some sense. Atkinson was Romie's therapist, after all. Wouldn't he have seen all of Romie's memories?

Dosset reaches down to his oxygen tank, where a black bag is slung along the top. I hadn't noticed it in the shadows. From the dark folds, he pulls something shiny and metallic.

At once I recognize the EMP.

"I told you to come alone!"

The voice comes from the trees to our left. Bushes rustle, and then Atkinson charges out of the foliage and into the glade, eyes savage and wide. In his fist, I can see the detonator—a short metal wedge. Dosset ambles out to meet him.

"Hello, Marcus," he calls. "I'm glad you made it back."

Noah emerges from behind a maple, trailing Atkinson. They're halfway between the explosive and Dosset when I, too, step forward. Realizing who I am, they both stop short.

"Lizzy?" Atkinson asks in disbelief. "W-what are you doing here?"

"I asked her to come along. Given the part she played in all of this, I thought it only fitting that she attend. Don't you agree?" asks Dosset.

A current of wind ripples through the trees, stirred up by the distant pollen fans. Atkinson doesn't speak. He's looking at the EMP. Probably thinking the same thing I am. That if the device goes off and the bombs don't detonate, we lose all of our leverage. We need to back away and detonate *right now*.

But still, he hesitates.

"Yes," Dosset says. "An electromagnetic pulse. Truly, Romesh is one of our brightest. With a knack for making dangerous things. Tell me, what would happen if I were to set it off? Would your detonator be rendered useless? Would your bombs?"

As he turns the block nervously in his hands, Atkinson's face wrinkles with uncertainty. "I suppose there's only one way to find an answer. Why not try and see?"

"For the same reason you haven't detonated the bombs," says Dosset placidly. "These tools are simply a means for threatening one another. But you and I both know you don't want to destroy these biomes. If you did, you would've already done it. Some part of you—the dominant part, I believe—wants to end this peaceably. More than anything, Marcus, you want peace. Just like me. And I can give it to you."

"I want my family!" Atkinson shouts at him as he waves the detonator. I can't help but gasp, afraid he might accidentally set it off with Noah so close. "Can you give them to me? I want my family!"

Dosset manages to remain calm.

"No, Marcus. You don't."

"What did you say?" Atkinson breathes, aghast.

"Your family is dead. You know that. What you want is peace with their death. Isn't that what we've given these cadets so many times over these months? Cadets like Elizabeth?" He gestures at me. "And you were happy to give it."

"Does she seem at peace to you, Adam?" Atkinson's voice roils with emotion. "Do I? You took away my reason to live!" His whole body trembles as he screams at the older man. "What other memories have you warped for your benefit? What else have you taken?"

Watching them go back and forth, I have an image in my mind of two animals tearing at each other. Ripping bits of flesh, drawing blood, matching wound for wound, but never enough to kill, only to maim.

I'm reminded of my parents. Of me and Terra. And suddenly I realize that I'm again caught in the middle.

Again, this won't end if someone doesn't step in to end it.

"Okay, enough."

They don't hear at first, so I step forward and raise my voice as loud as I can manage. "I said *stop!*"

Surprised, they falter—both of them.

"Whatever you two might believe, you're wrong. You're both hurting the people you think you're protecting."

"Elizabeth—"

"No. Now you listen. Dosset,"—I turn on him—"you think you're saving the human race, keeping us locked in here. But you aren't. All of us, every cadet—we're miserable. Only, the others don't know why. Because you took away the reason. Which means no matter how much we might want to change, no matter how hard we try, we'll always be stuck living out the same problems, stuck with the same habits, over and over. All because you can't trust anyone. Instead, you just control them like they're robots. But that's not life. It's abuse."

I wheel to face Atkinson.

"And you... you think you're so much better than him? You could've killed me when you uploaded the Memory Bank that night. You said it yourself. The other cadets went brain dead after Dosset put them through the same procedure. But because you wanted answers, to find out what he was doing, you risked someone else's life. You risked *my* life."

"Is that what he told you?" Dosset asks, sounding amused.

"That's the truth."

"Elizabeth, when will you learn? Not all wolves hunt in the shadows. Some of us are happy to bare our teeth. Some of us *know* what we are." He smiles pleasantly as he turns to Atkinson. "Others, well... they would rather deceive themselves."

"I'm not like you," Atkinson says, withdrawing. He nearly trips over a honeysuckle bush but manages to catch his balance. "I'm not like you."

"You see, Marcus was the one behind *all* of the brain-damaged cadets, not just your own experience. He was the one who destroyed their neural pathways. I simply placed them into the cryobeds to keep them alive."

"I... I knew he was up to s-something," Atkinson pleads, looking to me now. "I tried to find out what it was, but—"

"We tried to stop him, of course," Dosset interrupts. "But it took time to figure out what was going on. Why cadets were being found in their pods on Monday morning, eyes vacant, devoid of brain activity. You see, he chose them at random to prevent any tie back to him."

The words cut a trench through my heart, filling me with disbelief.

"Is that true?" I whisper.

"Lizzy, I—"

"The night he chose you, Elizabeth, was the night we finally figured out what he was doing," says Dosset, sighing as he steps toward Atkinson. "But when we caught up with him, he had already given you the Memory Bank. And rather than face responsibility for his actions, he took a double dose of Verced to erase the evidence from his mind. Or perhaps he was simply attempting suicide, to take a coward's way out."

"You don't know!" Atkinson croaks. "You draw your conclusions and call them facts. But you could have given me the dose yourself, and who could argue? None of us remember!"

"So I decided to make him disappear," Dosset murmurs, unfazed by the outburst. "Just like I made all his victims disappear. A fitting punishment for an unforgivable crime, wasting life that way." He shakes his head as if saddened by the memory of the lost cadets. "But it would seem, Elizabeth, that he told you only half the truth. Just like you did to your friends, such as Noah here, when you kept secrets. Isn't that right?"

Heat creeps up my neck, exposing the validity of his words. I glance at Noah and see the questions written on his face, just like with Romie. I want to tell him that I can explain. But the words turn to dust.

Even if it's only part of the truth, it's still the truth. Isn't it?

"You see, you both had the same choices I did," Dosset continues. "The same choices you have now. And I believe that, regardless of the EMP, you'll make the right one."

"She made the choices she had to make, and so did I," Atkinson gasps. "The choices you forced us to make!"

"No, Marcus. No one is forcing you to do this. In fact, you don't *want* to do these things. You don't really want to condemn us all to a life out there in this infant ecology. You know how hard it will be. The kind of suffering it will cause. The death. You've already seen it yourself. Are you really willing to go to these lengths just to cling to the past? Are you willing to hurt everyone on this planet? Think of the cadets whose lives you already ruined. Think of Elizabeth and all of the pain you've caused her."

"No," I say, finally recovering my voice. "That isn't how it is. He would never have done any of this if not for you."

"And that justifies him?" Dosset prods. "You said it yourself—he risked your life, all for selfish reasons. You can argue if you like, but you know the truth."

But I've finally stopped listening.

"He's manipulating you," I say, turning back to Atkinson. "If we don't go through with this, he'll keep the system going like before. You can't trust him. Just detonate the bombs before it's too late! Marcus—" I snap my fingers at him, finally locking his gaze onto mine. "You can't let him win. He's a liar!"

Atkinson looks at the bomb and takes a labored breath. When

he raises his head, tears are etching streaks on his weathered face.

He doesn't look at me now. Only at Dosset.

"But my family..." he chokes out.

"...is gone," Dosset finishes, stepping closer. His voice is bright and warm as a sunbeam. "It was your memory of them that drove you to this place of fear and violence. You've become the very thing we knew the cadets would become—a product of emotion. One that could destroy everything we've worked so hard to build." Another step. "You don't have to be this way."

"Marcus," I begin again, but he still won't look at me. I dig into my pocket, seizing the Verced. Across the clearing, I see that Noah's fists are balled white.

"My family," Atkinson moans. "My family, my family..."

"Yes, your family," Dosset says. He's only centimeters from Atkinson now. "Sometimes it's better not to know, Marcus. Sometimes it's too much. It can be better to simply forget."

His whole body trembling, Atkinson lifts his arm like a withered tree limb. Head bowed, he places the detonator in Dosset's palm. I watch our very last hope trade hands. Then I pop the cap on the Verced.

It's time to move. Time to act. My heart is pounding so loud, I'm sure they can hear it. I step from the shade with a deliberate stride, ignoring the blade in my knee.

"Yes," Atkinson croaks. "Sometimes we have to forget."

Dosset's fingers close around the detonator. I see that Noah has begun to move—

And then Atkinson whips his head up, eyes clear as glass.

"But sometimes we have to remember."

With one hand he reaches out and tears the cords from the oxygen tank, pulling them free, wrapping them around Dosset's throat, and around and around. I freeze in disbelief, my feet rooted to the spot. Feeling as if I'm watching from somewhere else, somehow far away.

Atkinson jerks Dosset backward by the neck, making his head

bounce up and down sharply, horrifying and unnatural. I find myself shouting, moving again, Noah with me, and we try to pull Dosset away. But Atkinson uses the body as a shield, dragging it, limp, too limp, Dosset's face quickly shifting from pale to purple.

Finally, I get a grip on Dosset's arm, and then Noah as well. I'm not much help, weighing so little, hanging on like a feather in a storm. But with the combined mass of all four of us we go over, a hysteria of shoving and fists and pulling—and the noise and the noise and the noise—and I manage to get the inoculator into Atkinson's forearm at last.

His hands shudder and release, and Dosset falls away.

"*Why?*" I scream at Atkinson, raving. "Why did you do that? What is wrong with you?"

I hardly know what I'm saying. My whole body quivers as beside me, Noah tries to unwind the cords. But Dosset's eyes are vacant. My mind can't understand it.

He can't be dead.

Atkinson is whimpering something.

"What?" I demand, gripping him, fevered.

"I never t-trusted him to let us be free," he says, looking up at me with his cloudy eyes again, shaking with a palsy. Already he's growing faint. "I n-never trusted him. So I called him here. And I set the bombs to go off in twenty minutes."

My mind is stuck. All I can think about is Dosset's body lying next to me in the grass. That it might only be a body now. I can't make sense of anything, least of all Atkinson's words.

"He's not breathing," Noah shouts up at me, his face near Dosset's mouth. "I can't get a pulse." And then he begins chest compressions and emergency breathing, and I fear I might throw up. I turn back to Atkinson.

"What are you talking about?" I choke, shaking him by the shoulders. He cowers like a child beneath me.

"The detonator," he whispers. "It was a fake. The b-bombs are on a timer. I set them for twenty minutes. Twenty... minutes."

And then his eyelids flitter and close.

Everything seems to stop. I look up, his words bridging a connection that my mind has been too battered to make. Atkinson telling Dosset that he had twenty minutes. Using Dosset's own motivation to bring him close enough for this. To make him vulnerable.

I don't have space for words or movement, just a second to feel numb fireflies filling my lungs and throat, dotting my vision like embers. I see Noah placing his hands on Dosset's ribs, beginning another round of compressions. Dosset's horrible face, swollen and blue. It's a moment of perfect clarity, ingrained.

There can be no erasing this. The white eyelashes, the weight of the pollen, the clinging jumpsuit, the blotched skin, the cracked lips, the breathing that comes so heavy, the breathing that comes no more.

It all catches up with me at once.

"Noah!" I scream, starting toward him. "We've got to—"

That's when the bombs go off.

From behind the force takes me, lifting me off my feet and throwing me with the power of a jet engine. It feels like I'm airborne for an eternity.

I find myself in the grass, the world shaking under me. I realize that all I can hear is a faint ringing, like a far-off alarm, meaningless. I try to sit up, but my vision swims and I find myself lying back in the grass, nausea wringing my gut.

When I manage to steady myself and look up, I see Noah. Far away, his face streaked with his own blood, staring dazedly at the world around him. Cool air rips past me, drying icy tears on my cheeks. It's strangely refreshing. Then, just as in the Polar Biome, I see the reason.

Burned trees like charcoal prongs, licked by tongues of fire. Scorched grass and flowers, bowed and flattened around a sunken crater. The pillowy dome canvas riven, a gaping fissure streaking upward in a jagged line, and the dissonant sight of swirling dust and the red-white rocks of Mars.

It feels as if I've been transported to a different world, my brain unable to link what I'm seeing now to the glade of a second before. I'm numb and dizzy. I can't understand any of this. It isn't real.

Again I turn to Noah, but now he's lying facedown in the grass, unmoving. *No, no, no, no, no*—my heart lurches, and I crawl on my hands and knees, trying to reach him.

Then I see them: the white coats. Doctors running, two kneeling by Noah, and I shriek at them to leave him alone until my throat aches. But I'm still too far away, my world still ringing with cold silence. The doctors see me, and then there are more of them, all around.

Hands are lifting me easily, carrying me away. I thrash and twist, but I have no strength left. I see them take Noah. As I'm spirited off, all I can think is that he can't be sedated. He won't be able to breathe.

The hallways go by in a white, senseless flash. When I reach the Sick Bay I'm laid out on a surgical table. Doctors whirl above me. I can barely keep my eyes open. Did they give me Verced? I don't know. I can't remember.

The world feels distant and cold. All I can think is that it's over. If Dosset is dead and the bombs have gone off, then we won. Didn't we?

"It's over," I whisper.

And that's my final thought. My vision blurs and the world goes still as the darkness opens like a flower.

Chapter Twenty-One

Dreams are meaningless. That's the official scientific theory. Involuntary, random blips on an electroencephalogram. When I was a child, they sometimes brought me joy. Or adventure. More often, they caused me terror.

And all of it meant nothing.

Nerve endings. That's what it all comes down to. Billions of rooted synapses, like trees entwined in erratic soil. Lightning strikes every millionth of a second, the charges scattering across the gaps and down a spinal braid.

I once learned that lightning almost never hits the same place twice. Three times, four times—the odds are astronomical. It would be nothing short of miraculous for repeated bolts to strike the same spot.

So what miracle brought us to this place? That the human brain can not only experience these flashes of brilliance, but change them as we see fit? How wasted on people who regard it as a thing to be controlled.

How wasted on me.

This is my unconscious reverie, floating between wakefulness and sleep, where I'm not quite able to get it straight. All these troubling thoughts that keep spinning around my head on an axis, over and over in sickening orbit.

Dosset is surely dead.

And I could have saved him.

I can see the exact moment that he died, when Atkinson ripped the oxygen tubes from his nose and wound them around like a garrote. When his feeble neck probably snapped, jarred by a single, swift motion.

And I wonder—is this cryosleep? Is this what I'll be seeing for the rest of my life? A lucid, continuous loop of a gruesome murder?

A murder that I contributed to. If not for me, Atkinson would have simply disappeared. And I would've vanished with him. If I'd acted sooner, I might have inoculated him before he was able to end a life.

Next, I see Noah lying motionless in the grass. And I know that this, too, is my fault. Then it all fades to black, and lazily, carelessly, the sequence begins again.

I wonder if Dosset's death changed anything. If the doctors will just erase my mind, not knowing what else to do. If Terra tried to take control, or if our shaky truce was simply an act.

Maybe this nebulous state is a kind of punishment. Maybe they've decided to leave me here in an endless theater of horror. Torture for all the pain I've caused.

Because really, it is torture. To not only see all your mistakes so vividly, but to be forced to relive them. No hope of moving on. No way to change or begin again.

Voices echo in the corners of my mind, though I don't know whether they're dreams or memories. At times I feel a pressure in my wrist, a dull pain in my arm, a tickle of air across my forehead. But when I strain to open my eyes, I drift away, lost in a swirl of dust.

Dust, dust. We all live in a world of dust.

In the end, how much dust can a body make? Little specks of death. Measuring life in millimeters. Dancing in a careless bar of sun, one last twirl before they join the rest in the layered waste of existence.

Though in a certain way, I guess dust is evidence of the new life that we're making. Every single day, we shed the past and start again.

Everyone but me. Now my life is only memories.

Like saltwater, wakefulness bears me up. When I fully rise from my stupor, I find myself in a white bed with a curtain pulled around. All I can hear is the distant thrum of an oxygenator, more labored than I remember, like the wheeze of tired lungs. Someone has dimmed the ceiling tiles to a twilight glow.

I move to stand, but my wrists are caught by restraints.

"Hello?" I say in a rusty voice hardly above a whisper.

As much as I'm able, I crane my neck to see beyond the moth-like tremble of the curtain. But I can't reach far enough.

What day is it? What's happened since the bomb went off? Was the Revision carried out? I still remember everything, so they can't have erased my mind—yet.

Maybe again, as with Noah, they've had to wait until I'm healthy enough to endure the procedure.

When I try speaking again, my voice is a little louder.

"Is anyone there?"

I hear a clatter, then quick footsteps. Abruptly Chloe is at my bedside, looking down at me, catching her breath in relief.

At first, I can't believe it's really her. But she's sitting on the edge of my bed, and she's wrapping her arms around me. I can't think of anything to say, I'm so overwhelmed. Then my disbelief abruptly dissolves into tears of relief, and she runs her fingers through my tangled hair, whispering softly.

"Oh, Lizzy," she murmurs. "It's okay. Shh, it's okay, it's over. You're safe now."

I laugh, pulling back to look at her. It feels so good to hear her say those words that I just keep laughing.

"What's so funny?" She puts a hand to my forehead in concern.

"Nothing," I say, wiping my nose. "Just... you. Always trying to comfort me."

"Someone has to bring you up for air," she says with a small smile. She looks weary. And changed in some way. Maybe a shade of innocence gone from her eyes.

My last memories come flooding back, and I suddenly realize that she's here with me, when last I knew she'd been locked inside the Helix.

"Wait, Chloe... what... what's going on?" I drop my hands. The buckles rattle as they fall. "Why am I tied down? What happened with—"

She shushes me, beginning to pull the straps free. "We had to keep you still. You kept thrashing in your sleep, and we were afraid you would pull the tubes loose."

"Tubes?"

It's then that I notice them connected to my left arm. A deep blue liquid flows around a yellowed bruise and into my body. "What is that?"

"Visce... Viscerect?" she says uncertainly. "It's to speed up your recovery. The doctors said you lost a lot of blood."

One arm free of the restraint, I begin massaging my wrist to get some feeling back into it. "Dosset's dead, isn't he?"

Chloe nods gravely.

"Atkinson broke his neck when he tried to... to choke him. He was frail, we all knew." The way she looks at me, it's as if she's studying me. As if she hasn't seen me in weeks. "Lizzy, what happened in the glade?"

The memories move in like a black cloud. Having just relived them so frequently, I'm surprised by the way they fluster me.

"I... I think that after we returned to the colony, Atkinson decided that Dosset could never be trusted. So he set a trap for him. And Dosset fell for it." I tug at the sheet, rubbing the cotton between my fingers. "Dosset brought me with him into the glade on purpose. He thought he could use me against Atkinson. I think he wanted to prove that, even without the EMP, he was still in control. Maybe he wanted to prove it to me. Maybe just to himself."

Again I see it so vividly in my head. The oxygen tubes. The hysteria. The bomb. I shrug off a shiver, curling my knees to my chest.

"I tried to stop them," I say quietly. "I thought if I could make them see what they were doing, if I could make them understand each other, it might change things. But it didn't. They just did what they wanted anyway. Nothing I said made any difference."

"Oh, Lizzy," she says softly. "It wasn't your fault. They were very misguided men." She sighs heavily. "No wonder Noah wouldn't talk to me about it."

I feel a weight lift off me.

"Noah? Is he...?"

"Don't worry, he's fine. They gave him Viscerect as well, after the explosion caused his nose to bleed again. Thankfully, it was only a hairline fracture to begin with. He woke up a few hours ago and has been helping with everything."

"Everything?" I ask, sitting up. The motion makes me woozy. "Chloe, how long have I been asleep? And how did you escape from the Helix? What's—"

"Relax, Lizzy," she says soothingly. "You've got to take it slow."

"Okay. How long have I been out?"

"Almost twenty-four hours. Zonogal said the sleep deprivation, poor nutrition, and blood loss had put you into a state of exhaustion. But we've been having people sit with you around the clock, just in case."

"In case of what?"

Beyond the partition, I hear a door slide open. A moment later the curtain is thrust aside with a rattle, and a bespectacled cadet blinks at the two of us.

"Elizabeth," Romie says with visible relief. "You're awake."

"Am I?" I ask, glancing between them. "Because I'm not totally convinced."

"I'd be willing to provide evidence if you require," he replies with a grin. He casts an eye at Chloe. "I apologize for intruding, but I have a few, um, logistics to discuss with her before this evening. Do you mind if I steal her?"

"Of course," Chloe says, rising primly. "I'll... catch up with you later," she tells me, giving my palm a squeeze. Then she hurries off with a sway of the curtain.

Romie's grin drains away like water through a sieve.

"I apologize," he repeats awkwardly. "I don't mean to rush you. But there are things that we should probably discuss."

"Are there?" I ask. The familiarity of his directness might be comforting if it wasn't for the concern etched on his brow. "I was hoping to talk about a few things myself."

"No doubt. Per doctor's orders, I've been told you must eat. Are you able to walk?"

His words remind me of the conversation Noah and I had, just hours ago in this very room. Only this time it isn't déjà vu.

"I can try."

Romie disconnects the Viscerect drip, and I swing my legs off the bed, testing my weight. My knee feels better, though it's still a little stiff. I change into a jumpsuit behind the curtain while Romie waits. Then he guides me out through the frosted doors, back into the world of the living.

The colony feels jarringly normal. Or *almost* normal. As we make our way to the Xeri cafeteria, we pass a gathering crew holding blue produce buckets, and I can't help but notice how tired they look. And how they stare. Not necessarily with pride or admiration. They look at me as if I'm an alien.

Self-consciously I tuck my hair behind my ears and hurry on.

In the cafeteria, Romie points me to a table in the furthest corner of the room. I'm alone for less than a minute before he returns with a dish of root vegetables and greens, topped with printed grains and chicken. He doesn't seem in a hurry to talk, and since the smell of food has awakened my hunger, I pick up a spoon and dig in.

"Not too quickly," he advises. "Or it could come back up."

I obey, but in a moment his caution is unnecessary. My stomach must've shrunk over the past week of hardly eating, because I'm full almost instantly. I push the bowl away and get a good look at him as he picks at the edge of the table.

His eyes are puffy and swollen, a sure sign that he hasn't slept. I'm reminded of Noah's bruises.

"You look tired, Romie."

"I am," he admits. "But there is a great deal to be done. After lengthy deliberation, we've decided the best course of action is to deconstruct the biomes and repurpose the canvas. But I think that's talk for later."

"What's the talk for now?" I ask. "Maybe you could tell me how you got out of the Helix? Or why I needed a babysitter while I recovered?"

He adjusts his glasses and bobs his head.

"Of course. I apologize. Terra was the one who insisted you be watched over. I believe she wanted to ensure that the doctors didn't try anything."

"Like altering my memories?"

"In a manner of speaking," he replies. "As I understand it, after the bombs went off, Terra took charge of the cadets... though to be honest, I have no idea how she managed it. Yet, once she had their support, the doctors surrendered immediately. Perhaps they would have resisted had circumstances been different. But with the biomes rapidly depressurizing, they must have seen little point. Sedating cadets in a power struggle would only mean fewer hands for gathering seeds." He leans back in his chair. "The entire colony has been on task, working through the night, attending to the most sensitive habitats first. It's an incredible undertaking."

"But we did it," I say, almost afraid to speak the words aloud. "We actually did it."

"More or less."

"And we've been working together. With the doctors."

"Yes. We outnumber them five to one. They are rather at our mercy." He looks up, his eyes tracing a strand of ivy that hangs near our heads. "As for Chloe and I, we were released from our holding cells because of Terra."

I try to imagine Terra giving orders, demanding that the doctors surrender. It's actually not very hard to picture. But despite our vulnerable talk in her pod, in my heart I still feel a bit uneasy about her being the one in charge.

"What happened next?" I ask, doing my best to sound neutral.

"Terra made several stipulations. The Helix was opened. The Stitches were confiscated. The production of Verced was halted and the remainder sealed away. At least for now. Without Dosset, the doctors haven't refused anything. Though if I'm honest, I don't see them as much of a threat anymore. Their previous program could only work with Dosset as their leader."

"So it all falls on Terra?"

"In terms of authority, yes. Shiffrin has been acting as stand-in director, helping to carry out all of Terra's wishes. She and Doctor Mercer have been working with me to figure out how to comply with Terra's most complicated request."

"And that would be...?"

"Restoration of the memories to their previous owners."

His burdened posture gives me pause. Wasn't that always the plan? Yet as I sit and consider it, I feel a tension grow as two halves of reasoning stretch in opposite directions.

When we give back their memories the cadets will take on years of buried problems. Everything from Earth that the doctors deemed too troubling, everything on Mars that bred negativity. Such heavy strain at such a volatile time, while everyone is under so much pressure—it could push the colony to the brink of a meltdown.

And then there's the news about Earth itself. If we tell the cadets now, it could result in the very chaos that Dosset always feared. But if we don't, we become like Dosset: We allow our fear of what could happen to dictate what will happen.

We continue keeping secrets.

"Needless to say, things are moving very quickly. I've been try-ing to figure out how to tell the others," Romie says, as if channeling my thoughts.

"About Earth."

He nods soberly. I remember the look on his face on the Bridge when he overheard the truth. Until now I hadn't considered how he must be handling it.

"So you haven't told anyone yet?" I ask gently.

"No. And neither have the doctors, to my knowledge." He hesitates. "I wasn't sure what to do, given the present circumstances. Everyone is deeply shaken by the detonation of the bombs. According to Terra, there was quite a panic. How she managed to enforce order... as I said, it's beyond my understanding."

I watch as a pair of cadets enters the cafeteria. When they notice me, they stare just like the gathering crew did. Then they quickly turn into the kitchen.

It occurs to me that the last thing most cadets heard from Lizzy Engram was my bluff about the virus. That, followed by rumors of my hand in Dosset's death.

"Well, it seems as if she exerts quite an influence over them," I mutter.

He frowns thoughtfully and returns to picking at the table. "Yes. What I suppose I mean to say is, we're all in a fragile place."

"When is this final Revision supposed to happen?" I ask.

"Tomorrow. An announcement will be made tonight at dinner. To be clear, Terra isn't the only one anxious to have her memories back. I confess that I, too, am eager. And yet once everyone remembers the past, I'm not sure if..."

He seems unable to find the words. While he cleans his glasses, the overheads state fifteen hundred hours.

"You think we should wait to tell them about Earth," I finish for him.

"Not necessarily. I think we should be *careful* about how we tell them. And I think that you should speak with Terra."

"What do you mean?" Something in his tone makes my jaw involuntarily clench. "About what, exactly?"

"Not anything *exactly*," he says delicately. "But as you said, she exerts an influence. It's a great deal of pressure, to lead others.

I saw how it weighed on you, and I can see how it weighs on her. When she learns the truth, she'll need you. We all will."

A cluster of Clovers and two doctors enter the cafeteria. This time, when they notice us, they head straight in our direction.

"Just... consider the future," he says. "Once everyone has their memories back, you will surely have a better idea of what to do."

I glance at the approaching group, which is nearly upon us.

"What are you saying, Romie?" I say, barely audible. "That I'll need to take over once Terra finds out about Earth? That she won't be fit to lead?"

He gives me a half-shrug. "I'm saying that I trust you." Then he turns as the others reach the table. "Gentlemen. Are we ready for the next reclamation phase?"

"If you are," says one. The others all stare at me, just like the rest of the cadets. With a conscious effort, I force a smile.

"Excellent. I'm right behind you." As he stands, Romie glances down at me. "I'm glad you're feeling better, Elizabeth. You should get cleaned up and organize your thoughts for tomorrow."

"Sure thing."

He heads off with the group, falling immediately into a brisk conversation.

As soon as I'm alone, dread begins to work its way down my throat and into the pit of my stomach. Does he expect Terra to become tyrannical just because she's grieving? Or that she'll be susceptible to an insurgency by the doctors?

I can't overthrow anyone. Not this time. Like he just said, we're all in too fragile a place. Doing something drastic will almost certainly end in anarchy.

And here I thought bringing down Dosset would fix things.

Unable to sit still any longer, I take to the halls. The cadets stare, and the cameras keep silent watch. I wonder if anyone is in the Comm Room to see me as I hurry away, desperate for space free of prying eyes.

My steps lead me to the showers. It must be around mid-afternoon because the stalls are dry and empty. I kick my clothes into a heap, welcoming the tiny, uncomplicated nook. As I turn on the water flow, the pressure feels higher than normal. Maybe because the biomes are no longer drawing on the colony's supply.

I clear my mind by dialing the heat as high as I can bear, blocking out the world, and reveling in the sensation of being *clean*, even though it stings my wounds.

When I'm finished, I work out the tangles in my knotted hair, first with my fingers and then with a brush. I clean my teeth. Wrap myself in a microfiber robe, being especially careful with my shoulder, which has already begun to mend, thanks to the Viscerect.

The methodical tasks give me a small reprieve, but as soon as I finish, my thoughts sink back into turmoil.

Exactly what does Romie think I should do? What *can* I do?

I almost regret the hours lost to sleep, hours I could've spent sorting this out. But I quickly realize how necessary they were. By the time I return to the corridors, I'm exhausted. And hungry.

Since dinner isn't for another hour, I decide to retire to my pod until someone comes for me. Or at least until I can frame up some kind of reasonable plan.

Nothing in my pod has been disturbed as far as I can tell. The lamp still lies on its side from where I knocked it, the bed rumpled from when Chloe sat beside me and held my hands, telling me that everything would be all right. That we'd get through this together.

But will we?

I sink onto the bed, smoothing the sheets. In the midst of everything that's happened, I've hardly had a chance to think about our friendship. About what our future holds now that she will soon have her memories back.

Once she knows about my history with Noah, will she cease to be my friend? How will I explain everything to her?

And what about him? It seems as if Noah has already caught up to where our memories left off, in certain ways. Finding out about our past may just push him over the edge, into...

What?

It's stupid, but even now, even after everything, I don't really know what I want from him. Could I allow him fully into my world, knowing the power it will give him? As I've just so painfully learned with Dosset and Atkinson, my honesty doesn't guarantee anything. You can't control other people. Only yourself.

So the question is, do I really trust him?

I don't have an answer for that. I think I do. But I'm not sure I'm prepared for what he'll think once he knows what happened.

Will he see my kiss on the cheek as a sign that I'm ready to move forward into something more? Will he seek assurances I'm not ready to give?

Assurances I can't give, I remind myself. Not until I talk to Chloe.

If I can let her down gently, maybe we can find a way to still be friends. And that conversation will be much easier after her memories are returned and we're both working with the same set of memories.

The same truth, as Dosset would have said. Once the truth is out in the open, everything will be different.

I just don't know if "different" will be better or worse.

These thoughts and a million others burn like the tail of a comet hurtling through me as I lie in bed with the lights low. Green numbers count the minutes away. When they finally reach eighteen hundred hours I roll to my feet and a take a long, shuddering breath.

Whatever comes next, I'll just have to figure it out. If people are going to insist on trusting me, I should probably start trusting myself.

Outside my pod, I slip into a stream of cadets who are too weary to notice who I am. We arrive at the Scrub cafeteria, where dozens upon dozens have gathered, packing out the tables with extra chairs, squeezing into narrow spaces and lining up along the walls. From the look of things, each and every cadet is present.

In the corner near the doors to the kitchen, the doctors can be seen wearing their white lab coats and murmuring softly to one another. Neither Shiffrin, Terra, nor any of my friends are apparent, so I slide in at the back and stand awkwardly beside a group of Clovers, their jumpsuits stained green at the knees.

Several minutes pass like this, and I can sense a kind of unrest growing. Then the kitchen door bounces open and Terra strides boldly forward, her hair braided back in an elaborate waterfall. Chloe's handiwork, I feel certain.

"Hellooo, everyone," Terra trills as, behind her, Chloe, Noah, and Romie enter. Shiffrin is last, looking just as fatigued as the rest of them. I can't stop my gaze from following Noah. Just the sight of him causes a nervous weight to sink in my chest. "How is everyone feeling?"

A general murmur rises in response. More cadets enter from the kitchen, bearing trays of cups, which they begin handing out at the front.

"Perfect." Terra walks directly to the center of the room and turns slowly, surveying them all. "Well, we did it. In less than twenty-four hours, we managed to save at least one of each specimen from every single biome."

It starts slowly, but the room applauds the announcement.

"I know you're all tired," she says with affected sympathy. "And I know we'd all like to send Romie into orbit for insisting that we work through the night. Right?" She shoots him a look and earns a collective chuckle. "Kidding, of course. Thanks to him, things should go much smoother moving forward. Now, what else?" Her eyes find me and she smiles. It's not entirely genuine. But it's not entirely fake, either. "Oh, right. Lizzy is back from the dead."

As the room follows her gaze, I feel my cheeks flush. The cadets nearest me draw back as if I've become contagious all over again. I do my best to return her smile.

"Couldn't let you take all the credit," I say, trying for a light tone.

She cocks her head as if trying to decide whether I'm being sarcastic or not. I see a flicker of the animosity I usually get from her. Then her smile slides back into place.

"Always making it a competition," she smirks. "Well, I think I speak for everyone when I say 'Thanks for everything—especially not giving us your weird blood disease.'" More uneasy chuckles, but I can tell the room is loosening up.

"Now," Terra continues. "I've got a few things to cover before dinner. First, we're having lasagna. Our new administrator, Chloe, says that in order to preserve rations, we'll need to start watching our diets after tonight. So be ready to stuff yourselves."

This is met with real enthusiasm. Hoots and pounding fists on tabletops. As if roused to join in, my stomach growls.

"Second," Terra goes on. "Second, a lot of you have asked when I plan to get your stolen memories returned to you. After having a talk with Shiffrin, Romie, and Mercer, we've outlined a process of making that happen. Then it'll be over. No more lies. No more secrets. And, of course, we'll be taking back your memories from Elizabeth as well."

It shouldn't, but the proclamation catches me off guard. I try not to let it show, keeping my face impassive as I hear grunts of approval around me.

What's the problem? I don't need the memories anymore. I don't even have a right to them in the first place.

So why does it feel as if they're trying to take away a part of me?

"I'm afraid I can only partly agree to that," Shiffrin interjects, stepping forward.

The momentum of the speech grinds to a surprised halt.

"You aren't giving the orders anymore," Terra says, flicking the imposition away with a snap of her wrist. "We are."

"This isn't a matter of authority, Terra," Shiffrin replies patiently. "I would simply be violating my oath as a doctor if I allowed you to risk the memories of your fellow cadets."

Around me, I can feel tension returning to the room.

"What risk would we be talking about, specifically?"

"The Memory Bank has always been stored inside the Helix, but it wasn't the only copy," says Shiffrin. "There was another kept inside Dosset's mind. Now that he's gone, there is only a single transcript of each memory left. It would be irresponsible to destroy the only backup when the original copy has recently suffered an electromagnetic blast." She glances at me, and there is something I can't quite identify in her gaze. "Until every cadet's memories have been safely returned and we can be sure none of those memories were damaged, Lizzy must retain everything."

"Is that true?" Terra asks, pivoting to Romie.

"I suppose," he replies slowly, frowning at the floor. "I hadn't considered the possibility that the storage drives might be damaged. But it never hurts to exercise caution. At least, not until our task is complete."

Terra looks at me again. This time I can't read her at all. But her hesitation passes quickly, and she cracks her neck.

"Great," she says. "She can intrude on our memories for a couple more hours. Happy?" When Shiffrin nods, her gray hair falls in and out of her face like a curtain. Terra turns to Noah. "You wanted to say something?"

"I do."

He steps forward, face pale, and the room goes silent. I stare at him in disbelief.

What will he say? Because I know how hard this must be for him. Standing up in front of a crowded room, all eyes on him—this is exactly the kind of situation that triggers his panic.

My own heart is racing.

"For those who don't know me, my name is Noah," he says, his voice thin. "I was one of the ones who helped stop the doctors... er, Dosset." He glances at Shiffrin almost apologetically. "I just wanted to say that, even though some of you have questioned how we got here and why certain risks were taken, Lizzy was brave to do what she did. She lived in hiding for an entire week, in constant fear. And she did it for all of you."

The crowd shifts uncomfortably, but as he speaks he gains conviction. I stare at my shoes, face burning.

"Yesterday, Lizzy was forced to run away from the colony. But she came back. To stop Dosset and to ensure that each of you had a chance to know the truth. No matter how extreme you might think her actions were, they were brave. They took wit and fire and intelligence and the most courage that I've personally ever seen."

His words send a thrill through me, making my skin crawl with pleasure and discomfort. I steal a look at him and see that the purple and green splotches under his eyes have faded, leaving faint, tawny smudges. He looks much better after the Viscerect. Almost normal.

I avert my gaze as he glances at me, a wave of heat rolling through my chest.

"So I'd like to make a toast," he says in a voice stronger and more confident than I've ever heard from him. "To Terra, for reacting under pressure to bring us all together. To Romie, for the guidance he gave. To each of you, for doing what had to be done to preserve the future of our planet. And lastly to Lizzy. For giving us all a brighter future."

A cup is placed into my hands, and I look down at the bubbly liquid, the color of amber. Carbonated tea. Only slightly fermented, and I suppose our best stand-in for champagne. I curl my fingers around the plastic and take a sip, aware that everyone is looking at me. One by one, I return their gazes.

Romie, looking unabashedly proud. Terra, wearing one of her fake, dazzling smiles, though her gaze is brighter than before. Even Shiffrin, watching me steadily with a kind of approval.

Noah raises his cup, flush with relief at having made it through his speech. I realize that anyone could see how he feels about me. It's written all over him.

And that's when I see Chloe.

Her eyes are wide with anguish and jealousy, emotions I've

never seen on her face before. It belatedly hits me that Noah praised each of us except for her. Even though he probably didn't mean anything by it, it's an oversight that speaks loudly. His words were unfiltered and honest, and they had the careless edge of a knife point.

The tea turns to acid in my stomach, my whole body abruptly cold. I want to reach across the room and explain, but what can I say? Her face clouds and she turns away.

I'm only vaguely aware that Terra has concluded and cadets are rising to dish their plates. Chloe breaks from the crowd, half-running toward the exit. I set my cup aside and follow.

It isn't as easy to keep up as it was before. My knee slows me down, and it isn't until I've reached the Scrub Biome that I catch her.

"Chloe," I call out. "Stop!"

She's opened the portal and made it several meters into the ruined habitat. The strange, tangy wind of Mars pushes back at me, sharp and thin, whistling through the passage. She faces away, but she doesn't move.

Cautiously I draw nearer, easing into the shadow-washed dome until I'm only a few steps behind her.

"He didn't mean..." I begin, but what didn't he mean? It's obvious how he feels. And I knew all along. I had every opportunity to discourage him if it was what I wanted.

Still, she won't look at me.

"I wanted to tell you," I say. "When I knew, when the memories came back and I knew how he felt, I wanted—"

"Do you think I didn't see?" Chloe demands, whirling to face me. I catch the flash of tears in her eyes. "Do you think I didn't know? I *knew*, Lizzy. All along, I knew. But I kept telling myself no, no, she would tell you. Lizzy would never hurt you on purpose."

"I wouldn't."

"Stop lying!" she cries out, the sound desolate. "Just stop." Her shoulders sag as I stare at her helplessly. Finally, she wipes her nose and mutters, "I don't blame you. I blame myself. I didn't want to face it. So I saw what I wanted to see."

The wind picks up, carrying a copper-like chill that makes me shiver. Even after everything that's happened, even after Dosset, I haven't learned.

How could I have let things get this far? For days I've had the chance to tell her. I've known the path we were on would eventually cut her deeply. Yet here I am. Because I didn't want to admit the truth either.

How can you be honest with someone when you know what that honesty will do to them?

"And yet," Chloe says, straightening as the wind dies back. "I *do* blame you for other things. Like letting me trust you." She shakes her head. "Do you know, I used to wonder why you didn't have any friends. Why it was just you and me. And now I know."

"It... it wasn't that simple," I say, my voice shaking. "What was I supposed to tell you, Chloe? That we've been through this with him before? I didn't want to risk hurting you, but I didn't know what to do. I couldn't—"

"You should have told me the truth," she hisses, and I'm taken aback by her fierceness. "Is that so hard? To be honest with me?"

"No. Yes! What would you do if you knew you had the power to ruin everyone's life, just like that? To use everything they care about against them?"

"I would've chosen not to," she says without hesitation. And I know she's telling the truth. She wouldn't have done anything that I did. She wouldn't have even struggled.

For her, the right choice is the easy choice. She would have been loving and forgiving, and as a result, Dosset would probably have caught her and erased her mind immediately. It took someone who thought like him to finally bring him down. Someone like me.

The knowledge is sharp in my throat, like a knife between us.

"It's not that simple."

"It is if you want it to be." Tears leap back to her eyes. "Do... do you love him?"

The question is so unexpected it hits me like a force, like the wind, pushing me back. I stammer and half shrug, at a loss for words.

"Don't be stupid," I say, and then I realize how harsh I sound. "This... we're... this isn't about love, Chloe."

"No? Then what is it about?"

"I don't know. Something else."

"Not for me," she says softly. "But I guess you must have known that."

I shake my head, surprised by a surge of irritation. She doesn't even know him. And if I'm deeply, truly honest, neither do I. "I don't feel like I know anything," I reply instead.

"No? Here I thought you knew so much," she says, a cynical light entering her eyes. Another new look for her. "But you're probably right. The truth is, you have all this information, but you don't really know any of us. Hm? You don't even know yourself. I'm not sure anyone does. Once I thought I did. But I didn't. Did I, Lizzy?"

A sob is caught in my throat, white and grating, and hot tears fill my eyes. But I turn away, not daring to let them show.

Because I don't want to believe it, but it's true. Isn't it? Everything she said, I deserve. I have no right to feel pity for myself. Even when I tried to be different, I was thinking of me first. Still not seeing the big picture. Still blundering along, not noticing all the damage I leave in my wake.

Not until it's too late.

"What else?" she asks. "What else haven't you told me? Other than lying about Noah, what secrets have you—?"

She halts mid-sentence, her eyes widening as she looks beyond me.

"N-Noah," she falters.

Knowing what I'll find, I turn to see him silhouetted in the open portal. He blinks at me, then at Chloe. Then again at me.

"Sorry," he says, the word hardly audible over the fluttering of the torn canopy. "I didn't mean to interrupt, I just—"

"What did you hear?" I ask.

He swallows.

"I didn't mean to—" he begins again. But he's cut off as Chloe pushes past me, then him, hurrying through the portal and disappearing back into the colony. The portal closes, a whisper.

Then Noah and I are alone.

Chapter Twenty-Two

I've never seen Noah so grave. In the soft light that filters through the ruined canvas, his face could be carved from marble. Silence fills the monochrome world between us.

"What did you hear?" I ask again.

"That you lied about me," he says reluctantly. "That you've been keeping secrets. But I already knew that, after what Dosset said." He takes a hesitant step forward, his gaze wandering over the gray dirt before finding its way back to me. "So what did you lie about?"

I take a moment to choose my words. It feels as if the ground might fall out from under me if I'm not careful. But I guess it kind of already has. "It wasn't so much lying as leaving out the truth," I finally say.

"The truth about what?"

"About what you... think of me."

His expression shifts, a reminder of the way he looked at me just a few minutes ago in the cafeteria. I wonder how much longer he'll look at me that way. What calamity was Dosset trying to avoid when he chose to erase our friendship?

Was he protecting Chloe or me? Or Noah?

"I see," he murmurs. "And why would you 'leave out the truth' about that?"

"Because I'm a bad friend," I say bitterly.

"No, you're not."

"And how would you know?" I ask, shifting my weight to favor my knee, which has begun to ache. "You don't remember enough to know."

"The doctors didn't erase *all* of my memories, Lizzy. What, you think I met you for the first time every Monday?"

I shrug. "Maybe."

"No," he says, taking another step forward. "I'm not sure exactly when we met, but that doesn't mean I don't know things about you."

"Like what?"

"Well, like..." His brow creases. "Like that you're highly competitive. That you always do a long run on Sundays, and your favorite trail is on the West Coast. That everyone in your family has dark hair except for you."

"How do you know that?" I ask, surprised, and a little self-conscious. I had assumed the doctors erased all those details, if he ever knew them at all.

"I just... pay attention to you," he says.

The emotions dissolve in a single swallow, replaced by a lump of nerves. "You think you love me," I correct him.

Another step forward, and his face is hidden in shadow. "I do love you," he says, and then he emerges with another step, and even in the dim light, I can tell he's blushing.

"You can't know that," I say, indignant.

"What?"

"I said you can't know that," I repeat. "You don't know me that well. Even if you do remember a few details, as far as you know we've only been friends for a week. Less than a week! You think people just fall in love that quickly?"

His eyes widen in surprise. Then they narrow and he folds his arms in a defensive posture. A new look for him as well. "Oh, so because of my memories, you know everything about me? Is that it?"

"Let's just say I have a better perspective."

"And that means you're sure, without a doubt, that I don't love you? What inside your head has you so convinced? Did I ever say that? Did I ever do anything to hurt you?"

My breathing is growing shallow again. I'm not being fair. But I can feel myself shutting down anyway, Chloe's words still ringing in my head like the echo of a bomb.

"I... I don't know," I say hoarsely.

I lock my jaw in exasperation, sealing any more thoughts from escaping. Why am I being this way? Why am I so sure he can't love me?

Because... because... I'm not. Because maybe he actually does. But even if I deserved him—which I feel certain that I never will—I think Chloe was right: I don't know myself. And if I don't know who I am, then he can't either. Can he?

What happens when he learns the truth about me? When I let him inside my head and he discovers my selfishness, my flaws?

When he learns what I did to Chloe.

"Lizzy, what do you not know?" he presses. I can hear the vulnerability in his voice, and it makes it so much worse. "Did I do something wrong?"

He takes another step closer. I could reach out and touch him now. And I'm surprised to find that I want to. That despite all of these fears, I *want* to let him in.

I'm overly conscious of my pulse thrumming in my palms and down my bone-weary body like the sparkling tickle of Verced. Every heartbeat a syllable for words I can't speak, to explain what I want from him. What I want from myself. To know and be known, totally and completely. To be someone worth knowing.

"Tell me," he says gently.

His eyes glimmer as they search mine for understanding. I open my mouth, but nothing comes out.

Again I feel a rush of that same longing in my fingertips, in my veins. More than anything, I want the comfort of his nearness. I feel as if gravity is pulling me toward him, toward his lips, an unseen magnetism.

But... it wavers.

Because in his bright gaze, I can see my reflection. And I remember the wonderful person he believes me to be. The wonderful person that I'm not.

"There are things you don't know," I finally say, a whisper.

"Like what?"

The question strikes me as so absurd, I almost laugh. The vast quantity of memories he doesn't know about.

My thoughts skim them, and in an instant, I see a girl with a heart-shaped face and freckles just like Noah's. His sister. And I see a thin, lofty man with horn-rimmed glasses, and a petite woman with fiery red hair. His parents. They're in a sunroom, waving for me to enter.

I can feel the love in these memories rising with profound bitter-sweetness to take my breath away. These caring people, these sweet memories, they're what formed the boy who stands before me now. And they're gone.

And Noah still doesn't know.

How selfish would I be to let him comfort me—to use him yet again—with such looming tragedy waiting for him?

"What are you so afraid of, Lizzy?" he asks, growing insistent. "What secrets are you hiding?"

There are only centimeters between us. He's so close that I know he'll kiss me if I don't pull back.

So I do.

"I just..." I shrink away, inexplicably numb. My hands are shaking. "I can't."

He blinks, the light dimming.

"You can't?"

"Not yet," I say faintly. "Tomorrow, okay? We'll talk tomorrow. I promise. After you have your memories back."

"Why?" he asks, almost pleading as he steps closer again. "What did Dosset take that you can't just tell me?"

But I withdraw even farther, keeping space between us.

"Trust me, okay?" I ask. Knowing I don't have the right.

I watch as a blank expression falls into place like a stone. And it cuts, it crushes me, knowing I could be the one to help him through this. But I can't. Not yet.

"Okay." His voice is hollow with confusion. "Tomorrow, then."

"Tomorrow," I nod.

He turns to go, looking as if he wants to say more. I almost stop him. But instead, I wait until he's gone and then find my way back to my pod, my heart aching with a fresh new bruise.

As I punch the code, I glance at Chloe's door. The image of her face, anguished at my betrayal, appears in my mind. Another blow. This one throbbing with a sense of incompleteness. That I was meant to do something, but didn't.

That I should have said something, but couldn't.

Inside my room, I sit on the bed. Now that it's over, now that everyone will soon have their memories back, reality edges in like a shadow unbound by the retreat of the sun. Other faces float before me, joining Chloe—Dosset, Atkinson, my mother and father. All the people I knew on Earth and will never see again.

And I realize that in many ways I've already begun to let them go. Even in my memories, they've been thrust into the patina of the past, sanded into obscurity.

Because they have to be. Time will never stop, and neither can we.

Tears sting my eyes once more, building up and rolling over my cheeks with the heat of a dying star. Isn't that what death is? It's forgetting. It's letting go. We make peace with the dead to say goodbye.

Maybe the problem with holding onto memories so tightly is that they don't allow us to make room for the future. Maybe the gentle decay of the past is a blessing that dulls the sharp blade of regret, allowing the possibility of rebirth.

When the lights click off I climb into bed, again feeling weightless. For hours I lie awake, staring into the blackness of the universe as it whirls above my bed. A strange calm patterns over me. I imagine that the stars are out tonight and I'm swimming through them, each one on a slightly different path than it was before.

I'll never see them again from my old world. Earth is gone forever. We have a whole new planet to explore. And now, a new Elizabeth to go with it.

Eventually, I drift off to sleep. When I wake, the lights are on. I sit up, overcome with the strange, panicky feeling that I've overslept. I'm just zipping my jumpsuit when I hear a knock at my door.

My first thought is that it's Chloe, but when I anxiously pull the handle I find McCallum standing in the passage.

"Can I help you?" I ask, my surprise coupled with fear.

"The cadets are about to be called to their theaters," he says gruffly. "Shiffrin asked that you wait with her during the procedures."

"Do I have a choice?" I ask without thinking. After all, I don't have anywhere else to be. The question seems to catch him off guard.

"Not today" is his reply.

"Sure."

I close the door and follow him down the stairs.

During my clandestine trips through the halls, the colony has seemed empty at times. But today it's like walking through a morgue.

The lights glare, but I hear no distant footsteps. No voice to announce the time. Just dead air heaved from overtaxed oxygenators. Filling the halls, suffocating me with its frail, stilted vacancy.

On instinct, I continue to glance at the cameras as we pass, but I no longer feel watched. It's the opposite. I feel almost forgotten.

McCallum leaves me as I enter the cafeteria. Behind, I hear the whoosh of distant doors, the clunk of weighted boots entering halls, the hiss of nervous voices. As if they were waiting for me to pass before emerging.

I let the doors close, muting them all.

Shiffrin sits alone at a table, a steaming cup and two covered bowls before her. I catch her eye, and she smiles wearily.

"Good morning, Elizabeth," she says.

"Hello," I say cautiously.

"Care to sit?"

"Why not."

I sink onto the hard plastic, watching her. She gently squeezes her cup between aged fingers and blows on the liquid.

"There's coffee if you'd like some."

"I hate coffee," I say.

"Tea?"

"You know, doctor, I've never really liked tea either."

"Oh? You never mentioned it. How about hot chocolate?"

"I'm fine, thank you."

She shrugs, sipping from the cup. "Well, if you'd like breakfast, you're welcome to it. Personally, I'm starving."

I peek beneath one of the lids and find a tofu scramble with mushrooms, onions, and wilted spinach. Potatoes on the side.

"Trying to butter me up?"

"We don't have butter on Mars, Elizabeth," says Shiffrin lightly. "The rations depleted two months ago. That's another memory we had to alter." The joke is soured by its plausibility. She seems to realize it and turns her attention toward the doors. "Unfortunately for your fellow cadets, a Revision requires a brief fast of one to two hours. I'm afraid it will just be us for breakfast today."

"A pity for them," I mutter, seizing my fork.

My portion isn't large, and I'm done quickly. While Shiffrin finishes eating, I stare at the ridged tabletop, listening to far-off footsteps.

They must be calling the cadets to the Wellness Suites one by one. I guess they'll have to inoculate them and take them back to their pods in the transport carts. As before, the notion makes me twitchy.

But it's necessary, right? When I woke with the Memory Bank, it was excruciating. Of course, the amount of memories was much greater.

I realize that I'm cracking my knuckles and stop myself.

"How are you feeling, Elizabeth?" Shiffrin asks, returning to her cup.

"Fine." I smile ironically, recalling that this was the question she would lead with before erasing my memories. "Want me to tell you about my week?"

"If you like," Shiffrin says.

"No thanks."

I begin drumming my nails on the table. After a few minutes of the incessant drone, she asks, "Are you sure you wouldn't like to talk about something?"

"Nothing to talk about," I reply. "Actually, yes. I've got a question. How come you aren't helping with the Revisions? I thought you were in charge of all this."

"I oversaw preparations. Mercer, Terra, and Romesh are more than capable of managing the procedures themselves. In my opinion, I have a more important responsibility."

"Breakfast?"

"You."

I snort.

"I'm well beyond *your* responsibility," I say. More feet clunk past the doors, and I chew on a nail absently, wondering who was summoned next. "Kind of a missed opportunity, really. You could have used this as a great excuse for altering our memories all over again."

The plausibility of this hits me as well, but Shiffrin's laugh is easy.

"Well, I think we all know that the Revisions can't go on without Adam."

"Right," I mutter. "One less self-serving person to worry about. Had enough of those to last a few lifetimes."

"Like your parents?"

For a second I think I misheard her. "E-excuse me?" I say

breathlessly.

"Of course, I know all about them," she says, holding my gaze. "I was your therapist—even if I didn't do a very good job, given the circumstances."

"My parents are none of your business."

"Perhaps," she concedes. "But then, I think you're very familiar with the burden of truth you cannot share. Such as last night, with Chloe."

I feel the blood roll out of my face, replaced swiftly by fire.

"What, are the cameras still on?"

"She came to see me," says Shiffrin softly. "And I think it only fair to tell you the same thing I told her. That over time, you may reconcile. That you both might grow to a place where you can be friends. Maybe part of the reason your parents were unloving to you was because they never knew real love themselves. You might have been the one to change that." She pauses. "Of course, in the case of your parents, I'm sorry to say this is all hypothetical. But I thought it may come as some comfort."

"Comfort," I say with a bitter laugh. "Yes, well, did you consider that my parents and I may have just had a toxic relationship? That they might've grown worse with age?"

"It's possible," she says.

I fold my arms, feeling old resentment and anger creeping into my shoulders. "Yeah. Well, I guess we'll never know, will we?"

"No, I guess we won't."

Silence settles in. More feet pass. Shiffrin rises and ambles into the kitchen. When she returns, she's holding a fresh cup. Without a word, she sets it down in front of me.

"What's this?"

"Hot cider."

I frown, filled with suspicion.

"We still have cider?" I ask, smelling the fragrant mixture. I've always loved hot cider. Especially when it comes with fresh donuts. But since it isn't likely that she's about to start pulling pastries out of her lab coat, I settle for circling my hands around the warm plastic.

The heat radiates up my arms, more soothing than I expected.

"You know, for a therapist you aren't very consistent. You attack me, you give me a treat. You erase my memories, you help me escape. You try to sedate me, you give me Verced."

"As Adam was fond of saying, there are versions of the truth. Perspective can change a lover into a thief or an enemy into a friend. But just so we understand each other, I've always hated the Revisions. Even when I first had the idea, I hated them."

Yet again, I feel I must have misheard.

"Wait—are you saying the Revisions were *your* idea?"

"They were. The first time." She stares into her cup. "After the ruin of Earth, the cadets didn't know how to carry on. We were unable to console them, and we began to fear for their health. I presented my idea as a theory, but we waited. Then a cadet took his own life. A boy named Jacob. So we decided to use the Stitches to reshape their memories. And it worked—for a time. But then they became troubled, expressing feelings of loneliness, frustration, anxiety. Only now they didn't have a reason for those feelings."

"Because you erased them," I say impatiently. "Dosset already told me all this."

She leans back in her plastic chair, away from the table.

"I'm sure he did. He may have also told you that he was the one who suggested we repeat the process on a regular basis. In his mind, doing so would allow us to monitor how well the cadets were doing mentally, and also to clean up any lingering trouble-some memories. We all put it to a vote."

"And you all agreed."

"No," she says.

"No?"

"No, we did not all agree." Her sigh is heavy. "At the time I was colony director, and Adam was our neurologist. The Stitches were his, brought to study the mental health of not only the cadets, but the doctors as well. To be sure we weren't developing cabin fever, among other things. But that was before Adam became the surrogate for the Memory Bank."

"Hold on... *you* were the colony director?" I say in disbelief.

"Adam was as brilliant as he was cunning," she says wryly. "The day before the vote, he went about his routine check-ups. And when we gathered the next morning, I found that my fellow doctors no longer believed me to be the director, but rather Adam. The vote was, not surprisingly, in favor of the Revisions. Unanimous, except for one."

"You."

She takes another long drink from her coffee.

"Why did he let you keep your memories?" I ask, bewildered. "Why not just tie up loose ends and be done with it?"

"On my own, I was powerless to stop him. And I believe he trusted me. Over time, he felt, I'd see the sense in it all. I think it was also some comfort to know that at least one person could be honest with him—really, truly honest."

"Even if it meant a disagreement."

"Especially if it meant a disagreement," she replies. "With my administrative experience, I helped him devise a plan to carry out the Revisions week by week. Meanwhile, he knew the science behind the Stitch. Once we had a roadmap of each cadet's mind, we let the brain work to our advantage. Any phantom memories that were missed in a procedure would be thrown out as an idle dream or the workings of the imagination." She stares out over the cafeteria as if lost in the memories. "It would've never worked without both of us."

"And so time moved on," I mutter, not bothering to hide my contempt.

"It did. The cadets continued their weekly therapy sessions. The doctors took notes and monitored behavior. Adam compared the notes with the Memory Bank, of which he kept a copy in his mind. He told the psychologists what to watch for, where the cadets were struggling. In turn, the doctors focused on those topics, asking questions for Adam to review. Gradually it becomes routine. Habits formed to make the process run more smoothly by the week. And so the entire population was kept happy and docile. Except for Adam, I suppose."

"You mean Dosset wasn't happy with his little utopia?"

"The constant strain took a toll on his body. Perhaps because he shouldered the burden of an entire colony. Or maybe because his mind endured the constant upload of new memories. First came the fatigue, then the oxygen tank. After a while, he ceased to leave the Helix at all."

I think back to when I first received the Memory Bank. How much pain it caused me; how the doctors said it could have been fatal.

What quantity of memories did Dosset have stored in his mind? He told me he had everything—surely even secrets he kept from the Memory Bank. Could that have been the reason for his frailty?

Did such a powerful strain on his mind end up crippling his body as well?

Shifting in my chair, I feel the creak of joints, the hiss of cuts, the dull torment of aching bruises. And they don't even include the stress my body received at the hands of my headaches.

"Poor him," I grunt, giving voice to my thoughts. "I guess that's the price of manipulating everyone on the planet."

She gives me a strange look, scrutinizing my face like a jeweler looking for faults. I shift uncomfortably in my chair again, running a finger around the rim of my cup.

"Then what?" I finally ask, trying to make her stop staring. "You came to your senses at last when you gave me the inoculator?"

"Long before that, actually. I knew shortly after you evaded Adam the second time that he'd met his match. Yet I needed to protect the cadets. That was always my primary concern. That's why I did my part when Adam asked it of me. Because all along, in spite of everything he did that I couldn't agree with, I knew he was doing the right thing."

"The right thing?" My hands grow still and I stare at her, incredulous. "He manipulated everyone. He stole their memories. We've all been his slaves."

"For your good, Lizzy. It was always for your good. He did what he had to do. And now more than ever, what we *still* have to do."

All at once I'm cold with nerves, though I don't entirely know why. What she's saying doesn't make any sense.

"Still need to...?"

"Without the Revisions, the cadets are prone to self-destruction," Shiffrin says calmly. "Adam showed me that. And you proved him right. Your actions nearly destroyed the entire colony. Since Saturday night we've been careful not to risk anything that could arouse suspicion. Especially as it relates to you. You must know how valuable you are."

Threads of a terrifying idea are unspooling in my mind, knotting loosely as they meet. But there are strands that don't make sense yet.

I push away from the table, almost tripping over my chair as I whip my head over my shoulder, expecting to find Sarlow and McCallum lurking behind me. But we're still alone.

"What are you saying?" I demand, and my voice cracks. "I don't get what you're saying."

"Simply that your fellow cadets will need you now more than ever," Shiffrin replies, still seated as she rolls her empty cup in her hands. I think of Romie saying almost exactly the same thing, and I feel sick. "We are the last of humanity. It is simply too high a cost and too great a risk to leave these things to chance."

"You're wrong," I shout. "The lies, the tricks, the secrets—they're the reason! They're the reason Dosset is dead!"

"No, Elizabeth," says Shiffrin gently. "You are."

I recoil as if she hit me.

"Me?"

"If you hadn't released Atkinson and helped him overthrow the system, Dosset would still be alive. Now we must build a better system. One that you sustain and I control."

"I will never help you," I spit, again looking for more assailants to come forward, to force a Stitch around my head. But still, the cafeteria is empty.

"Perhaps not now," says Shiffrin patiently. "But once we adjust your memories, I think you'll help us in any way you can, like the other doctors do. Your friends certainly will, once we inoculate them and finish the Revisions." She glances at her watch thoughtfully. "Which should be any minute now."

On top of everything else she's said, I don't immediately take her meaning. But some intuition is humming through my thoughts, and like an echo in a cave, it builds steadily louder until the truth hits me in a rattling shock—

The doctors aren't returning the cadets' memories.

They're erasing them.

My whole body has gone hollow. They plan to continue the Revisions *now*. And so they'll get healthy cadets with no dead parents, no guilt, no baggage to weigh them down.

I can almost see the sense in it.

Shiffrin's eyes bore into mine, hard and black as onyx. And suddenly all I can think about is Noah and his golden eyes and everything I didn't get a chance to explain.

"What have you done?" I say weakly.

"Only what is necessary," she replies.

Without thinking I turn on my heel and charge the doors, blasting into the hallway as Shiffrin calls behind me. Her voice fades, sucked into a vacuum.

Empty. All empty. I charge the Wheel, a desperate weight hanging in my throat. How could I have let this happen? How was I so blind, so distracted that I didn't even think about what Shiffrin might be wanting? What she might've been waiting for all along.

Please... please don't forget me. Please, don't let Noah or Chloe or Romie or even Terra have forgotten me. I'll learn from my mistakes. I'll untangle my selfishness and put my old habits to rest.

Just don't let them forget.

The halls fly by, and then I burst into the Polar domes. But I'm going too fast, and I ram right into a pair of doctors. We fall, and I scramble back to my feet just as I recognize the cadet they were helping toward the Wheel.

"Noah," I gasp.

He's awake. If he hasn't been inoculated, maybe he hasn't had his memories changed. Maybe we can still get away. "Did they—?"

My words fail. He slowly climbs to his feet, looking confused. Speechless, even.

And then I feel tiny teeth pinching my arm, and I turn to see Sarlow holding an inoculator against my skin. She pulls it away, keeping me steady as my knees turn to water. My body is abruptly drifting.

I look at Noah, who still stares at me in shock.

"Do I... know you?" he asks.

My whole world stutters as if it spun off its axis and tumbled out of orbit. I can't make sense of anything. If he doesn't remember me at all, that means... that means...

"Relax, Lizzy." Shiffrin's voice brushes my ear. "As our new surrogate, we need to keep you in good health—mentally, emotionally, and physically."

I'm falling into waiting arms. And then I know—

They're never going to stop. To make it work, they just need someone like Dosset, like me, to interpret the memories and predict what comes next. Until they're absolutely certain that our race will survive, they're going to keep us living in the smallest bubble possible. Away from anything that might upset the balance: hardship, betrayal, fear... even love.

And the fee for that prison will be my body. My freedom.

My mind.

Gently I'm being pulled back, away from Noah, who blinks after me until Zonogal takes him by the arm. And that's the last I see of him. I try to resist, but the drug makes everything fuzzy, and I know I don't have long.

Someone bends my knees and lifts me up. I think it's McCallum, but the ice-cold numbness is trickling through my ears. My eyelids beat one last flutter like the wish of a dying moth, and I look up into Shiffrin's eyes.

In those eyes, I see grim intention. I know I'll be seeing her again. I'll be seeing all of them again.

I just don't know what I'll remember.

TO BE CONTINUED.

ACKNOWLEDGEMENTS

I never liked the term "self-published." In my mind, it hinted at amateurism—and more perplexing, at isolation. Writing is an inherently solitary business. Before *Biome*, the notion of also undertaking marketing, design, proofreads, and a thousand other small tasks on my own sounded like a special kind of masochism.

Yet for several very good reasons, self-publishing ended up being my path. And I was surprised (perhaps naïvely) to find that, when I shared that path, I was joined by an enthusiastic tribe of machete-wielding companions.

To you incredible individuals, this is where I say, "Thank you," rather than sending you an elderly bottle of bourbon. (For that, I'll need more sales.)

In the truest sense of the word, to my "partner," Carissa. This story—from its content, to its personality, to its distribution—could never have happened without you. Thank you for the endless nights, the feverish work, the laughter, and the frozen yogurt. Oh, and for marrying a novelist even though you don't like fiction.

To Jill, my dearest mother and fellow author. You quite literally taught me to write, for which I am ever grateful. (You also taught me to hold a pen incorrectly, but whatever, you know?) I can never thank you enough for all the help you've provided over the years. This book could not be what it is without your insight and home-made pie.

To Randy, my loving father. You showed me what it means to be a man—patient, caring, and ever the buoyant spirit. Thank you for the talk in the driveway. I wouldn't be here without you. (I mean that literally.)

To Jeff, my brother. For the conversations that could go on for another hour; for being an editor, a sounding board, a steadfast videographer, and a generally awesome fellow. Thank you for the overwhelming support.

To Chris, my other brother. For nurturing some ideas, and rejecting others. Thank you for the beautiful artwork and the rye—and for the drive to the airport that meant so much.

To Kevin, my long-time writing companion. Thank you for always listening, beta-reading, contributing, and falling asleep halfway across the prairie.

To Christian, who slept on my couch. Thank you for the word-play, for going to bed early, for avoiding the black hole, and for being cut from the same cloth.

To Kathryn, for the avocado-inspired desserts. Thank you for throwing that snowball, and for reading another book about Mars. Your encouragement warms my heart.

To Masen, my kindred spirit. Thank you for the chess, the poetry, and the inspiration. Our talks will always nurture my soul—no matter how early they come.

To Beth, John, and baby, the kindest people I know. Thank you for being among the first to read *Biome*. I will never forget your baked goods.

To David, for reading twice, for taking meaningful walks, and for shared depth. You set a wonderful example.

To Danae, for loving literature and thinking critically. Your perspective never ceases to surprise and delight.

To Katie and Joe, for being the coolest people in the city. Thank you for helping make this a reality in so many ways. Also, thanks for making me look good. It's quite a feat.

To Molly, for always keeping me on my toes. Thank you for the phone calls, the open invitations, and for sharing so much of your partner.

To Anne Elisabeth, India, Cheryl, and Tosca for being among

the first to give these ideas a chance. Your kindness is one of the reasons I'm writing this. Thank you for being incredible.

To Jill, for being a truly outstanding last-second copy editor. Your sense of humor, your craft, and your patient professionalism could not have been more appreciated.

And finally, to the mischievous Drew Hudson, the vibrant Angela Ficorelli, the unflagging Chris Smith, the ever loving Randy and Jill Smith, the kindhearted Elaine Bills, the clever Shirley Smith, the prosaic Todd Arnold, the inspiring Marianne Falk, the genuine Jen Rock and Mike Buslepp, the wonderful Ericka Gutierrez, the noble Courtney Smith, the heartening Jean and Curtis Birky, the subtle Luke Turalitsch, the altruistic team at Lazlo, the wholehearted Deena Tucker, the classy David Lowe-Rogstad, the thoughtful Cheryl Hodde, the ingenious Joe Bauer, the benevolent Matt Farley, the remarkable Erin Congdon, the explosive Steven Wise, the encouraging Lissa Forsterer, the enterprising Jeff Zimmerman, the dauntless Danielle Miller, the scholarly Danae Dracht, the inclusive Jett Harsh, the profoundly generous Mike and Amy Hudson, the wonderful KC Cook, the buoyant Gregory Moyerbrailean, the expressive Rachel Avallone, the vastly creative Kyle Sullivan and Renee Yama of Cyclops LLC, the enigmatic and supremely giving Duke Johnson, the powerful Phil DeAngelis, the philosophical Michael Masen, the big-hearted Beth and John Gibbons, the openhanded Jill Stengl, the peerless Lauren Stuart, the legendary Peter Dean, the brilliant Kate Bowers, the talented Stefanie Norlin, the authoritative Ron DelVillano, the inquisitive Kevin Osborn, and the caring Tim, Jessica, and Jovie Perry—

From every chamber of my heart, thank you for being early adopters; for supporting *Biome* at such a critical phase; for being remarkable and memorable; and for quite literally telling a story with your actions. You're all heroes in my book.

Lastly, to my readers old and new. Without you, these worlds and words would be nothing.

ABOUT THE AUTHOR

Ryan Galloway has been writing books since he was twelve years old. He is an advocate for trail running, Pokémon, mental health, coffee, sustainable fashion, and medicinal science. He also believes art should make you feel something—and that such a human connection can only be achieved with honesty.

Born and raised in the suburbs of Detroit, Michigan, Ryan now lives in Portland with his wife and delightful friends, imaginary and otherwise. *Biome* is his debut novel.

CPSIA information can be obtained
at www.ICGtesting.com
Printed in the USA
FSOW01n0003271116
27812FS